Dragonfly

Jana Begovic

Manor House

Library and Archives Canada
Cataloguing in Publication

Title: Dragonfly Slayer / Jana Begovic.

Names: Begovic, Jana, author.

Identifiers: Canadiana 20220429774 |

ISBN 9781988058917 (hardcover) |

ISBN 9781988058900 (softcover)

Classification: LCC PS8603.E42848 D73 2022 |

DDC C813/.6—dc23

Cover art: Viktor Zagrai / Shutterstock / (Dragonfly close-up).

First Edition

Cover Design-layout / Interior- layout: Michael Davie
324 pages / Approx. 108,560 words.
Published November 2022 / Copyright 2022
Manor House Publishing Inc.
452 Cottingham Crescent, Ancaster, ON, L9G 3V6
www.manor-house-publishing.com (905) 648-4797

Description: Captivating story of several people, all medical professionals, discovering they are interconnected through the bonds formed in a past life. One bond between two psychiatrists is of a romantic nature and spans several incarnations - and further extends into a future reincarnation…

This project has been made possible [in part] by the Government of Canada. ***« Ce projet a été rendu possible [en partie] grâce au gouvernement du Canada.***

Funded by the Government of Canada
Financé par le gouvernement du Canada

Canada

For all those who have been the wind of love and support beneath my wings of imagination.

"Writing is both mask and unveiling," as E.B. White said, and I am one of the many writers who has felt jittery and unnerved by the unveiling process, by laying themselves bare before a judging public. Had it not been for an immense amount of love, support and encouragement from my family and friends, I may have never dispelled the gnawing self-doubt about my writing ability.

I am forever grateful to those who have been the wind beneath my creative wings, my mother Masha, husband Miro, son Andrej, daughter-in law Virginia, sister Dijana, aunt Seka and uncle Cinca, as well as numerous friends: Sanya, Julie, Karen, Mary Jo, Kosa, Goga, Mira, Jenny, Edith and Tanya for acting as my Alpha and Beta readers, and calling my novel "unputdownable", riveting and mesmerizing. I am also deeply grateful to my editors, Nancy Bayer Curran and John Scanlon, as well as to the poet Patrick Kavanagh for permitting me to use his poetry in a chapter of this book. And last, but not least, I am more than thankful to Michael Davie from *Manor House Publishing, Inc.* for his infinite patience while waiting for me to submit to him the final manuscript version, and for giving the book its finished artistic look.

- **Jana Begovic**

Praise for *Dragonfly Slayer…*

"A story of "uncovering," *Dragonfly Slayer's* characters' past and present synchronicities are mindfully crafted layer by layer before revealing a surprising conclusion. In her distinctive passionate, vivid prose, Ms. Begovic skillfully blends the intellectual and emotional infused with a magical realism that both intrigues and excites the imagination—a rich, mythic journey well taken."

- **CK Page**, author, ***Fabulistica***

"A chance meeting between a scientist, Weylin McLaughlin, and a homeopathic shaman, Keith Wilson becomes a catalyst for self-discovery while exploring the revelatory effects of a psychedelic drug. A former lover, Leandra, and a cancer patient, Annette, team up with them and travel across Ireland on a path that leads to past life regression, the permanence of love, and an ancient curse kept secret from the visible world. Begovic's literary prose is poetic, accessible and provides the perfect genre-bending marriage of myth and medicine. Will the painful truths these characters discover restore health and rekindle a romance as immortal as the Celtic lullabies sung on the green hills of an emerald paradise?"

- Mark Antony Rossi, writer-Host, Strength to Be Human podcast

"Weylin and others – discover they share past incarnations after taking the psychedelic drug - Jacacia. This drug provides past-life regression therapy and a source of self-knowledge. The fire and enchantment of erotic sex between Weylin and Leandra contrast her attempts to remain faithful to her husband. The interlaced past lives also reveal a long-standing curse, which requires the help of a shaman to lift the spell. The rugged encounters are well written by the author. **Jana Begovic** skillfully creates a dark love story that burns through time. Excellent writing for a difficult prospect."

- **Dr. Ian Prattis**, author, ***Four Phases*** and, ***Shattered Earth***

Key Characters Whose Life Paths Intersect:

1. **Weylin McLoughlin –** Psychiatrist from Ireland
2. **Kieran –** Weylin's name in the past incarnation from 17th century Ireland
3. **Leandra Springfield** – Psychiatrist from Canada and Weylin's ex-lover

4 **Jilleen –** Leandra's name in the past incarnation from 17th century Ireland where she was a healer, a chieftain's wife and Kieran's lover.

5. **Adrian Springfield –** Prosecutor and Leandra's husband in the present life
6. **Aidan –** Adrian's name in the past incarnation from 17th century Ireland where he was a chieftain
7. **Ariadne Quigley** – Weylin's patient in the present
8. **Ailionora** – Ariadne's name in the past incarnation from 17th century Ireland where she was a healer and a high priestess
9. **Hugo** – Ariadne's lover in the present
10. **Egerton –** Hugo's name in the past incarnation from 17th century Ireland where he was Alionora's fiancé
11. **Annette Walsh –** Psychiatrist and Weylin's boss in the present life
12. **Lady Tyrone** – Annette's name in the past incarnation from 17th century Ireland where she was a noble woman

1

Weylin

Another rainy day. It did not even make sense to mention it. After all, I was born in Ireland and have lived most of the fifty years of my life in Dublin, so logic would have dictated I'd be used to rainy weather to the point of not even noticing its gloominess, but such was not the case. Especially on a day like this that marked the transition into the second month of feeling depressed.

I had never been severely or clinically depressed, but from time to time, I found myself enveloped in a cloak of melancholy. My effort into hiding this period of inner night from my children sapped my mental strength. And their presence in my life had been like a bright lantern that not only dispersed and lighted that shadow, but also warmed it with renewed hope that I would feel alive again. And what irony to be a psychiatrist susceptible to moods ranging from mild moping to moderate depression.

It felt as if my soul suffered from an unknown malady that no psychoanalysis could allay. And how could one even psychoanalyse a soul that retreated into its penumbral abode somewhere deep within us, and seemed to be averse to too much probing and exposure to light.

Once I allowed the misty veils of blues to swathe my mind, I would start feeling not only invisible, but also forgettable. And for some reason, I have always been plagued by fear that people whom I loved would forget me. After all, the sinkhole of time swallows and fades all memories. Perhaps, the source of that fear was my father who never came back from India to visit me, and who never wrote to me after leaving my mother. How is it possible to forget one's own child? And why as an adult have I not been able to completely erase his imprint on my psyche?

I had a dream about Leandra last night. I had not thought of her for quite some time, but the strange encounter on last week's flight made me think of her again and write to her using a work-related pretext. And even though I had broken off that illicit relationship years ago, and healed from the pain of loss rather fast, I never wanted her to forget me. I also did not want her to remember me as a delicious but inconsequential fling, and an episode easily covered by oblivion. I know it sounds paradoxical, but that impulse came from the depth of my soul.

The experience on the plane was one of the strangest I had had in my entire life, one that I had difficulty understanding on any rational level. My family and I were flying back home from Malaysia where we had spent three weeks on vacation. Travelling had always been my lifelong passion and there was nothing, except being in love, that could fill me with such a sense of extreme aliveness as stepping into new worlds and cultures, and anticipating the unexpected behind each new street corner or bend in the road. During my travels, I may have suffered occasional bouts of subdued moods, but never depression.

The British Airways flight was oversold, and many people could not get seats together. My wife sat with our children three rows behind me, and I found myself sitting beside a man whose shoulder-length grey hair was tied in a ponytail with a red elastic band. What caught my attention was the drawing pad he kept on his knees and the image of a magnificent dragonfly. The man was colouring its wings using three different hues of green. He was taking pencils from a case protruding from the seat pocket in front of him. He was so absorbed in his work that he did not hear the flight attendant ask him to put his seat belt on, and push his backpack farther under the seat in front of him. When she touched his shoulder, he looked up startled and buckled up. At the same time, he smiled at me and said, "Once I start drawing, the world around me disappears."

"That dragonfly is incredibly beautiful. Are you a professional artist or is it just a hobby?"

"Drawing is one of my passions. Expressing myself through art is a deep-seated need. I don't know if that makes me an artist," he said.

I couldn't help noticing how blue his eyes were. I introduced myself, mentioning also I was a psychiatrist from Dublin, and at the same time thought how out of character that was. Normally on planes I stick my head in my book, try to sleep, and have no desire to chat with the people sitting next to me. After all, I am an introvert of an extreme kind.

The man looked at me with curiosity, proffered his hand and said, "Keith. Your name is very unusual. I'd never heard that name before. Does Weylin have some kind of meaning?"

"Yes, it means son of a wolf. It's an old Celtic name. My mother loved wolves and old Celtic names. When my children were younger, they used to call me, 'a big, bad wolf.'"

Talking to him, I forgot that the plane was taxiing and when it suddenly took off, I grabbed the seat handles firmly. Even though I have seen most of the world through my frequent travels, my fear of flying had never left me.

"No reason to be afraid," Keith said calmly.

"How can you tell I'm afraid? Is it the way I gripped the seat-rest that made you think it was out of fear?" As I was asking the question, I felt a slight stutter in my voice. As a teenager, I had had a much more pronounced stutter that would make me feel mortified in front of girls. Now, it only appeared when I was inordinately tense or nervous, and for some reason I was feeling rattled. There was something in this man's eyes that seemed to reach the core of my soul, stirring ripples I had not felt in a long time, ripples the nature of which I could not even define. Under his glance, it felt as if some primordial longing awoke in me, a yearning for something, someone—some vital piece of self-knowledge. How do I find what I'm looking for when I'm not even aware of what it is? I just know it whispers to me from the dark corridors of the labyrinth of my soul, and I'm unable to decipher the message. And why was I still talking to this guy? His reply took me completely off guard. Could he have heard my silent question?

"I read people's energies."

"You what...?"

"I'm an energy reader...and a healer."

"I've heard of energy healers, but not of readers. Is that some kind of psychic?"

"I don't like the word psychic because I have yet to meet a genuine one, someone who doesn't scam people for money. Yes, you can say it's similar, it's just that I don't have a shop with a crystal ball or Tarot cards, and I do not charge for readings; in fact, you couldn't even order a reading from me."

"So you're an energy reader who doesn't provide readings for money or otherwise? Do you heal people for money?"

"I do neither readings nor healings for money. From time to time, I agree to use energy for healing purposes, but only in cases when the energy reading tells me I can help. I do not advertise my ability; in fact, most people do not even know I possess it. Recently, I decided to let a group of paranormal researchers study me, so I'm stopping over in Frankfurt for a few days."

"Were you on vacation in Malaysia?"

"Yes, I travelled around the country for two weeks. My wife died two months ago, and I had to get away from home."

"Sorry to hear that. What did she die of?"

"Cancer. Pancreatic. No cure. As an oncologist I knew it, and as an energy reader and a shamanistic healer, I'd read her illness in her aura before the tests confirmed it. I tried to heal her...and for a while, she seemed to be on the mend, and then her condition worsened so much that she died within three weeks. It was her time to go, and nothing could reverse that."

His voice was soft and sad, and his eyes turned misty. We were interrupted by the flight attendant offering drinks and snacks. I opened my bag of nuts and wolfed them down.

"Low blood sugar, right?" He startled me again with his remark because my blood sugar tended to drop, and I could not wait for too long before eating. I looked at him with widened eyes thinking how in the hell could he guess something like that, but then I thought that as a doctor he wouldn't have found that hard to deduce. I didn't say anything, but just gave him a strange look, got up and went to the row in which my family was seated. They were eating sandwiches my wife had packed. My eldest son, Thomas was reading a book, while Jonathan was showing something to Jenna on his computer. My wife Maureen was working on a crossword puzzle in a magazine. On her lap, she had a collection of fashion magazines, and those containing crossword puzzles and Sudoku. I could never understand her reading preferences, and her general aversion toward novels and fiction.

She lifted her head when I leaned my arm on the back of her seat.

"Are you alright in your seat?" she asked with a tone of neutrality that provoked an unvocalized thought in me of, 'As if you give a fuck.' I always harboured a small hope that during our vacation time we could somehow reconnect and reignite the long lost love and passion, but we were like two semi-strangers who slept together, lived together, traveled together, and functioned well enough as a family. In fact, we functioned so well that outsiders, and hopefully not even our children, could easily notice any fissures in the fabric of our marriage.

"I'm Ok. An interesting guy's sitting next to me, so I'll try to kill time chatting with him.

Well, relax and try to catch some sleep. It's gonna be a long, long flight."

I spoke with the kids for a few minutes and then went back to my seat where I found Keith colouring the dragonfly's wing with a shimmering green pencil.

"It's a truly magnificent dragonfly," I said.

"My wife adored them and whenever I draw them, I feel her subtle but unmistakeable presence."

"I also knew someone who loved dragonflies." It was at that precise moment that the memories of Leandra started swirling in my brain coupled with surprise that I would volunteer that kind of information to a stranger. Thoughts of her gathered in my mind, and time seemed to lurch to a halt like an abruptly anchored ship.

"Is it the woman whose imprint I feel in your energy field?"

"What? What imprint and what woman? What are you talking about?" Jesus, man, you're starting to freak me out!"

Keith's voice was calm and soothing. "We all have energy fields and auras. Other peoples' energy can reach us, and we can connect through energy over vast distances. I'm talking about the woman who loves dragonflies...the dragonflies you slew, metaphorically speaking."

"Wh…wh…what the...fuck are…are you rambling about?" My voice was brimming with incredulity and the stutter came back. I am not a rude guy, and I don't often use crass language, but his outrageous remark provoked a vulgar retort.

"Are you saying I'm some kind of fu…freaking dragonfly slayer? And excuse my language. It's not my habit to curse in front of strangers. You just...you just say the weirdest stuff."

Then I heard myself laughing and shaking my head in disbelief over what I'd just heard. Just my luck to end up sitting beside a nutcase! As if I didn't see enough of them in my psychiatric practice. But what he said next made my jaw drop to such an extent that I caught myself gaping at him.

He seemed unfazed when he said, “She loved you and you know that. For her, it was not sheer infatuation; it was connectedness on the soul level. The energy imprint reveals, in fact, not only soul energy, but also past-life energy. She thinks you slew the dragonflies. The dragonflies were part of the magic that your two energies wove while you were together. There’s also energy of another woman mingled here. That energy was stronger and pulled you away from the woman who loved dragonflies. Her name begins with...with...the letter L. Yes, it is definitively L. Yes, the name of the woman who loved dragonflies starts definitively with the letter L."

I was at a loss for words as never before. How could he have guessed all of that? The role of the two women he was alluding to was not something I was proud of. Both were affairs. With Leandra, it was pure erotic magic. Breaking up was dreadfully painful, but like with all the pain, disappointment, rejections and other bad things that happened to me, I buried her deep down in my soul, hoping the pain would never start oozing out of unexpected places. Jorunn helped me get over Leandra. She was someone who would sweep everyone off their feet, with her charm, appeal, beauty, and a contagious smile.

I sighed and looked at Keith waiting for more creepy revelations, but he was drawing again and not looking at me. The plane started to shake and creak under the assault of sudden turbulence. Keith stopped drawing and leaned back. I felt my face drain of blood as anxiety flooded me. There was always something to fear.

“No reason to fear. It will stop in a few minutes.”

Keith’s voice almost made me jump in my seat. He was sitting completely relaxed as if the captain had not announced the turbulence was serious, and that no one should leave their seats including the flight attendants.

I did not reply. Fear and anxiety turned my stomach into a tight knot. There were so many things I was afraid of. Flying scared me, getting old, sick, losing hair, losing my children through accidents, illness...As a boy, I feared my mother would abandon me and forget me like my father had. The bitter taste of abandonment had intensified when my wife turned cold toward me, and started rejecting sex until our lovemaking would happen only once or twice a year. It wasn't even lovemaking; it was her laying herself down on the sacrificial altar of marital duty making me feel humiliated and so forgettable and unwanted. In spite of our alienation from each other, I did not want a divorce, and I did not want to ruin family life for my children. Most of all, the thought of somehow losing my children through an eventual divorce terrified me. Luckily, my affairs ended without Maureen ever suspecting anything. I could have wrecked my life so completely had she found out about Leandra or Jorunn.

"You let fear define you too much," said Keith amplifying my nervousness.

"You know no...thing about me." A veneer of annoyance in my voice masked the fear.

"You are just saying random things hoping for a hit. Yes, I'm afraid of flying like many other people. Nothing unusual about that."

"Fear of flying is the least of your fears." Keith's voice was still calm and soothing.

"Ok, tell me everything you can read about me. I'm listening. In fact, as a psychiatrist, I spend most of my life listening to other people talk about themselves. Bloody high time I learned something about myself. So, you have my full attention." The sarcasm and antagonism in my voice were caustic, but he paid no heed to the tone of my voice.

I was so annoyed that I had not even noticed that the turbulence had finished until the flight attendants came by and started serving dinner. I ordered pasta and wished I had also brought a sandwich along because I was starving, and the pasta could not fill me up. The red wine I was served tasted like vinegar, and I asked for a white instead. After a sip, I looked at Keith with expectation and defiance wishing to prove to him that he couldn't know shit about me and that energy readers were scammers just like mediums, psychics and others who preyed on people's vulnerabilities and gullibility.

Keith was chewing his food slowly and told me he would talk to me after dinner.

That both raised my impatience level and aroused my curiosity, and still shaken up by the violent turbulence I realized that my appetite was ruined. The tomato sauce in the pasta tasted rancid, and the bun was as cold and hard as a golf ball. I ate it all anyway hoping I wouldn't get a stomach ache. Travel was my passion, but flying invariably spoiled every experience.

I ordered more wine and asked for more peanuts. The flight attendant brought me four packages. I wished we could afford business class, but for the cost of five tickets I could probably buy a new car.

"Are you ready?" Keith startled me again.

"Sure! Bring it on!"

"I'm no quack, Weylin. I'm a doctor who happens to have some, let's say, unusual interests and abilities. Where they come from, I can't say. They have always been there. As I said, I don't do readings either for money or entertainment, but occasionally I indulge researchers of the paranormal or those rare doctors interested in exploring novel ways of treating mental disorders, such as using shamanism."

"As a psychiatrist who has been accused by his boss of not being innovative enough with his treatments and of being too averse to prescribing medication, I'm certainly interested in hearing about novel ways of treating mental illness. So please tell me more," I said with enthusiasm.

"One of the reasons I was in Malaysia is my interest in shamanic rituals. I have been studying shamanism for many years, and last year, my wife and I spent six weeks in Honduras and a month in Peru. I have developed my own shamanic and energy reading and healing techniques, and will be demonstrating that ability over the next few days. The reason I'm doing this for you is that I like to help, when I can, even if it is not solicited of me."

"So what do you notice about me?"

"Your aura is very strong, and your energy reveals a lot. In fact, your aura is so intense that it is pulsating in different colours. When I get close to it, images appear, and that is how I was able not only to sense the strong imprint of the woman who still loves you, but also to trace back that energy to past lives. Now, you realize that I had no way of finding out any information before I met you. I know nothing about you, except that your family is sitting several rows behind. I'm not a psychic who will fish for information and who will use what you say to construct my next statement about you. Therefore, I don't want you to validate anything I say."

Keith's voice was relaxed, and I thought that probably nothing could rouse a significant reaction out of him.

"Your energy reveals anxiety. You're always worrying about something. There is also energy of contraction about you, telling me that you are very introverted. You often experience social anxiety in a crowd of unfamiliar people, and that anxiety sometimes produces a sense of panic in you."

He stopped and took a sip of wine, and then did something strange. He took out his drawing pad and scrutinized the dragonfly. What he had said so far about me was bang-on accurate; however, by witnessing my fear of turbulence, he could have extrapolated about my generalized anxiety. And yes, I worried a lot...in fact I always referred to myself as a worrier-in-chief, self-deprecatingly.

The plane started to shake again, increasing my nervousness. I was also starting to sweat and feel queasy from the rancid pasta. Out of nowhere, the memory of Leandra and our long drive from Glasgow to the Ring of Brodgar hit my brain like a bolt of lightning. I remembered how she was touching my knee during the ride, feeding me sandwiches and fruit, whispering she could hardly wait for us to get to the hotel and make love. I also remembered my fear of being caught cheating. But how great it had felt to be wanted so much, and so often! No wonder that rush is so intoxicating that some people are always in search of the beginnings of love.

When we arrived at the stone circle, it was late afternoon already. She was touching the stones one by one as if transfixed. I remembered how she had said that the henge had reminded her of the White Circle, and I did not understand what she meant by that, so I asked her where the White Circle was located. She looked at me perplexed, and then laughed saying she had no idea where that name came from, or why she mentioned it. With her usual insouciance, she kissed me and said, "Never mind. Who knows from which dark recesses of my subconscious that name and image surfaced?"

Having stayed at the circle for a few hours, we drove back to our hotel in Kirkwall and had a romantic dinner in a quaint little restaurant. I was happy with her, and yet terrified that my wife might somehow find out and leave me. Breaking up my family life was never an option, even though I would sometimes daydream of spending the rest of my life with Leandra.

Turbulence snapped me out of my reverie, and I looked at Keith wondering why he stopped reading my energy. I noticed he was still colouring his dragonfly and smiling while absorbed in that work.

"Now, that you have piqued my curiosity, aren't you going to continue reading me?"

"Your negative energy, anxiety and skepticism weakened my own energy and ability to read you. The people I'll be helping this week with their experiments with the paranormal assured me that the energy in the lab would be if not highly positive and friendly, at least open-minded and neutral."

"I'm sorry. I'm a nervous flyer and I have a self-diagnosed generalized anxiety disorder. So, I'm a psychiatrist who treats others with anti-depressants and anxiolytics, when drugs cannot be avoided, but is reluctant to take any himself. So, an energy healing would actually do me good. It's natural and kind of supernatural at the same time."

"I cannot do an energy healing here. You would have to lie down and I'd have to hold my hands above you and move them up and down your body. It would also involve both of us drinking a special herbal concoction. During that slightly altered state of consciousness, I'd be able to read your past lives and through me, you'd be able to remember them. If the source of your fear and anxiety can be traced back to a past life, there's a good chance you might be able to expunge them from your current life. In other words, with the help of that drink I can both read and heal ailments. Without it, the reading is only partial. What's the name of the woman who loves dragonflies?"

His smile was nonchalant, but also full of conviction that the person behind it knew what he was talking about.

I hesitated for a moment, but then whispered her name. Keith did not say anything for a minute, and when he spoke, his words punctured my heart with pain.

"You have tried everything to kill that love, but its imprint is still in your energy field. That woman has never stopped loving you even though she has learned how to live without you, and deny her feelings. The other woman whose name begins with...with J, loved her own reflection in your eyes. She is a wounded soul, a broken soul who siphons energy off people's admiration for her. She needed your energy for a while, but not anymore. She has found meaning and stability in her life, and her well-being no longer depends on seeking and finding adulation. She is also connected to one of your past lives. That connection was of a violent nature, but I am not able to see or feel more details about the circumstances you had shared."

I looked at him speechless. Everything he said sounded true. I had no way of knowing if Leandra still loved me, but I had also noticed Jorunn's need for adoration. She would have probably grown tired of me quickly and moved on in search of more intense attention from others. As to the past lives, I never believed in reincarnation. We go back to dust, and it is the end of our brief existence.

"How can you be sure Leandra still loves me?"

"As I said, I detect her energy. The energy contains residues of deep pain, but the energy of love vibrates strongly and unmistakably. You did not want her to forget you, and she hasn't. In fact, your soul energies are so co-mingled because it seems you have incarnated together several times. I cannot say, that is, I cannot predict if you will incarnate again...even though that is possible, too, but you will definitively enter each other's lives again. There seems to be something unresolved between you…some truth you both need to learn."

Keith stopped talking and resumed colouring the dragonfly. As I looked at his drawing, the dragonfly seemed to move its eyes in my direction. In its look, a shadow of reproach floated. "Keith, can you tell me anything about my wife's energy imprint?" Even though I felt horribly uncomfortable revealing to a complete stranger the intimate parts of my life, I continued.

"She left me...I mean...emotionally she left me and forgot about me years ago...we lost intimacy and have turned into roommates who tolerate each other for the sake of family. How can I put it; it is no longer the marriage I thought I had. When we married, I thought everything would be ideal, and that love and passion would never be lost."

Without moving his eyes from his drawing Keith said, "She feels she was abandoned by you at a critical time, the time when she needed you most. You indulged in something selfish..."

And then he did something strange. He placed the palm of his right hand over my head and started moving it slowly without touching me. I felt a sense of embarrassment well up in me in fear other passengers might notice his bizarre behaviour. Just as I was about to get up and fake having to go to the washroom, he said, "You went on a long trip to indulge your wanderlust and you left your wife alone with your firstborn twins."

I dropped my glass on the floor and the last drops of wine in it spilled. My surprise was of ineffable magnitude. How in the world could he have guessed that I did go alone to the Amazon to fulfill one of my travel dreams? And Maureen stayed alone with Thomas and Jenna, but her parents were there two houses down and helped her daily, and even spent most of the nights in our flat.

"Wow, you're really creeping me out, man. I've no idea how you do it, but so far you've been spot on.

Perhaps you can tell me how I can reconnect with my wife and what it is I'm doing wrong. Even though I have a full-time job, I still help a lot around the house, cook, clean, take care of the kids...but I must be doing something wrong."

"Your gloomy outlook does not help. Your moping and your long face turn your wife off. Your constant allusions to the lack of sex grate on her nerves. She is no longer physically attracted to you, but she appreciates all you have provided for the family. She thinks you are an extraordinary dad, and she is content with the life you have. She does not fully understand the source of your discontent and why you are so sex obsessed. She does sometimes think that you may be unfaithful, but she also tells herself that if you get sexual satisfaction elsewhere and it's only sex, she does not mind too much. If I sat next to her, I'd be able to read her better. This is only what I get from your own energy, which contains traces of hers. And, as a psychiatrist you must know this. Like most people, you let your sense of happiness and fulfilment depend on others. If you loved yourself more and reconnected to the internal source of love hidden within you, the love from without would penetrate you more easily...like an echo or a boomerang it would come back to you. Also, just like so many other relationships, yours has suffered from numbing and alienation that comes through familiarity. Familiarity makes it so easy for us to forget or no longer see the mystery in each other. To resuscitate your marriage you both need to work at breaking out of the stranglehold of familiarity and rediscover the mystery of each other."

Again, he seemed to have hit the nail on the head, and I no longer felt surprised. At that point, I expected he would simply know everything about me and it no longer unnerved me. In fact, I wanted him to provide me with insights into my life realizing that as a psychiatrist I was never successful at self-analysis.

"I still have no idea how you guessed so much about me. It's most fascinating, I must say. I wish I were that insightful with my patients."

I looked at him and noticed he was starting to nod off. We were already four hours into the flight and most people around us seemed to be in deep slumber. The conversation with Keith sparked a million thoughts in me. I still wondered how he could have guessed so much about my life, my relationship with Leandra, my wife, my anxiety... I knew Leandra had loved me with a most fiery passion. Her lovemaking was fierce, and of such sensuality that I could not even begin to describe. I could not remember any woman taking so much erotic pleasure in my body. And then on impulse, I opened my computer and searched for a secret folder in which I kept the erotic stories she wrote for me. I was looking for the one in which she chronicled our weekend in Glasgow and our short visit to the Ring of Brodgar. I still cannot believe I had taken such a huge risk, spending a weekend with my mistress in another country, but my mind was completely drugged with infatuation.

After a few minutes, I located the folder deeply buried under a few other folders, opened the file and read it. Images of us splashed across my mind and my heart suddenly beat not only with a longing for her, but also for a longing to belong to someone again, someone who loved me.

VIGNETTES FROM AN ENCHANTED LIFE

I am waiting in a restaurant close to the car rental office where Weylin went to pick up a car for our weekend escapade. The unquiet in my heart is turning into clamouring anxiety. I feel tremulous and catch myself pacing to and fro from where I am sitting to the staircase landing, from which I can see the door leading to the main restaurant level. He should have already completed the transaction; it cannot take that long to rent a car. Could he have gotten cold feet and left me stranded in Glasgow? I sent him a text message, but he has not responded. From where I am standing, I can only see people from their waist down. I know I will recognize his gait; and then I see him walk into the restaurant in a relaxed and leisurely manner as if he is not about to spend a weekend with his secret lover in the Scottish countryside.

****

Sitting beside him in the rented Alpha Romeo, touching him, whispering love and lust to him feels as surreal as all the fantasy stories we have written for each other. Anticipation of blissful hours ahead of us makes me feel faint. Love swells in my breast; desire drenches me like springtime rain that breathes new life into thirsting flowers. The freeway stretches before us. I feel I have stepped into a dream, into a fairyland in which we are travelling surrounded by verdurous nature, overflowing with the excitement of being together, stealing time from life. I take pleasure in feeding him as he drives, laughing as I pull my fingers away from his hungry, biting mouth. I want that mouth on my skin branding me with fiery kisses. In my head I am weaving dreams of enduring love, as if love can be captured and tamed, and kept forever verdant like the meadows on this pagan summer day.

****

Entering the town of Kirkwall is like walking into a picture book. Under the September sun, stone houses exude inviting warmth. The inn in which we booked our room looks just like in the pictures we had seen on the Internet. We walk into it through a shady, slightly unkempt, but utterly enchanting garden. And our room is what we had wanted; an old-fashioned room that has character and looks like somebody's bedroom and not a typical, impersonal hotel room. The ceiling is tall, the windows large and covered with draperies the pattern of which depicts fairies, butterflies and daffodils. The bed is a four-poster bed with fluffy white pillows and down filled duvet. The wardrobe is ivory-coloured just like the walls.

****

We find ourselves on the bed in no time. My hands are under his white and grey cotton T-shirt hungrily travelling down toward his belt, having no patience for slow lovemaking. Time becomes a blur in my head; I am raw emotion, I am love, I am a body wanting to disappear in another body; I am tongue and lips tasting his skin; I am scent mingled with his scent; I am that peak that mortals reach when they touch heaven for a fraction of an instant and feel immortal; I am a distilled antidote to death.

****

I walk the town with my head in clouds. There is a service in the St. Magnus Cathedral, and we quietly sit in the pews listening to a choir sing. No one suspects that we, two grave sinners have violated the sanctity of this church. We walk around and admire the architecture. But back in the sunshine, my enchantment with the stone houses surrounded by lush gardens with blooming flowers, ivy and wrought iron fences is depthless. The dream continues....

****

Soft candlelight casts warm flickers of light across the ivory coloured room walls. We are dancing slowly to the music coming from a TV channel. He does not like to dance, but he readily agrees to dance with me in the privacy of our room. I have no doubt he would do the same in public under the right conditions. I am breaking through his inhibitions, and that makes me feel so special. Soon, we are naked, kissing hungrily, thirstily, wanting each other like the very first time. His head is between my legs and his lips are sapping the sap oozing out of me and revealing my constant want for him. He wants to eat me and drink me and absorb me and I want to be fused and welded to him both physically and spiritually. His lips are delectable, ambrosial; I know his skin, I feel his blood flow under my tongue; my fingers roam every crevice of his body; I want all of him, his every cell, I want him to be a part of me that I can never lose, forget, or love less....

I am lulled to peaceful sleep with his arms wrapped around me as if they would never let me go....

****

Another glorious summer morning. The market is beguiling with its display of fresh fruit and vegetables, a variety of cheeses and olives, pies, breads, smoked and fresh meats. After breakfast at the hotel, we decide to buy bread, cheese, tomatoes and fruit and have a picnic around the Ring of Brodgar, our destination for the day.

****

The scenic drive makes me feel as if we are driving through a picture book, expecting fairies to start flitting through the air. Perhaps the scenery is not as beautiful as my brain, muddled and intoxicated with love, perceives it.

****

The Ring of Brodgar. Huge stone blocks towering over us puny mortals. I am in awe, barely breathing. I had dreamed for many years of visiting this mystical site, and now, I am standing in front of it, having difficulty processing the impressions. If someone had told me two years ago that I would visit this henge with my lover, I would have laughed in great amusement and would have added, "And after that, I will have afternoon tea with the Queen of England."

I am trying to feel the energy of the site by running my spiritual fingers across the stones and trying to feel their cragginess. Who erected them and why? What do they symbolize? They stand mute before us revealing no answers. In their splendour, in their sheer magnitude they look indestructible and triumphant over us humans whose days on earth are so brief. I sit on the grass feeling my energy mingle with that of the whole universe. I feel gratitude for being given such precious moments. And at that moment, a memory of a different stone circle flickers across my mind and I see the words, "White Circle." And I feel love and pain and I taste disappointment and loss. And then I feel a tender touch on my cheek and look into Weylin's eyes that are brimming with concern. I whisper, "I'm fine, Kieran. For a flicker of a moment I thought I was somewhere else."

"Did you just call me your husband's name?"

I am as confused as he is because my husband's name is Adrian.

****

Sunshine is drizzling on us like liquid honey. We are sitting on a cragged rock gazing at the waters of the Loch of Stenness. There is so much beauty in the brackish water and untamed landscape. Weylin, who is always hungry, opens our bag and takes out bread and cheese. While Weylin is wolfing down the food, I am unable to eat, overwhelmed with the impressions of nature around us, and the mere fact that I am with my lover in Scotland.

****

We are lying in a field near the Ring of Brodgar. From a distance, the stones look even more massive, more imposing. My head is on my lover's stomach, and I want to kiss him and touch him and make love to him, but there are other tourists walking the site and my lover chastises me jokingly that we could be arrested for fornication in a public place. He says,

"Sometimes I think that if I didn't have kids..." and I cut him off not allowing him to complete the sentence. I know what he wanted to say.

****

On the way back to Glasgow, we take a different road that takes us across a bridge. The river underneath is twinkling with translucent hues of green. Ducks are swimming in abandon. All is peaceful and green; the landscape reflects everything I had imagined the Scottish countryside to be. Feelings of enchantment do not subside.

****

The river appears and vanishes on my left side. Stone houses, covered in climbing roses and ivy are on my right. A slideshow of countryside images is playing in my head, and I have no time to process the imagery. We are looking for a place to have tea. From time to time, his hand is on my knee. We touch while we are driving. I love him.

****

I remember the book "The Enchanted Garden" at the moment we step into a coffee shop surrounded by a garden. I feel that there is or should be a river or a creek bank below the lawn with tables and chairs, but I do not explore much. My lover brings a tray with tea, sconces, crème fraîche and jam. The landscape around us, the tranquility, the charm of the coffee shop, the plants in the nursery behind the coffee shop, the Golden Retriever named Benny who sits between us, the sight of my lover so near, so mine for a few brief hours, make my eyes well up with emotion. We know that we will have to part, all too soon. Our conversation seems somewhat fragmented, and among the fragments are our words expressing openness toward the possibility that some day we could be together. A shadow of melancholy clouds my lover's eyes. I tell him that many of our daydreams have become true, so let us make a wish. He says he does not dare. I ask him if he fears the wish may not come true. He replies that he is afraid it might come true and that is a no-win situation. I suggest we make a win-win wish so that whatever happens, no one gets hurt.

****

He wants us to dress up for dinner. We are to eat on a patio of a lovely restaurant even though it is a bit cool to sit outside. I ask him to choose between the brown or black dress for me to wear. He chooses the brown one. I wear a sequined leopard print sweater over it. I also ask him to choose the panties I will wear. He chooses black lace. He tells me I am beautiful and that he is being objective. I smile knowing that love paints everyone beautiful. He is dashing in his white shirt. Later over dinner, looking at him, I feel as if I am dream walking, and will awake at any moment alone, feeling hollow, starting to fade and pine for my lover...but we are still here, in Scotland and I am clinging to every moment. We talk about his children, who are the centre of his universe. I, who come from an outer circle of his life, make some observations about his relationship with his children and my comments touch something deep in his heart, some hidden, intuited but not fully acknowledged truth. His heart opens to mine and I walk into it.

****

Back in the room, his passion is burning brighter than ever before. He looks at me as if he sees me for the first time, his look revealing boundless love. He whispers repeatedly, "I love you, I love you, I love you"...He pins me against the wall, pulls up my dress...his lips are on my inner thighs, right above my stay-ups, exploring me, caressing me. He stands up...his white-hot kisses are bruising me deliciously, and I am drunk with love and lust again. He whispers, "I will make love to you, and I will show you how much I love you." The candlelight flickers like the electrical and chemical signals in my brain that have gone haywire...Again, I am love, I am lust, I am melting into him, into his body that looks like smooth-sculptured stone...I find myself on the bed under him...he is inside me and the feeling is beyond a mortal man's power of description...the path to my culmination is brief and I moan softly and then loudly, and twist and writhe in the sweetest of agonies, and my heart is like a brilliant star throbbing against his heart.

****

After breakfast, we drive to the airport, planning to leave the rented car there. I watch him drive, and tenderly touch his stubble. At the airport lounge, I realize that time is ticking away much too quickly and that I will have to leave soon. The time spent with him was sheer magic, the most beautiful dream...Do I dare crave more...is it ingratitude to wish for more and more for myself when so many people have not known love and passion...We stand up to embrace and say goodbye and I wince in pain, and my chest is constricted with heartache. On the way to the gate, numbness sets in like a protective membrane ...but I know that there is another nick of painful loss etched in my heart...

2

Weylin

Another bout of turbulence startled me from a shallow dream through which Leandra trod lightly. I cursed loudly. Keith looked at me quizzically, but remained silent. My computer screen went into a sleep mode, so I turned it back on because I wanted to close Leandra's chronicle of our weekend in Scotland. In fact, I thought I should have deleted all traces of her, including my secret email account I used to write to her, and send her the erotic stories I wrote about us. The sexual energy between us had had the strength of a nuclear reaction, so no wonder Keith could still detect its traces in my energy field.

"What you said about Leandra makes sense," I said to Keith who looked at me with a flicker of incomprehension in his eyes.

"I want you to tell me more about my connection to her... I always believed there was a special bond between us that even the passage of time has not completely dissolved. Can you tell me more...please? "

"The energy between the two of you, and between the two of you and your other lover is intermingled. It is the energy of past lives. I cannot tell you more now. As I've already mentioned, to tell you more, I'd have to get you into an altered state of consciousness to enable you to access your past lives and understand the nature of your connection."

"How do you do that? Tell me more about it because I'm not sure I understood what you had previously mentioned. Do you use hypnotherapy?"

"I discovered another method in Honduras during my shamanic apprenticeship. I am in possession of a recipe for an herbal concoction that not only allows you access to the spirit world and the Source that some call God, but also to the gate beyond which lies the path to your past lives."

"Ayahuasca?"

"Ayahuasca has become the buzz word among psychedelic users and tourism is booming around it. What I'm talking about, however, is unknown in the mainstream circles. In Honduras, I met a young woman who told me her grandfather was a shaman in a very remote mountain village. She said that he could summon spirits, and cure most illnesses, but also enable people to access their past lives. This way, they could better understand the lessons recurring in their present life. And I heard a voice in my head nudging me to seek out this man and learn from him. My wife was not happy about my decision to travel for two days through a jungle, but her curiosity was also piqued."

Keith stopped talking and asked a flight attendant for some water. I was impatiently waiting for him to continue, but he was taking his time sipping his drink.

"Anyway, the journey through the jungle was difficult even though I hired two experienced guides. The heat was unbearable, the mosquito bites were burning our skin and I was tempted several times to turn back, but surprisingly, my wife insisted that we continue on and find the shaman. And so we persisted and reached this secluded village and spent seven unforgettable weeks there. I am fluent in Spanish because my mother was Mexican, so I had no communication problems."

"What was the shaman like?"

"An old man with the body of a middle-aged man. A fascinating person, who could talk to trees, animals, and plants. He was also very inquisitive and wanted me to show him my healing powers and to read his energy. Friendship and trust quickly developed between us. Three weeks into my stay at the village, he told me he felt I was ready to try his herbal concoction that could take me onto a journey into my past lives. He said that once I accessed the world of spirits, I'd need to find one who would take me through the hole in time. He said he'd help me communicate clearly my desire to go back in time as he would also drink the tea and the plant power would connect us."

"That sounds pretty crazy to me. I thought that psychedelics produced in you the sensations of connectedness to the entire universe...but that they cannot regress you to past lives...at least that's what I read...not that I was ever interested in it all that much."

"It's only this particular brew that can do that. The chemicals in it unblock suppressed memories. One of the chemicals is DMT, better known as the spirit molecule that can produce both effects of either unimaginable terror or bliss. It has been associated with the near-death experiences because some believe that it is released at the times of extreme stress. In some studies, the volunteers to whom DMT was administered were able to gain clear insights into their mental conditions, and were able to overcome anxiety and depression. However, the herb I possess and grow can do much more because it is composed of a mixture of DMT and more potent psychedelic chemicals. It does produce hallucinatory effects, but with the right dosage, it enables those who trip to not only pull aside the veil and get a glimpse of parallel worlds, but also to open the portals to past lives. I experienced it first-hand by gaining access to a past life during the 17th century, when I was a seventeen-year-old boy who drowned when the ship I worked on sank in a raging storm. The ship was Portuguese and was on its route to Latin America. That certainly explained my fear of swimming."

"A bit hard for me to suspend disbelief. What's the name of the brew you drank that enabled you to go back to a past life?"

"Jacacia. As I said, this shaman concocted it through experimentation with several plants. By crossbreeding a few hallucinogenic plants, he was able to grow Jacacia. It took him ten years of trial and error to create a new breed of psychedelic plant. He taught me how to boil it and use it. A chemist is currently running a series of tests on it in his lab to determine what other chemicals besides the DMT the plant contains. Phil Grey, a psychiatrist friend has gone through a quagmire of hoops and loops trying to get permission to use the plant to try it out on schizophrenic, psychotic and terminally ill patients. You cannot imagine the mountains of paperwork he had to fill out to obtain permission to trial it on human subjects. Phil is also listed on the approval request form as the person owning the herb. I was his supplier, but that was not mentioned in the application forms. It was only stated that there was enough of the drug for trials on about twenty individuals. If approved, and he should be getting an answer any day now, I'll be working at his side."

"How do you import it from Honduras? It must be illegal."

"I grew it at home from a seedling I brought back from my trip. I built a solarium, which I keep heated and humidified. I have a banana tree in it, and all kinds of tropical plants. No one could ever recognize a psychedelic plant among them, especially one that is practically unknown."

"So does it do anything else except awaken past life memories?"

"Yes, of course...what good would it do you to access your past lives without some effect on your current one? I also know a few people who were cured from anxiety and depression after ingesting it a few times. Under its influence, they were able to access their past lives and were illuminated with the knowledge of the meaning of their life, of their soul's path and purpose, and of the reasons behind their current problems. My wife took the brew after she realized she was dying and the result was peace and acceptance. She was the one who ended up comforting me. A part of the research in Frankfurt will focus on the effects of Jacacia. I have it in my suitcase masked as tea. Unfortunately, I can only make enough brew to try it out on one person. Imagine me, a reputable oncologist smuggling a few grams of psychedelic herb into Germany!" His laughter was wry.

"At that moment, an idea flashed across my mind. I wanted to convince my boss to seek permission for trials with this brew on some of our patients. It would be a limited study. I was sure if I presented this correctly, there was a chance she'd buy into it and seek approval from her high-flying friends in the Ministry of Health. After all, she receives plenty of research money and finding volunteers would be easy. Such an initiative on my part might redeem me in her eyes. She had always found me too stuck on traditional treatments and psychoanalysis, and reluctant to prescribe psychopharmacology products. Something this radical coming from the traditionalist like me would probably shock her.

"A study of this kind could result in an article that could revolutionize treatments of serious clinical depressions. And then Leandra came to mind again, but for a different reason. I remembered helping her collect clinical data on the effects of a new anxiolytic; I planned to ask her if she'd be interested in collaborating on this project. There was no reason why we could not collaborate and let bygones be bygones. I didn't expect her to hold any grudges against me. She would have forgotten about our affair a long time ago. It could not have possibly meant a whole lot to her, anyway."

"Listen, Keith. I find what you've told me very exciting and I'd like to propose something. If I manage to persuade my boss to seek approvals to conduct a small-scale research on a group of severely depressed or anxious people, who are resistant to conventional drugs, would you supply us with the brew and train us on how to use it? Of course, we would fund your travel expenses and pay for the training."

"I think it's a brilliant idea to have a government-sponsored study. The problem is, no one really knows I have the plant and bringing it to Ireland would be illegal. You said you were from Dublin, right?" asked Keith and continued without waiting for a response.

"How would I declare it at the customs? I'm growing it in secrecy. But if we get approvals without anyone grilling Phil on how he came into possession of the herb, we could include you and your boss into the study."

"Where are you located?" I asked.

"In Montreal."

"What a coincidence! Leandra lives there." I said with surprise.

Keith looked at me briefly without commenting and continued. "Before testing it out on patients, I believe we should all be part of the experiment first, to gain firsthand knowledge of its effectiveness and safety. After our trials have been documented, and after we receive a full license from our authorities to use the drug, you could then initiate your own study with our assistance. You would then be able to refer to our study and licenses in your approval request forms, and obtain the drug legally. We now have one more form to fill out and that one requires that we identify the source of our drug supply. We are yet to come up with something credible that will not put our whole study into jeopardy."

"Alright, I will discuss it with my boss, and you and I will stay in touch. As soon as you have received your approvals, and if my boss agrees, we can start planning to visit you. I was just thinking of inviting Leandra to participate as the two of you live in the same city. She is a renowned and well-published psychiatrist, and I am sure her contributions would be of great value. Isn't that the strangest of coincidences, come to think of it?" I detected a change in the timbre of my voice as a wave of embarrassment washed over me and I could not explain its source.

"Perhaps, it is not a coincidence. Your life paths need to cross again. There is a purpose behind it, even though I cannot tell you what it is."

"What happened between us was pure folly. Sometimes, you fall under the spell of infatuation and you take risks in search of pleasure denied at home. Luckily, it all ended without anyone getting hurt."

As I was speaking, I was still in disbelief I was revealing so much to a complete stranger. At the same time, it felt good to confide in someone I did not know well. Strangers tended to be less judgmental. My own thoughts and feelings confounded me.

Keith must have turned his attention to my aura again, as I noticed his eyes slowly scan across my body, and then off to an unseen distance. "You're wrong about nobody getting hurt." His finger traced off to that same distance. "Her pained energy still reaches out to you even though you do not sense it, but it is clear that she was horribly hurt. You obviously got over her much more quickly than she got over you." His eyes snapped back to mine, and he half-smiled. "I can see you're puzzled. But thoughts are energy, so thinking about something or someone creates a connection to it. And when the thoughts harbour strong emotion, even more energy flows to the object of its attachment.

"I never intended to hurt her in any way. I did not know what I wanted. I did not know what to do any more, how to behave. I was too torn and too afraid of losing what I had. Before we broke up, I could only see the negative sides of adultery. The horrific burden of it. Breaking up was painful for me too, but the sense of freedom that came with it was tremendous. I'm sure she's well over me and we can collaborate as good colleagues."

"Alright! We'll explore that vein of discussion if we get permission to conduct this study, and permission for you to join us. It should all be aboveboard. I have no desire to act like an illegal drug dealer, so I have to declare how I came into possession of the plant."

Keith fumbled in his backpack and extracted a somewhat crumpled business card. I told him I did not have any with me, but that I'd write to him once I was back at work to discuss this further. All of a sudden, I felt hopeful that by trying something so unorthodox I would find answers to the many questions semi-articulated in my subconscious mind. I had never believed in past lives, but now the mystery of reincarnation seemed to have imbued every cell of my being, and I could not wait to try the secret brew and reconnect with whatever experiences lay behind the veil.

Perhaps I would gain insights as to what was missing in my marriage, and if it could be repaired. And perhaps, I would discover the source of the longings, the echoes of which I have continually felt as deep stirrings within my soul.

I got up to use the restroom and talk to my family, but they were all asleep looking contorted and uncomfortable. I thought once again how torturous air travel was.

As I got back in my seat, the late hour registered. Keith was snoring lightly, and the cabin lights had dimmed, but slumber escaped me. I put on the headset and found a channel with soft instrumental music.

Like unexpected lightning flashing across a cloudless sky Leandra's face flashed across my inner eye as soon as the first notes of the old instrumental, "Kiss," started to seep languidly into my ear. The old melody, to which we had danced during the last weekend we stole from life, resurrected memories that flooded from under the patina of oblivion, and unexpectedly filled my eyes with tears.

I faulted Keith's bizarre comments. 'She is just a ghost, a mere ghost from the past,' I heard myself mutter. I did not want to dwell on the past. After all, I'd stuffed so many painful memories deep down into my soul and I did not want to lift the lid on that casket. And I didn't even like that too-sugary melody. That was Leandra's taste in music. To me it sounded like elevator or department store music. But her body had felt like an extension of mine, like a perfect fit at the nano-level. I wanted to abandon that train of thought and stop thinking about her. *Goddammit Keith! Why did you have to mention traces of her energy on me? There's no such bloody thing. Such assertions go beyond any lunacy I've ever heard.*

My hand went to my face and touched a trail of wetness sliding from my left eye. Fucking dry airplane air! I needed eye drops, but did not feel like rummaging through my backpack.

My thoughts went to my marriage. For many years now, I had felt disconnected from my wife. I believed I had tried everything I could to revive the spark in our relationship, to rebuild the bond of intimacy, until I finally realized that the cold, dead embers were impervious to ignition. Or maybe the fire had simply stopped burning in me after the countless times my wife rejected my amorous overtures. And yet, even such dead embers held much deeper worth than any forbidden fire, albeit one of volcanic magnitude and intensity.

Guilt had always gnawed at me while I was living parallel lives. It was loathsome to lie to my family about business trips and meetings that just happened to take place on weekends and yet, I could not resist the illicit pull.

Every time I would return home from my escapades, the contrast between a weekend filled with breathless lovemaking, giggles and star-filled gazes would be achingly stark, making me feel as if I were surfing ocean waves, the troughs as frighteningly deep as the soaring heights of the crests. Such emotional rides would make my stomach drop as if the ride had been a physical rollercoaster.

The black and white contrast became a source of anxiety, bringing brief bouts of depression. But whenever my mind would manage to escape the shackles of what felt like temporary insanity, and access the wan light of lucidity, I would get a glimpse of the nature of love affairs. They were castles in the air built on chimera and fantasy, and their lifespan was that of a dragonfly. So it was better to slay that dragonfly before anyone had a chance to catch me straying.

At that moment, I remembered dragonflies hovering over a pond in the park Leandra and I had walked alongside holding hands like two teenagers in love. And like magic one of them landed on my face just as Leandra exclaimed how much she loved them. *This must be a case of Jungian synchronicity;* I had thought and mentioned it to Leandra.

She said how fascinated she had been when as a first-year medical student she had read that a female patient was telling Dr. Karl Jung about her dream of a beetle, when that same species of beetle banged against the window. That was how Jung's theory of synchronicity or meaningful coincidences was born. From that moment on, she had always been on the lookout for these meaningful coincidences. And there were so many of them whilst I was secretly meeting with her. The Universe seemed to have conspired to give us sunny days and starry nights for our trysts, flights that departed and arrived on time, favourite songs that played on the hotel room radios, free room upgrades…

But I was a child of fortune who had extricated himself from the quicksand of a love affair and regained his integrity. And my short fling with Jorunn did not even count as a serious infidelity. Leandra never tried to fight for me or convince me not to break up our relationship. Even though her devastation over the news that I could no longer maintain our relationship was palpable, she said she understood. No one should live a double life. That is unworthy, so beneath a life of honesty.

No, I did not really miss her. After all, she may have been right in her observation that my feelings for her were only born out of a fleeting infatuation that wore the cloak of love. Yes, I was infatuated with her green eyes and her blonde hair piled up on the top of her head.

I had also admired her ability to turn any small talk into an intellectual conversation, and her sense of compassion that would make her weep over the injustices and immeasurable suffering in the world.

More memories started flooding my mind. After I left her, I buried her memory deep in the coffin of my subconscious mind, the same coffin in which I had stuffed so many painful memories of past rejections, betrayals, hurts and disappointments, hoping they'd never return to haunt me. That was how I always dealt with pain. I was a man who buried his demons nine feet under because I believed that if ignored long enough, they would vanish for good.

Another recollection pierced my heart with the vividness of an event that had just happened. We were in the elevator going back to our room. We had just swum in the hotel pool and were dressed in bathrobes. Unlike our elevator rides in most cities, this one was different. Something was amiss. And it was clear that it was the nature of our love. Like a noxious substance seeping insidiously into our relationship, it corroded our joy of being together. The stars in her eyes did not have the same lustre. Perhaps the secrecy was too heavy a burden to bear. I pretended everything was all right and planted playful kisses in her hair.

I had no reason to remember Leandra, except for Keith's crazy remarks, but it worried me that the buried memory chest seemed to be leaking unwanted recollections. After all, more than five years had passed since I had left her in a state of shell-shocked disbelief by telling her I had undergone an inexplicable transformation and wanted to break up. Every choice came with consequences, and my fear was that the consequences of my affair would ruin my life if my wife discovered my infidelity.

I was not able to give Leandra time to adjust to losing me because I had no energy left, not even for friendship. It was simply the right thing to do. It was simply immoral to be unfaithful. And I didn't question if it was honourable to be unhappy. I never meant to hurt Leandra, but I was tired of our painful partings and most of all, of the secrecy and fear of being discovered, threatening the loss of my safe and comfortable life.

I buzzed the flight attendant and asked for a whiskey. She was kind and said she would bring me some from business class. I had always disliked its taste, but somehow I found it went well with the maudlin instrumentals the airplane station was playing.

One shot turned into two and I blamed the alcohol and Keith for the memories that began swirling in my mind, making me dizzy and nauseated. With my fingers, I began to trace my thinning hairline, and all of a sudden felt the need to look in the mirror without understanding what secret impulse prompted me to do so. I got up and went to the restroom.

My reflection alarmed me. The lines in my face had deepened over the last year and the grey in my hair was drowning out the last black streaks. My temples were balding and my eyes had the hollow look of a man with a hardened shell devoid of love. "You look so lifeless," I whispered to the shrunken stranger in the mirror, his state brought about not so much by aging, but from a lack of love. Then I noticed a shadow of sorrow cloud the face in the mirror as another memory surfaced from the dark recesses of my mind.

On the bed, with legs folded into the lotus position, Leandra had reached for my white shirt that was lying crumpled on a pillow, and put it on. She brought one lapel close to her nostrils and inhaled its scent. She said that remembering my scent helped dissolve the physical distance between us. Then she began to cry unexpectedly.

'Weylin, I feel it deep in my soul that we are reaching the end of our road together. Something is happening to you and I cannot stop it. I also feel that both my love for you and the pain when we have to say goodbye are changing me. The guilt of being in a relationship with a married man and cheating on my husband keeps me awake at night.' Emotion choked her. When she looked up again, tears were glistening in her eyes.

'I've had another premonition and this one said you'd leave me soon, and I will rely on my work as therapy…it will be my self-medication and, hopefully it will bring healing. After all, my purpose is to bring healing to others and in giving to others I will hope to heal the wounds you will be inflicting on me, albeit unintentionally.'

'Don't say such things! We will be together for a long, long time. Feelings do not change overnight or from one week to another.'

She had lowered her gaze and turned her head toward the wall. Her weeping was mute, silent, and her body immobile. I pulled her toward me and almost instantly, the scorching fire of desire alchemized the moment of deep sadness into ecstatic lovemaking. And that was the last time we saw each other. Once I was home, exhaustion burrowed a deep hole in my heart. And I could no longer live a life of duplicity. I had to tell her because I had always told her the truth, and that brought shocked silence on the other end of the telephone line. We both sobbed, not able to articulate the pain, and our final goodbye reverberated in silence.

For weeks on end, I suppressed impulses to call her or write to her, telling myself she had been a brief fling and that my thoughts had made the pain of loss appear bigger than it was. Little by little, by exerting extraordinary willpower, I succeeded in pushing her out of my mind.

Developing a bond with Jorunn, a colleague from Norway helped immensely. Her sparkling charm and seductive power wiped out the last traces of Leandra. She flirted with me and teased me, and when she shook her mane of black hair before me, I felt I was losing my mind again. I wanted her and finally at the conference in Barcelona she let me have her.

Afterwards, she only wanted to be friends. Leandra also came to that conference. Before that, we had exchanged a couple of emails and broken the nine-month long silence. She confronted me about seeing Jorunn and replacing her so easily. I felt so utterly uncomfortable under her accusatory eyes, and I said I had no need to justify myself for having a good time. She asked me many questions to which I had no answers. I just wanted to get away from her as soon as possible.

I went back to my seat feeling physically and mentally exhausted. I wondered why my life had not gone the way I had imagined and hoped it would.

When I got married, I expected my life to unfold smoothly; I expected love and passion to persist and withstand the onslaught of time. Extreme naiveté? Was I unconscious of the inevitable change that everything in life is vulnerable to, emotions, physical bodies and all existence?

Suddenly, feelings of depleted energy, corrosive sorrow, aimlessness and hopelessness enveloped me. This melancholy in me seemed to be rooted in something I, as the vessel that bore it, could not explain. My psychiatric knowledge was helpless before my own barren soulscape and my yearnings for something I could not clearly delineate in my mind, for some truth I had yet to uncover.

What did I need? Psychotherapy with a colleague? Meditation? A divorce? Like gyres and eddies in an untameable river, questions without answers were swirling in my head. And then I knew with a certainty I had not felt for a long time, that I would visit Keith and try his mysterious substance. And I would invite Leandra to participate and try to forge a new relationship with her, one of warm collegiality.

3

Weylin

After our return to Dublin, I still had two days of vacation left and spent them reading and lounging around the house. I was tempted to watch a rugby game, but heavy sheets of rain flooding the city forced the organizers to cancel the match.

My energy level was still high as travel electrified me unfailingly. Maureen was also in a lively mood, and we talked quite a bit about our experiences in Malaysia. Jonathan was planning to give a presentation to his classmates about this trip and spent a few hours sorting through the pictures.

My in-laws and my mother came for dinner and all of us regaled them with our travel stories. My mother returned our cat to us, joking that next time we left she would keep Trixie because she was growing more and more attached to the white and fluffy feline. As far as I was concerned, she did not have to return the cat because I did not care much for cats, but I knew the children would protest vehemently as they adored their feline sibling.

The first day back at work was hectic. I was overbooked, and by the time my last patient left, I felt in need of another vacation.

Before leaving the office, I sent an email to Keith telling him I was still interested in trying his mysterious psychedelic drug. I was deeply intrigued by what he had told me and started to imagine treating my own patients with Keith's concoction and affecting their healing, or significantly improving their mental health. I have always had the desire to make a name for myself and leave some kind of permanent professional mark, ensuring thus I would never be forgotten.

The next day I arrived at work feeling under the weather. I thought I may have a caught some bug on the plane, and was happy to see only seven patients were booked due to three cancellations. The first patient was new. It was an attractive woman with curly blond hair and a firm handshake.

"Ariadne Quigley. Pleased to meet you Dr. McLoughlin. I'm so happy I was able to get an appointment with you."

"Make yourself comfortable, please. Tell me why you needed to see me."

She sighed deeply, looked at her fingernails and then bored her gaze into me.

"I'm having anxiety attacks and believe I need medication. It is crippling me and as a cardiac surgeon, I'm afraid if it goes untreated, it will have an adverse effect on my work. My greatest fear is that I will experience an anxiety attack while performing a surgery, and would not be able to complete it, or even worse, that I might make a fatal mistake and lose the patient."

"Do you have a history of anxiety or is this new?"

"Relatively new. I divorced my husband two years ago and the process leading up to the dissolution of our marriage had been stressful and painful. It was not easy to explain to my two teenage children that their parents were joining the dismal statistics of failed marriages. Both my son and daughter blamed me for the break-up of our family. In spite of the horrible turmoil the divorce created, I did not feel anxiety. I felt sadness, sorrow, anger and disappointment, but not anxiety over the future. Especially because my husband and I managed to maintain an almost amicable relationship and contact. My anxiety was precipitated by another event that shattered my soul."

"I'm listening."

I noticed a sudden tremor in Ariadne's chin as she was collecting her thoughts in preparation of telling me her story. Even the most articulate persons find it difficult to give shape to their grief, losses or mental illness using mere words. What words cannot convey, the anguish in their eyes expresses giving shape to a fuller picture. And it was anguish misting her blue gaze.

"About eight months after my divorce, I received a call from a man I'd been madly in love with some thirty years ago. I was a medical student and Hugo a plastic surgery resident. The relationship seemed ideal, the power of attraction between us volcanic; we seemed to know what the other one was thinking, we'd easily complete each other's thoughts; I felt I was walking in dreamland. And then one day, out of the blue he called me to say he had to break up with me...that I had come too close for his comfort...that he was no longer capable of handling that surge of emotion...that I was sapping the energy he needed for his residency. You are probably aware that it is a very prestigious field and few surgeons could access it."

Choked up with emotion she stopped speaking and I told her to take her time.

"It took me a long time to recover from that shock, but I was young back then, and I survived and fell in love again. I was fortunate enough to have had parents who were well off, and funded my travels all over the world, and it was during such trips that I'd fall in love again and enjoy life to the fullest. But back to what I started to tell you...a few months ago I received a call from Hugo and I was in disbelief that he contacted me after what seemed like centuries of silence. He said he was in town and wanted to see me, and I agreed to meet him in his hotel lobby. He lives in London; in fact, he moved back to London from the US a few years ago."

Her sobs interrupted her narrative and I got up to offer her a box of tissues. She readily accepted it and placed the box on her lap. She wiped her eyes and I noticed a discreet twitch in her right eyelid.

"What Hugo told me rattled me to the core. After many years of successful and lucrative practice, he suffered a terrible and freak accident. He fell out of a tree while apple picking and smashed several bones including some in both his hands. His surgical career was over, even though he healed enough for everyday tasks. After that enormous setback, he began working for an NGO delivering humanitarian aid to countries in need, and working with Doctors Without Borders. He still could not do anything of a surgical nature, but he was in charge of a UN-sponsored vaccination programme. Unfortunately, the fall was not the worst thing that happened to him. He developed cancer and underwent a radical cystectomy. So his whole bladder and prostate were removed, and a stoma for urine collection installed. Since the cancer was of a highly invasive type, he has been living in fear of its spread. When I asked him why he contacted me, he told me he had never forgotten me, and that I'd always been the love of his life. His marriage was unhappy, he told me, but he stayed because of his children."

She paused and looked at me. "Doctor, you have a strange look in your eyes, all of a sudden. Did I say something inappropriate?"

She stopped talking and looked at me expectantly. I could feel myself blush. Hearing her mention Hugo's unhappy marriage made me think of my own, in which I'd felt trapped without seeing any way out. Yes, divorce in modern society was easy enough, but I viewed it as a failure, and I did not want to fail at marriage even though I may have failed at it a long time ago beyond any chance of redemption. I also could not help but notice the ubiquitous cliché about the unhappy marriages that men seeking affairs tell their mistresses. Hadn't I been one of them, too?

"No… of course not," I assured her. "You did not say anything unusual. Please continue."

"I cannot even explain how I ended up in his room. Having had two straight gins on an empty stomach does not justify or explain the pull toward his arms. What happened that night was pure and distilled bliss. I felt myself glow in his arms as I had ages ago when we were young; I felt the time and distance that had accumulated between us melt away in an instant; his joy in being in my arms was intoxicating; the beauty of his soul that merged with mine elevated and ushered us into a new dimension. I touched the stoma on his stomach as a portal into the divine and sacred. My love gave him back his manhood that he thought he'd lost forever after the surgery; he told me I was his antidote to his impending death...Yes, he said he was dying, and it was only a matter of time before the Grim Reaper knocked on his door."

Her words reflected some of the feelings I had felt while I was illicitly in love with Leandra. Her love had been an antidote to my self-doubt and my lack of self-love.

"After he left Dublin, I expected we would continue seeing each other; however, after the initial exchange of texts, he stopped writing to me. He suddenly began to ghost me and that flung me into unspeakable agony and anguish because I was madly in love with him all over again. Imagine, to resurface out of nowhere in my life, only to leave me suffocating in his silence. I continued to write to him, but he was not responding. I felt as if I was walking a tightrope between death and insanity...I felt I was losing my mind, but had to compose myself...I had no choice but to go back to work hoping the surgical knife in my hand wouldn't shake, that my children would not have to suffer additional stress from seeing their mother in another type of emotional disarray. I was also plagued by fear that he might have died and that was the reason behind his silence."

Now, Ariadne started coughing and I could see she had difficulty swallowing. I poured her a glass of water from the pitcher on my desk. I always kept it there because I tended to forget to drink enough and stay hydrated. She thanked me and continued.

"His silence was devastating, and its weight felt like a cumulative and combined effect of every single heartbreak and rejection I had ever experienced. I wept for days on end not understanding why he would do that to me again. How can you tell someone you love them and then vanish? I wondered if such cruelty, intentional or unintentional, could inflict so much hurt as to fling someone, like me, into despair so deep that they could die of a broken heart. These are all rhetorical questions, I know, but that is how I felt. Anyway, after two months of silence he called me again to tell me he was in Dublin and wanted to see me. And that was another weekend during which he loved me again purely and completely, he a man dying and broken fulfilling every fantasy of mine, awakening in me feelings of ultimate aliveness and belonging, a soul-warming joy that just felt like pure wonder. Being with him felt like crossing into a dimension of exquisite purity, transparency and comfort."

Ariadne's breathing was laboured, and I asked her to take a few deep breaths to calm herself. At the same time, it was obvious to me that her anxiety must have deeper roots than those stemming from heartbreak. She was looking at the floor and then she bent down to retie her shoe before resuming speaking.

"So after such extreme emotional and physical intimacy we experienced, after moments of complete spiritual fusion, he did the same thing again. He vanished without a trace and would not respond to any of my texts. He erected a wall between the two parallel worlds he was living in, and once back to his family nest he severed all contact with me, as if I never existed, as if I never mattered. And my anxiety level grew exponentially after each of his visits, and there have been several. But the last one ended with even more profound heartbreak. After I sent him several messages, he finally replied saying he was in hospital suffering from complicated sepsis and he wanted privacy and space and for me to withdraw gracefully. In other words, no more contact. With cancer as his underlying condition, I have expected him to die any day. Every morning, as soon as I get up, I google obituaries in London. My heart lurches in my throat every time I see an obituary of someone with the same name. And my anxiety mounts and mounts and I feel I am descending into a dark well of madness."

She took another gulp of water and after drinking it, she shook her head signalling to me that she was still not able to continue speaking. I waited patiently for her to regain her voice.

"So you haven't heard from him anymore?"

"No, not a word, not a thank you for the birthday greeting I sent him. I feel I am doomed, I feel like the living dead, experiencing fits and spurts of anguish, fury, sadness... I also feel as if some negative, dark souls have been preying on both Hugo and me, and that they control him and will kill him, and then invade my mind completely and possess me. Am I going insane?"

"I think what you are describing are the symptoms of repeated and abrupt withdrawal.

His intermittent showing up in your life hooks you onto feelings of love intoxication, and then he lets you go into freefall of withdrawal, of craving the drug of love, the dispensing of which he controls. You need to find ways to help yourself get out of…"

"I'm aware of that and I've tried to sublimate the pain through my hobbies of painting, ceramics and photography, but nothing has helped. I feel I'm living in a vacuum of disappointment of being abandoned and dismissed by him ...his presence galvanizes me and infuses me with life while his silence brings agony and is brutally rearranging my entire existence. I feel this painful shearing of my heart, I feel ravaged, and pillaged, and seasick from this ride into the realms of ecstasy and the abyss of agony. He is my true love, but I cannot have him, and I do not know what to do with this pain...it has nowhere to go, but keeps accumulating. What is also challenging is that I have no harbour to return to for safety. I feel I'm forever weathering storms... even in the silence and relative calm there always seem to be storms brewing on the horizon."

"Do you have family and friends that can offer support?"

"Few friends can relate to such emotional excesses. Most feel I am the one feeding this obsession by giving it energy. One of them is my sister. And I would never reveal my feelings to my parents because there would be no understanding on their part... only an infinite number of whys. Why did he come back if he knew he was dying, why did he not communicate? Questions without answers."

"How is your relationship with your parents?"

"In a word, superficial and that has always bothered me. I'm exhausted of playing the role they imposed on me and expected of me. I was always supposed to be strong and perfect and accomplished, a great mother and wife, and I feel I have failed in each one of these roles.

My husband used to be my pillar of strength, but I lost his love, too, and feel like an invalid."

"Give me some examples of your interaction with your parents."

"They treat me like an idiot. It's all these details and all this subtle nagging...or asking banal questions showing they do not even trust me with being able to make an omelette. They'd ask how many eggs I used or what cheese, or why did I cut bread in such thin or such thick slices, or why I served breakfast on these particular plates instead of those flower-patterned ones because these are not dish-washer safe, or how overfilled the glasses are....They do not treat our relatives that way, only me. With everyone else, my parents are pure sweetness. In a nutshell, they have always been hypercritical of me, of my weight, clothes, cooking, boyfriends...they are simply brutal with me, and yet expect constant help and support from me."

"Have you brought that up with them and told them how that makes you feel?"

"I tried so many times only to be told I was being melodramatic, and I acted like a Prima Dona or a drama queen. Things only get worse when my daughter started showing a total lack of compassion and kindness toward me. I feel deserted by the entire world, and feel that my existence is in shambles. I see it as meaningless, and I feel like I'm walking in a deep muddy rut, barely able to lift my feet. I feel surrounded by a wall of pain, and I am finding myself unable to peer over its edge to see hope...so I thought medication might be of help."

"I wish I could offer a pill to make it all better instantaneously, but as doctors we both know medicine has its limitations. I do not prescribe anxiolytics easily, and unlike some of my colleagues, I recommend we try first a few sessions of traditional analysis. Do you have other siblings besides your sister?"

"I have an older brother."

"How is your relationship with him?"

"Polite and distant."

And then she broke down into sobs.

"For many, many years I never even acknowledged it to myself. I had dissociated myself from those horrific memories, as kids tend to do when the trauma to the psyche cannot be processed or accepted. But I could admit it to Hugo, I could share with him my own shameful secret of my brother molesting me sexually, and strangling me during the act so that I would pass out. I am an incest survivor, and a survivor of miscarriages with my first husband, and a survivor of parental coldness because I never received any emotional support from them. I am a survivor of so much grief and pain that your office cannot even hold it.... So has there been any breakthrough in anxiety reducing drugs that could help me?"

"There are many drugs on the market and some seem to work wonders especially in case of generalized anxiety disorders; however your problems run deeper than the anxiety stemming from your current circumstances. If it were only that, I'd say that once sufficient time had passed from the traumatic event of the breakup, your anxiety should dissipate on its own. But your childhood trauma has never been resolved; your relationship with your parents is yet another source of pain. In your case I'd recommend psychoanalysis."

"But psychoanalysis takes time and I dread the thought of coming to see you for the next three years to learn more about myself and try to shed light on my soul only to find it has receded even deeper. This does not make sense, I know. What I'm trying to say is I need a quicker solution. What drug would you use on yourself if you were plagued with anxiety?"

"I've never given it any serious thought because I have always avoided taking meds as much as I could. So in light of that it is strange that I'm considering experimenting with an unorthodox drug…but that's another topic…we should schedule another appointment for you."

I stopped talking astonished that I would even hint at the possibility of trying Jacacia. I never revealed anything of a personal nature to my patients, and I quickly tried to steer the conversation toward her next appointment with me. But the words were out and she'd heard them, and curiosity lit up in her eyes.

"What drug are you talking about? I'm willing to be part of any experiment for a chance to lead a normal life again. Please tell me."

"Well, I've just recently learned about an herb-derived drug, or rather a type of psychedelic that can supposedly assist people with accessing their trauma and connecting them, so to speak, with it and helping them understand it. In fact, I've always hoped to find a more revolutionary and direct way of helping patients deal with and overcome mental illness, and I am planning to try this drug personally to see if there is any merit in the claims made by the person who believes in its potential."

Ariadne's eyes suddenly lit up and she exclaimed, "Please, include me in that study if you plan to conduct one here. Or, if it will be conducted on any other site, I will gladly go there. I can always rearrange my schedule and get a few days off. I volunteer and will sign any waiver…so please include me."

"It's too premature to talk about it. The study will take place in Canada if my contacts obtain approvals for conducting it. However, if it materializes, I will want to include a couple of my own patients, if my boss allows that. But as I said, it's still premature and I haven't given it any deep thought yet... there are simply are too many 'ifs'."

"Allow me to say something else, which you may attribute to the fragile state of my mind. When I was going over the list of psychiatrists trying to figure out which one to seek...we both know that not every doctor in any specialty is of the same calibre...anyway, as I was scrolling down the list and came to your name...Weylin is such an unusual name, you must agree...it was like I heard a voice whisper to me I should see you. So there is a reason why I came to you. I know this may sound bizarre, but in this disarray of thoughts and feelings, there was a knowing I had to meet you in order to get to the answers on some deeper level, and I have no idea what that level might be."

She paused a moment, then continued. "I was sent to you even though I had to try hard through my connections to get an appointment with you. I feel there is a bond of some sort...And one last thing…I have been having nightmares in which I see myself hovering over a white stone circle. I am naked and bleeding because I had suffered some trauma— I do not know what kind. Anyway, as I hover, I shout curses and ask some Goddess to erase the memory of my shame. I wake up from that dream shivering and feeling I'd lost something of myself, something important that I had preserved to give as a gift to someone. I've been having this dream for several months now, but lately, whenever that dream comes back to haunt me, a voice whispers that I need to lift the curse I had cast on a place in order to be liberated. I do not know what curse I cast, or what curse needs to be lifted, but the voice tells me that some memory needs to be restored before he and I are whole again. I do not know who the 'he' is, but I believe it is Hugo. When I told Hugo of these dreams the last time he was here, he said that he had dreamt a few times that he was on his way to see me, but when he arrived he could not find me and knew I was dead. That dream filled him with fear that he would never see me again. So you see, all these strange happenings keep adding to my sense of panic and I often fear I am losing my mind. I sound crazy even to myself, so I can just imagine what you might be thinking. But, please, please, consider me for that study if it materializes."

There was urgency and conviction in her voice, and tension in her body.

The look in her eyes held a plea and its energy reached me and I heard myself say, "For your next appointment, please see my secretary. There have been a few cancellations in the next two weeks, so she may be able to give you an appointment soon. If you do not feel better after a few sessions, then we'll discuss a prescription. And if this study materializes, I will consider including you."

At that moment, I glanced at my computer screen and saw Keith's name pop up in my inbox. Leandra would have said it was a definite case of synchronicity.

"Fair enough and thank you. I somehow feel things will get better."

After she closed the door, I wrote down a few notes in her file. Her story was somewhat unique, but it revealed to me the universal need to find completion through love. It also revealed a brokenness and wounding inflicted by family, and I wondered if there was anyone who grew up unscathed by family-inflicted trauma.

From Ariadne, my thoughts turned to self-reflection and my own family and marital situation. I'd never forgiven my father for abandoning me and I've never forgiven my wife for no longer desiring me, and withdrawing her love from me.

I'd always expected my marriage to be perfect. Maureen and I met when we were both students. From a casual encounter in a bar to a wedding was a relatively short distance. And now, many years and three children later, we were almost complete strangers, and I wondered why all my efforts to resuscitate our marriage had failed.

And yet, whenever I tried to talk to Maureen about the lack of passion in our marriage, she would roll her eyes at me not comprehending. In her view, love just changed form and there was nothing wrong with our marriage. It was where it should be after so many years of togetherness.

She thought I was unrealistic in my expectations, and that, in general, daily exchanges of 'I love you' were fake and meaningless. I often wondered how many people managed to stay content in their marriages.

Before my next patient came in, I opened Keith's email.

"Dear Weylin,

I wanted to share the good news as soon as I could. But first, I'd like to mention that my stay in Frankfurt was excellent, and I left some fine scientists doubting everything they'd believed before meeting me. I will tell you in more detail about the experiments they conducted.

The great news is that we have received the initial approvals to conduct a limited study using Jacacia. It will take us a couple of weeks to set it up because the guidelines are strict and multiple layers of control have to be implemented. We had applied for approval to conduct the study in Phil's home in order to have a comfortable and pleasant ambience, but that was refused. Now, Phil suggests we redecorate his hospital office space. His wife offered to take care of that. Remember that I mentioned Phil the psychiatrist, and my friend Luke Burton, the chemist, running tests on the herb. We would like to include a couple more psychiatrists in the second round of experiments, but if you wish to contact your colleague Leandra to see if she'd be interested in this first session, please feel free to offer her the opportunity to participate in the study. In the first cycle, the study would be done on about eight people at the most. We decided to include a limited number of patients in this round. Phil already has a couple of his patients in mind. I know you'd be interested in trialling it on yours as well, so if there's a way you can bring one or two to Canada, that would be great.

More to follow soon.

Stay well, my new friend!

Keith."

After reading his email, I decided to get in touch with Leandra and ask her if she'd be interested in this study. After all, I planned to spend a few days in her hometown and it was appropriate to contact a local colleague. I wrote a few lines to her, and after that, I called my boss's secretary Linda to ask if my boss was in, and if I could have a word with her. After a couple of minutes Linda called back to say that Dr. Walsh could see me immediately, but she only had fifteen minutes to spare.

Infused with optimism and excitement uncharacteristic of me, I knocked on Annette's door.

Upon entering, I saw her turn away from the window and point wordlessly to a chair. I sat down and looked at her noticing strain in her pallid expression. I did not dare ask her if she was alright because a steely look in her eyes warned me against trespassing on her privacy.

"If this is not a good time—", I stuttered blushing over my discomfort in talking to her.

I have always had a feeling she looked down upon my expertise not only because of my reluctance to readily prescribe drugs, but also because of a plain dislike of me as a person. I hoped I was wrong.

"Not at all. I have a few minutes to spare and since you come to see me so rarely, I'm curious to hear what it is about. I also need a distraction from some news I've just received."

"I wanted to consult you about participating in a study. You know me as a traditionalist when it comes to treatments, so I expect you'll be surprised when you hear what I have to propose."

And then I relaxed and began to tell her about my encounter with Keith, his description of the Jacacia effects and the history of this plant, the approvals his team had received for a small-scale study, and what a breakthrough it might mean for the treatments of severe anxiety disorders and depression, possibly without any side effects.

I told her of Keith's belief that the chemicals in the herb he possessed assisted patients in accessing their past lives, and suppressed emotions, propelling them towards processing, and alchemizing blocked feelings and helping them heal.

Her expression was inscrutable, and my enthusiasm started to wane under her unblinking stare. In a more hesitant voice I mentioned that Keith was, also, an energy reader and healer trained in shamanistic rituals, and I noticed a soft and sudden flicker of light in her eyes.

"Tell me more about his healing abilities."

"He told me he could read his wife's illness in her aura, but could not cure her because it was her time to go. However, he successfully healed a few other people by detecting their illnesses and offering healing. He does it for free when he knows his unusual abilities can make a difference. He's no quack. He's an oncologist. Although one may not exclude the other...anyway, that is what I learned from him and it sparked my interest."

"Oncologist?"

As soon as she uttered that word, she slumped in her chair, leaned against the desk and put her head in her hands. Sobs racked her body and I almost jumped out of my chair taken aback by this unexpected outburst of anguish.

"Sorry, Weylin. Before you came in, I just got a call about my biopsy results. Normally, you have to make an appointment to discuss your results, but the pathologist is a good friend from med school. I have breast cancer in an advanced stage and you know what that means. A death sentence. Not immediate, but who knows...a few months...a year at the most. It has metastasized to the liver. I am going for an MRI tomorrow and after that, I will undergo aggressive chemotherapy in hopes the monstrous disease and its metastases can be blasted into remission. A doctor friend suggested I go to Paris to a special institute where they remove metastases and offer experimental immunotherapy treatments. Apparently, they have had considerable success in prolonging life expectancy."

She fell silent and was crying softly while I was standing speechless and shocked over the sudden shift in conversation. My palms were sweating and my discomfort level was rising by the second. That was the facet of my character I loathed. As a medical professional, I should have been able to show the empathy I felt, but awkwardness invariably got the best of me.

"Did you have any symptoms...I mean how come it was discovered so late? Breast cancer is curable in many cases. My wife has two friends who survived it."

"I saw my doctor late...You wouldn't believe how cowardly I am when it comes to my own health. I discovered a lump in my left breast over a year ago, but ignored it, hoping it would go away. Randy, my husband, and I lead a very active lifestyle outside working hours...we swim competitively, sometimes we train for triathlons...and I just did not want any illness to get in the way of our lifestyle...or of our vacation plans. I did not want to disappoint him."

"But...but, Annette, what are you saying? How could you disappoint him by reacting promptly and getting treatment in an early stage? And what made you decide to seek help now?"

My confusion and disbelief were palpable from the tone of my voice. A doctor to neglect a symptom of potential cancer! Unbelievable!

She looked crestfallen and her lower lip was quivering.

"I started bleeding from the nipple. The cancer disfigured the nipple...your disbelief is clear, Weylin. I know, I should've seen a doctor as soon as I felt the lump. One does not need to be a psychiatrist to know that fear of a diagnosis does not change that diagnosis. I told myself we all must die from something..."

"But you did not…do not have to die from that...sorry, I...I simply always thought you were extremely health conscious. After all, aren't you a vegan, and don't you cringe when you see the office staff eat pizza and store-bought cake? And you cycle to work and are such a paragon of healthy living. It is paradoxical you would ignore a lump in your breast."

She sighed deeply and said, "Weylin, you know nothing about me. Your impressions of me were formed based on the image I was projecting, and that was the image of a woman who was a strong administrator, as well as a good diagnostician. I have always tried to be perfect because...because ..."

She stopped speaking and began to wipe her eyes with a tissue. She got up from her chair and went to the window. With her back turned, she continued her sudden confession.

"As a child, I always thought my mother never loved me. She always criticized me expecting perfection I could never reach. She had a much deeper connection with my sister, and I always felt like an outsider in their company. Even my dad's love could not protect me from feeling unloved and unwanted. My self-esteem and especially my self-love have always been low, and I have always placed everyone else's needs before my own. Maybe that is the reason I didn't react immediately when I noticed the lump. I didn't want to inconvenience my family with my sickness, or the department with my sick leave, which I now have to take anyway. I lived in denial, and denial has now caught up with me, and as of tomorrow I will be on prolonged sick leave...and may never come back here. I'm meeting Dr. Kelly after you. She will cover for me."

She was facing me again and her face looked as if it had aged ten years within the last few minutes. I heard myself speak again.

"We all see patients with deep childhood traumas they have never been able to process. I am not surprised to hear your childhood left a lot to be desired...but then again, is there anyone who reached adulthood unscathed from some kind of parental injury. Do you remember the lecture you gave last year...the lecture in which you discussed how impressionable children were and how helpless before the enormous shadow of their looming parents. And then you stressed that even though the parental imprint on a fragile psyche of a child could be deeply negative and painful, it did not need to stay permanent. You said that as adults we could and should regain our power, and shake off any bad traces of parental neglect or abuse... you said... we could reverse and change our thinking and emotional patterns."

She was looking at me with patience and gentleness in her eyes. "Yes, I said all that and more. I was trying to convince myself we should not let past injuries bog us down in any way."

"After your lecture, I felt so feeble in my inability to forget and forgive parental abandonment. Both my father and my step-father abandoned me, and that sense of abandonment has never left me completely...there are times during which a dark mist of depression moves across my soul, and that abandonment washes over me. There have been times during such downward spiralling that I'd recall your saying that we needed not stay small and helpless, and had to mature and forgive the sins our parents committed against us. We had to transcend the hurt of their errors toward us; we had to develop understanding for their failures as parents...we had to rise above their fallibilities, inadequacies, frailties and recognize the good in all the bad they did."

"I remember saying all that," replied Annette and continued. "I wrote that lecture one evening when sadness felt unbearable. I imagined myself following my own advice to the letter and erasing all traces of parental neglect I'd felt for so many years without having had the knowledge of labelling it correctly. I did not want to feel defeated by what my parents could not give me. I believed that by showing strength on the outside, I would start to feel it on the inside, and it would become an organic part of me. Yes, I said we had to grow up and take full responsibility for our happiness, and as a caterpillar grows out of its cocoon, so we, too ought to slough off the emotional states that felt like childhood shipwreck. Because blaming our actions, our emotional handicaps on what we suffered as children are just lame excuses. And yet, that self-talk did not help me feel worthy of seeking immediate medical help because that would have meant somehow taking care of my own needs and neglecting my family...my children. I know…irrational does not even begin to describe it, and now I'm dying and what is worse, I have difficulty understanding my own motives and actions. Who am I, Weylin?"

Her face looked tired and haggard, but a mysterious luminosity in her eyes was pregnant with unanswered questions.

"Would you consider coming with me to Canada and seeing Keith? I know this sounds like quackery and a preposterous suggestion, but perhaps he does have some unusual abilities. He has studied shamanism, and he is an oncologist, so you could get a second professional opinion. And perhaps trying Jacacia might be of some help with the trauma of this terrible diagnosis."

My voice was tremulous before a boss who just minutes ago had looked like a woman made from nails and steel, and who has now morphed before my eyes into a human withered with fear and fragility. I wanted to hug her and tell her there was hope, but my social ineptitude quickly curbed the impulse.

She suddenly looked up and there was a glimmer of excitement in her eyes. "You know what, Weylin, I'm interested...I want to meet that guy and take part in that study, and if it is not all quackery and I get better, I will use all my influence to get that drug here for more studies. And if Keith says I am beyond help, I will then tell my family about my diagnosis, but until then, I'll pretend all's normal. I hope fate will allow me that much time. How soon can we go?"

"I will write to him to say we are interested, and then we have to wait for him to give us the dates. He said he needed a couple of weeks to set everything up, so this is happening fairly fast. I'm glad to see you so open-minded, but then again, unlike me, you have always been in favour of enriching our treatment protocols by new approaches."

As she looked at the clock, I could see her mental preparations start up. "Sorry to have to kick you out now, but I must talk to Dr. Kelly about replacing me for a few weeks. I will give you my new cell phone number so we can stay in touch. What incredible timing and coincidence, or maybe there are no coincidences, as some tend to believe!"

With a smile and her professional persona fully restored, she saw me to the door, and I went back to my office to retrieve my briefcase and go home.

As I opened the door to my car feeling perplexed by the latest developments, my heart skipped a few beats seeing a bird land on the windshield and flap its wings.

I stared at the beady eyes and a hooked bill of what I thought must be a hawk or a buzzard because I could never tell the difference. It was cocking its head from one side to the other as if trying to relay a secret message to me.

I dropped the car key under the seat feeling utterly unnerved over the bird's appearance. With a hoarse screech, and one last look at me, as suddenly as it had landed, it took off the car and vanished.

Only a brown spotted feather remained on the windshield as if some kind of omen. My hand shook as I was trying to find the key and turn the ignition on.

When I finally managed to start the car, I winced at the pain in my temples indicating the onslaught of a massive headache. Headaches frightened me because they made me think I might have a brain tumour instead of a simple migraine, which I tend to get when I'm overly stressed.

Once home, I baked a store-made quiche for dinner, and made a salad. I felt too nauseated to eat and excused myself from the table, telling my family I'd take a painkiller and lie down.

I took a Tramadol despite knowing that it tended to give me the most bizarre dreams, and even nightmares, but I could not rely on any other drug to work better and faster.

4

Weylin

As expected, my migraine lessened after about twenty minutes and I entered the realm of lucid dreaming, and as soon as I awoke, I wrote a detailed account of the dream in the diary I have kept since the age of fourteen. The headache was gone, but now I wondered how I would be able to fall back to sleep, as I had taken my nap at an inopportune time, and woke up at ten pm. I started to read my diary entry when my wife came into the room ready for bed.

"Is your migraine any better?"

"Yes, there's only a slight throbbing in my left temple. I'm feeling a bit nauseated, so I'll go sleep in the guest room in case I need to get up and vomit. You need to rest, too."

I took my diary and my glass of water with me and left our bedroom. I heard Maureen say to call her if I felt unwell. At that moment, I tried to remember the last time we'd fallen asleep in each other's arms, but could not. It was just too long ago.

Once in the guest room, I turned the light on and read my diary entry. I stopped reading, closed my eyes, and let the strange dream replay in my mind.

I was on a trip and the journey seemed to take forever. But then, moving was what I truly appreciated; when travelling, arriving always quickly turned into an anti-climax that soon triggered impatience and yearning to see what was around the next bend in the road. I was walking on a road to a remote prairie town, and the trip had been extraordinarily strenuous and exhausting. I remembered enduring terribly long stretches caged in horse-drawn coaches, while other legs of the journey had been traversed in a canoe with a fellow traveller. The last many miles, however, I'd been walking the dusty highway in solitude;

sometimes enjoying but also cursing the eternal sun that baked the landscape into a hard surfaced monotonous brown wasteland, and made me sweat profusely. Nights were cool, though, and always the highlight of the day. The starry canopy above not only never disappointed me, but also every new night increased my awe of the profusion of twinkling lights. My backpack was getting less heavy, which was a sure sign that my food was running out, so I hoped the next settlement was indeed as close as I had been told; travelling without anything but a rudimentary map certainly offered some hellish challenges. But it had to be this way. I wanted to travel slowly and enjoy the movement itself more than the destination I would eventually reach. I was aware that my way of travelling had many people shake their heads in either pity, or disbelief. Not that I spoke to a lot of people when on the road. My taciturn, slightly misanthropic shyness meant I could spend days in the company of people without really communicating with them. Some people interpreted this as the characteristic of a condescending and arrogant man, whereas others just found me to be constantly angry or overly proud, or even a little mad. Sometimes this lack of social contact bothered me, and I envied the close bonds enjoyed by long-time friends or couples. But then, I'd be on my way into another expanse of territory devoid of people, and I'd feel good again.

The aim of this trip was to experience the aurora borealis for which this part of the world was so famous. I'd read about it so many times, and wanted to see first-hand whether it was nearly as magical as it was typically presented in books. Every journey of mine had a goal: a sight to see, an animal to behold, an experience to endure, a fear to face, a challenge to overcome. There had been volcanoes in rage, salmon leaping determinedly into the jaws of complacent bears, icy rapids traversed in panic, the turning of the leaves to their autumn colours in endless and serene forests, desert moonscapes, tornadoes closing in on me, earthquakes rumbling below my feet, whales defying gravity when hurtling themselves out of their element.......

So here I was, entering the outskirts of a little town whose name I couldn't even recall. It was to be my base for a few days, as I restocked my provisions and recuperated from the many days on the road. I was actually looking forward to savouring the spoils of civilization for some days, my top priority being to clean up and get into some fresh clothes. I checked into a fashionable hotel on the main street. Having showered, shaved, and eaten a big, not very healthy breakfast, I went to the library to read up on the news and get some details on the local environment. I found a quiet corner and sat down to read a paper. And then she walked in, and I recognized Leandra. She walked in as someone set on a goal, in a fast, no-nonsense, determined way, as if she had things to do and wanted to do them quickly. She searched for a book and when she looked at me, there was no recognition in her eyes before she left the library.

Later that day, I went to a main-street café for lunch. The place was busy and only one table was unoccupied. I made my way towards it, but stopped in my tracks when I saw Leandra sitting at the table next to the one I was approaching. She looked up briefly at me, and made the vaguest of smiles. I was flooded with a sense of burning disappointment. How could she have forgotten me so completely! I sat down, ordered my food, and while eating, I felt heartache over Leandra's not recognizing me. How was that possible? I felt erotic vibrations radiate from her to me and yet she did not seem to know me. So I continued eating, bemused by the situation. And then I decided to say the same thing to her I had said when I'd seen her at dinner at the conference when we'd met for the first time.

"Excuse me, but I have to say this. You look stunning."

Even before that last word had crossed my lips, she looked me straight in the eyes and with a happy gleam in her eyes said, "Thank you." And still there was no sign of her recognizing who I was. But soon we started chatting; however I did not dare ask her if she had forgotten me, and so decided to pretend we were strangers who'd just met.

Time flew by, I was enjoying myself, and quickly my disappointment over her not recognizing me evaporated. Leandra told me she had been dispatched to the town on a mission for her government, using her special skills in several different languages to solve a conflict between two local families. She was a professional mediator, the one who resolved seemingly intractable conflicts. I found this fascinating, but especially when she told me that her real goal while in this part of the country was to observe the air-borne mating dance of a local species of dragonflies. When asked whether she was a zoologist, she laughed and explained that to her dragonflies were a symbol of transformation and synchronicities. I was taken aback by the complexity of such a concept, but she happily obliged me when I asked her to explain what that meant. As anything was possible in dreams, I did not ask her if she still was still a psychiatrist or why she did not recognize me, or how dragonflies could mate at the same time the aurora borealis appeared, but rather I let the strange dream unfold.

She showed me pictures of dragonflies and described in detail how their mating dance was a performance of mid-air acrobatics, and how she had been admiring them for a long time, turning the insect into a kind of talisman for her. And so lunch became the occasion to ask her out for dinner that night. And after that dinner, I offered to walk her to her hotel under the stars, and it turned out she was staying at the same hotel; in fact her room was on my floor, adjacent to mine. At her door I finally said, "Leandra, it is me, Weylin, don't you recognize me? May I come in?"

"Of course I recognize you. I've never forgotten you because you asked me not to during our first lovemaking."

In her room, we embraced as never before, clinging to each other and kissing as if for the first time, our lips fusing. My hands took on a life of their own as I found them sliding down her buttocks and thighs. They let themselves climb up her summer dress and settle on her behind. She responded to my touch with deep sighs and her body melted into every part of mine creating a perfect fit. We paused and looked with incredulity into each other's eyes. I gently spun her around so that she was facing the wall, cupping her breasts from behind her body, pressing rhythmically against her rear, my hands once again travelling down her abdomen and resting in the moist-laced hollow between her legs. She threw her head back and moaned with desire, guiding my hand into her panties, turning her head and licking my ear. Somehow, we managed to cover the couple of meters to the bed, kissing incessantly.

Though the air was still thick with erotic intensity, we now made love deliberately slowly, savouring the languid undressing of each other. Leandra ended up under the covers still wearing her stockings, panties, and bra. In the warmth generated by our bodies under the duvet, we were rediscovering each other. She was looking at me with eyes at once giddy with pleasure and love, yet also gleaming with a combination of puzzlement and seriousness. I was about to tell her I'd never stopped loving her when I woke up. Would that have been a lie, I wondered.

I closed the diary and shook my head over the recent events. The dream about Leandra was the result of the Tramadol. Nothing else made sense, but my body still tingled with the ripples of erotic pleasure it had experienced as if the dream had been real. The cells in my body seemed to remember what the mind had forgotten. My body felt a belonging that was not anchored in this space and time, but somewhere else. And suddenly I was infused with sorrow, the darkness of which was paralysing. And before my spiritual eye the contours of Leandra's face rose, and I simply knew I had to see her again if I ever wanted to uncover some long-forgotten truth.

5

Leandra

Passing by the mirror in the hallway upon my return home, I glanced at myself and saw a subtle smile light up my eyes.

That feeling of lingering joy and lightness after having spent a couple of hours with David and Mia, and their nine-month-old baby girl Victoria, warmed my whole soul. I was so delighted to see David blissfully married. At the same time, I realized how much I'd missed his company at work as he took a few months of unpaid paternal leave to enjoy being a dad.

For someone who had never believed he'd have a family of his own, he now looked as if he had always been a devoted husband and father. Next week he'd be coming back to work and his mom would babysit Victoria. And his mother's decades-long period of isolation, brought on by her grief and compounded by her divorce, had finally ended; she had rediscovered the joy of living. With that, the years of having been alienated from David had simply been erased. For his part, he'd finally found forgiveness in his heart and compassion for her having neglected him after his twin sister Victoria had tragically drowned.

Interestingly enough, David's mother Glenda even believed that her daughter had reincarnated in her granddaughter to bring her back to life and reunite her with her son. David, as a psychiatrist who used hypnotherapy and past-life regression in treating his patients, did not try to dispel her belief.

I took off my shoes and texted Adrian asking him if he wanted to eat at home or out. I was hoping he'd say out because I did not feel like cooking, but rather like having a glass of wine with some Italian food. His text came almost immediately saying he was on his way home and was bringing dinner from Mr. Bianchi. As if he had read my thoughts! So it would be Italian, but at home. I smiled again.

I set the table, lighted two shimmering blue candles, and freshened up by taking a quick shower and putting on a light and simple lavender coloured dress. I never wanted to take our relationship for granted again, and wanted to savour to the fullest every moment of our togetherness. A few drops of perfume completed my simple, but chic attire, but before I had time to brush my hair Adrian was already at the door. I let my hair flow loose and semi-dishevelled, and went to the door to greet him.

"Hey, sexy babe, how was your day?"

"Pretty good. After work, I went to see David and Mia. Victoria is such a doll. I'm in love with that baby."

"With Cassie getting married next year, we may soon be grandparents and you'll have babies in your life again."

"That will be something! Imagine! And it feels you and I were young not so long ago. Where did our days and years vanish?"

"On the wings of time they ended up in our memory, and that is where they will gather forever more." He smiled. "I'm starving. Why don't you unpack the delicacies I brought us, and I'll go wash my hands and get rid of this suit. In fact, I think I'll give it away. It no longer fits me and is pretty worn actually."

"Of course it is. It must be twelve years old and is old-fashioned, just like you." I laughed and landed a light kiss on his stubble. Since we'd decided to give our marriage a second chance, we'd never mentioned my infidelity or Weylin's name. It had turned into a taboo subject, but at times, the dark memory of the near demise of our marriage and my treason would resurface between us, and fade again unacknowledged. It usually emerged at the moments Adrian would catch me daydreaming, and in his look, there would be the unspoken question of whether I was thinking of Weylin, and reliving memories of my relationship with him. I did not know if it was wise to pass over that subject in silence, but I could not bring myself to reopen that painful topic and wound.

"Wow! You bought so much food as if we were having a bunch of guests." The tantalizing smell of fried zucchini, fish, and calamari made me dizzy with sudden hunger. I transferred the contents from the boxes onto a large crystal platter, and poured white wine into the glasses that used to belong to my late mother-in-law. It took Adrian a full year after her death to accept both his parents were gone, and to start thinking what to do with the house they'd left him and all its contents.

While waiting for Adrian to join me at the table, I checked my emails on the phone expecting to hear from our daughter, Cassie. My heart skipped a few beats when I noticed an email from Weylin. I had not heard from him for several years, and the frenzied swirling of butterflies in my stomach could only be explained as an involuntary reaction stemming from shock. I clicked on the email and without reading it, scanned it for length. When it came to business exchanges, Weylin was a man of few words, so I was surprised to see a rather long text. For a few moments, I was undecided about what to do, and then I knew. I would wait for Adrian and read it together with him. There could never be any more secrets between us.

He joined me smiling. He was wearing a black long-sleeved T-shirt and jeans. As soon as he sat down, he filled his plate and raised his glass.

"Cheers, my love! And that colour looks really good on you. Have I seen that dress before?"

"You bought it for me in Greece years ago, remember? I found it crumpled on my closet floor."

My laughter sounded hollow and nervous because my thoughts were neither on the dress nor on Adrian's typical forgetfulness of the gifts he gave me. My glass quivered in my hand reflecting the tempest in my mind, and my attempt to find the right words with which to disclose the arrival of Weylin's email without ruining our evening. Before I could compose my thoughts and broach the topic, Adrian said, "I've something important to tell you. As you know I wasn't able to reach any decision as to what to do with my parents' house, but tonight I finally decided. We have just hired a new prosecutor who's moving from Alberta to work for our firm and he has been looking for a house.

Last week when he was here house-hunting, I showed him Aggie's house on impulse. Sorry, I didn't tell you...I had to be sure I was ready to sell it. He and his wife fell in love with it, and especially with the furniture and decorations, and offered to buy all of it. They do not want to transport their furniture, but will just sell their house's contents. So I decided I was ready to let go of my parents' home. Of course, I will pack up the things I want to keep and put them in our basement. I'm sure there is a lot you would like to have as well. And would you mind going through Aggie's wardrobe and deciding what to do with her clothes."

His face was beaming with the obvious relief at having been able to let go of a house that he had never stopped considering his home. I was happy to see his pain of losing both parents start to subside. Time was, indeed, the ultimate layer to rest. Adrian had had to sail some rough seas when he lost his mother, and found out about my adultery. He'd believed our marriage was doomed, and he would never be able to forgive me such high treason. I now felt uncomfortable about having to tell him that Weylin wrote, and about mentioning the unmentionable name. He was still chatting about the house, the exorbitant amount of money we would make on the sale, and the long vacation we could now afford to splurge on that I simply did not dare trespass onto the territory of this unexpected email.

But, as the time would never be right, I inhaled deeply deciding to mention it regardless of his reaction or the consequences. I also considered deleting it and never finding out what had prompted Weylin to contact me, but I thought that would be both cowardly and uncouth. And after all, he was still a colleague whom I was bound to run into again at a conference, sooner or later.

Once Adrian stopped talking and focused on his meal, I raised my wine glass and tried to give my words a celebratory tone, "Here's to the happy news about the house sale and to our vacation!" I stopped to take a sip and continued.

"Adrian, there's something I need to share with you now because I want to continue being transparent in my words, thoughts, and actions. We have not mentioned my transgression in a long time, and I can only hope you forgave me not only in your outward conduct, as you certainly seem to have done, but also in your heart. We do not talk about it and maybe there's nothing left to say. But something unexpected happened, and I need to tell you about it. Weylin sent me an email. I've just seen it but have not read it. I want to read it together with you because there cannot be any secrecy between us."

His eating slowed down and he was scrutinizing his plate as if something unusual had just appeared on it. I noticed he was separating the bones from the fish, and pushing them to the rim of the plate.

"Well, dinner's going to be spoiled either way; let's hear what he has to say."

Even with the turmoil he must have been feeling, he kept his voice neutral and his thoughts opaque. He was still looking at his plate and cleaning the fish. I sighed deeply, clicked on the email and read it aloud.

Hello, Leandra,

Hearing from me will probably come as a surprise; hopefully, not an unpleasant one. The reason I'm writing is to inform you of an interesting study that will be taking place in Montreal, and to check if you might be interested in it. It will be conducted at the Pine Shade Hospital with the intention of examining the influence of a new psychedelic drug on the human mind. Our hope, and the ultimate aim, is that the drug might reduce anxiety or eradicate depression, as well as allay fears and suffering in the terminally ill. The drug is derived from a plant grown in Honduras. My boss and I, and possibly one of our patients, plan to participate in the study, not only as observers, but also as the study subjects.

I'm excited over the prospect of revolutionizing the way we treat mental illness. Apparently, this drug opens portals to past lives and by reconnecting to them, we may also find healing or our life purpose. According to Keith, the person who invited me as a participant, the chemicals in this psychedelic herb facilitate a kind of conversation between the subject and their inner self about painful emotions and unresolved issues, and also help them feel reconnected to the natural world, and thus achieve states of deeper healing. Of course, there is always a possibility that this whole thing might be some kind of voodoo or wishful thinking on the part of the researchers, but I've decided to try it myself, and if I, or my boss, experience something worthy of further exploration, we plan to propose it be studied further at our hospital. I have my boss Annette's full support, and in fact, her interest in this study is both personal and professional. Thanks to this project, she and I are building a new relationship.

If you remember me mentioning it before, Annette had considered my treatment techniques too old-school, and not innovative enough.

I don't know how open you would be to trying something so very unorthodox, and if any of your colleagues might wish to join us. Anyway, if you're in town the week of the nineteenth, I'd like us to meet and discuss this. I hope you do not think I've lost my marbles completely by proposing such a strange collaboration. I'll be able to give you more details when I see you because I myself will have learned more by then.

Take care.

Weylin.

I reread the email silently trying to make sense of it. Adrian was still eating, and when I glanced at him, I noticed the tension in his jaw.

"You're not eating," he said.

I no longer felt hungry, but started picking at the food with fake relish admonishing myself for that gesture of insincerity. Weylin's email did rattle me, after all. An email in the form of what resembled a business proposal rang strange after so many emails in the past that were brimming with love and passion. Perhaps ex-lovers could turn into close colleagues, or even friends. But doesn't friendship taint what used to be love? Suddenly, my head was swimming as confusion and uncertainty set in.

"So, are you going to join that study?"

"I haven't been able to process this information yet. I would need more detail to understand what it's all about. David, in fact told me today about a patient he was treating for a couple of years, and who eventually went to Peru to try Ayahuasca, and came back healed. That's what he told David after he stopped seeing him. He stayed for three months in Peru and learned about shamanism. Ever since my hypnotherapy sessions with David, I`ve started to believe there's more than meets the eye. After all, remember how shocked we both were at your own revelations under hypnosis. I still cannot believe I did not dream that session, and your revelations that you were my husband Aidan in one of my past lives."

"Do you want to see your ex-lover?"

His tone was tinged with acerbity even though the effort to sound disinterested was unmistakable. And the air around me felt cooler, and the food looked unappetizing and tasted bland. Perhaps there could never be true forgiveness. I might have gambled his trust away for good even though he stayed with me, and we seemed to have rebuilt happiness. I swallowed hard as a piece of fried zucchini seemed to be lodged in my throat. When I spoke, there was a raspiness in my voice and an underlying apology.

"I did not contact him. I did not expect this mail. I need not reply to it. The last thing I'd want is to resuscitate the pain we had to live through. I hope you believe that."

He raised his gaze from his plate and muttered, "I would like you to reply to him and tell him you want to meet him and discuss the study. And the reason I want that is because seeing him in person will be the ultimate test of whether you have expunged him from your heart. And after that, I may finally find some peace, and feel more secure in the knowledge that it is truly over."

I was moved to tears by his magnanimity and composure, but most of all the trust his demeanor was exuding. He trusted me to meet Weylin and he hoped I would come back home with a heart full of love only for him. His eyes were warm and moist, and I got up from the table, sat on his lap and wrapped my arms around his head. I kissed the top of his head and thanked him not only for enduring the worst of injuries, but also for putting so much effort into rebuilding trust. And the moment that had been laced with pain and doubt turned into giggles and then laughter. It was so surreal that we would be talking about my ex-lover at our dinner table one moment, and then making light of it the next. Adrian was truly an extraordinary man, and I was a daughter of fortune to have married him in more than one lifetime, as my hypnotherapy sessions with David had revealed.

I reached over the table to get my phone and write a brief reply to Weylin saying I'd be happy to meet him and hear more about this intriguing study. I read my response aloud, and then turned the phone off. We finished the wine and decided to watch a movie. I sighed with relief that the crisis stirred up by the email seemed to be over.

That night I dreamed of Weylin and ascribed it to the effects of his email. The dream could not have any deeper meaning than the simple processing of reality in a surreal way.

In my dream, I was sitting outside in the backyard looking up at the night sky. Its bedazzling beauty and iridescent sheen made me forget for a moment about the pain lacerating my soul and shredding my heart to pieces. I did not know the nature or source of that pain but felt it pulsate through every cell of my body. My gaze was following the full moon. Against the clear dark sky, the glittering silver of the moon made me blink as its brightness was hurting my eyes. A shiny star, positioned close to the moon, looked as if it were pulling the moon on a silver cord across the sky, and the moon was trailing behind it with reluctance.

My lips were moving and I heard a soft prayer escape them. "Oh, Mother Goddess ruling our earthly life, and weal and woe, I implore you to give me back my lover...please, make him look into his heart and rediscover his love for me...please, stir up in him the resplendent memories of us...over all incarnations in which we loved each other!" My whispering sounded feverish and delirious...my hair fell dishevelled on my shoulders, and if anyone happened to cast a look upon me, they would find my sanity suspect. I was kneeling barefoot in the backyard of our house in sub-zero temperature. I was wearing a long, white cotton nightgown that could not have kept me warm.

Having gazed at, and prayed to the moon for a few minutes, I lowered my head on what looked like a stone altar, a simple arrangement of two vertical stones with one lying across them. I continued praying, but my words soon turned into uncontrollable sobs. I was aware it was irrational and immoral to want my lover back, because Adrian and I had saved and rebuilt our marriage, and I did not want to jeopardize it ever again. I was telling myself I had to let go of him and this dream did not make sense. I would wake up and forget about this strangeness. It had happened a long time ago. The curse could not be coming back. I should have forgotten him and buried him under the darkness of oblivion by now.

As I was weeping and drenching the stones with hot tears, a moon ray descended from the night sky and fell upon the stone on which my weary head was lying. I noticed the light and raised my head. The moonlight danced on the wet spot my tears had left, and I suddenly realized I could see myself in the stone's surface as in a mirror. The image frightened me. Pain and suffering had aged me, and had dimmed the sparkles of life in my eyes.

All of a sudden, behind my haggard face distorted with anguish, I saw Weylin's face. His look reflected the gloom that was coursing through his blood; the lines on his face looked deeper than ever and unhappiness radiated from his eyes, creating a dark aura around him. 'He is also in pain', I thought, and forgot about my own anguish wanting to kiss his away. We were both imprisoned by the pain and torment of not being able to be together, and not being able to erase each other from our hearts. At that moment I felt possessed by a fury I had never experienced before. I screamed and hurled a stone toward the moon cursing the Goddess for her cruelty, for allowing me a glimpse of heaven only to condemn me afterwards to the agony of loss.

Exhausted, I fell on the ground feeling that through my suffering I had come close to the doors of death. 'Do people really die of a broken heart?' I thought and remembered in my dream that I had fully recovered from heartache, and was no longer in need of any ritual of grief. Confusion thickened in my head. I felt I was sinking into a warm darkness, and when I, finally opened my eyes, and looked at the sky, I felt numb, but at the same time anchored in that moment in which there was no past and no future, no pain and no suffering.

I had dived so deeply into my inner depth, behind my mind and thoughts so that when I heard a voice in my head, I thought I had crossed over from sanity into deep madness. 'Despite the impossible circumstances, you will not lose your lover and you will not hurt anyone around you. The two of you were meant to meet for the rest of your incarnations until there are no more lessons to be learned and your cycle together is complete. One day, the wish you made in that enchanted garden will come true. Believe it! In this incarnation, the yearning for clarity that is clamouring in your hearts will be satisfied, and all the answers from your previous lives will come to you both. Your souls will no longer be split but united...soon, it will be soon, for only moments lapse between incarnations...trust the moon.'

'But who is talking to me and why?' I heard myself whisper in my dream.

The same voice continued softly calling me 'daughter' and telling me that I have forgotten how to dance to the rhythm of my inner nature; that I am no longer listening to the cadence of my soul that once was so intimately attuned to and intermingled with birdsong, with the colours of the sky, with the movement of the wind, and with the pulsing of the earth.

The anonymous voice told me that my soul was shrinking under the accepted ballast of conformity; that I needed to relearn to dance to the music of moonbeams and the song of ancient forests that my soul once could hear. The last thing I heard was that Kieran was coming back to help me relearn the tongue of nature that I had allowed to sink in the subterranean recesses of my soul.

I woke up with a start and a heavy chest. My bewilderment over a dream that made no sense did not allow me to fall back asleep, so I got up softly in order not to disturb Adrian's sleep, made myself a cup of chamomile tea and went to sit in the sunroom wrapped in a blanket. Our cat Meeko jumped on my lap and nestled there. The clock was showing three a.m.

The pain I had felt in the dream lingered in my chest. In the dream, I had relived the pain of losing Weylin whereas in real life, that pain had dissipated a long time ago, and there was no need left to perform autopsies on my grief. The voice in my dream clearly said there were answers to be learned, even though I thought I had found all of them during my hypnotherapy sessions with David. Those sessions had clearly revealed that Weylin, whose name was Kieran in one of my past lives, betrayed me in every lifetime, and Adrian was my true love, each time and forever. I could not have imagined finding any more answers, for I had had no more questions. But then, I suddenly knew that the dream had nothing to do with my current life, but rather was a remnant of a past one.

It could only mean I was delusional when I had believed I had regained control over my life. Weylin was coming back because the two of us seemed to be an unfinished story.

6

Leandra

When I came into my office, I glanced at the schedule and noticed a cancellation. I decided to use the empty slot to read some of the latest research, but before opening the journal on my desk, I checked my email and saw that Weylin had written. I had not heard from him for weeks, and had been expecting he would write to give me an update on the study in which he planned to participate. I opened the email feeling calm and composed.

Hey, Leandra,

Happy to let you know that Keith and his team have put everything in place for the study I wrote to you about. I'm feeling slightly nervous about agreeing to take this herbal concoction of his. If you recall, I'm very averse to taking or prescribing drugs. Even though I'm having second thoughts now, I've decided to go through with it and hopefully be enriched by the experience, as weird as it may be. Also, my boss has high expectations not only of the drug itself, but of Keith's healing powers. She allowed me to reveal to you that she has advanced cancer of a highly invasive type, so Keith may be her last hope.

Anyway, I'm arriving tomorrow late in the evening and would like us to meet for dinner the evening after, if you are free. Any restaurant works for me.

Looking forward to catching up.

W.

I sat at the screen for a few minutes trying to process the information. After a most painful and heart-shattering break-up with him, and the subsequent revelations that emerged during the past-life regression sessions I had undergone, how was it possible that he and I were now exchanging casual, neutral-sounding work-related emails? My head started to swim at the thought of meeting him for dinner and hugging him as a colleague instead of a lover with whom I had been madly in love over several incarnations.

At least, that is what the hypnotherapy sessions with David had unearthed. And he is not even aware of our past-life connection. But, perhaps, fate was bringing us together again in order for him to find that out. But what if under the influence of the drug he accesses the same lifetimes I was regressed to, and reveals information about us I had no knowledge of? I gasped at that possibility.

The next two days were so busy that I almost forgot about Weylin's arrival. I replied briefly to his email suggesting we meet at 'Ambrosia', my favourite Italian restaurant, which I loved as much for the delectable food as for the operatic arias playing in the background. I knew Weylin did not care for opera, but I was sure he would appreciate the cuisine. I had called Mr. Bianchi to make reservations saying that I was not coming with Adrian, but rather with a European colleague.

When I told Adrian that Weylin was in town and I was meeting him, he went quiet and looked down. I had to crane my neck a bit to hear him. “Don’t mess this up for us.” He looked back up, and his eyes sought out mine. “Do what you have to do, but don't you dare hide anything from me. I went once through hell and want this to be the final chapter. Call it closure or whatever. Also, I can see how one dinner may be normal, but any more meetings alone I disapprove of. I have to go back to the office and work on these new trial preparations, so don't wait up."

"I will wait up and I will tell you all about the evening."

Normally, whenever I would have dinner with Adrian at 'Ambrosia' I would dress up, but tonight I felt no desire to go out of my way to look particularly good. I put on a pair of black slacks and a turquoise-coloured sweater.

I arrived at the restaurant ten minutes early and chatted with Mr. Bianchi at the bar while our table was being prepared. He served me a big glass of chilled white, and I drank half in two gulps realizing how nervous I was all of a sudden. Gabriel Fauré's Requiem was playing in the background and the lugubrious tones painted my mood with melancholy that turned into nervousness, and then a feeling of suppressed fury. He had shattered my heart during several lifetimes, and he is now reappearing in my life for the most bizarre reason. It was insane to agree to see him and talk about some bogus study.

I started fidgeting in the chair, and considering getting up and leaving. I took out a notepad from my purse and started scribbling a message for him saying that something unexpected had happened, and I could not meet him, but that I wished him a successful study and a pleasant stay when I heard, "Hello, Leandra. It's been a while."

I raised my head and there he was, somewhat aged and a bit more weathered looking than the last time I saw him, but with the same twinkle in his eyes, and a slightly crooked smile. I dropped the pad on the floor getting up to greet him. His hug was firm, warm and friendly.

"Nice to see you again." I muttered sounding like an idiot to myself, and wondering if either of us would allow ourselves to trespass into the past, or if we would keep the conversation on neutral grounds.

"What are you drinking?" he asked.

"Oh, I had a glass of house white." I realized the glass was empty, as I had downed it from sheer nervousness.

Mr. Bianchi approached the table smiling warmly. I introduced him to Weylin, and he shook his hand. I wondered what he would have thought of me if he knew I was introducing an ex-lover to him. He was so fond of Adrian who had saved his business from racketeering attempts by successfully prosecuting a gang.

Weylin said he was starving and ready to order. I ordered roasted vegetables and took a sip of wine from my refilled glass. As I was listening to Weylin order his dinner my head started spinning from disbelief that he and I were sitting in my hometown, in my favourite restaurant, owned by Adrian's friend and former client, Mario Bianchi. How could it be? What was the meaning of this unlikely encounter or reunion? Was this how fate or gods played with us humans?

As if reading my thoughts Weylin said, "I know this is utterly surreal, but throughout the flight I felt some inexplicable sense of compulsion...as if I had to come here and participate in these strange experiments. How can I even explain the feeling? My whole experience with meeting this guy Keith was one of the strangest things I've ever encountered. He claims he reads people's energies and has healing abilities...I...I...just had to come, something pulled me like...as if there was some truth to be discovered...something I had to learn, a longing I had to fulfill. Am I making any sense?"

For a moment, the conversation fell silent. In the background, Maria Callas sang "Un bel di vedremo" from Madame Butterfly and the notes filled me with disquiet.

"I never thought I'd like opera arias as my dinner background music. What is this music?"

"An aria from Madame Butterfly."

"What is it about? You know me, I can talk rugby, but not opera."

"It's about a Japanese girl whose heart gets broken by her American husband, and who kills herself. Just another story in which a man breaks a woman's heart by betraying her. Anyway, back to what you said about expecting to find some truth in the study you're about to participate in. How utterly unexpected and intriguing that you came to my hometown seeking some elusive truth!"

"I know, it is more than bizarre. Have you ever experienced something that you could not explain rationally?"

I was tempted to say, 'falling in love with you,' but instead I decided to tell him the whole story about my experiences with David; my past-life regressions in which he, Weylin, was the man called Kieran and Carlo, the man I had loved so profoundly in all of my past lives, the man who always betrayed me, and wounded me almost mortally. His look was one of utter incomprehension. I added that I could send him recordings of the sessions if he wished to learn all the details.

"I'm speechless, Leandra. I had never expected to hear something so far-fetched and mindboggling. That goes against all my beliefs. I've never believed in past lives or hypnotherapy, which is why I had no interest in attending the session your colleague David organized a couple of years ago, the one Jorunn attended. She told me about her experience and how it helped her improve her life. But I hope there is some kind of scientific explanation about what happens to the brain under hypnotherapy, and how it creates events, and false memories. As an aside, you certainly did not paint a flattering picture of me and my actions in your past lives."

"As opposed to your actions in this present incarnation." I regretted the words as they were leaving my mouth, but it was too late. I couldn't believe that I would have said something so recriminatory. I had had no intention of mentioning our affair and creating an awkward situation. I should not have agreed to meet him. It felt as if I had just made another big mistake. I tensed up and felt an energy shield rise between us like impenetrable armour.

"I'm deeply sorry if I ever hurt you in any lifetime. It was never my intention. What we had was unsustainable from every aspect. We did not want to hurt anyone in our families, and I could no longer maintain our relationship for fear we might be discovered. But, please, send me the recordings of your sessions. I've decided to be more open to different kinds of treatments, and am curious to find out what David uncovered. Maybe I've been too rigid in my approaches to treatment, and generally in my way of thinking."

"What do you expect to gain from participating in Keith's study?" My voice was now cold, and I disliked its timbre. Everything about this evening was unnatural and strained. The man I used to love with every cell in my body, the man who hurt me beyond measure, was now sitting across from me bantering about a study, and about a doctor who was a shaman. I watched him sip his wine and eat his rare steak at leisure, as if he had never blasted my heart into smithereens, or loved me with volcanic passion that carved fiery riverbeds in my skin and my soul. Looking at the food on his plate, I felt a wave of nausea hit me; I had stopped eating meat a few years ago, and found it difficult to look at a piece of meat still oozing blood. I turned vegetarian when eating meat began to feel like burying animal souls inside me, souls that wanted to live. However, I refrained from making any comments about his choice of food.

"I'm really hoping this herbal concoction can help patients face their traumas, inner demons, maybe, and as Keith says, reconnect them with their past lives. And even though I find that hard to accept as a possibility, I do hope for a miraculous drug that can revolutionize the way we treat mental disease, that can increase our success rates, or just be an additional weapon in our psychiatric arsenal...I don't know...I'm not sure what to think about all this. I haven't seen his protocol, but I expect all subjects will undergo blood testing and other check-ups to ensure there are no risks linked to their taking the herb. I'm sure their vital signs will be monitored throughout the sessions. So, are you interested in participating?"

"After my experience with past-life regressions, I have no desire to personally try anything like that again. After all, I have no more questions for which I would seek the answers via such unorthodox routes; however, I would like to participate as an observer who might then contribute to your subsequent analyses and discussions."

"Maybe I'll be able to reconnect to my past lives and give you my version of my role in yours. Maybe, you will still get some answers or some clarity." He smiled and the energy between us changed, thickening and pulsating with the vibration that reminded me of the time our souls had been fused in deep love. Recognizing the danger of such feelings, my body stiffened anew, and I diverted our conversation to safer grounds by asking him about his work and children.

He talked animatedly about his boys, but it was obvious he harboured a special tenderness for his daughter. When I asked about his wife, he said nothing had changed and they were still as estranged as ever. After the exhaustion on his face became too evident to ignore, I said that he must be jet-lagged and we should call it a night. I promised to send him the recordings of my past-life regression sessions, and he said he would listen to them tomorrow before going to the airport to meet his boss. He reminded me of our Monday meeting with Keith and his team at eight a.m. and I said I'd be there.

We hugged goodbye and I did not allow the touch of his hand to linger on my back longer than a couple of seconds before disengaging. My body felt wooden, and my smile icy and artificial. I did not offer to give him a ride to the hotel. He could get a taxi. After all, this must be a business trip for him with all expenses paid.

When I entered my car, I turned the car on and immediately jumped in my seat when a loud crackle of static blasted from the speakers. Before I managed to hit the off button with my fumbling fingers, I thought I heard a female voice sigh in exasperation, 'Poor she,' but it quickly turned into a long 'sh sh sh' sound.

My heart was racing, and I turned the ignition off and sat in the dark shivering and staring at the wheel. The sound of an incoming text message helped me regain my composure and I looked at the phone. It was Adrian. "*Can't focus on work. Why the hell did I encourage you to meet him thinking I could deal with it? It's now unbearable. Furious as fuck.*"

I replied immediately saying, "*Nothing to worry about. Meeting over, business talk only. Won't see him again one-on-one. Study starts Monday. Love you.*"

Adrian did not reply. I decided to wait up for him regardless of how late he came back home. This was one night when talking to him and assuaging his fears was necessary.

7

Weylin

I woke up early, feeling disoriented for a few seconds. I got up and opened the drapes to look at the morning sky. The clouds looked dark and ponderous, and I hoped it wouldn't rain. My boss was arriving at five p.m., and I had a lot of time to kill before going to the airport. Normally, she would not need to be met, but would just take a cab to the hotel, but when I offered to meet her flight, she readily accepted. She said her illness brought on panic attacks due to her fear of dying, and she'd take a sedative to help her endure the long flight. Her cancer was spreading, and Keith and his study were her only hope for a miracle.

When I checked my phone for messages, I noticed Leandra had sent me three audio files via Dropbox and I remembered she'd promised to send me her recordings from her past-life regression sessions. Curiosity made me impatient to listen to them and assess their credibility. I quickly showered and called room service to order a large breakfast. After eating, I went back to bed with my laptop to access the files and play them.

And then my inner and outer worlds were rattled to the core by the strangeness and, at the same time, uncanny believability of Leandra's accounts of her past incarnations, and my role in them. Her story of our being inebriated with love for each other sounded so real that it touched my heart, and ignited it with the memories of us. There was a sudden flutter in my soul when I heard her mention the name of Kieran. It somehow felt part of me, a part of me that penetrated deep, all the way down to my DNA and I knew with certainty that I had been Kieran in another life. Leandra's storytelling was so vivid that I could visualize her on the floor of a 17th century jailhouse in some Irish village; in the cold river swimming for her life after she was thrown off a bridge accused of witchery.

In that lifetime, Leandra's name was Jilleen and she was known as a healer, and a girl who loved to roam. Chronicling her past life under hypnosis, Leandra also spoke of a secret hand-fasting ceremony performed on her and Kieran by the high priestess called Ailionora. She described a masked ball, during which the woman by the name of Lady Tyrone stabbed to death her husband's lover Morgana; Leandra also revealed her pain over losing both her lover Kieran and the child she carried.

My arms were tingling with goosebumps, and the hairs on my neck stood up listening to her tragic love story in Italy. Had I been the man named Carlo who betrayed her? That could not be true. But my heart was racing as I was trying to grasp at some distant memory that was swirling in my mind like a wisp of fog only to dissipate before I could touch it. As I was straining to make sense of what I was hearing in the recording, I had the strangest sensation. My surroundings turned dark, and I felt as if I were floating inwards toward my very soul.

Before my eyes, I could see a circle of stones bringing back memories of the Ring of Brodgar. I could feel myself step within the stones searching for some silent and secret memories that would illuminate my life with meaning. The atmosphere around me was numinous, and a voice startled me by whispering, 'He shall now learn the truth and reveal it to her. Our work shall be done.' I somehow became a witness of my own inner world that belonged to a distant past. And whose voice did I hear? I then remembered Leandra's mentioning the White Circle when we visited the Ring of Brodgar, and calling me Kieran, and then feeling bewildered because she could find no reason for mentioning names unknown to her.

Shaken, I looked around trying to make sense of the experience that had left my heart pounding. I got up to take a sip of water before returning to Leandra's narrative. And again I felt proximity to some piece of vital knowledge, but I had no means of accessing it. Something in me was trying hard to remember. Utterly spellbound, I continued listening to Leandra's account of the incarnations in which she had loved me. What a curse it was to love and be loved with feelings of such depth, and yet be able to experience it only for a brief time in every lifetime we seemed to have shared, including this one? I wondered if she and I would be able to stay together in a future incarnation, and as soon as I caught myself thinking such thoughts, I felt disbelief that I would entertain them even for a moment. What was happening to me? And yet, there was something so credible in the hypnotherapy sessions she underwent with David!

So Leandra and I were lovers throughout time, and would be through all eternity! I gasped at the thought, and then felt enveloped in a calm certitude. It felt right that we would have been lovers in past incarnations. After all, not only her body, but her very soul felt like an extension of mine. Hadn't I even said once that we were a perfect fit at the nano level? And she'd thought I had cursed her with the whisper, 'Don't you ever forget about me.' During our last phone conversation before our break-up, she told me she feared she'd never be able to forget me, for I had cursed her by whispering that to her during our lovemaking. But, even if I had whispered that, I never would have meant it as a curse. I have just always felt diminished when people would forget me, as my father had forgotten me, and I always feared self-effacement.

When I looked at the clock on the nightstand, it was already one p.m. I had just spent five hours listening to the stories of my and Leandra's love relationship spanning lifetimes. And she portrayed me as a betrayer, and a fickle-hearted duplicitous lover. But that was her version of the events. Perhaps she had interpreted my actions wrongly; perhaps my circumstances had dictated such behaviour, and she did not know the entire truth behind Kieran and Carlo's motives and actions. I caught myself bursting into an incredulous laughter over trying to find possible justification for her lovers' conduct. I had never believed in past lives or reincarnation. That was pure nonsense. But I was still wondering at the same time if I might get a chance to prove her wrong. If

Jacacia had the power of opening up windows to past lives, maybe I would glean a different truth about Kieran and Carlo, or one of them at least. Circumstances beyond our control made it impossible for us to stay together in this life. The same might be true for other incarnations in which our paths crossed. I could not imagine myself ever having been a bad person. Maybe a coward, but there was never any malevolent intent in me against anyone.

I walked the city the next couple of hours dazed from what I had learned. I was also impressed with David's skill as a hypnotherapist and psychoanalyst, and hoped I would have a chance to meet him. I became aware of how closed my mind had been to anything but traditional psychoanalysis as a treatment option and a strictly scientific explanation of the world. Perhaps my soul was impoverished by the lack of any true spirituality. And now, all of a sudden, I was ready to embark on a mystical journey into the world of Jacacia. The change in me was inexplicable, as if a higher force were leading me toward an unknown fate.

Once the first raindrops fell on my face, I went into a coffee shop and found a table by a window. I ordered a sandwich and a large cappuccino and sat still for a long time, still unable to process recent events. A stirring in my soul was whispering softly that this was only the beginning and that important revelations were yet to come.

When I saw a cab park in front of the coffee shop, I got up in haste wanting to get a ride to the airport. The streets were wet and a light breeze rose. The ride to the airport was slow because of the heavy traffic, so when I arrived at the terminal, I only had to wait half an hour before Annette's plane landed.

When I spotted her, I was alarmed. She looked pale and frail, and painfully thin. I wondered if she would have the strength to go through the study.

"Hello Weylin! Don't look so concerned. I'll be fine. The flight was turbulent, and I was nauseated most of the time. A long, hot bath and some warm food should help. And I heard from your patient Ariadne. She is arriving tomorrow, so she'll miss day one. She had lots of things to organize; kids, her three dogs...not easy being single."

"Let me help you with the suitcase. I asked the cab driver who drove me here to wait. We negotiated a flat rate so our hospital budget won't go bust with the expenditure."

"Did you see your colleague last night and is she going to take part in the study?"

"Only as an observer. She's gone through past-life regression therapy and has no more desire to try non-mainstream treatments."

"Why did she try past-life regression?"

"Curiosity," I caught myself lying realizing I should not have even mentioned it. She may grill Leandra about it.

"I feel wiped out and can't wait to go to bed. I hope I have enough strength for tomorrow's meetings. I also feel trepidation over meeting Keith. What if he says he cannot help me? I will then have to tell my family that I'm most probably going to die within a few months."

"You should not be having such thoughts now. You need dinner and bed."

"I'll have a bite in my room. Too tired to go out."

I helped her check in and after I left her in her room, I went out for a walk looking for a restaurant. I thought of Leandra and hoped her husband did not mind her going out for dinner with a colleague last night. But was I just a colleague?

My phone beeped and I saw Leandra's text letting me know she had to see a patient first thing in the morning, and would arrive about an hour late to our first meeting. I texted back to say I did not expect it would be a problem and that my patient Ariadne would miss the entire day. Exchanging work-related texts with Leandra marked a new phase in our relationship.

After a quick dinner at a small Greek restaurant, I strolled leisurely back to the hotel thinking about Leandra's revelations under hypnosis. I could not make any sense out of them, and especially could not fully understand the reasons behind her decision to subject herself to such an unconventional treatment. I also thought about how reserved she had seemed during our dinner. She must have felt uncomfortable seeing me after such a long time. I'm sure she regretted having had an affair with me, and having risked her marriage. We were both foolish. I fell asleep thinking about her, which must have been the reason for the most bizarre dream that ensued.

In the dream, Leandra and I were approaching a building in silence. Actually, the word "building" seemed ill suited for the bizarre structure in front of us. It appeared to be an unworldly hodge-podge of architectural wet dreams; organic Gaudi met cubistic Picasso, who met a Gothic castle-like fortification. Strangely, it was not scary or frightening in any way; it seemed to beckon us inside, inviting us to explore and probe its secrets. Leandra was wearing the light, wavy knee-length summer skirt I had noticed on her before and admired so much; it flattered her and delicately but unabashedly hinted at the curves and wonders it covered. It went well with her soft beige-colored blouse, buttoned in front. Her heels echoed when she walked on hard surfaces. I wore my comfortable Dockers pants, not too casual, but not unnecessarily business-like either. My shirt was one of my favourites; the checkered white and red one. The sun was out, so I was sockless in my loafers.

When we entered the building, we were struck by its vastness and couldn't grasp if it was spatial misconception, or some trick of the bright light that streamed through numerous skylights and floor-to-ceiling windows. We looked at each other and smiled. We didn't talk; not because we didn't want to, but because we didn't need to. Hand in hand, we started casually ambling down a corridor lined with brick walls. The longer we proceeded, the more we were reminded of the impossible architecture favored by someone who reminded us of Escher; doors and gates led to other rooms that appeared to spiral off into new doorways; above us staircases wound this way and that, curling around each other like spaghetti frozen in mid-air, defying gravity. Nobody else was in the building. This was our space.

I wanted to look into one of the rooms and let go of her hand, but when I turned around she was gone. This shouldn't be possible; there were no staircases or doors in the immediate area around us. I was puzzled, yet not worried. So I walked down the hallway, looking for her, calling out her name. Even though I felt a longing inside me, I rejoiced at being in a position where I have to call for her; it signified our connectedness and underscored the vibrations that existed between us, a bond that thrived on love and infatuation even when we were physically apart.

And then I saw her on a ledge-like staircase; it seemed to hang suspended in mid-air yet somehow it was connected at unfeasible angles to other stories and corridors. She walked down hallways, disappeared in rooms, and then reappeared looking fascinated by what sh'd seen. I called out to her, but she did not seem to hear me. She strolled along; unhurried, allowing herself time to take in the impressions of various shapes and forms.

On our solitary wandering, we would occasionally get close enough to see each other, calling out to each other. Sometimes we could even touch when the stairs we ascended were close enough. But we walked on. At one point, I could hear the echo of her heels getting louder and louder as she walked on. And all of a sudden, we met; simultaneously we descended stairs that led into a large atrium, complete with light coming from a roofless opening in the middle of the building. We moved straight for each other with no hesitation. Our embrace was intense, and carnal and loving. When we looked around again, we noticed five doors in the pentagonal atrium, placed in exact 72-degree angled recesses in the surrounding walls. A painting of a huge dragonfly covered the first door. The door opened and we found ourselves in a white room with a king-size bed sprawled in its middle. Candles were ablaze on little tables, and our favorite wine sat waiting for us in a cooler. The light in the room was dim, and from somewhere we heard music playing. We were frantic with desire. Gasping and panting we tore clothes off each other, and only then did a certain calm settle on us.

Lying naked on the bed, we kissed, slowly and lovingly, making all our emotions emanate from our lips and tongues. I grabbed the wine bottle from the cooler and poured some between her breasts watching the little rivulets run toward her navel where my tongue thirstily awaited them. Our lovemaking turned into a dance of utmost intensity during which we moved sometimes in slow and perfect rhythm, and at other moments like ferocious animals in flight, never taking our eyes off each other. I admired her body. She was so erotic and fiery. We continued rocking gently like a boat on water, only the boat and the water were complementary; one couldn't exist without the other. She looked at me with the glazed gaze of a person hypnotized and when we fused, we became like one organism that could not be separated into entities because we fed on each other; the room spun and I knew that these were moments that simply might not be recalled later because the intensity transcended understanding.

And then something happened that ruined the moment. Something landed on my face and I smacked it away. To my horror, a dead dragonfly fell between Leandra and me. She looked at me with inexpressible sadness in her eyes. With tears spilling down her cheeks, she whispered, 'You slew a dragonfly. You sinned against our love. You destroyed the magic.'

I woke up in a sweat remembering every detail of the strange dream. This was my second dream about Leandra in a relatively short time. I was over her. We were colleagues now. Our affair was a mistake that could have cost us our marriages. So why was I quivering with longing again?

8

Leandra

I arrived at work almost an hour early. I woke up feeling restless and disquieted, almost anxious. I had tossed and turned all night long and the main reason I could ascribe to such a state of mind was Weylin's presence in my hometown. Somehow, though these feelings of disquiet were compounded by a vague recollection of a dream in which I roamed a bizarre- looking building, entering and exiting rooms with symbols on the doors, ascending and descending staircases with someone that felt familiar. I remembered my deep sadness over the sight of a killed dragonfly, but I could not recall who it was that slew it. Something was telling me I was missing a vital piece of information, that there was something I could not grasp, or something I was misinterpreting, but I could not put my finger on it. I briefly talked about it with Adrian over coffee and his first thought was that it had something to do with Weylin.

His arrival here had upset my emotional equilibrium, and Adrian could hardly wait for the study to be over. I could not convince either him or myself that I was not thinking about Weylin, and that I was feeling as disinterested in him as in the study itself. However, after a few sips of coffee, I realized I was deceiving myself about my reactions to Weylin's presence here. After all, he was the person who marked my life and fate with a clear before and after, and his reappearance on my life path must have unsettled me whether I was ready to admit it or not.

I had another cup of coffee in my office waiting for the patient whose appointment I did not want to reschedule as my colleague Diane had asked me to see her. Diane said it was her closest friend who needed a consultation, and she felt her friend Monique should talk to someone who did not know her. Diane did not elaborate on what prompted her friend to seek psychiatric help, but just said that her friend had waited a long time before confiding in her that her life was not as rosy as she had led her friends and family believe.

My cell phone rang and I took it from my purse. When my hand shook unexpectedly, I dropped it on the floor, and it fell out of its casing. As I was picking it up and trying to put it back into its case an epiphany struck me. I had spent the last year doing everything I could to save and repair my marriage, and I had invested utmost effort into being the best wife and mother I could be, and the best psychiatrist, friend, and person, in general. Feelings of guilt over my infidelity were always simmering under the surface of my awareness, and I was using all my willpower to keep Weylin out of my thoughts.

I generally felt happy and optimistic, and enjoyed my life seeking stimulating conversations, developing new friendships, and attending cultural and other events with or without Adrian, but only now, at the sight of a broken phone did I start to realize that no experience, regardless of how enriching or motivating, could compare to the highs I had reached with Weylin in my current life, and Kieran and Carlo in the past ones. In addition, it was not hard to see that the reason for such intensity lay not only in the secrecy that had veiled our love, but also in the energy that seeped from previous incarnations into this one, heightening the experience powerfully. My life felt as if I were living it in a pool of tepid water, swimming contentedly, but never experiencing the bliss and exhilaration of the moments spent with Weylin. Yes, secrecy and fantasy amplified the depth of experience, but one would be foolish to risk losing real-life happiness and contentment for transient feelings of exhilaration. I also became aware of the wall I had erected around my heart so that Weylin's presence could not ripple it with skipped beats.

My musings were interrupted by my secretary Fiona's knock; she opened the door and ushered in Monique. Monique was a beautiful and willowy woman who radiated eternal youth and spiritual mellowness through her pale blue eyes. I already knew from Diane that Monique had just turned fifty, but I would never have guessed.

"Thank you for seeing me, Dr. Springfield."

"You`re welcome. Make yourself comfortable, please. Some patients swear they feel relaxing vibes emanate from this new chair. "

"It feels like sitting on a fluffy cloud. I can easily imagine your patients not only relaxing but also dozing off. "Her laughter had a tinkling sound to it, and her eyes glistened with warmth and amicability.

"Tell me about yourself."

"I`m a mom to four lovely children, a wife, a midwife, a painter and a spiritual teacher in my sparse spare time." She halted her speech looking at me with an expectation for further prodding.

"How is your general health? Are there any serious illnesses in your family history?"

"We have been blessed with great health. Both my parents had been physically healthy until their eighties when they started to suffer from arthritis. My two siblings do not have any major health issues...that is ...there are no genetic diseases running in our family."

"Any mental disorders?"

She sighed deeply before whispering, "My mother is the only one suffering from a mental illness...schizophrenia, but she has kept it in check with meds."

"Are you married?"

"Yes, I've been married for twenty-five years."

"Are you happy in your marriage?"

"My husband is a wonderful man...a humanitarian trying to make the world a better place. You should also know that we are polyamorous...we took that decision in many years ago while living in the New Age international community called Findhorn in Scotland. I was twenty- eight at the time when we opened up our relationship. I hope you are not one of the people that judge polyamory negatively."

"There's nothing to judge about consensual adult arrangements. Tell me more about it. You are the first polyamorous person I've met. How did you go about it?"

"We were the first in our community to be public about it. We worked on the mutual agreements for about six months. Our list of agreements had to do with letting each other know as soon as an attraction arose. Another condition was that the person we got involved with had to be spiritually aligned with us. We also had to let each other know once we decided to enter a new relationship, and we both had the right of veto if it felt like it threatened our marriage. And we had to take precautions not to contract STDs. We had more agreements, but I can't remember them all."

"How difficult was it to abide by the agreements?"

She sighed deeply before replying, "We broke all the rules at one time or another. We hurt each other and failed often. We fell in love with other people and came close to divorcing, but in the end, we realized how much our family meant to us."

"What has been the greatest challenge in leading a polyamorous life?"

“When you don’t have a lover while the other is having a great time with theirs.”

“What has been your greatest fear in this context?”

“Being bored in the marriage and wanting out.”

“I imagine in any kind of relationship, jealousy becomes an issue?"

"Yes, but more so for the travel and fun outside the marriage, especially while raising small kids and being stuck at home while the other is having an adventure."

"Have you ever felt negatively judged by those who found out about your lifestyle and how has such judgement affected you?"

"When we first did this in our spiritual community, I had a girlfriend who said, 'How come you have two men? I can't even get one.’ Others told my husband to 'Just go get her and drag her back by the hair', and 'You are being cuckolded', and my lover was told, 'You are getting in the way of their marriage.' But we endured in that lifestyle. It's a great way to get the truth out about the primary relationship. It helped us at different times of life, for example, when the kids were small and when life was hard, boring, frustrating, or stifling. When needing stimulation spiritually from a different mind and soul. Spiritual growth has always been more important than sexual variety."

"Am I wrong in assuming you came to see me because of some problems in your love relationships? Because I'm not really a marriage, or a relationship counsellor, but I can recommend one."

"No, that is not it. I came because I need help with finding forgiveness. Diane described you as understanding and compassionate...and as a wise doctor and woman. So I do not need a psychiatrist who will treat me for mental illness, because I do not have any problems or symptoms that might be considered as a mental disorder. I need someone to guide me toward forgiveness because the fact I cannot forgive my mother makes me feel anger, and that anger feels like an acid corroding me from within."

Monique sighed deeply looking uncomfortable and edgy.

"What did your mother do to you that you need to forgive her?"

"She called me horrible names for embracing the life of polyamory. She said my children should be taken away from me because of the sinful life I was leading. At one point she even called child protection services asking them to intervene, but the social worker witnessed a happy home."

"Tell me more about your mother."

"She claims she is a devout Christian, but she never goes to church. She also smokes and drinks a lot, so only on very rare occasions can my children feel a softer and more traditional kind of grandmotherly love. She always finds things to criticize and the only time she behaves normally is when I invite her to celebrate my husband's successes and awards. She feels happy to share some of the limelight dressed to the hilt. But even then, she always finds something to criticize...my children are dressed too formally for such young girls…I was flirting with the photographer...the white wine wasn't cold enough or dry enough...as if she knows anything about wines etc. She also never forgave me for having children because that made her a grandmother when she felt too young to be one."

"What was her relationship like with her mother?"

"Strained from what I have heard. Her mother died when I was three years old, but my mother never talked lovingly about my grandmother."

"Forgiving parents is generally not as easy as forgiving others. The reason, as you are most certainly aware, is the fact that mothers are supposed to be sources of unconditional love and giving. We often feel let down by our romantic partners, colleagues, even friends, but we expect our parents to always be there for us. But parents are also people that have been wounded, betrayed, disappointed...people who may be ill-equipped to be parents. Their behaviour is conditioned by their social circumstances and beliefs imprinted on them. The first step toward forgiveness is trying to put ourselves in their shoes. Would we have behaved differently if we had suffered from mental illness, or if our minds had been entrapped in religious dogma that rejected behaviours other than those condoned by the Church. Polyamory can attract scorn and judgment even from non-religious people, who may perceive it as a threat to the known way of life. People are often unconscious of their behaviours, of why they do what they do. I'm sure that by not being able to forgive your mother...by continuing to hold grievances against her, you are also unable to achieve real freedom."

"I wanted to see you because no one was ever able to tell me what to do to achieve forgiveness. Whenever I try to follow the advice given to me, very soon I find myself facing a wall of anger toward her once again. And that wall turns into a wave that threatens to drown me if I dwell on it for too long, so I try to divert my thoughts from it and think of happier things. As I am talking to you, I am already starting to feel that anger."

"Is it only anger you feel when you revisit painful memories?

"I think I use anger to mask the pain underneath because it is easier to feel anger than the renewed pain that always takes me back to the place I no longer want to remember. I try not to remember because remembering the hurt feels like watering anew poisonous plants someone else planted in my garden. I don't know if this makes any sense at all."

"It makes perfect sense. You feel poisoned by other people's actions and that poison has seeped into your heart and became entangled with the positive emotions of love and happiness. But before you can disentangle your heart from the pain you no longer want to feel, you need to lift the curtain and face it again."

"It is too hard to process those memories. I always wanted to feel safe with my mother, but never did due to her unpredictable behaviour, her drunkenness..."

"Did you ever ask her why she had to drink? What was it she needed to escape from?"

Monique fell silent and her expression revealed deep contemplation.

"Mental illness, which she could not understand, or which she either could not or would not acknowledge as a source of her problems. But I was a child...I needed a mother...someone who would orient me when I felt disoriented, who would comfort me when I felt hurt."

"Was your father supportive of her?"

"No. He left after she was diagnosed with schizophrenia. He sent money regularly because he was a successful realtor. But we did not see much of him. So no, she did not have much support from anyone. The few friends she had also disappeared over time. In retrospect, I realize her own life must have been hell. I find it so hard to relive those memories. Coffins filled with pain should be left buried."

"On the contrary. I believe healing can only be accomplished if we exhume those coffins and rummage through them until we leave no piece of pain unturned and unexamined. And I also believe in the healing power of tears. They help dissolve and wash away the pain of the grievances we cradle."

Monique began to cry. Through sobs, she managed to say, "I have not cried in a long time… and it feels good to let go, to weep, to let it out."

The tension, so evident in how she held her body, slowly ebbed out over the next few minutes as her shoulders shook. After a short time, she looked up and dried her tears. With a wry half-smile, she said, "Maybe...maybe that was my first step towards healing, and forgiveness, and freedom."

"We all carry wounds. It is simply human. And our wounds are hungry creatures. Some may seek vengeance, some are brimming with white-hot anger, but if we are able to forgive the people who had caused them, we can close those wounds forever and make them fade, leaving no trace they had ever been there."

"That is so nicely said. But what if I can never forgive? I am, in fact, angry with myself for not having been able to forgive."

"You need to forgive yourself first for not being able to forgive your mother. Acceptance of your non-forgiveness might be the first step toward the eventual full forgiveness. Whether you forgive her or not, forgiving yourself should result in the acceptance of either state and bring you peace."

"So if I cannot find forgiveness in my heart that's ok, too."

"As long as you can accept that; however, if you cannot accept your inability to forgive, you need to go deep within yourself to find the reasons, to remove the blocks to your inner sense of freedom and healing. Because by not forgiving, you are causing suffering to yourself. Also, remember, a few minutes ago you said you realized that your mother's life must have been hell. That statement is a sign you are able to feel compassion, and your compassion comes from your awareness of her situation. That awareness of others is one of the steps towards forgiveness, and things like meditation can help you build upon it. Have you ever tried meditating?"

"Yes, but it hasn't helped"

"If you try to meditate from the perspective of compassion, you may be able to enter your mother's world and try to gain insight into what it might have been like for her to live in her skin. What often happens, when children are hurt by their parents, is that they dissociate from that pain, and their feelings become numb, so to speak. Numbness diminishes our capacity for compassion. So an essential step toward forgiving her is for you to imagine yourself living your mother's life. You are an adult woman, a mother, a midwife, a wife. Now it is time for you to step into your mother's shoes. It is much easier to condemn than to view with mercy and understanding the life of someone who has hurt us. In your polyamorous life, and your life as a midwife, you must have felt enough love, enough belonging and expansion, as well as compassion to allow yourself now to bridge the gulf between you and your mother. Forgiveness through compassion simply brings us freedom and soul renewal."

"Ah, that is so nicely said...I..."

Her phone rang and she apologized for having to take the call. After talking for a minute, she got up apologizing profusely, and said that a patient had gone into premature labour. It was a young woman suffering from anxiety and Monique had promised her she would be there when her labour started. I said it was not a problem, as I had to be at another hospital shortly. I called a cab because my car was at the mechanic's for ignition problems. As soon as I sat in the back seat, I started feeling trepidation over seeing Weylin again. Why? Why did he have to re-enter my life?

When I arrived at the hospital, it took me ten minutes to find the room among the maze of corridors. When I opened the door, feeling nervous and agitated, I was welcomed by a friendly atmosphere and warm smiles. We shook hands as I was introduced to Keith, Annette, and Phil and I nodded briefly at Weylin. "Sorry to have missed the first hour."

"We haven't started yet. We discussed the protocol and as you are only observing, I will ask you to read this sheet. Your observations will be helpful once we start discussing and comparing our impressions. "Who is the first one to try the psychedelic drug?"

"I will go first." Weylin said. “It is out of character for me to even entertain the idea of experimenting with a drug, and accessing who knows what, but it is high time to open my mind to what seems impossible, improbable, and even crazy. My patient Ariadne should be here in the afternoon. She is coming straight from the airport, and we decided to wait for her before we begin. Keith believes this is no random gathering and that we are all somehow interconnected and need this collective experience."

"While we are waiting for her, I'd like to go over the protocols, dosages and procedures to follow in case the subjects' blood pressure drops or rises too high." Keith said and continued. "Annette asked me also to perform an energy healing on her. You, Leandra – I hope it's alright to call you Leandra - probably do not know that Annette has cancer and her reason for being here is to undergo energy healing sessions with me. She allowed me to reveal that. I see you look surprised. Yes, I have some healing abilities and I read energies."

Keith looked at me quizzically and I felt I was blushing under his penetrating gaze. I felt my armour go up in fear he may detect something I did not wish him to find out about myself...something about me and Weylin. My reaction had had nothing to do with Annette. All of a sudden, I became aware of my effort to obliterate Weylin from my consciousness and my existence, to ignore his presence in this room. I felt the impulse to get up and leave, and slam the door, and defy this turn of fate or events that brought us together again. In my mind, I began to articulate an excuse, a reason why I could no longer participate in this study, when my gaze fell upon Annette whose eyes were filled with hope.

"Leandra, I am very sick, perhaps terminally, and this is my last hope. I never expected to believe that anyone had any energy healing powers, but I have nothing to lose at this point. I am clinging to a thread of hope after Keith examined me this morning and told me he felt huge energy blockages that had caused my cancer. He also said it was not my time to go, which means there is a chance he can help me. I also need to change many things about how I live my life, and I am ready for a big change. I will also take Jacacia in order to reconnect with my past lives, and see if there is some trauma that has followed me to this one, and caused my cancer. Facing death has changed me deeply. Yes, I am fighting for my own life, and it is mostly out of self-interest that I agreed to take part in this experiment; however, if Weylin and I see any value in including Jacacia in the treatments of our patients, I will start the paperwork upon our return to get permissions for our own limited use. For me, it took dying to open up to something so radically new."

"I suggest we go to the cafeteria first and get some coffee, and when we come back, I will conduct a healing session with Annette." Keith got up and we followed automatically.

9

Weylin

I tried to chat with Leandra on the way to the cafeteria, but her body language was rigid and her responses cursory, so I abandoned the conversation. She was silent during our coffee break and was sipping water absent-mindedly, or that's what I thought. I hoped she harboured no bad feelings regarding our past. I was aching to talk to her about her extraordinary experiences with past-life regression in which I apparently played a role as a lover who had always betrayed her, and once Keith and Annette were absorbed in their discussion about energy healing, I turned to Leandra and said, "Is something wrong? I get a distinct impression you do not want to talk to me. And I'm dying to hear about your past-life regression therapy. I...I was in disbelief listening to the recordings...in fact they moved me and shook me up in a way I've never been shaken up before. I no longer know what to think. What seemed to be rational now looks irrational. It's like all of a sudden, everything is upside down and I feel like Alice in Wonderland."

"This is not the time or the place to talk."

"Let's talk while Annette is in her healing session with Keith. She told me she'd prefer a private session. She wants to share her experiences with the rest of us after."

At that moment, Annette turned toward us and said, "Yes, I'd prefer a private session, not only an energy healing session, but also one during which Keith will administer Jacacia to me. I have agreed only to Phil's presence, as he is a critical part of the experiment. I feel nervous and terrified of the possibility that Keith cannot do anything and that Jacacia will have no effect on me. At the same time, I am fearful of actually accessing a past life. As I am a control freak, it unnerves me to be subjected to experiences I have no control over. What unsettles me most of all is not knowing how to tell my family I'll be dead in a few months, or even sooner if I find no help in these sessions. So even though I want a private healing session, I want to tell you about it later, and I want your input. I hope this is alright with you, Leandra, and that you understand."

"Of course," said Leandra. "Under such circumstances I would also want to have a private session."

Her voice was strained and was laced with a coldness and detachment unusual for her. Something seemed to be bothering her. Perhaps she regretted agreeing to take part in the study. Or maybe my presence disturbed her. I could only hope she harboured no grudges toward me.

Annette and Keith got up to leave and with a sigh of irritation, Leandra said she could have seen another three patients had she known the study would be postponed.

"I'm sorry about the change. Ariadne could not come yesterday, and now Annette messed up the schedule by insisting on a private session. I was supposed to be the first one to try the drug, but I guess that should not matter much," I said and continued, "but tell me, please, do you really believe you were regressed....do you really believe we knew each other in past lives?"

"Yes, I absolutely believe it, feel it and know it without a speck of doubt. I always fell for you, and you always hurt me. I never learned the lesson, and that is why I had to repeat it in this lifetime. I can now only hope there are no more lessons left to be learned."

"What lesson... or lessons?"

"That I always fell for fake love instead of appreciating true love... that I could not forget you throughout the lifetimes because you freaking cursed me with that whisper to never forget about you...that I trusted fickle love, and believed infatuation was love when it was only fleeting sexual attraction...Sorry, Weylin, I should not have said all of that. It sounds accusatory and unfair because it was my conscious decision to have an affair with you. But I still firmly believe that under regression, I accessed memories of the past lives in which I knew you and loved you with all I had in me. As insane as it sounds."

"But what if ...if it did not happen like that...what if you misinterpreted the situation...what if your information is not complete. Perhaps if I met Keith in order to access the knowledge from my own past lives and finally still this feeling in me that something is missing and incomplete in my life...I don't even know how to explain it. Maybe there are no coincidences. Maybe you were always right about synchronicities, and this is one of them. I am here for a purpose, and you are here for a similar purpose. And perhaps, that purpose is for us to understand the complete story of our relationship. There must be some things you did not know about me in those lifetimes?"

"I'm sure I didn't misinterpret anything. You never loved me on any deeper level."

She said that in a neutral tone and her eyes remained expressionless. And then it occurred to me she was behaving in a detached way in order to ensure none of the old feelings of love she had felt for me would escape under her defences. She did not trust herself, and she certainly did not trust me after our history of painful encounters and goodbyes during our fiery affair.

"Leandra, now I cannot wait to try Jacacia and ask Keith to help me go back to the incarnations in which I knew you. I need to know if I was really the kind of creep you think I was. I believe that's the reason I'm here. You're well aware I never meant to hurt you. Under different circumstances we could have stayed together...in fact, I have no doubt had we been free we would have been an ideal couple...but it simply was not sustainable, the way it was. I could no longer tolerate the ups and downs...the secrecy...the fear of my wife finding out and divorcing me."

Leandra looked like an ice statue.

"Of course I understand. No need to explain again what you once said. You were quite clear when you said you could no longer maintain our relationship."

Her words did not match her tense body language or the way she avoided looking me in the eye.

"While waiting for Annette's session to be over, I'll sit over there and catch up on reading a couple of articles on my phone. Talk to you later."

That was a lame excuse to get away from me. I regretted inviting her to participate in the study, and felt anger over my decision to get involved in something as far-fetched as finding potential cures in psychedelic drugs.

I left the building to take a walk on its manicured grounds. As I was passing under a tree, a brown bird flew low over my head and landed on a branch of another tree. Our gazes fused and I was rattled by the intelligence radiating from its eyes. I expected the bird to start speaking to me at any moment. What could this encounter signify or herald? And then I remembered the hawk that had landed on my windshield, and a sense that an important discovery was ahead of me rose as unmistaken knowledge from within my soul. I did not come here by any kind of random coincidence. It was to find missing pieces of some semi-veiled puzzle. There was no doubt in my mind that Leandra was part of the puzzle, and that she and I were mysteriously entwined. And I believed that I saw that clearly in the bird's eyes, even though if anyone else had stated such a preposterous belief, I would have recommended a period of intense observation in a psychiatric ward.

I returned to our study room after an hour of walking aimlessly, trying to make sense of events. Once back in the room, Annette's wan smile greeted me. I tried to read its meaning and believed hope radiated from it. I looked at her again and noticed an unusual glint in her wide- open pupils. She looked drugged and it seemed the effects of Jacacia had not worn off yet.

"Weylin, I need to share with you what happened. Please ask Leandra to join us, too." Annette's speech was a bit slurred, and Keith nodded, looking at me, and said that she was still under the influence of the drug but felt compelled to share her experience with everyone as soon as possible in fear she might forget the details.

I sent Leandra a text message and she replied immediately saying she was on her way up. As soon as Leandra entered and took a seat, Annette began to speak. Every now and then, she would look at Keith in search of affirmation. While she was talking, he was nodding at her with smiles and almost imperceptible nods. She still looked intoxicated, and her breathing was somewhat laboured.

"Keith has given me so much hope...I...I'm so excited I don't know where to begin. It is hard to describe his healing technique...I never believed in alternative medicine before and am not even quite certain I can believe my own experience now...I am still trying to process what I felt and witnessed as Keith's patient and his study subject," Annette said.

She stopped for a moment, closed her eyes, and inhaled deeply before continuing.

"Hovering his hands over me, Keith was able to detect energy blockages in my body...at various points. These blockages prevented my immune system from protecting me from illness and from fighting it. He said that by suppressing my emotions over many years, I had created a body of dark unprocessed pain energy that turned against me by transmuting itself into cancer. You should have seen how much I wept once his own energy unblocked some of mine. I felt as if pent-up pressure was released from my body, and was gushing from multiple openings with a hissing sound. But that was only the beginning. After the energy healing session, I ingested Jacacia in hope of reconnecting with a past life and clearing the traumatic experiences from that period.

That almost indescribable trip began with an explosion of colours in so many shades of brightness that my vision was momentarily saturated. I could hear Keith's voice echoing softly in the foreground of a much more powerful voice, which introduced itself as the spirit of Jacacia. It all felt like a dream in which memories of a life that happened centuries ago revealed themselves to me. And I saw my past life with utmost clarity, and I remember every single detail, even though I am not sure I can find the right words to relay it all to you faithfully. My experience was one of floating and observing my own life in 17th century Ireland, and then fusing with it and reliving it."

At that moment, Leandra gasped in astonishment and Annette opened her eyes and looked at her with puzzlement in her eyes.

"Your mentioning that time frame came as a surprise because the past-life regression therapy I underwent a couple of years ago revealed I had also lived in that time period and the same country you had lived. So I was just wondering if I might have known you. But the mere fact that I have been brought here makes me believe I must have known you and we must all be connected. I no longer believe in coincidences. Please continue," said Leandra in a voice brimming with anticipation.

Listening to Annette and Leandra's exchange added to my sense of disbelief that I was actually witnessing all of this. What happened to my highly sceptical mind? How can all of this be? Is that the same Annette whom I'd known as a demanding, intimidating, and most of all inscrutable boss? She leaned back in her chair and gripped the arms of it as if she had just experienced a dizzy spell. She continued her story.

"When the colours stopped playing in my field of vision, the first thing I saw was an elegant yet formidable looking manor house with huge white pillars adorning a wide entrance. I found myself hovering above the house and marvelling at its beautifully manicured gardens before I saw myself. The woman sitting on a white bench in a gazebo covered with climbing white roses was unmistakably me. I could feel all her emotions, her turmoil, her tears clamped up inside her heart. On the outside she looked peaceful and composed, but on the inside, she was torn up and oozing pain out of every pore. She felt humiliation, degradation, and betrayal because her husband's infidelities had not only multiplied, but had also taken a form she found too difficult to tolerate. Even before she had gotten married, she had made a vow to herself that she would never allow others to see her suffering the way her mother had let everyone witness her own humiliation at the hands of her husband, who had beaten her and yelled at her when he was drunk as well as when he was sober.

Observing myself in the woman below, I could feel and relate to her stubborn decision to never show hurt nor ever allow anyone to pity her. Her husband, Lord Tyrone had invited his lover Morgana to a masked ball he had organized to mark his wife's birthday. Ah, the humiliation! She was expected to play the role of the gracious hostess and pretend she did not know he had a lover, let alone that the heinous wench would be desecrating her home with her presence."

Annette gulped down air before she continued her story. Interestingly enough, she also switched from describing herself in the third person to speaking in the first person.

"The night fell and dressed as a queen and king, my husband and I stood outside our house, welcoming the guests. I felt like screaming and smashing everything in sight, but as always, I managed to appear regal and dignified in my role. Men and women in lavish and elaborate costumes were coming up to us to greet us. I smiled and welcomed them even though I feared the pain would suffocate me. I had no one in whom to confide, and the feelings I kept pushing deeper and deeper into my soul were poisoning me and threatening to choke me. They had turned into a monstrous beast that was tearing at my insides. My curse was not only my unfaithful husband, because most husbands were unfaithful, but also my barrenness. Neither Jilleen's nor Ailionora's herbs could do anything to help me conceive. And now rumour was spreading like wildfire that Morgana, my husband's harlot, was with child."

I looked at Leandra and noticed a soft smile light up her face. She looked as if Annette's story held no surprise, and she had just met another friend from a past life, and it was perfectly normal to expect such encounters. I, on the other hand, felt an utter sense of incredulity over hearing Annette mention the names I had heard in Leandra's recordings from her regression sessions. I looked around the room as if needing confirmation that the observers and participants were highly educated professionals with scientific backgrounds, and not psychiatric patients suffering from delusional disorders. But all of us were professionals from medical fields and we just had to try to make sense out of these peculiar experiences. I also wondered if any of us would dare present at any psychiatric conference on what we have witnessed so far. I turned my attention again to Annette, who continued her story in a voice laced with hatred and agitation. Her body language exuded the tension of someone who was physically and spiritually present in the story she was narrating. In that moment, she still inhabited a different dimension from our own.

"There she is! Dressed in a crimson dress befitting a strumpet. She thinks I do not recognize her behind her red mask. Her red attire with a deep plunging neckline reminds me of blood and plague, demons and hell. Her screeching laughter also reveals her vulgar soul as much as her shameless flirting. The garish dress with all its folds and pleats does not hide her swollen belly. And she flaunts it as if the bastard will be known and recognized as Lord Tyrone's child. Powerful men have mistresses, but do not recognize the bastards born out of such unions. But what if my husband decides to get rid of me and marry his whore? I must not allow that.

Whilst the guests are revelling and drinking, and while they later disperse in the gardens searching for a hidden treasure of rubies my husband had hidden as part of the celebration, I stay inside seething, cursing, and plotting revenge. At the same time, a smile never leaves my face. I have learned to veil my feelings with a masterful deception.

I shall not suffer humiliation anymore. After all, had it not been for my dowry, my husband would not be half as rich. It is with my gold that he bought the string of rubies he gave me tonight as our anniversary present. What diabolical duplicity to give me a gift of precious stones and humiliate me with Morgana's presence!

I find myself alone staring at my opulent portrait, commissioned by my husband five years ago, when he had still fancied me. Unseen, I go to his chamber and fetch his prized dagger. Fury consumes my soul and muddies my thoughts. When

I turn around, I am startled to see Jilleen standing before me. Her beautiful aquamarine dragonfly costume is wet and ruined, and her long brown hair is falling in wet strands around her face, and cascading down her shoulders. It is full of dry leaves and tiny twigs. She is a woman like no other. Happy and insouciant, she roams the fields, yet I have heard evil tongues say that she meets a secret lover during her walks. A woman adored by her handsome husband Aidan need not look for any other man's attention. Few men can compare to her tall, muscular, and valiant husband.

I hear her say something about having fallen in the brook on our estate, and needing a dry dress, but I shove her to the side, and go outside with resolve beating firmly in my breast.

Morgana has taken off her mask and is laughing among a group of masked men. Shameless whore! She shall laugh no more. Hearing myself scream in madness and fury, with all my might I ram the dagger into Morgana's white throat and chest, holding her by the hair at the same time. Blood spurts everywhere onto the revellers surrounding her, the rosebush behind her and onto my face. I stab her and stab her until her blood makes my grip on the knife wet and slippery, and until the strumpet has drawn her last breath. Strong hands claw into me tearing me away from Morgana's limp body, and I scream, and flail and kick with a fervent desire to kill every single witness to my humiliation and revenge.

I lose consciousness and slip into a warm darkness. When I come around, I hear horse hooves click monotonously against the hard ground. It is hot and suffocating in the carriage. A hand proffers a cup, and I drink from it recognizing the nauseating taste of valerian root, which leads to the darkness enveloping me again.

When I awaken from what felt like death, I find myself lying on a hard surface. I slowly get up trying to feel my way in the dark. The floor is earthen but level and swept clean. Moonlight is drizzling lazily into the small chamber from a window that is too high to be reached even when I stand up fully. My eyes are able to discern a narrow cot in one corner, and a pitcher of water beside it. I drink from it tasting not only water, but also my own blood oozing from a cut on my lower lip. I am not afraid. I am calm and content that I killed Morgana, and whatever happens to me now, I am ready to accept with equanimity.

Exhaustion helps me fall sleep. A creaking sound awakens me, and in the pale light of dawn, I see a silhouette of a nun.

She comes in and says in a stern voice, "Your husband brought you here last night. You are to stay with us and expiate your sin of murder. Wash yourself and put this on. You will meet the Abbess through whose grace and kindness you have been embraced by this nunnery. If you are wondering about this place, it is the Abbey of Our Holy Mother. Your husband brought you in an unconscious state and implored our Abbess to give you shelter. Your heinous sin broke his heart. Your husband believes you committed the murder out of madness, and you can no longer walk free, or live in his home. But God is all merciful and here you may atone for the sin of extinguishing an innocent life."

I feel fury well up in me again and I am tempted to spit at her and scratch her face, and tell her I took no innocent life, but that of a harlot, but I decide to remain silent and keep my thoughts and feelings under an opaque veil of inscrutability. My husband must have brought me here so justice could not reach me. Once my deed is forgotten, he will come and fetch me. But what if he brought me to this convent so that he could be rid of me, so that I remain buried and forgotten here? I must find a way to escape.

The nun, whose name is Maria, brings me before the Abbess. I kneel at her feet and listen patiently as she talks about damnation and hell awaiting sinners of my kind. Her words cannot penetrate the shield around my heart. She asks me questions, but I remain mute. Both she and Maria conclude that I lost my power of speech due to the shock I endured, or perhaps it was God who punished me for my sin by taking away my speech. In the end, they decide that my loss of speech is a sign of God's punishment. My road to eventual redemption would be strewn with fasting, kneeling on the bare floor in prayer, and toiling in the Abbey gardens. And so after a life of utmost comfort, a new life of extreme hardship begins.

I rise at dawn to join in their prayers of gratitude for the new day, and the nuns accept a mute figure standing beside them with her head bowed, or her eyes raised toward the sky. They all believe that even mute, I am expiating for my sins in silent, but devoted and sincere prayer. My blank expression hides my inner states that alternate between periods of calm and numbness, and tempests of rage against God, my treacherous husband, and this dismal prison. Even in my cell, I do not allow myself to weep or moan from the pain caused by hard physical labour in the gardens full of rock and infertile soil that needs endless tilling. But I endure for months on end, carrying out all assigned tasks without a whimper. Any pain, spiritual or physical, I just push deeper and deeper into the darkness of my soul until the feelings turn to stone.

The Abbess sends me to confession every time a priest visits the abbey. I kneel mute waiting for the session to end. His words wash over me like a light breeze one barely feels on one's skin. I overhear the priest, whose name I cannot recall, tell the Abbess I was a lost soul beyond salvation. He sees wickedness in me and declares that I have not come any closer to God by living in this saintly place. And I just smile inside continuing to plot my escape by climbing over the stone wall one night when everyone is asleep. I have already found a place where the stones protrude enough to provide narrow ledges onto which I could place my feet. I do not know what the wall will look like on the other side, but I plan to hold on to the top edge, extend myself by my full length and then jump, for the remaining height should allow me to land uninjured.

I notice that Sister Maria starts looking at me with smiles in her eyes and that puzzles me. She brings a cup of tea to my cell and tells me she wants to help me regain my voice. When her hand trails across my cheek, I look at her with cold indifference without cringing on the outside. Her touch repulses me.

One evening as I am shelling peas at the kitchen table by candlelight she comes in and stands behind me at the very edge of the table. What she does next shocks me, but I pretend I neither notice, nor understand the nature of her movement against the table's edge. She is leaning firmly against the corner gyrating her hips. Her breathing turns into soft moans and I shudder at the realization that she is sinning shamelessly in my presence in the house of God. She is pleasuring herself against the dull wooden edge as her left hand is squeezing my shoulder. *Oh, what depravity*, I think! I am tempted to reach for the knife lying on the table and plunge it into her throat, and it takes all my willpower to remain immobile. When she finally leaves, I shudder in revulsion.

From that evening on, every time she sees me alone in the kitchen, she repeats her ritual of rubbing herself against the table until a plan hatches in my head, a plan that should stop this most repugnant deed. As one of my duties is to kill and pluck chickens, next time I kill one I squeeze its blood into a leather sack.

That afternoon I take potatoes and carrots into the kitchen and start peeling them. It is a dark and cloudy day and I work by candlelight. The kitchen table stands in the corner where there is no window, so I light another candle to help me see better. The leather sack with chicken blood is on the table and I carefully drench the table's edge with it. Then I place a piece of rag on the floor to absorb the blood drops so they cannot be seen by anyone. The other nuns are getting ready for the evening service, which will be held by a visiting priest. For that occasion, they will wear their white scapulars over their brown habits.

Maria comes into the kitchen flushed and in a haste. Her gaze reveals both lechery and stealth. She makes me think of my lecherous husband and I taste the bile of hatred in my throat. How I wish I could kill her.

She begins her dance of self-pleasure while I am peeling the potatoes. It is clear to me that part of her enjoyment is my silence and seemingly powerless presence. As someone who does not speak, I cannot tell the Abbess of the sin committed with impunity. Inwardly, I smile thinking of the red stain she will have on her white scapular. I hope she does not notice it before she goes to service. I want to witness her shame and inability to explain the blood on her habit.

After I finish peeling the potatoes, I rub the edge of the table clean and I go to my cell and change quickly because the service is about to begin. In the meantime, the sky opens up and sheets of rain fall on the monastery. Even with candlelight, it is not easy to see well in the damp corridors leading to the chapel. I was the last to come in.

The chapel is dark, and I can only see the silhouettes of sisters holding unlit candles in their hands. I stand in the second row behind Sister Theresa. I recognize her because she is the tallest and the most devout among us.

The Abbess walks from one sister to the next lighting their candles with her own. Once the last candle is lit, we begin to sing welcoming the priest into the chapel. He appears at the first note and stands at the pulpit. Just as he starts to speak, his face contorts into a mask of fear, his eyes widen and with a quivering hand, he points out at a sister in the first row and shouts, "The Devil is in our midst!"

Fear and panic thicken in the room as the sisters start shuffling, whispering, and looking around disoriented. The priest in the meantime takes the candlestick from the altar and gingerly, with eyes still wide open walks toward a sister, stops before her and lowers the light so that the candlestick almost touches her crotch. The rest of us muster up our courage and encircle him. And I suddenly see what had unnerved the priest and is now making everyone gasp in horror. The candlelight flickers across the red shape on Sister Maria's white scapular. Her crotch area looks as if someone had painted an angry red face with horns and a gaping mouth drooling blood; rubbing herself against the blood-covered table's edge, she had somehow drawn a contour of the Devil's face itself. I shriek in delight over her punishment, but my scream goes unnoticed among the cacophony of gasps, fear-drenched screams, and stifled screeches.

"Remove the Devil's daughter from this holy chamber," shouts the priest with his eyes bulging and sweat trickling in rivulets down his brow and neck. No one dares approach Maria, but when she suddenly moves and dashes for the door, I intercept her and grab her with all my might. Wordlessly, I wrestle her to the ground tearing off the wimple around her head. She screams and kicks, but she is no match for me, for a woman brimming with fiery rage. I pin her arms to the floor and hold her tight until she begins to sob and her body goes limp. I stand up and look around surprised to recognize awe in the eyes of the sisters that surround me.

The priest shouts again that Maria be escorted to her cell and not let out for twenty days. She is to confess her sins, for clearly, she has copulated with the Devil, and he has left his mark on her. She is to be given only water during the time of her atonement. He adds that he is too disturbed to lead the service and orders that we all retreat to our cells.

The next morning a clap of thunder wakes me up. I shiver underneath a threadbare blanket and think about my old life when I was rich and spoiled, wrapped in silks and fur, fed the best delicacies. My husband's infidelity now seems insignificant, and I regret killing Morgana, thereby losing a lifestyle few women are given to enjoy. I decide I absolutely must escape this wretched life and find my way back home. I still have family who should give me shelter if I appear on their doorstep.

I dress and go to the chapel for our morning prayer. I can hear sisters whisper and when I come near them, instead of them averting their eyes and ignoring me, the murderess they tell me that Maria was found hanging in her cell. She killed herself over the scandal the red blot caused. We are to bury her immediately because the Abbess does not want word to leave the convent and reach the villages around it. Maria is, after all, known to the local people as the nun who knitted beautiful scarves and sweaters. Should anyone ask about her, we are to say she had fallen ill and died.

The rainy days are followed by unusually hot weather. On the day I decide to use the cover of the night to escape, the heat is almost unbearable. The habit I wear is made from rough black cloth that makes my skin scream from prickly itchiness. I never found out what the nuns had done with my resplendent gown, which I was wearing on the night my husband left me to rot in this place. I want to tear off the hellish garment, and stand naked in the garden, but I know how restricted my actions are. My frustration and anger know no depth.

As I am weeding patiently among the cabbage heads, my breathing starts to come out in gasps followed by a piercing chest pain. Sister Annabelle who is working on my right side screams when she sees me keel over and moan in agony. The pain in my chest intensifies and I faint. When the blackness around me disperses, I find myself lying on my cot with Sister Annabelle putting a cold and wet cloth on my forehead. My chest is still constricted in pain, but my breathing is somewhat less laborious.

I try to move my legs and arms, but to my horror, I cannot. I try to speak and want to expunge through words and tears the sediments of pain, betrayals, regrets, and disappointment with myself and others, but my tears have hardened and would not flow, and my words have frozen and nothing can thaw them. I try to express with my eyes the agony of being imprisoned in this unmoving body, and Sister Annabelle's face reflects her understanding of my plight and my terror. She speaks softly to me trying to assuage my fear. She says that God will help me and not to fear anything in his presence. I do not fear dying because death is salvation. Again, I attempt to talk but all I manage to produce are weak gurgling sounds followed by trickles of blood.

Behind Sister Annabelle, right near the door, I can see a dark silhouette with folded wings on its back. I know my hour has come, and I will leave this world carrying with me all the burdens that have weighed on my soul with crushing heaviness for so long. Had I known I would die without spilling out the poison of my many grievances, I would have never chosen silence; I would not have ceased speaking, and I would not have withheld my grief from these good women. Who knows what disappointments their own hearts cradle, and by talking, we could have lessened each other's pain. But it is too late now.

"Your eyes are saying so much. They bespeak of pain and terror, and I wish you could unburden your soul before you give it unto our Lord," whispers Annabelle, stroking my cheek gently.

I open my mouth again, but only rattling sounds escape it. The room around me becomes flooded in bright, white light. That light penetrates me and lifts me off the cot. When from above I cast a glance on the cot, I see my stiff body, a gaping mouth, and eyes frozen in terror.

Annette stopped speaking and began weeping silently with her head bowed. When she raised her head, she looked at us one by one and said, "Both Keith and I agree that the past life I accessed showed me how deep the trauma went... so deep that it followed me into this life and who knows how many others. By blocking and suppressing traumatic events, I poisoned my body in that lifetime, as well as in this one. My unshed tears and suppressed emotions in this lifetime compounded that and were the spark that ignited the fire of illness. What I experienced through Jacacia is miraculously cathartic, as crazy as it may sound to you and me alike. I feel... feel a sense of lightness, a sense of being unblocked. Emotions and sensations are flowing more freely through me than ever before. I believe both Keith and Jacacia unblocked passages in my body and soul so that true healing can now begin from within."

Even though teary-eyed and visibly shaken up by the experience, Annette still looked radiant. "That is the colour of hope," I thought. I also wished Keith had indeed effected a miraculous healing. If that turned out to be true, then all my medical knowledge and scientific beliefs would be in question. Or, perhaps, science does not need to exclude the mysterious and the inexplicable.

Keith just smiled warmly and said he would conduct a few more healing sessions with Annette without her having to ingest Jacacia. He said she had responded readily to his energy and her blockages were almost fully removed. He also said something that I never expected to hear from an oncologist unless I thought the oncologist needed psychiatric help. In a perfectly neutral voice, he said Annette was surrounded with spirit protectors who would assist her along the healing process. I looked at Leandra with eyes wide, seeking her reaction to Annette's story and Keith's diagnosis. She smiled at me nodding slightly, and when Keith suggested we take a break, I beckoned her to follow me out.

As soon as we found ourselves far enough from the office door, I asked her to tell me if I had lost my mind the last two days, and if Annette's account of her past life was shocking in its revelation that she was the same Lady Tyrone who had known the same Jilleen, whose name Leandra had also mentioned in the recordings of her past-life regression sessions. I could just imagine Annette's reaction once she learned that Leandra had been that Jilleen in the same past life.

Leandra looked at me and said, "I now know you had to come. I am sure that there are forces that impel us toward crossing each other's path repeatedly and that there must be a reason. Annette came to find healing and you came to provide both of us with the rest of the answers. I am not as astonished as you are, because under David's hypnotherapy sessions I discovered things that made me shake my head in disbelief. Now you are witnessing the same. There is a reason behind all of this, and something is telling me we will learn what it is soon enough. The look of incredulity on your face amuses me."

And then, looking at me, she began to laugh, and her laughter lightened up the atmosphere. Seeing myself through her eyes made me burst into laughter, too. And that laughter was laced with warm feelings for each other, genuine fondness and I wondered if in the fondness we could still find the tempestuous love that seems to have tethered our hearts to each other throughout the centuries.

Just as the warmth between Leandra and me started to transmute and thicken into a deeper energy, Keith approached us saying that he and Phil had to spend some time together adjusting the Jacacia administration protocols. Annette's blood pressure had spiked up making them reconsider the dosage. He apologized for the change in plans, but said he would like to call it a day and resume the experiments tomorrow morning. Ariadne's flight was also delayed and Annette had already sent her a message to go to the hotel and rest in preparation for tomorrow's session. I was slightly disappointed as I was impatient to experience Jacacia firsthand, but I said I understood.

Leandra hugged Keith and left. For a fraction of a second, I wished she had hugged me, too, but she just smiled half-heartedly.

10

Leandra

I left the hospital feeling a mixture of emotions that were hard to label or distinguish. Astonishment, confusion, disbelief, pleasure...I just knew I had to remain open-minded and dive into the experiences before me, trusting that the Universe or the gods wanted Weylin to re-emerge in my life to relay an important message. I also felt relaxed realizing that our spontaneous laughter had shattered the wall of coldness and discomfort between him and me.

After all, we were both professionals, and if I had still been able to act professionally at the conference during which we became lovers, I was certainly able to maintain composure and collegial countenance over the course of this study. The only thing that concerned me was the undeniable existence of an energy chord between us, and a wisp of fear that I might start feeling more than just friendly affection for him. With a slight shudder of unease, I opened my car and went back to work as I still had a whole afternoon before me.

As soon as I entered my office, I called David to tell him about these new and unexpected developments, and my agreement to observe Keith's experiments with an unknown psychedelic drug. David's response did not surprise me. He said he believed my lessons were not completed, and that the new events had been aligned so that I could learn more about my connection with Weylin. There was obviously more to the Weylin and Leandra story despite my previous belief that my past-life regression sessions with David had provided me with all the answers.

After all, I had only known Jilleen's side of the events, but have never learned Kieran's side of the story. I gasped at that realization, and shivered with unexpected anticipation about learning more. I wondered at the same time about the role Weylin's patient Ariadne might have in the constellation of our interwoven destinies. Could it be coincidental that Weylin had selected her over all of his other patients as one of the study participants? Was I connected to her, too, in one of my past lives?

I spent the rest of the afternoon working on a few patients' files and extracting information for an article I was co-writing with a colleague. But I felt a deep sense of disquiet and had difficulty concentrating on work. Again, I felt I was being pulled into an eddy of happenings I could not control or resist. I felt tempted to call Weylin and discuss all of this with him, because we seemed to be partners in a karmic dance we had never chosen. Or, perhaps we did.

Over dinner, I told Adrian about Annette's session, and that her revival of hope Keith might cure her cancer with his energy. Looking off into space, Adrian shook his head lightly, but then he smiled and said, "The weirdness obviously continues." He kissed my forehead and said he had work to do in preparation for a trial.

I spent the evening reading medical journals, and chatting with a friend who was contemplating leaving her husband, but who at the same time was conscious of having no compelling reasons to do so. Marital boredom, familiarity, and the loss of mystery with each other…is there any couple that does not reach that stage?

At nine o'clock, I turned off the lights and fell asleep almost immediately. Weylin came into my dreams, unbidden once again. *I dreamt that our life paths crossed once again at a conference, and I wondered who it was that was pulling the strings of our twinned fates. He should have disappeared from my life forever, but he kept coming back. With each new encounter, the wall between us seemed to get taller, and I sensed its cold and impenetrable presence. I looked at Weylin askance noticing his thinning grey hair and for a flicker of a second the desire to extend my hand, and run it softly across his face, welled up in me. The invisible wall stopped the movement like a jolt from an electric fence. Our conversation was stilted, the smiles forced as the past hung between us like a curtain neither dared part. We had turned into each other's taboo, into strangers afraid of trespassing into the forbidden zones of what once was.*

I steered the conversation toward his art and his gallery, and it began to flow more easily. It was strange to talk about art, knowing that he did not own a gallery, but was a psychiatrist like me; still, I did not question that strangeness. After all, it was just another dream.

I pretended to be my old insouciant self, unmoved by his apparent indifference toward me. My light banter was another mask hiding my memories of dizzying love and its ultimate demise. And these memories lived in a place filled with incomprehension over how abruptly bonds between souls dissolve into nothingness. As if we were never inebriated with love, as if the power of our bond never made us feel immortal and god-like! How did those feelings vanish? And why was I still meeting him in unexpected places? Did we really meet across different incarnations? Will we meet in future lifetimes? Questions without answers.

Looking into his sky-coloured eyes, I tried to still my throbbing heart, as he no longer looked like Weylin, but like Kieran. For a few moments, silence fell between us like an opaque veil covering the unspoken. Anger rose in my throat leaving the taste of bile. I despised myself for loving a man who had stopped loving me long ago. That weakness of mine marred my soul and felt like an unbreakable curse, or like a tragic flaw in my character. And the thought he might somehow see through my pretence terrified me. It was time to retreat behind the wall again.

I woke up with a start. It was only midnight. Adrian was sleeping peacefully, and did not even stir when I left the bed, took a blanket from an armchair and went into the backyard. The moon was dripping silver tinsels down our flaming willow branches. I sat on a garden chair and gazed at the midnight sky hoping that the night's stillness and magic would provide the answer to the question, "Why did he show up in my life again. Why, why, why?" And why did I dream about a wall when the wall seemed to have vanished after we both burst into laughter?

A light breeze rose, creating a susurrus among the willow leaves, and within the rustling I heard, "The knowledge is incomplete."

I shivered and went back into the house with a heart full of trepidation.

The next morning when I arrived at the hospital room where the Jacacia experiments were to continue, I almost collided with a woman with short, blonde hair. As I started to apologize, we looked at each other and recognition flickered in our gazes. I felt a strong connection to her. I was certain I knew her but could not place her anywhere. She was the first to say, "We know each other, don't we?"

"I'm sure we do...from a conference? You do look so familiar." I laughed nervously unable to recall where it was the two us had met.

"Ariadne." She introduced herself and continued, "Weylin's patient, eager to undergo whatever it is this guy Keith claims his secret drug induces."

"Leandra. Lovely to meet you. I'm Weylin's colleague."

As soon as I uttered the words, the look in her eyes revealed she sensed Weylin was more than a colleague to me. She cocked her head ever so slightly as if wondering why a thought like that would have crossed her mind.

Weylin was already sitting in the chair designated for the study subjects. He smiled at me warmly, but I smiled back perfunctorily, avoiding again any kind of closeness with him, even the kind of intimacy a mere smile might generate. I did not trust my feelings for him and felt the need to withdraw again. When Keith began to talk, my attention shifted to him.

"We are ready to begin. Weylin will go first and then Ariadne will follow. The observers should sit in the chairs under the window so they remain unobtrusive. We will discuss Weylin's experience afterwards…by the way, it will be videotaped. We did not videotape or record Annette, but I did take copious notes. Also, she's allowed me to say that we had another energy healing session early this morning and that I can no longer detect any blockages in her, or signs of illness. As you can see, she looks healthy, feels great and can't stop smiling with optimism."

"I've spoken with my doctor in Ireland this morning and it was clear he thought I'd lost my mind and had fallen for quackery," Annette chimed in. "But he agreed to run a series of tests on me as soon as I get back home."

"Phil should be here any moment and then we'll start," continued Keith. "Weylin, as I mentioned before, once you ingest Jacacia and start feeling its effects, you will have to frame clearly within your mind which part of your life needs illumination with knowledge…or, which part of yourself you need to face and gain insight into…are you aware of any unhealed trauma… do you suffer from anxiety that needs to be addressed, or do you believe you need to access memories of a past life in which you might find answers to the questions weighing down on you? The spirit of Jacacia seems to have the power to reconnect everyone to what they desire to discover about themselves. For example, my wife wanted answers on how long she had to live, and was told it was her time to go. Her purpose on this plane had been fulfilled and she surrendered unto death with peace. So Weylin, after you drink Jacacia from this cup, let the spirit know I am only serving as a guide and an observer so that I can go on the same journey as you, and witness and chronicle your experience."

"What quantity of the drug should I take," asked Weylin.

"We are not sure about the right dosage, so we will err on the side of caution, and ask you to drink only half a cup. If the effects are not strong enough, Phil will give you more. From my own experience, though that should suffice. Are you ready?"

"Yes, I am."

At that moment, Phil entered with a tray. From a large white bowl, he poured some greenish liquid into two wooden cups. Perhaps Jacacia released its potency from wooden containers! He handed one cup to Keith and one to Weylin, and turned on the video camera propped up on a desk opposite the armchair in which Weylin was sitting.

After gulping down the proffered liquid, he closed his eyes for a couple of minutes, then opened them and said he could already feel the effects. He said he felt warmth rising from his chest to his head. He then looked at me, raised the empty cup as if making a toast, and said, "I want Jacacia to take me to the same lifetime in 17th century Ireland in which Leandra lived. I feel compelled to prove to her, among other things, I was not the bastard she believes I was. Something is telling me that's where I need to go for answers I'm not aware I'm seeking."

I felt myself blush crimson as if Weylin had divulged the details about our affair. Ariadne's smile seemed to reflect inner knowledge of our secret, and I wondered if I was simply imagining things. The energy in the room felt familiar and pleasant. It vibrated love and understanding. At the same time, I became acutely aware of an invisible, but pulsating cord between Weylin and me, the cord I had tried to sever so many times without success. That energy still lingered, and its sudden presence filled me with impatience to hear Weylin's side of the story.

11

Weylin

I drank the liquid, and its cloying taste made me shudder in revulsion. It reminded me of the Sangria I'd tried on a restaurant patio one summer night in Madrid. I'd barely been able to drink half a glass while Maureen had enjoyed several. That memory was immediately replaced with a feeling of apprehension over the effects Jacacia would produce. My palms and my lower back began to sweat and I just hoped my often profuse sweating would not produce an odour.

Apart from feeling a warmth rising in my chest, nothing happened for a few minutes, but then with a suddenness as if I had been sucker-punched, voices began to thunder inside my head. One of them was Keith's, yet it sounded like an echo of a more powerful and resonant voice that spoke to me.

"As you are entering the realm of Jacacia remember that all is one and one is part of all. I am in everything, and everything is contained in me. You are because I am, and we are parts of the depth of unity. In me, your memories reside and can be resurrected at will. Through me, you can return to the ancient rhythm of your soul, the place you had inhabited before the consciousness of birth separated you, and before you belonged to the Earthly plane."

Keith drew a deep breath, and as he continued, his voice lowered and the cadence changed. "Surrender your spirit to the gentle power of Jacacia, and trust it to guide you where you need to go to find complete knowledge of thyself and appease thy soul's longings. In me, there are places calling to those seeking sacred wholeness and belonging. In me thou shalt discover that nothing is ever lost that cannot be found on another plane."

A myriad of blindingly beautiful and vibrant colours exploded before my eyes. At the same time, my body seemed to be hurling toward the sky and was travelling at what must have been the speed of lightning. The colours parted, unveiling a dark spiral plunging downward, and with frightening speed, my ascent turned into a dizzying descent. I expected to feel nauseated, and to lose consciousness, but to my astonishment, the travel and descent down the spiral were not unpleasant. Even though I heard Keith's request to the spirit of Jacacia that I was seeking answers surrounding my role in Leandra's life in 17th century Ireland, I could not imagine that based on such a cryptic and vague description, I could end up in that lifetime out of an infinite number of possible incarnations. And why was I even grounding my thoughts in such suppositions instead of questioning my sanity? Why I would start considering this experience as normal was beyond my wildest conjectures. I just felt my complete trust in Jacacia and the spirit or spirits behind it speaking the words that I somehow could automatically translate into English.

"Where are you Weylin?" Again, I heard Keith's voice as a weaker echo of another voice.

Choking on tears, I could not reply for a moment. I found myself sitting on the ground behind a large stone house and sobbing. I'd left the house so that no one could see my pain and breakage. All my life I'd tried to appear braver than I was because fortitude was expected of men. Somehow, I was always aware that my spirit lacked warrior traits. That is why I was jealous of Jilleen's husband Aidan, who not only was our Chieftain, but a man of huge physical and mental strength, a man valiant enough to wage wars and yet soft enough to capture Jilleen's heart. And I wanted Jilleen for myself, but I knew I could never claim her. Even daring to be her lover terrified me because her husband Aidan would kill me with ease if he found out. Many a time I was tempted to break off our dangerous liaison, but her passion and love for me overpowered my fear and clouded my reason.

"Why are you crying, Weylin?"

"I am not Weylin. My name is...it is Finnian… no, that's my elder son's name. My name is Kieran. I'm crying because God doesn't seem to hear my prayers. I've sinned too gravely against him and his laws. I've loved a woman that is our Chieftain's wife. The magnitude of my sin is now weighing heavily on me... and fear is ravaging me... fear that my son will die for my sin, that my wife will expel me from the house because her parents hate me, and they're the custodians of the wealth we enjoy. I feel my whole life is lying in shambles around me, and all I can do is pray."

"Why would it fall upon your son?"

"He tried to save a lamb that a group of children threw into a well. My elder son is a lad of great strength, but also has a heart overflowing with kindness for people and animals. He pulled the wretched animal out of the well, but because it had a broken leg, it had to be killed so it would not suffer more. During the climb, he cut his knee against the sharp wall of the well, and the gash bled heavily. Soon, it turned red and swollen, and the redness spread to his thigh. Fever began to rock his body and his words became garbled. He is now lying unconscious in his chamber, and I fear we are losing him. I know God giveth and taketh away, but I cannot accept that now; I cannot imagine my life without Finnian. He is the light of my life. He helps his neighbours and has a smile for everyone. He makes people laugh with his imitations of others. He invents jokes and funny stories and makes money at the inn by amusing guests with them. Finnian is one-of-a-kind lad."

"Who is with him now?"

"My wife Moira and the healer Ailionora. She cleaned his wound and put poultices on it. She's been feeding Finnian tea made from secret herbs, but nothing helps. My wife is kneeling at his bedside and refuses to eat or drink as penance for whatever sins she may have committed to deserve losing her firstborn. She doesn't answer my calls or respond to my touch. Her body feels and looks like stone. Grief and fear have petrified her."

"Did you marry out of love?"

"I fancied Moira. She was a merry girl and one with a huge dowry. Her parents never wanted me as their son-in-law, but loved Moira enough to allow her to choose among her suitors. My parents had a small estate that did not yield much, and by marrying Moira, I found myself in a life of wealth and comfort. But that did not satisfy me because I have always felt a longing for more, a yearning for someone to awaken me. I felt I was living my life in a state of semi slumber."

"How did you meet Jilleen?"

"I had met her in my dreams many times before I met her during a summer solstice celebration. In my dreams, she would take my breath away by wanting me so much. Moira never wanted me, but subjected herself to my will as wives are expected to do. I discovered the meaning of love in my dreams, and I believed those were visions sent to me by God.

When I met Jilleen, the recognition that it was the woman from my dreams struck me like a bolt of lightning. Her touch felt so familiar that I realized I had always known her. I could not explain such knowledge or from whence it stemmed. She and I were one twinned soul that walked in two bodies. My knowledge of her was primordial, and the realization that I was powerless to change our life circumstances, and make her permanently mine, caused me excruciating anguish.

One day she vanished, and I thought I would die. I learned she had been accused of witchery and thrown off the bridge to drown. My beautiful Jilleen who nurses both people and animals back to health, who gives money to the poor without her husband's knowledge, who venerates nature and all its spirits, who bursts into mirthful laughter when dragonflies land on her arms, and who is saintliness incarnate except for the sin of loving me. Miraculously, she survived the ordeal, and we heard that the inquisitor himself had saved her. Her husband had quite a few people hanged in revenge for what had been done to his wife, but I am not sure if the person who had accused her of witchery was ever brought to justice.

Ah, how happy she makes me when she showers me with sweet kisses and responds to my touch with moans of sensual cravings. Our favourite flight of fancy is to imagine a child born out of our love. At times, we would stop daydreaming aloud about our child for fear of God's wrath. How can something that feels so right and natural be so sinful at the same time?

Once, after we made love on a rock by our favourite lake, we began to talk about our child again. We even had a name for our son...it was always a son we dreamed of. His name would be Conor because it means a wolf lover, and Jilleen not only loves wolves but also has often been followed by one, a she-wolf that comes close to her and allows Jilleen to caress her head. Our son Conor would grow into a just and valiant man who would be remembered by history. Afterward, every time we would meet, we would tell each other stories about our son Conor and how he would be the one to save the world. We would describe in detail not only his physical appearance, but also his characteristics, flaws, and virtues until we would laugh in great amusement.

One day Jilleen told me that Conor was appearing in her dreams. He was five years old, had a round face, golden hair, and sky-coloured eyes. Whenever Jilleen would extend her arms to hug him, he'd move away saying, "Don't be sad mummy that I shall be born, but shall not live. But one day I shall be born to live a long life. One day you will understand. I was sent to tell you that. Please, find me. Please, promise you'll find me, and you'll search to understand." Jilleen would ask him to explain what she needed to search for to understand, but he would smile and his eyes would ripple with mystery before he would disappear.

Conor appeared twice more in Jilleen's dreams and left her feeling haunted by his image and his words, the meaning of which she still could not penetrate. He was still asking her to promise she'd search for him and not allow the thread of ancestral knowledge to be broken. She was bewildered that such a small child would express such mysterious thoughts. She implored him to stay longer and help her understand, but he could not say more.

She did promise to search for him and the hidden knowledge he was hinting at, and that drew bubbly laughter out of him.

She became so haunted by our imaginary child that she felt compelled to commission a painter to paint a portrait of Conor based on her description. She wanted to capture his image forever before it faded from her memory. The painter, whose name was Hugh Collins, painted a golden-haired child with a face lit with a slightly mischievous smile. As in Jilleen's dream, the child held a glittery purple dragonfly in his hand extended as in an offering.

Jilleen's husband asked her about the painting, and she said a boy had been appearing in her dreams and it was a sign from God the meaning of which she could not penetrate. Perhaps it was an omen that they would conceive another son. She told Aidan that the child's image was so vivid that she wanted it immortalized in a portrait. Aidan was used to Jillieen's unusual and whimsical nature and was pleased to see how happy the painting made her once it was hung in their hall. He even said that he hoped Jilleen was right about the boy being an omen of the child he and Jilleen would have. Their son would be delighted to have a brother who looked just like the boy in the picture. Aidan added that instead of the boy holding a dragonfly in his hand, he would prefer his son to hold a bow and an arrow.

Even though Aidan marvelled at the masterful skill of Hugh Collins, who painted a life-like image of an unknown boy, the servants spread all sorts of gossip that included their questioning Jilleen's sanity. Some even intimated that the only reason she commissioned the painting was to be with the painter, but others countered by saying a woman married to Aidan would certainly not even cast a glance at the unprepossessing, short, and emaciated looking artist who also had a limp.

"Did you see the painting?" Keith prompted.

"Yes, one day when Aidan was away on a hunting trip, Jilleen asked one of her servants to order strawberries from our estate. She wanted to make jam. I brought them to her home and her servants ushered me into the hall, took the strawberries, and told me to wait for the lady of the house, who would pay me. Jilleen descended the stairs looking as pretty as a fairy in a white dress sprinkled with blue dragonflies embroidered with artistic skill. She smiled at me with eyes full of glitter and once again, I felt the deepest love for her. I blushed looking at her and the unease of being in her home filled me to the brim. She always had much more of a determined spirit than I had, and I could not but admire her fearlessness.

The painting took my breath away. The boy in it looked life-like beyond words. I recognized him not only from my and Jilleen's imaginings, but from somewhere deep within me. He was a part of me, even though he was not of this world but of another, a world I could sense but not reach. What unsettled me, was that his resemblance to me was uncanny, and I was afraid someone might notice it. Jilleen, however, remained unconcerned and laughed giddily looking at the picture. I said it was a fine portrait, and that I might ask the artist to paint my two boys and then wished her a good day. I hoped her servants who were standing in the hall did not notice anything untoward in my conduct.

"Why are you trembling now, Kieran? Did something dispel your memory of Jilleen and your son Conor's painting," Keith's voice reverberated through my past-life memories?"

"Yes. A storm is raging around me, and the black sky is splintered by white light and thunder. It must be God seething in anger over us sinners. I need to pray for salvation."

'In this dark hour of the night,
Hear and feel my heart in fright,
Protect and heal my elder child,
Forgive the sinful love I've felt,
Forgive the errors in which I've dwelt,
Shine the light on my tortured soul,
Through your grace let me be whole,
Father, Son and Spirit, Three.'

I am sitting alone in the rain and thunder with my forehead pressed against the wet ground. I am praying with a fervour I have never felt before. I am mumbling promises of giving up Jilleen and returning to my family in body and soul. I am bargaining with God and offering sacrifices if he will only let Finnian live. I am offering my own life in exchange for his. My words of prayer are interspersed with my thoughts about Jilleen.

I wish I could seek her help, for she is a healer, too, but I do not dare summon her. It would be sacrilegious to allow my lover entry into my home. I've not seen her since the masked ball at Lord Tyrone's manor and the horrific murder committed by Lady Tyrone, who disappeared that fateful day. People believe her husband spirited her away to protect her from facing justice.

My thoughts are wandering in myriad directions because I cannot tolerate even one thought of my son's impending death. I am smashing my forehead against the ground, imploring the Lord to spare my son. Over and over again, I swear that I shall give up Jilleen in exchange for my son's life. I am ready to abandon the love of my soul for my Finnian. At the moment when my despair threatens to split my heart asunder, and when in fury and helplessness I hurl blasphemies toward the sky and shout, 'What do you ask of me?' A deafening sound cracks the skies open and a hissing voice speaks to me.

"What is the voice saying?"

"Thy eldest son shall be spared, but thy newborn shall die in his place. A child for a child, a son for a son."

"What are you doing now?" Keith's voice probes further.

"I am running up the stairs to my son's chamber. My drenched clothes are dripping mud and water all over the stairs, and I slip, stumble and fall, and rise again. Blood is dripping from the laceration on my forehead into my eyes and I wipe it with my wet shirtsleeves. When I enter my son's chamber, I look at my wife who is still kneeling petrified at Finnian's bedside with her head lowered on his chest, while Ailionora is placing pieces of wet cloth on Finnian's forehead. He looks as pale and ashen as the first light of dawn.

When Ailionora sees me, she smiles wanly and tells me his fever has broken and my son will live. I am gasping from fright and relief. "Thank you, Lord for answering my prayers!" I am now shivering from head to toe from cold and Ailionora thinks it is from fright.

"No need to feel fearful anymore, Kieran, says Ailionora. Your son is out of death's clutches."

"He will live because it is God's will. God promised me he would live. My children are safe, praised be our Lord. Where is his brother?"

"Duncan visited Finnian briefly, kissed his forehead and went back to his chamber. I told him not to fear, for his brother's life has been spared. Come see, the swelling has come down and his forehead is much cooler."

I bend down and gently raise my wife whispering to her softly, "Moira, rise and look at our firstborn. Our son will live. God promised me."

She is now crying in my arms. Her whole body goes limp and she faints. Ailionora sprinkles her with water and makes her drink a few drops. Lack of nourishment has made her weak and I now fear she may fall ill. She regains consciousness, staggers to Finnian's side, and bends down to kiss his forehead. His blonde hair is matted and lustreless, but his eyelids flutter for a moment and he looks at us.

"Father." His voice is barely audible, but it is a clear sign death is no longer hovering over him. Ailionora bids us goodbye, instructing us to give Finnian strong broth in the morning, as well as the herbal concoctions she left on the table. She says it will not take long for him to recover fully.

The next few weeks I do not leave my son's side. Every day his strength returns more and more, and by the fortnight, he is able to ride out with me. We laughingly race each other up a hill and to the top, and I fall on my knees praising the Lord for giving me my son back.

Once back home I remember my promise to God that I would give up my life of sin with Jilleen. After a few months, I muster up the courage and send a messenger to her house. He knows he can only deliver the message to Jilleen in person. In my message, I ask her to meet me in two days at the foot of the hill where we have met so many times. On the other side of the hill is the lake where we have made love on the rocks surrounding the translucent green water, and where we disappeared into a world created by our fancy.

When the time comes to meet her, I find myself trembling with anticipation. From a distance, I recognize her blue cape. She seems to be walking more slowly than usual. Once I can see her clearly, I notice her laboured breathing, and discern a heavy shape underneath the cloak.

What ensues is too terrible to remember. Recognizing from my look of astonishment that the wide and thick cloth of the cape could not hide she was with child, she addresses me in a voice laced with anger.

“Yes, I am with child and no, I have no way of knowing whose child it is. If it is yours, my husband will not know and will love it as his own.”

I cannot find any words. My speechlessness infuriates her and I cannot recognize my gentle Jilleen.

“I want nothing from you.” Her voice gives me chills.

“Please, don’t be angry. I’m just... just... I didn’t think.”

“People who make love make babies. I may be carrying our Conor.”

"I know, I just did not think it would happen. Our child was part of our imaginings...our fanciful play. I did not think..." I sigh and add, "This is such unfortunate timing because I wanted to…I wanted us to talk and perhaps…we should, I think agree we should stop meeting in sin and secrecy. I am finding it hard to cope with two lives. When I am with you, I reach such heights of ecstasy and then I must go back home to my dismal and empty life with my wife. I cannot live like that anymore. I know I may sound like a coward, but we are both risking too much. The circumstances are impossible, you must see that."

"Kieran, are you now leaving me for another lover?"

"How can you even think something like that? Of course I am not." My voice has a quaver in it.

"Jilleen, let me explain the real reason why I can no longer...why I had to promise God I would abandon my life of sin...Once you hear the truth I am certain you will understand..."

Before I can finish my sentence, she turns around and starts to run back home.

"Jilleen, Jilleen," I shout. "It is not what you believe. My son would have died had I not promised God..." She cannot hear me as the wind that rises as if by magic drowns out my voice. Soon, she turns into a dark speck in the misty distance.

I want to tell her how it breaks my heart to let her go, but that I bargained with the Lord and have sacrificed my love for her for my son's life, but I lost that opportunity and can only hope to see her again and explain. I would rather pierce my own heart with a dagger than hurt my Jilleen.

The next evening as I am riding back home from our fields, I stop at the village tavern for an ale. A group of men are sitting at a table, and I catch fragments of their gossip. It seems a woman almost died in childbirth. Usually, men do not talk about birthing and deaths of babies, as it is a topic for womenfolk, but this, I sense, is somehow different. I overhear them say the baby died, and the mother is still so weak she may not live to see the dawn. When I hear the word 'Chieftain' I stop dead in my tracks.

"Whose wife almost died?" I ask tremulously nearing their table.

A big red-haired fellow who was recently hired to work on Aidan's land answered. "My wife heard from her sister that the Chieftain's wife Jilleen birthed a stillborn. It was a boy. Womenfolk are sayin' the wee lad had yellow hair, and ye' know the Chieftain's hair is dark like a raven's wing. Some say it was the Devil's child and Jilleen's a witch that dances in the moonlight with the Devil, and she shoulda drowned when thrown off the bridge."

His words make me stagger and I have to lean against the table at which the men are sitting. The realization that Finnian was spared so the angel of death could take my newborn, a son born from a depthless passion hits me a like a bolt of lightning. I lost Conor to save Finnian! A child for a child, a son for a son. My chest is burning with anguish. My poor, poor Jilleen! How I betrayed you by bargaining with God! My sins can never be expiated. God took our son Conor. The son we dreamed of, the son whose future we wove with our words, the son whose portrait Jilleen commissioned! But I say nothing, nod briefly and leave the tavern.

Once outside, I feel drained of all life. I stumble from one house to the next until I reach Ailionora's cottage. I knock on the door and enter uninvited. She is sitting on the floor looking transfixed into the flame of a big white candle.

"Sit down, Kieran. I was expecting you."

"Aili...Ailionora....," I hear myself stutter. “I am devastated by the news of Jilleen's child...and hearing she almost died." I crumple to the floor, fighting back tears. I have never allowed anyone to see me cry, except God to whom I pray from time to time.

"I could no longer maintain this dangerous relationship. I have been gripped by fear...there is more fear than love in my heart. I wanted Finnian to live and had to give up Jilleen. She was with our child...I just know it was my son. The sacred ritual you guided us through in the White Circle...I thought Jilleen and I would never part once joined by you...I hoped circumstances would align themselves, and we would be permanently together. Love made me blind...it prevented me from seeing real life...the perils of real life. Because of her strange ways, Jilleen almost lost her life as an accused witch, and now she lost me and our child, and I had to lose her. This is too much loss to bear."

"You may have lost her in this lifetime, for your fear made you partly dissolve the bond between your souls, but that bond can never be fully severed."

She is looking into the flame and moving her hands over it. The candle flame flickers and grows in strength, and I see shapes in it moving, and coiling and twirling.

"What is it you are divining?"

"You and Jilleen are one soul split into two. You are each other's mirror and neither of you will ever find peace until you are reunited. You will continue seeking each other from one lifetime to the next until you are irretrievably entwined. You will feel a longing for completion not understanding from whence that inner tension and discontent arise until you meet her again. But wait...there is more."

"Tell me!"

She's gazing at the flames and her expression does not reveal whether the images she sees bode well or poorly for me. "You will seek each other across lifetimes so you can unite...but there is something else...something that is escaping my sight."

I wait patiently for her to speak again. Her hair is so close to the flame I fear it will catch fire. When she moves away, she lifts her arms into the air and murmurs a prayer the words of which I cannot understand. At the moment when a hissing sound can be heard from one corner of the room, the candlelight turns iridescent blue. She opens her eyes and looks at it anew.

"Kieran, I see it more clearly now. Your son will be born again. The same son you lost now will be born again from your future union with Jilleen. He is another reason why your souls shall always remain enmeshed. He will be a great man, a man needed by the people of his time. He will bring important change, but I can see no further as that lifetime is too far into the future."

"But it is blasphemy to talk about lifetimes! We die and go to Heaven or Hell and that is it. If the folk hear you talk like that, you can lose your life...And how do you know Jilleen and I will not be united again before we die in this life?"

"My beliefs differ from yours just as my gods differ from your one god. I see worlds you cannot see, I sense events you cannot foresee. May it be a solace to you knowing that your and Jilleen's soul energies cannot be disentwined in spite of the separation imposed by time, distance, and the flow of centuries to come."

She gazes dreamily into the candlelight before continuing, "Your union will rise and fall, expand and shrink in dependence of your fear or your courage. In this lifetime, your fear has kept you in shackles. Your fear of God, Jilleen husband's wrath, your fear of losing your family and the wealth and comforts you enjoy. In another lifetime, similar fears will split you and Jilleen asunder. That is all I can say for now."

"Can you help me explain to Jilleen I never meant to hurt her? Yesterday, I wanted to tell her I had made a bargain with God and promised him I'd stop sinning with her, so that God could spare Finnian's life, and he did. I cannot continue a life of sin. I need her to understand that and to forgive me. I cannot live without her forgiveness."

"Sin is unavoidable. By leaving Jilleen, you have sinned against your soul and hers. You are sinning against your heart that desires union with hers. From now on, you may think you are no longer sinning, but you will be living a shrunken and shrivelled life. And that in itself is a sin."

"Did you see Jilleen? Do you know how she is?"

"They would not let me see her. She almost bled to death and her husband only lets servants wash her and feed her. He keeps her cradled in his arms, I was told. She always sought refuge in her husband's arms, even though it is you she loves."

Ailionora's words make me feel numb with pain and I descend into silence trying to compose my thoughts, but they are a tangled mess. I want to learn more about Jilleen, but instead I hear myself ask, "Why are you alone, Ailionora? Have you loved anyone, or have you always been a solitary healer, and a high priestess who has had to hide her role and beliefs from others?"

"I shall tell you my story one day, but not tonight. Go home, Kieran. May the Goddess be with you!"

"There is no Goddess, only God." She just smiles at me.

The next few months I ride out daily to the White Circle hoping to see Jilleen among the huge stones. This is her favourite place to stand and gaze at the sun or the moon, or to collect herbs that abound in the area. The mystical energy emanating from the stones seems to make the soil especially fecund. In that circle she and I had undergone a ritual performed by Ailionora, a ritual, whereupon under the spell of love, I forgot my own God and joined Jilleen in summoning spirits and asking them to let us find each other always. But she does not come.

Even without seeing her, I feel her pain while I am riding aimlessly. Her pain becomes my own. After all, she is the heart of my heart and the soul of my own. Grief and anguish over losing her are too much to bear and I begin to frequent the Whitehorse Inn, intoxicating myself to oblivion with ale and mead. My wife protests vehemently at seeing me in such a state. She now shudders even more than before when I touch her and pull her toward me in the middle of the night. I find no pleasure in her flesh.

One day, in a semi-drunken state, I fornicate with Jane, a woman whose gaze I had felt so many times on me before. Everyone knows Jane's history and how as a young servant girl she had been maltreated by her master, Bearach Drumgoole, a man who had not only abused her flesh, but also set his falcons on her to disfigure her face for his demented entertainment. There have been rumours that Jilleen healed her hideous scars and that Jilleen's father Bartley O'Farrell used his influence as a man of God to have her released from such cruel clutches.

Jane later married another man, but according to evil tongues found no happiness with him. When Jilleen was accused of witchery and thrown into the river to drown, some said Jane had been the accuser, but that was never proven. After I had lain with Jane for the first time, she mentioned to me in passing that she had always thought Jilleen was a witch. I was taken aback by the malice in her voice. It made her face look ugly and I shuddered in revulsion.

The first time I learned of Jane's interest in me was at Lord Tyrone's masked ball when she approached me asking me to accompany her outside, as she was feeling unwell. I wondered why she had not sought her own husband. When she told me she was in love with me I was flattered, and surprised at the same time. I behaved as a gentleman, telling her I would not insult her husband by making advances at his wife. Her eyes were filled with fury upon hearing that, but she just smiled and left.

Three weeks after my visit to Ailionora, at our annual fair, Jane follows me when I go into the bushes to relieve myself. I am drunk again, and it feels good to be wanted. Steeping heartache in rutting numbs the pain in my soul, but only for a short while. The pleasure is shallow, though. No touch feels like that of my Jilleen. My soul longs for her only, and pleasures of the flesh cannot appease the soul's longings and thirst for their only true counterpart.

I continue meeting Jane out of despair and despondence. I use her more and more to diminish my anguish. Escaping into memories of my secret encounters with Jilleen and resuscitating their sweet flavour only enhance the pain. Inconsolable longing dwells and stirs in the dark recesses of my memory. I am trying to find some meaning in my life, something I can rejoice in, but my existence feels like a sinful waste of God-given days.

One night I visit Ailionora again. She is the only person to whom I dare reveal my tumultuous feelings.

"Kieran, as much as it is a sin to do others harm, so it is sinful to harm oneself. By drinking yourself unconscious, and walking around dishevelled in torn clothes, you are bringing shame to your family. Drink this! It should sober you up enough to talk."

"Who in the hell are you, Ailionora?" I slur. "You must be a witch. Use your magic and help me see Jilleen again. My...my soul has been sick, and I know not how to heal it. I feel cursed. Love is a curse...have you ever known love and what it does to you? How it turns you into a stranger to yourself?" My words are knots and tangles of disjointed sounds, and I am not sure she understands what I say. The room is spinning increasing my nausea.

"Go outside and vomit. What I gave you will purge you. It will also make ale taste bitter for a few days and I hope it helps you abandon this path toward self-destruction. Life is a gift and it is a sin to waste it."

I go outside and retch violently, but after a few minutes, my head clears up. Exhausted, I go back, sit on the floor with my head in my hands, and whisper, "Help me, Ailionora, what do I do? How can I see Jilleen and end the pain of betraying her by leaving her so abruptly? I want her to know why I did it. I had to choose between her and Finnian's life. Why do we have to sacrifice one love for another?"

"I saw Jilleen yesterday and in a moment of lucidity, which comes and goes, she told me she was planning to visit the White Circle in three weeks to say her Summer Solstice prayers. Even though gravely concerned about her, her husband allows her now to leave their home unaccompanied in hopes that by going back to her old ways of roaming she finds healing. He also allows her solitary visitations to her son's grave. So the cemetery is another place where you may see her before the Solstice.

And I have been permitted to see her regularly to try to heal her soul, but souls do not heal as fast as bodies do. I have to tell you she has changed, and she may not recognize you. Every night she still roams the chambers of her castle looking for her lost baby. But she is not always aware of what it is she has lost; she just knows it is something important, something that belongs to the heart, something that if not regained will render life unlivable. I just want to warn you. You may not find the same Jilleen ever again...in this lifetime. She has enrobed herself in madness, temporarily, I hope, to guard her heart from pain. Her madness sometimes burns in flames and she needs to be subdued. At other times, she sits stone-faced on her balcony, gazing into the distance. But, seeing her, at least you may find some closure to help you part ways with her."

Hearing her words makes me roar in pain, "Are you telling me she has lost her mind because she could not bear the loss of our son? How can I part ways with her after causing her so much anguish? If she can no longer recognize me, how can I explain to her I had to give her up to save my son's life? Will she go to her grave not knowing the truth and believing I betrayed her?"

My questions come in gushes. I am gasping for air and daggers of anguish pierce my heart.

"Face the truth you must face, Kieran! You will always find each other, and truth shall be known to both of you. Trust that. This segment of time is a grain of sand in the vastness of eternity. You will always find her. Some souls coil around each other forever. Yours are like that."

"How do you know? Have you loved like this? I have asked you that before. Have you ever felt crucified between death and madness?"

"I have and I still love like that. The rose of my love often feels like the thorns of hell I have to endure. Your face shows that you want to hear my story, but all in good time. Go in peace, Kieran, and forgive yourself. You can do no more than say goodbye to her."

"You know more than you are telling me."

"It shall all be revealed. I have no power to change the leaden course of fate. None of us have any choice but to surrender to what must be."

Soon after, I hear from Ailionora that Jilleen has started to visit her son's grave almost daily, and I ride to the graveyard in the morning and in the evening in hopes of seeing her.

The first time I come to the cemetery, I go from one grave to another trying to locate that of our son. My heart is aflutter as I tread carefully in order not to disturb the solemn slumber of those gone before me. Some graves are overgrown with weeds and ivy; others are clean and well kept. I pass the large tombstone under which my wife's ancestors lie. One day my own body will be lain to rest there.

At the very edge of the graveyard, I spot a white slab of stone covering a small grave. My heart tells me Conor lies there and when I approach it, I see his name engraved in black letters. Around the name, a relief of dragonflies, fairies and flowers adorn the simple stone. There is no sign of a cross, and I have heard people gossip that only a witch would have a heathen grave for her bastard son.

I stagger under the weight of sorrow. I burn with guilt and grief, and apprehension of seeing Jilleen and finding her changed. I wait for hours, but she does not come, and stricken with disappointment I ride back home. I lie to my wife about my whereabouts and despise myself for unshriven guilt and dishonesty. God will judge me harshly once my time comes to leave this mortal plane.

When I finally see Jilleen it is a bleak and rainy day. I was just about to leave the cemetery thinking no one would come in such grey, dismal weather when I spot her. She looks frail and desiccated, shadow-like. My knees go weak and blood starts pounding in my temples. My stomach is a tight knot as I slowly approach her. I can taste the silence around us.

She lowers herself on the grave and kisses it. She lays flowers on it, and then lays her head on the stone oblivious of the raindrops. Her black clad figure looks like an injured bird squirming against the white stone surface. I come near her, but she does not hear me. I call out softly to her and she turns around and rises to face me. Her hand travels along my cheek and she peers into my eyes with curiosity. I swallow hard, fighting back tears. My Jilleen knows not who I am. But then, her eyes light up and she says, "You are so familiar to me. You feel like a part of me I lost and will seek forever. Did you come here to help me find Conor? You know...he expects me to find him...he's waiting to be found. I made a promise I would search for him."

"We cannot find everything we lose...not even ourselves. And just as I am a part of you, you are a part of me. I tried to tell you why we cannot be together, why I had to relinquish the dream of us. I know not if you will understand what I need to tell you."

My voice is soft but filled with pain. I caress her hair. I wish I could protect her and save her, and spirit her away from this place, from pain and loss.

"Hush, I must not listen to you. I still know not if you wish me harm."

"I love you, Jilleen. That will never change. I never meant to hurt you. I wanted to be a source of happiness for you. I had no choice but to end our relationship. Ah, you do not even remember...you do not know who I am...what I meant to you."

A smile frolics on her pallid face. “You have to leave now. I need to try to find my son."

"He is my son, too."

A shadow of confusion passes over her face. She looks around and says to my surprise, "Why am I here and who are you?" My heart breaks into an infinite number of splinters. I embrace her tightly, planting kisses in her wet hair. She looks at me again and says, "I know now I have always known you. My body and soul know you. You are me, aren't you? When I look into my mirror, I sometimes see your face. You are a reflection of my own soul, aren't you? But I need to go back home now."

Before I could utter a sound, Jilleen disappears and I wonder if my encounter with her was not merely a dream.

Crestfallen, I return home. My sons' merry chatter cannot penetrate my gloom. I barely hear my wife's questions about a horse that has fallen ill. I find an excuse, and leave the house and go to the tavern. One ale turns into several and the next thing I know I am stumbling back home.

On the way back, I stop by Ailionora's house to tell her about my encounter with Jilleen and to seek further counsel.

Drunkenly, I tell her Jilleen did not recognize me but still felt a connection between us, a special bond. She repeats what she told me days earlier that Jilleen is recovering slowly. Her soul and spirit are broken and mending them will take much more time.

"I will find no peace until I can tell her why I had to leave her. My biggest fear is that one of us will die before I can ask for her forgiveness. I know she will understand once she hears the truth. But if her spirit does not rejoin her body...if her madness keeps her prisoner...I cannot even bear the thought. You see her often. Please tell her about my bargain with God..."

"I will tell her, Kieran. As soon as the light of her spirit returns. I still hope she hears the truth from you."

"I will go to the cemetery every day in hope she recognizes me and can talk to me."

"In four days Jilleen will go to the White Circle to say her Summer Solstice prayers. In a moment of complete lucidity, she again asked me when Summer Solstice was and said that she had to pray on that day. That will be another opportunity to see her alone and unburden your heart, if you do not see her at the cemetery before the Solstice."

In spite of going to the cemetery and the White Circle the next few days, I do not see Jilleen again. The abyss of my desolation is depthless. I have become obsessed with fear and premonition that one of us will die before I can explain to her why I had to leave her. I consider writing her a letter, but am too afraid her husband might discover it. Also, her fragile state might not allow her to comprehend the letter's contents.

My despair turns into fury that consumes me like a most insidious disease. I try to hide my anger, but it seethes unchecked. I get into fights at the tavern, I yell at my family and at the peasants tilling our fields. I curse as I have never cursed before, hurling insults at people and God, knowing my soul is condemned to eternal damnation without a hope of redemption.

I still meet with Jane in secrecy and find it harder and harder to reach culmination of my pleasure. I keep pounding her flesh and ignore her wincing and squirming under my weight. Unlike my wife, she does not complain, even though I take too long and hurt and exhaust her in the process. With Jilleen, lovemaking was sacred and holy, poetic and divine. And I have no words to describe the pleasure given to our flesh. Eternal damnation is a price too small to pay for the idyllic moments lived with Jilleen. I wish I could believe Ailionora's prophesy that Jilleen and I will continue meeting after death. For a love this deep, death cannot be the final gate.

Two nights before Summer Solstice I am so drunk that I have no recollection how I came back home. When I come to my senses, I see Jilleen's father beside my bed. As our local priest, he is revered and loved by most people. Pure gentleness radiates from his eyes.

"My son, your wife summoned me. She says you act as if you were possessed by a demon. Your family knows not who you are anymore. Your own sons stay out of your way. I am here to listen and to help with advice, absolution, compassion—whatever it is you might need to unburden your soul."

"Father, my sins are too dark and grave to confess or for you to absolve. I am possessed by unholy desires...I do not understand the nature of life...I, I...you will think this is blasphemy, but I do not understand anymore God's messages and his expectations of us mere mortals. I have failed him, my family and myself."

"God loves you, my son, and his forgiveness is infinite."

"Can you tell me how your daughter Jilleen is doing? Have you been able to help her heal?"

His look is one of utter gentleness instead of surprise that our conversation took such a sharp turn. I wonder if Jilleen confided her feelings for me to her father.

"I saw my daughter yesterday. She wept on my breast and her tears showed me her tortured soul was on the mend. God gave us tears so that we may weep out the pain lodged in our souls."

"She knew who you are?" I ask in a voice overflowing with hope.

"She recognized me and called me 'sweet father.' She has always called me that. Why do you ask about Jilleen?"

"People have been talking about her escaping into madness after she lost her baby. I know you care much for your daughter. I feared I would lose Finnian, but God took mercy and gave my son back to me."

"God answers prayers and heals pain. But what is it, my son that made you turn from a docile man into a violent one?"

"Something heavy weighs on my chest. There are words that need to be spoken, a truth to be revealed and my fear of dying before saying what must be said fills me with fury."

"I am here to receive those words and unburden you."

"Those words are not meant for you, father, but for someone dear to my soul. Once she hears them and forgives me, I shall be at peace again. The pain of loss will still plague me, but it might become bearable. I see questions in your eyes, but I can say no more. Please leave me now. I am aware of the damage I have done. I will pay in gold for the chairs and tables I destroyed in the tavern, and will ask forgiveness from my family for turning them into the objects of my wrath."

As he gets up to leave, I notice a black leather-bound book he picks up from the armchair in which he was sitting.

"What book is it you are reading?"

"This is a book in which I write. I am chronicling the events that have befallen this region as far as I can recall, and as far as the oldest people in our village can remember. I also write about the more prominent of our co-dwellers. I have mentioned you and your family, too. I have divided the book into chapters about people and chapters about events. The years may not be accurate, but they are close enough. One chapter I devoted to the mystery of the White Circle."

"You must have mentioned your daughter in the book."

"I would have mentioned her even if she were not married to the chieftain. After all, she is my greatest joy. I have even described her house and that strange painting of the boy she saw in her dreams. I have been so concerned about Jilleen's state of mind. Thank God she is getting better. As to the book, who knows, one day it might be of interest to those who come after us. We shall all vanish one day and walk through the gate of death, but in this book, if it does not perish in fire or some other calamity, we will live forever on this plane of existence."

"Where do you keep it?"

"There is a recess in the floor under the desk in my study. I widened it and lined it with oilskins. I keep the book in a box at all times. Moisture cannot penetrate it unless the whole church gets flooded. I have left instructions in it for Jilleen, or whoever finds it asking that they continue writing in it. Even though we will all join our Father in Heaven one day, I do not want all traces of us to vanish from this earthly plane. That is why this chronicle is of great importance to me. It will preserve memories of our brief flickering against the eternity."

He gets up and leaves, blessing me with a sign of the cross. I order a servant to heat water for my bath and I wash myself. While lying in the hot water I suddenly realize what is wrong with me. I miss the ME I was while Jilleen loved me. I was not the same man as I am today. I was bristling with youthfulness, with passion and excitement. Her eyes mirrored back a man of strength, beauty, and valour, a man who was chosen by the most desirable woman in the world. That same man feels shrivelled and withered now, embittered and numb from the pain of loss. Without her, I can only sink into nothingness.

I find my wife and sons later and ask for forgiveness. I say I have suffered from a fever and headaches. I abhor telling lies, but I have heaped so many on them already that one more will not be noticed. They will never know it is not a fever in my body, but a feverish longing that leaves holes burning in my soul. I realize how I replaced the grief that was sapping my soul with fury and rage against the world. Neither can bring Jilleen back.

In the evening, I go to the tavern to pay for the damages to the furniture I caused by punching men in their faces and felling them on the tables, but words of apology stay frozen on my lips; instead I place a bag of coins on the counter.

"Damn your blood, Kieran! Why the feck did ye have to trash my place?" Alroy yells at me, raising his fist. I move away from him and mutter an apology. His curses follow me on the way out.

On the way back home, I stop at Ailionora's house. I never leave her house without bags of herbs. I tell everyone I buy tinctures from her to help me with headaches so that evil tongues do not start rumours about a solitary woman. What she tells me stirs me with renewed hope. Jillieen will go to the White Circle tomorrow to say her prayers to the sun and the Goddess. Ailionora saw her today and although still sorrowful, Jilleen no longer showed signs of madness. She told Ailionora that to celebrate Jilleen's return to the world of living Aidan gave her many gifts of jewels and fine dresses and entreated her to wear that finery. To please her husband, Jilleen had put on a lavender coloured dress and dragonfly shaped earrings.

When she descended the stairs, Ailionora noticed how all the servants gasped at her ethereal beauty. Her long brown hair cascaded down her back in soft curls. Her green eyes had sparkles of life in them again, making the sadness recede. Seeing his wife look like an apparition of beauty, Aidan lost his voice for a moment. Jilleen smiled and embraced him tightly. When Ailionora left their house, she could hear laughter and merriment. The entire household was celebrating the revival of Jilleen.

Jealousy burns in my throat as the image of Jilleen and Aidan rises in my mind. Again, I wish I could steal her from her family and take her away somewhere we will never be found. My own powerlessness reignites the rage in my heart and fills it with murderous desires. What have I become?

I thank her and leave.

The next day, I ride out toward the White Circle. In the back of my head, a nagging thought is reminding me I am to meet Jane there, but I disregard it. I was too drunk last time when we copulated to remember what either of us said about meeting again. I also decide firmly never to lie with Jane again. I sink in my own eyes thinking about my secret liaison with her. Her body satisfies my rut, but leaves my soul bleeding with emptiness and longing for that special caress.

Riding toward the Circle, I feel my heart beat with the wildness of a captured bird, thrashing and flailing in hope of freedom. My eyes are searching for any sign of my love. The midday sun is blanching the stone circle in white and gold hues, shrouding it in the Solstice magic.

And then I see her. She is entering the White Circle through the eastern gate. To see her roaming alone again must be a good omen. My Jilleen is well again, thank God for his mercy! Her hair is flowing in the light breeze. She is wearing a black dress and I find that strange. Jilleen would normally wear a white dress on Summer Solstice and her hair would be adorned with a wreath of flowers. But she is still mourning the loss of our son, and that is why even from a distance, she looks solemn. She stops from time to time to pick herbs, but as soon as she picks them, she drops them. She touches trees and then embraces their trunks. She then touches the stones as if absorbing their magic and energy.

Behind a large stone, a wolf appears, and Jilleen goes down on her knees cradling the beast's head. I have always known of her friendship with this she-wolf and have always feared for Jilleen's safety. She assured me there was no reason to fear. The wolf was her protector. The wolf licks Jilleen's face and hand, and trots away. I have difficulty keeping my horse in place, as it wants to run away, terrified by the wolf's presence.

She steps on the wide, cragged stone in the middle of the circle. That stone served as an altar during the ritual Ailionora performed on Jilleen and me. After the ritual, Jilleen and I made love on that stone, promising each other eternal love. One side of the stone shows the initials of our names I had chiseled with my knife close to the ground, so that they would not be easily noticeable. I will never lose Jilleen! She will always be ingrained in me, and nothing can erase the marks she left on my soul. There are few truths in life that fill me with so much certitude.

I am watching Jilleen as she raises her arms toward the sun. It looks as if she were embracing the whole universe. I come closer but she does not notice me in her rapture. Her lips are moving, and I recognize her prayer to the Goddess. She hides from everyone her belief in a female god and in a multitude of other deities. She has only shared her faith with me and Ailionora. I forgive her that heresy, and sometimes even wonder if she may be right, if there are magic and divinity all around us, but it takes special eyes to recognize them.

I come even closer, not daring to interrupt her prayer. The sun is shining so brightly it blinds me for a moment. Jilleen looks like a black angel perched on the stone, about to take flight. My horse neighs again, still alarmed by the wolf's vicinity. Jilleen stops her prayer, steps down from the stone and looks around. Seeing me, she seems taken aback and starts walking away quickly. I call after her, but she does not stop. She is now running toward Glenda's Bluff. My heart freezes in horror, recalling the legend of Glenda jumping to her death from the bluff after learning her lover was killed in a war. Could the agony of losing her baby make Jilleen do the same?

Fear cripples me for a moment, and then I run after her. I will not allow another opportunity to be wasted. I will talk to her and make her understand why I had to give up on us. I want her to understand my love has not diminished and will never wither even if we can never be together.

She is standing on the edge of the bluff gazing at the sun again. Below her, the ocean waves are crashing against the jagged rocks. She seems to have forgotten my presence. She is standing so close to the edge I expect her to fall into the abyss and be smashed against the sharp formations. Stones and earth can so easily crumble beneath her feet. I approach her gingerly, not wanting to frighten her. At the same time, I feel I am being watched. I turn around but there is neither a man nor a beast to behold.

"Jilleen," I whisper softly touching her hair. She turns around and in her eyes, I see both love and sorrow.

"After all that has happened, after all I have lost, we should no longer talk to each other. Healing can only be found in silence," she says softly.

"But I must talk to you, if for the last time. There is a truth I must reveal to you and seek your forgiveness. If I don't, I will never find peace again. So hear me out."

"But you slew the dragonflies I loved, we loved. You betrayed me, and left me feeling bereft."

At that moment, I notice soft flutters of wings, as dragonflies seem to fly out of her hair. In summer, they would always land on her arms or hands, hair or even face and I would watch them, transfixed. Once, when one alighted on my face I asked Jilleen what the meaning of such a visitation was. She explained they carried magic on their wings and messages from other realms invisible to most people. When I asked what the message was, she said it was love. Our love was not ordinary love, but one planned and fated from times long before this one. Our destinies were twinned.

"I did not betray you, Jilleen. I did not mean to slay our dragonflies or shatter our love. I did not want to leave you, and my heart bleeds for the loss of our child. I wish we could have married and had Conor and other children."

"I had a dream and was told you and I would meet Conor again...I will give birth to him in another lifetime. I trust the messages and visions from beyond and feel at peace again. I have forgiven you, Kieran, but I will no longer go back to my wicked ways of being your lover and betraying Aidan's trust."

"But I still need to explain to you what happened and why I had to give you up. You must listen. I cannot carry the unspoken words any longer. They are poisoning me and ..." My voice cracks with impatience. I need her full attention, but the look in her eyes strays from me toward the White Circle. She is squinting in her attempt to make out something behind my back.

She looks at me again and in a tender, whispering voice says, "I'm listening, Kieran. I'm strong enough again to hear the truth, whatever it may be. I trust you would never want to hurt me, or wish me any harm."

She raises her hand and touches my face scrutinizing my features and then trembles and says, "I will always carry a remembrance of you, for you are imprinted on my soul. Tell me now."

"A few months ago Finnian fell gravely ill, so ill my wife and I thought we would lose him. You know how much I love my sons...more than life itself. Finnian is my firstborn and when he was born, the midwife said he was not breathing and that he died.

And he did look lifeless...blue, shrivelled, and tiny. Just when we thought God called Finnian's soul to himself, he let out a cry and our anguish was replaced with joy.

When he fell ill after injuring himself by climbing out of the well behind the tavern, and when his knee swelled up and a fever ravaged him, I turned to God."

Jilleen is looking at me with eyes wide with anticipation. I smile and just as I am about to continue, the unexpected force of the blow I feel in my back makes me lose balance, and both Jilleen and I fly toward the abyss. Instinctively, I grab at a branch of a dwarf tree that was fighting for light and life by growing out of rock and meagre soil. The bough is resilient enough to hold my weight and I hold onto it tightly, trying desperately to find a crevice in the rock wide enough to support my right foot. I expect to fall to my death at any moment when suddenly I am able to plant my foot on a ledge, and grab the tree with the other hand. I look up and see a figure peek over the bluff. And to my horror I recognize Jane and realize she was the one who pushed me and Jilleen, trying to kill us both. Her laughter is that of a mad woman, and I hear her scream and shout obscenities. "Damn ye to hell, you whore...you witch. You escaped drowning but this time you will not escape death. No one falls off this cliff and comes back alive. Keep your lover now in death, you harlot."

Her screaming continues until her voice starts cracking from exhaustion. All that time I am hugging the tree and pressing my body into the rock so I can remain unseen. In her mad jealousy, Jane killed Jilleen and wanted to kill me, too.

Once I am sure she left, with knees shaking, I climb slowly back to the top. I had not fallen deep. The tree that stopped my fall is only a couple of yards away from the top. I do not even remember how I made it back over the edge. Breathing heavily, I lie on the ground not daring to look back, not daring to think about Jilleen's death.

It is clear to me now that it was Jane who had accused Jilleen of witchery, who had always hated her even though Jilleen was always kind to her and healed her horrendous scars. The murderous hatred I feel makes me stand up. I go back to the edge of the cliff and look down the abyss looking for Jilleen, but see no sign of her. Could she have survived the fall? Could anyone survive falling from this height? To go down I would need a rope and help of a couple of men. I call her name a few times, but the only answer is the sounds of the waves. Realizing I cannot do anything alone, I go home knowing I will find a way to take my revenge on Jane. Jilleen's murder will not go unpunished.

Bleeding from my arms and legs, I go back to the Circle. I call out to my horse, and it comes trotting toward me from a nearby grove. With huge difficulty, I mount the horse. Blood oozes from the cuts on my legs, but I do not feel any physical pain. I feel numb from shock and cannot even think of Jilleen lying dead at the rocky bottom. From a distance, I hear a wolf howling. I believe there is deep grief of loss echoed in her howls, but I cannot be sure.

I sneak into my house and change my torn clothes after washing the blood off my body. I throw the bloody clothes into a sack with a plan to bury it later. Exhaustion and shock make me go to bed. I shout to my wife that I am upstairs feeling unwell and do not want to be disturbed. She asks me if I am drunk and I assure her I had nothing to drink, but have the chills. She wants to bring me tea, but I say I just need rest.

My sleep is full of nightmares, and I wake up drenched in sweat. *Jilleen is dead. You have lost Jilleen.* The realization freezes my blood and I feel I will go insane. My wife comes into the room with a worried look on her face. I notice it is dark outside. I must have slept many hours.

"Why that look, my wife?"

"Jilleen has not come back home. There is a search for her. Folks are sayin' Aidan should not have let his crazy wife roam alone again."

I try to say something but my voice cracks. She continues, "It is too dark already. I heard them say they'll search around Glenda's Bluff. Someone said she may have killed herself. She pretended she was healed. Maybe she was always mad."

There is a hue of malice in my wife's tone. Her eyes bore into mine and at that moment, I realize she knew of my love for Jilleen. She must have known, but never said anything. I pity her for never having felt from me more than friendly affection. I also pity myself in silent lamentation.

After my wife leaves the room, I feel like weeping, but cannot. My throat is constricted as if a stone were lodged in it. I remember Jane's face distorted with evil and I suddenly know what my purpose is. I will kill her, and she will know why she has to die. I start hatching a plan and the same evening I know what I need to do.

The next few weeks I work in the fields like a madman. I hear that they found Jilleen's body and buried her. Those who had wanted her dead as a witch cried and wept at her funeral, calling her an angel. Like a thick fog grief descends on our village, suffocating us. It seems people are speaking less, moving more slowly as if in a dream, gazing at a distance with vacant eyes. I now know time has come to act on my plan, and I go visit Ailionora.

I knock on her door one rainy night. She opens the door as if she had been expecting me. She motions me to sit near the hearth and dry myself. Before I have a chance to say anything, she starts. "We will all grieve Jilleen for a long time. She was a special soul sent to this plane to touch the lives of many. Remember what I said last time. You will always find each other.

Your story is not finished. But I never expected her to take her own life by jumping off the bluff."

"She did not kill herself. Someone pushed her."

Ailionora gasps.

"How do you know? Did you witness it?"

"I was pushed, too, but I grabbed a branch on the way down and saved myself."

"Who was it that pushed you? Who would have wanted Jilleen's death?"

"Jane. She was the one who had accused Jilleen of witchery. I have no doubt about it anymore. She wanted her dead."

"Was she jealous... did you bed Jane? Is it because of you she wanted Jilleen to die?"

Ailionora's eyes are filled with fiery anger and disdain for me. "How could you do it when you loved Jilleen?"

"I was never sober when I was with Jane. I only hoped her body would appease my pain, but it could not. Her body was like a balm to me...something from the outside I hoped could soothe what was raw and bleeding on the inside."

I place my head in my hands and start swallowing hard to suppress tears.

"I am cursed, Ailionora. Jilleen was willing to hear my words. She would have forgiven me, and I would have been freed from the guilt of having had to leave her to save Finnian...but now, it is too late...and I cannot accept it that it is too late."

"It is only too late in this life. You will have a chance to tell her when you meet her again. You will know it is her because your soul will recognize her."

"But what if she is married again when I meet her? What if I am too old when we meet...there might always be obstacles...What if there's no God, or Goddess, or eternal life or any other life, but just this brief moment in time full of toil and torment?"

"If you were able to peer behind the veil as I have, you'd never have any doubts. I am looking at the candle flame, and an answer is rising before me. You will roam through eternity until the time your destiny with Jilleen can be fulfilled."

I notice Ailionora is gazing entranced at the candle flame. I ask her to tell me more, and while she is rocking slowly and revealing my destiny in whispers, I sneak into her back chamber - her apothecary - to look for poison I could use to kill Jane. The chamber is lit with soft candlelight illuminating countless jars and bags of dried herbs, tinctures and poultices. As a healer, she was given a piece of land and a house by the chieftain many years ago to receive patients from the whole region. Many folk swear they have been magically healed by her medicine.

A small table holds a book in which she keeps recipes for her concoctions and descriptions of treatments. I know I have little time, so I hold a candle close to the inscriptions on the jars...foxglove, chamomile, fairy thimble. Will I find what I'm looking for? And then I see it. A little black jar containing the extract of hemlock. I snatch it and stuff it in my pocket. I plan to come back and return what I do not use.

When I come out of the room, I find Ailionora rocking back and forth, still entranced. When she comes out her trance, she looks fatigued and pale.

"Go now, Kieran. We can do nothing more. Live the rest of your life the best way you can."

"I will come again. I still want to hear the story of your life and what love has done to you. You must have played at some point in your life on that playground created by the Devil himself. I want to see your scars."

She smiles and closes the door behind me.

Two days after I see Jane at the market. A red scarf hides half of her face making me think her husband has beaten her up again. There is no compassion in my heart, but murderous hatred that is seething and threatening to reveal itself in my voice.

"Good morning, Jane." My voice is soft and full of guile. "Will you meet me tonight in the White Circle? I have something important to tell you. And I've missed my cailín álainn." Calling her a pretty girl makes me realize how I never found her pretty, not because she was unattractive, but because something sickly and disturbing emanated from her.

She looks suspicious and somewhat skittish, unusual for her. When I smile seductively, her tension and mistrust leave her and she whispers, "Aye."

I nod and head home, but feeling a sudden premonition, I stop by the church. As if pulled by a divine force I go behind the building into the garden. Jilleen's father is sitting at the wooden table under the apple tree writing. When he spots me, he lays the quill on the table, and beckons me to come closer.

I take a seat and look at him. Grief has shrunken and aged him so much I almost let out a gasp. He reads the reaction in my eyes and says, "This may be the last entry I have made. The book ends with my daughter's death. In my heart, the will to continue living without my child has waned. Since the day my wife and I found her at the church door, we have loved her more than we could have loved our own child. God giveth and taketh away, and my hope is he taketh me now."

"I loved her, too, Father, and that love is a grave sin lying upon my chest. Life without her has lost its brightness, meaning and purpose. Yes, I have children and will do all I can to help them grow into decent, god-fearing men. Faith that she and I will meet again will keep my heart beating. I cannot expect your forgiveness, so I seek it not."

His eyes are misty with tears. He gets up and comes behind me. I feel his fragile, shaking hand on my shoulder as he says in a trembling voice, "You are forgiven, my son."

He does not ask me any questions and his countenance gives me the impression that he has known this secret already. Perhaps Jilleen had confided in her father. He picks up his black book and walks into the church. I remain standing motionless, not knowing what to do next. My gaze rests on the apple tree overshadowing the table where Jilleen's father had sat. The boughs are full of small green apples and I imagine them falling off in a few months and rotting on the ground if left uneaten. My soul has already started rotting.

When I meet Jane, it is a night of a full moon. I wait for her by the rock on which Jilleen and I sealed our promise to always find each other. For a love this deep death can never be the final gate. As soon as I remember the words Ailionora had said to me, I take out my knife and engrave them under our initials and whisper to the stone, 'Thou shalt now be the repository of our secret love.'

I put two candles and two chalices on the rock. In one, I pour hemlock mixed with wine and in the other just wine. And I turn into patience itself.

She is out of breath when she arrives. Her hair is down and partly covering her swollen cheek. She runs into my arms kissing me with delicious fervour, whispering that we can now stay together forever. I embrace her feeling utter revulsion. Her skin feels snake-like, and I shudder.

"My love, let us raise a toast to that. Let us drink this wine to celebrate this night. I want wine-flavoured kisses. I want the moon to be jealous of your beauty and our love." The words I speak sound strange to me, because they sound like something a poet with little verse writing skill might say, and I always scoffed at both, poetry and poets. Delight lights up her face.

I raise my cup to my lips and take a sip. My eyes never stray from hers.

“Sláinte!” I tell her to drink up, draining my own vessel. She does the same, but almost spits the wine out after she makes a choking sound. The wine could not mask the bitter taste of devil's flower and its repugnant odour. Fear that I did not use enough tincture from Ailionora's bottle grips my heart.

I take her hand and lower her to the ground on which I spread a blanket. I pour more wine for her, and she takes a reluctant sip. I tell her I want us to talk and make plans for our future encounters. We have to keep meeting in utter secrecy. I cannot leave my wife, but believe even if she suspects I might have a mistress, she will not protest much. She does not like my touch and will gladly be left in peace. As I am talking, I am observing Jane carefully. Her pupils are dilating and her face looks drained of colour. She is not listening to me, but I keep talking and stroking her hair at the same time.

She lies back on the blanket pulling her knees up to her chest. "What was in that drink, Kieran that is making me so sick?" Her question is barely articulated when she leans on one side and starts retching and vomiting. Her agony is of the kind that belongs to the torments of hell itself. She is sweating and salivating and convulsing in pain. I pick her up and carry her toward Glenda's Bluff. She is squirming and writhing in my arms, but I am a strong man, and carrying a small woman like that is not hard.

I am carrying her in silence fearing someone might ride by and catch me in the act of murder. She is moaning in pain and her body is getting stiffer and colder. Her legs stop moving as the poison spreads through her body. Soon it will stop her heart.

When I reach Glenda's Bluff, I stand still at its edge. The darkness of the abyss below swallows the moonlight and is ready to receive Jane's body. I lift her and then hurl her into the darkness to be ripped asunder by the rocks and carried away by the ocean currents. At that moment, a wolf howls close to me, and I know it is Jilleen's she-wolf. I hear solitude, yearning, and her name in the howl, and I shiver. I hope the wolf approves of the revenge I took, and she witnessed.

Quickly, I go back to the stone and remove all traces of Jane and me. Once back home, I fall asleep almost immediately wondering how I was able to commit a murder, and yet feel no compunction. I am a stranger to myself.

A few weeks after Jane's disappearance, two women claim they have seen Glenda's ghost walking around the White Circle beckoning them to follow her to the bluff. Fearful and yet curious, they walked behind the figure floating in a mist, but stopped short of the edge in fear of falling. The figure beckoned them a few more times before vanishing. The women say they were convinced that both Jilleen and Jane were lured to their death, and that Jane's body must be at bluff's rocky bottom.

A group of men gather and lower themselves on ropes down the treacherous slope, and find Jane's mangled body. There is no doubt in anyone's mind that Glenda's ghost is behind the tragic deaths of the two young women.

Even though I am relieved to know my crime will never be discovered, I feel haunted and changed forever. Joy has deserted me. Except for my children, who still put a smile on my face, my life has little meaning as days are strung together in a monotonous, drab-coloured necklace of time.

The lifelessness of my days is broken by two events. During the gathering for the Sunday mass, two men go into the Church garden to look for Jilleen's father, as it was uncharacteristic of him not to appear in church on time. I follow them soon after. We find the priest sitting at the table under the apple tree. It looks as if he had fallen asleep warmed by the morning sun. His head was resting on the black leather book in which he chronicled the events, and life stories surrounding our village.

When one of the men pries the book away from his fingers, I take it and on the last page I read, "*Our Chieftain, the beloved husband of my daughter Jilleen, moved to England to serve the King. The sense of betrayal is all-pervasive. His ancestors had died battling the English; our fields reek of the blood of our fallen soldiers; our village had never fully accepted the English version of faith because I, as its servant have not been imposing it rigidly, but allowing faith to be more open and fluid. Aidan, you had no right to desert us regardless of your need to leave the place where you lost your beloved wife. You have displayed cowardice. In times of pain and grief, we need to unite and comfort each other...* "

The words that followed were mere inkblots. His weary and grief filled heart must have given up on him at that moment. Semi-conscious of my own actions, I swath the book in the oilskin on the table and hide it underneath the altar. After that, along with the others, I go from house to house spreading the sorrowful news. God certainly has sent more woe our way that can fit in all of our hearts combined together.

We mourn his death and mix grief with rage over Aidan's abandonment. The ale we drink is bitter and honey can no longer make the wine taste sweet. I spend my days working my fingers to the bone even though it is not necessary as we have serfs to toil on our land. My yearning for Jilleen does not leave me in peace. The loss of her has displaced my soul in a permanent state of bewilderment. Aidan had ordered she be buried in Conor's tomb, and I go there from time to time and sit forlornly on the grave.

I do not even attempt to hide my grief. Passers-by cast strange looks at me upon seeing me mourn on the grave of another man's wife, but gossip about me turning mad leaves me unperturbed. My son and Jilleen, who was my wife wedded in the secret ritual performed by Ailionora in the White Circle, lie beneath my feet. I should be lying in their embrace of death, but I am still condemned to life.

I visit Ailionora telling her about my dreams about Jilleen, and asking her to summon Jilleen's spirit so that I can have closure and unburden my soul, but she says not all spirits can be summoned. Conversations with her keep my soul pulsating with bare traces of life. I remind her of her promise to tell me her own life story and one rainy night she finally obliges.

****

When I came out of my Jacacia dream, I felt disoriented. Keith was taking my blood pressure and once done, he examined my pupils.

"How much do you remember, Weylin?" he asked.

"Everything, I believe. Was I talking aloud?"

"Yes, you were, and I was able to follow your story as if watching a movie."

I looked at Leandra. She was stone-faced and paler than the whitest sheet. She wanted to say something, but choked on emotion and tears flowed down her face like abruptly thawed ice. She looked at me with a new knowing. She finally heard the words Jilleen never had a chance to hear, and she now knew what she had considered as my betrayal may have only been cowardice, fear of God's wrath, but never a lack of love for her. I even committed a heinous murder as revenge for her death.

My session lasted for over two hours and I felt both physically and emotionally exhausted. Keith suggested we take a long lunch break before Ariadne's session. I had no doubt in my mind that her story was somehow entangled with Leandra's and mine, and I was eager to find out in spite of feeling utter fatigue.

When I stood up, a feeling of nausea overwhelmed me and I staggered. Leandra noticed it and offered her hand. I grabbed it to regain balance, and in that instant I felt I was holding Jilleen's hand and leaning against her. Like electricity, the energy of recognition jolted through me, and Leandra's expression revealed she felt it, too.

She and I left the building wordlessly, while the others went into the direction of the cafeteria. We got into Leandra's car and she drove in silence. She parked in front of a little restaurant that had potted flowers in its windows. The tables were covered with lavender-coloured tablecloths and had vases filled with dry lavender. The name of the place was "Lavender Dreams" and Leandra said it was one of her favourite restaurants. The owner imported lavender from France and used it in the most delectable cake recipes. I asked Leandra to order for both of us whatever she liked, because I felt too weak to even read the menu. I gulped down a whole glass of iced water and motioned the waitress for a refill. I noticed a tremor in my hands as I was placing the glass back on the table.

Leandra ordered three different dishes saying I should try to eat as it would make me feel better. I refused wine, but she said she needed some badly to calm down.

"Weylin, I was shocked by the discoveries I made during David's hypnotherapy sessions. You listened to the recordings. And gradually, I got over the shock...the whole story and the drama of us more or less diffused under everyday life, big and small. Adrian and I repaired our marriage and life began to take its natural flow and normalize again...But this now...could you have invented that whole story having heard mine? But Annette couldn't have known anything about Lady Tyrone... I just don't know what to think. Confusion is splitting my head in two..."

"But if what I said under the influence of that drug is true, then you and I are fated to meet lifetime after lifetime until a destiny involving our son Conor is fulfilled! It does sound insane.

Psychiatrists do not have such crazy conversations among themselves. We are not supposed to even entertain ideas of such preposterous possibilities. I've never believed in reincarnation. I barely believed in psychiatric drugs and always preferred psychoanalysis."

I sighed deeply before continuing. "I would have never believed it had I not experienced it. And after experiencing it and witnessing Annette's regression, I'm not sure I can believe my own senses. I'm so glad Annette's here. She's even more sceptical of anything outside mainstream science than I am. I just don't know what to think."

Our meal arrived smelling divine. Poached eggs, smoked salmon, quiche, lavender cakes...All of a sudden, my appetite returned and I started wolfing down the food. Leandra cut a piece of quiche and offered it to me on her fork. Just as I put it in my mouth, she blushed and said, "Why do I always have this urge to feed you, even now? It's embarrassing and strange."

"Because as Jilleen you always enjoyed feeding me morsels of food or berries, remember? And I always tried to bite down on your fingers in sensuous play."

And then we burst into laughter realizing we were talking about 17th century memories. I looked at her, and in her eyes, I spotted glints of love, Jilleen's love for me, and my throat constricted not only with emotion, but also with the knowing that we have always belonged together. The suddenness of that realization made me cough. Leandra looked at me quizzically, but I dared not reveal my epiphany. Instead I said, "Well, all of a sudden I know what to think..."

Leandra stopped eating looking at me attentively. In the meantime, the waitress asked us if we enjoyed our meal and laid another dish on the table. The intoxicating smells wafting all around us prodded me to eat some more. The bread was hot and garlic butter melted on it instantly. Before I continued speaking, my glance fell on the napkin I took out of a napkin ring, and I saw a picture of a beautiful dragonfly. They seemed to be following me and leaving signs that I was on the right path. I ate and smiled, impressed by the ambrosial tastes. I also changed my mind about wine and ordered a glass of sparkling white.

"You were going to say something, Weylin."

"Yes, answers to this mindboggling mystery and this surreal experience we've both had cannot be found in suppositions, explanations, or some weird theory. None of that would satisfy me. The only way of making sense out of this experience is to do real research and uncover hard evidence. Without that, I would tend to ascribe it all to the processes happening in our brains, processes that must have basis in science. If we continue with the experimentation and gain more understanding of the brain, we might be able to find irrefutable scientific explanations, but for now, I want to look for other types of evidence."

"What do you mean? What evidence would you be looking for?"

"We have enough information to go on. We need to travel through Ireland, or even maybe Scotland and search for evidence. We need to find written records of the time in which locations, such as Glenda's Bluff, or White Circle are mentioned. There must be records of the monastery to which Lady Tyrone was banished. Jilleen's father's book may still be lying under the floor of an abandoned church. Your husband Aidan's name may have been mentioned in a book and so on."

"Yes, you said that Jilleen's father kept a book chronicling the events and we know he kept it in his study...but which Church? After my hypnotherapy sessions with David, I did try to search the White Circle, but there is no such name describing the stone circles in any part of the UK."

"Maybe the name was changed. Perhaps, Ariadne will now reveal more facts we can use in our search...more clues. Would you be able to take a couple of weeks off and go on this wild goose chase with me?"

Our excitement was slowly brewing. We gazed into each other's eyes feeling a primordial connection. I felt Kieran's blood coursing in my veins and in Leandra's eyes, I recognized Jilleen's reflection, and my heart fluttered with the longing for love I had not felt in too long a time.

"I now know why you had to hurt and desert me in our past life, but what about this incarnation? Can you even fathom the depth of my anguish over losing you? I do not think I was able to fully recover," said Leandra.

Her eyes welled up with tears and her lower lip quivered with pain.

"I could no longer lead a double life. The pressure became horrendous...unbearable. I was fearful my wife would somehow find out and divorce me, and my children would not want to talk to me. But now that they are older and that I am fully aware nothing can save my marriage...it is so completely dead, thoughts of wanting out have become more and more frequent. I no longer dread divorce. We simply cannot resuscitate dead feelings...we can only perform an autopsy on them to try to understand what happened. And what happened through the lifetimes is us, we happened to each other. That we are here cannot be a coincidence."

"Weylin, the idea of travelling through Scotland and Ireland with you makes my head spin with thrill, anticipation, but I can't justify it to my family. What would I say to Adrian? I can't just say, 'Hey, I think I'd like to search for evidence of having lived in 17th century Ireland or Scotland, so I'll just drive around with my ex-lover in search of proof.' How would that sound? What would you tell your wife?"

I was silent for a few moments. I took a sip of coffee and looked at her.

"Jilleen...Leandra, I am going to divorce my wife. And I feel it in my heart and bones she will be relieved to be offered a chance to find true happiness with someone else. I am sure this kind of knowing is the result of Jacacia. Something in my brain or mind just opened, and clarity seeped in."

"I will never leave Adrian for anyone."

"I am not asking you to ruin your life for me. I'm now ready to start a new chapter in mine whatever it may bring. I no longer want to live a life without passion...I no longer want to find substitutes for the love missing in my life. And I want to become a better psychiatrist, a better dad, a better man. And maybe even a friend to my wife. And I fervently want this travel adventure through my home country or further. And if I find no evidence of us in the past, so be it. I cannot imagine experiencing what I have just experienced, and letting it turn into a distant and forgotten memory of a strange event. Some force brought me here, and it wants me to search and find the complete truth. There has to be more to this."

"I'd also like to delve deeper into this and to uncover real evidence, but even if I could join you in your search for evidence, I'm not sure I could stand it...What I'm trying to say is that memories of you are still painful...especially memories from this lifetime. It is time to go back. Let's hear Ariadne's story. This is too weird not to get even weirder. I wonder how we knew her."

"No need to wonder. Everything's telling me we knew her closely. I know who she is, but will let you discover that for yourself."

12

Ariadne

Dizziness and mild nausea washed over me as I entered the room. Everyone was already seated and I introduced myself.

Keith offered me a cup of tea and remarked that I looked pale and unwell. He also added, as if it was an everyday thing that he could read people's energies, and that my energy clearly revealed I was feeling ill. Then he added, without even waiting for me to confirm that, indeed I was feeling slightly sick, "Ariadne is next, but we will wait until she feels better. I will take this time to comment on what has transpired so far and what I read from everyone's energy here."

Everyone was quiet. I was certain we all shared a sense of disbelief, a sense of being trapped in a dream. I was eager to hear what Keith had to say. At the same time I was questioning my own sanity of having travelled so far to take part in a most bizarre experiment with complete strangers.

"I can see incredulity in your eyes, and you are probably tempted to pinch yourselves to see if this is real. Rest assured it is. I can also tell you that it is not coincidental you all ended up here...even though I cannot explain why circumstances aligned themselves in a way for us to meet and make this happen."

Keith then looked straight at me and said, "Ariadne, you, Weylin, Annette, and Leandra are connected by past-life energies, and I can easily read them now. Ariadne, you are seeking important answers, and aren't even aware of all the questions you have. I hope you find them here."

"The only way I can fully believe in the experience I've just had is to do some serious research by trying to uncover physical evidence of my past life," said Weylin. "And that is what I am planning to do. I also hope Leandra joins me. Under hypnosis guided by her colleague David, she had discovered she was Jilleen, the Jilleen I loved so much."

Weylin looked at Leandra and her cheeks flushed with embarrassment. The bond between them was palpable and visible to everyone. I was feeling impatient about finding out in what ways I was connected to them. More than that, I was curious to learn about my own fate in my earlier lives and if those experiences had spilled over into this life.

"I'm feeling better now, Keith, and am ready. The tea you offered seems to have helped, I said."

"Are you sure? I noticed tremor in your hand as you were raising the cup," Keith replied.

"That sometimes happens when I'm exhausted or jet lagged. But I'm eager to do it and would not wish to postpone it."

"First, we'll take your blood pressure to make sure it is alright. Your energy does reveal that you are well enough now to undergo the experiment."

Fifteen minutes later I drank the tepid liquid Keith handed me and my head started to swim. Random thoughts swirled in my brain, colours meshed, blended, and separated in vibrant bursts before my eyes. I felt sucked into a vortex and hurled into empty space. A voice sounding like an echo asked me where I wanted Jacacia to take me and someone, who seemed to be a part of me responded on my behalf that I wanted to go where the answers to my questions from my current life were to be found.

At the same time, a deep knowing within me revealed the destination where I needed to go in search for answers. It would be the same place and time Weylin and Leandra lived. And it felt so natural to go to that same place out of all the possible places and past-life times. In the world of Jacacia, the impossible and the mysterious seemed to be just ordinary occurrences.

As if by magic, the spinning in my head caused by the sudden travel through time and the blinding vibrancy of colours cleared, and I found myself sitting on the floor of a small house. I was sorting herbs and putting them into small bags. Sunrays were dripping into my room through two small windows, painting the floor a warm hue of gold.

When the door opened after a knock, I knew it was Kieran. With my spiritual eye I had seen him walking toward my house. He was a changed man after losing Jilleen. His eyes were dimmed and hollowed, his face hardened even more than his heart. I had no herbs for such a state of grief. He found no solace in my words that his and Jilleen's souls would coil around each other for eternity. There was a destiny to be fulfilled in another incarnation. He warned me against speaking such heresies, for I may be accused of witchery. There are no other lifetimes, but heaven or hell, he said, and he was certain hell would be his eternal home, for his sins were too grave for any God to forgive.

When he entered, the rancid smell of ale permeated the room and overpowered the scent of lavender.

"I've come to hear the story you promised to tell me. Who the devil are you, Ailionora? Are you a witch, are you even of this world? Who loved you and whom did you love?"

"Sit down, Kieran. I am ready to tell you the story of my life. You have been curious about it for so long."

He lowered himself on the floor and said, "Your role in my and Jilleen's life has been so important and yet you never revealed much about yourself, and how you came to live among us, and become part of us. You witnessed our love and wedded us in a secret ritual in the White Circle. I want to know if you have ever loved as much as Jilleen and I did, if you have ever been suspended between madness and death after losing someone you love. That is how I feel now...I am living and yet not living. I feel as if my soul has left my body, leaving me hollowed out."

"I have loved and I have lost, but I am still waiting for his return. He is coming back. His message in my dream was clear."

"Who are you, Ailionora, and who turned you into a High Priestess, a Druidess? That is what you called yourself before Jilleen and me, knowing we would not reveal your heresy and your belief in a Goddess. Perhaps your shared belief connected Jilleen and you. My faith has never strayed from the one and only God, our Father in heaven, even though I sometimes rage against him for having allowed Jilleen to die. But now…tell me the story of you."

"I was born in a hamlet at the foot of a mountain. I still carry memories of the brooks I splashed in, and glens I used to play in during the summer, and rocks I climbed. The smells, the sights, the textures, the animals, insects, people's voices...it is all still alive within me.

My life was carefree. I was an inquisitive child fascinated by nature and thirsty for knowledge. My grandmother and mother were healers, and they taught me not only about the medicinal powers of herbs, but also about the magic residing everywhere. They said one day I'd be able to peer through the veil and see the world invisible to most people. Once I turned fourteen, my mother would teach me the secrets of druidesses, and initiate me into following the ways of the Goddess who had many names."

"What or who is that Goddess?"

"She is the feminine energy that imbues all there is. She is the magic that only some can feel, taste, and drink. Once you enter her energy, she guides you through life and helps you find your purpose. She is the mother of all of us, including the fairy folk."

"Who was your father?"

"He was chieftain of our village and the neighbouring five. He had blue eyes and long red hair. He and my mother were always exchanging secret glances, and even as a child I could see the deep bond of love between them. As a couple, they looked striking. My mother had thick and long black hair and large dark eyes, and people were wondering how my grandparents, whose hair was reddish, and who were rather short, could have such a black-haired, tall and willowy beauty of a daughter."

"How did your mother become a high priestess?"

"She was initiated by my grandmother Etain. Once she turned fourteen, my grandmother revealed the secret codex to her. That codex, passed in a yellow leather-bound book from the times unknown to me, contained the rites and the rituals of those selected to walk the path of the Goddess. My grandmother had five daughters, but only my mother had the sign of the Goddess inscribed on her body...under her breast. The secret can be passed from mother to daughter, grandmother to granddaughter, aunt to niece, or any other girl in the family, or even outside the family circle, if there is a child in the village bearing the mark of the Goddess."

"What does the mark look like? Jilleen had a blue mark under her left breast that I used to kiss without trying to look at it more closely. It looked like a fairy or something with wings."

Unabashedly, I lifted my dress and showed Kieran the mark under my right breast. He got up, walked across the room to the table on which a candle was burning, lifted it and brought it back. He kneeled and shone the light over the mark. His eyes widened as he said he had recognized the same sign Jilleen bore under her breast."

"It looks like a dragonfly. It is….it is a dragonfly. That is why she loved them so much, and that is why they were always landing on her. Does it mean she was also a high priestess?"

"I wanted to offer to her the initiation into the secret code, after I saw the mark on her while her servants were bathing her. I do not even know if she was too old to be initiated, but I was willing to try. Unfortunately, she left this world too soon."

"How did your mother initiate you? I understand it is a secret codex, but I am curious to learn about everything you are allowed to tell me." Kieran's gaze bore into me with burning curiosity.

"My mother could not initiate me. One night, the English army attacked the village, pillaged it, burned it, raped the women, and beheaded my father. My mother had been restless days before the attack, warning everyone about the need to leave, and hide, but no one took heed. My mother, who as a high priestess had special powers and could fend off evil, was pregnant at the time. These powers become dormant while a druidess is carrying a child. Otherwise, if she had unleashed them, the baby would have died from such a violent force. Both my mother and grandmother could also shapeshift into animals, but in pregnancy, that power could also not be summoned.

That night we would have all perished had my grandmother not awakened me before the attack. In great haste, she packed a few things and took me into the night, never to return. She told me later she only had time to reach our house once my mother's premonition and fear reached her. My father was asleep when she entered the house, and my mother would not leave my father. I remember my mother hugging me with tears in her eyes and asking me to run with my grandmother and never look back. And so we left the village.

Running through the woods, I remember stopping suddenly and starting to scream as pictures of my mother's bloody body appeared before my eyes. That was the first time I became aware of my second sight. My grandmother grabbed me and covered my mouth with her hand. I fought and bit her hand trying to escape, but she was still a strong woman. When I finally collapsed on the ground, I muttered through tears what I had seen. My grandmother rocked me gently, whispering that soon she would initiate me into the secret code, and I would be the next high priestess. She said we must go on in spite of the horrors that had befallen us; it was our duty never to give up, and to be the repositories of our ancestral memories. We must never allow the English to erase our heritage and those memories. Our ancestors lived in us and were there around us to offer us their wisdom. I sobbed as we continued walking, and I continued mumbling about my lost family, my shattered childhood innocence and happiness. I did not understand why my grandmother would be mentioning our ancestors at the time of our indescribable family loss that made me wish for my own death.

The memory of my mother's blood-covered body would make me stop and I would start convulsing. During the convulsions, my palms felt so fiery hot that when I grabbed onto a branch to keep my balance, it burned in my hands and disintegrated into ashes. My fright and confusion reached a fearsome height, threatening me with suffocation. My grandma slapped me a few times to make me come to my senses. The terror and trauma were awakening my powers before I was ready to accept them.

We lived in the wild for what seemed to be an eternity, living off mushrooms and other edible plants. From time to time, my grandma would shapeshift into a hawk and go hunting for rabbits and other small animals she would later roast over an open fire. Waiting for her to come back would be a constant source of terror, as my greatest fear was that I would lose her, too. Many a night I would wake up screaming because blood appeared in my dreams. And every time, the ground around me bore signs of singeing. The heat of my body produced that effect.

It was Aidan who found us one day as he was hunting. I wanted to run and hide but my grandma said she sensed he was good man. He and his party were carrying a dead boar dripping with blood. I was horrified and wanted to scream, but my grandma held my hand firmly and pulled me along to face the men. My fists were burning holes in my threadbare clothes, but I was able to exert control over my feelings and thoughts, and stopped thinking about blood. At the age of nine, I understood that I was not an ordinary girl, and that I had to learn to master the power within me, inherited through the long lineage of druidesses.

Aidan brought us to his home and asked his servants to let us bathe and give us clothes and food. Even though a boy of some sixteen years himself, Aidan already had the air of a leader. Fate would have it that when we arrived, Aidan's mother was lying in bed gravely ill. Grandmother overheard the servants whisper about the mistress' illness that had kept her bed-ridden for over two weeks. Aidan's father, who was a powerful chieftain, was pacing the manor up and down distraught, irritable, and frightened at the same time that death had entered his home and lay in wait.

Once washed, fed, and clothed, my grandmother told a servant that she was a healer and if the master allowed it, she would like to see the mistress. The servant looked at her suspiciously and left the kitchen without saying a word. Soon after, a male servant appeared and beckoned my grandmother. Her red medicine bag had never left her side and she took it with her. I do not know what happened, or why the mistress was dying, but several days after, she appeared in the kitchen, and called my grandmother. She thanked her for saving her life and said that she and her husband were appointing her as the village healer and were giving us a small house on their land. And so this house became our home.

"When did your grandmother reveal to you the secrets of the codex? Did you have to undergo a ritual?"

"It was not just one ritual. It was a long process of teaching me about herbs and their healing properties. Once she thought I had gained enough knowledge she began initiating me into the ways of the Goddess. She read to me passages from the book of secrets, but told me the most important signs and messages could only be found in nature. So she instructed me to listen to the wind, to lie in the sun and let my skin absorb secret messages, to stand naked under waterfalls and learn from water, and to gaze into fire until my initiation was complete. I had to learn the language of the four elements."

"What did you learn?"

"Nothing, for a long time. I learned to be quiet. I learned to lie or sit in complete stillness. Months passed and I was still waiting for the secret knowledge to seep into me. I developed patience and a knowing that once time was ripe, that knowledge would come to me, or rather rise from within me. And it did. One day, the whispers of the wind turned into the ancient words of wisdom and in the air around me, I could feel the presence of the spirits of our ancestors. The sunrays warmed me with old truths, and the fire and water left their imprint in my soul. All of a sudden, I was able to understand the ancient conversation between the sea and the shore, the wind and the trees, the water and the landscape. I was destined to be a healer, a protector of nature, a mediator between people and spirits that lived behind the veil. The invisible became my second home.

My grandma imparted all her knowledge to me and guided me for many years until the day she fell ill and died. One of the last words she whispered on her deathbed was that she would always try to guide and protect me, and that as a druidess, she would shapeshift into a hawk until it was her time to reincarnate again. She also made me swear I would always honour my role as a druidess and keep the memory of our ancestors in sacred reverence. She said our ancestors were everywhere around us, incarnated as animals, stones, or plants. That is why everything in nature was holy."

"So your grandmother believed that we incarnate again. I wish you could convince me I will see Jilleen again. Tell me I will, and I will believe you."

"Our souls travel through eternity seeking their other halves. I have told you many times that your and Jilleen's destiny has been left unfulfilled in this life. Your story will continue. You live in each other. Her soul is mirrored in yours just as yours is mirrored in hers."

"Ah, how I long to touch her, smell her hair..."

Kieran's eyes were misty and his chin was trembling.

"You still have not told me whom your heart has loved."

"My heart has only loved one man. Our hearts and souls have been connected since the day we met and touched. That touch, along with the look in his eyes, were words written and spoken in the language of bliss and ecstasy."

"Tell me about him. I want to hear a happy love story."

"Ours has been a story of painful longing and separation. But he is coming back. At last, we will be reunited and my wait will be rewarded."

"Is it because of him you never married?"

"I have always felt married to him. Our souls belong together, just like yours and Jilleen's. You can be happily or unhappily married to many people, but your soul's destiny belongs to only one person. He is that person for me. Even though you and Jilleen were married to other people, I still officiated the secret wedding for you two in the White Circle because of the entanglement of your souls."

Kieran sighed deeply and pain clouded his gaze. He put his head between his hands, and I could see his chest heave. I offered him a cup of tea and asked him to drink it all at once. The brew contained an herb that soothed ailing hearts.

"My story begins in the year Jilleen married Aidan. I helped prepare the wedding feast. My grandmother was too old and frail for any kind of work, and I took over her role as a healer. Aidan's family was always kind to everyone working for them and never forgot how my grandma healed Aidan's mother. As a healer, I was especially revered, and no one dared call me a witch for fear of Aidan's parents' wrath. Jilleen and I were close friends and she wanted me to be her maid of honour. She and I talked for hours about her wedding gown. Once it was sewn, we took it to the White Circle on the night of a full moon. We laid it on the altar stone in the middle of the circle, the same stone on which you and Jilleen made love after I wedded you... I prayed to the moon until she spilled her rays over the dress, making it sparkle in the dark. The Goddess had blessed her dress and her wedding.

"It was at Jilleen's wedding I met Egerton. His back was turned to me when I noticed him. His curls were as yellow as yours, only longer. A voice from deep within my heart whispered, 'It is he.' I expected him to turn around, and recognize me, so I waited for that to happen with a most delicious anticipation. And he did.

"He turned around, and his blue eyes squinted as if the light had been too bright. Never taking his gaze off me, he approached me. We just stood there. Our silence needed no words. Our hearts fluttered in recognition of each other.

'Where have I seen you before, sweet damsel?' he asked.

'In your dreams, perhaps.'

'I must see you tonight!'

"I told him I was busy with wedding preparations, but could see him after the wedding.

"Throughout the week he was staying at the manor as Aidan's friend from England, we exchanged furtive glances. One day he came after me into the cellar, pulled me behind a barrel and kissed me. His kisses inebriated me and filled my blood with a fire

I had not known before. Before I disentangled myself from his embrace, he whispered to me, 'You will always be mine.'

"I knew that already. I was ready to marry him and follow him anywhere.

"Egerton was not only handsome and brave, but also full of wit and merriment sparkling from within his eyes and soul. The girls giggled in his company, pretended to have some business in the chambers he was in, offered sweets and ale to him, but he smiled at them good-naturedly and paid them tasteful compliments that made them blush. I felt no jealousy, for he and I had forged a bond of secret and eternal belonging.

"After the wedding, when Aidan and Jilleen retreated to their marital chamber, I went to the White Circle to wait for my love. The stones were washed in moonlight and were glowing in a bluish hue of the night. My heart was beating wildly and my frenzied state turned into fear that love would rob me of my powers and my ability to commune with the Goddess and other deities. I knelt in the middle of the Circle and raised my hands toward the moon in prayer. Once I reached a state of complete stillness, I was again able to receive messages from the Goddess. They were full of warning, and I knew something was amiss. My fear was spun from the threads of foreboding, and I tried to understand the meaning behind the cold gripping my heart. And then I knew. Egerton's life was in danger. He was hated by Aidan's circle of noblemen and other clan members. Egerton was English and the fact that he saved Aidan's life in a battle could not diminish the flaming hatred against the English felt by our entire region. How foolish of Aidan to invite him and of him to accept the invitation! I must warn him. He must leave at once. He must not wait for the dawn because he will be slain.

"Just as I was tempted to go back and warn him, I heard horse hoofs and knew it was him. He dismounted from his white mare and ran to me. Our kisses were feverish and his hands lost themselves under my dress. My breaths came out in rasps and moans and no wisdom I possessed helped me understand the force that took me captive. I also could not understand where I found the strength to push him away from me, and in a voice broken by arrested passion I told him he had to get away if he wanted to live. My words came in a torrent. I told him about my past, about the powers passed down to me, about my second sight and my communion with the Goddess...and he believed me. He still lingered and wanted to make love to me, but I urged him to leave.

"'Promise me you will wait for me...promise me to remain chaste...no one must touch you...ever. Promise me you will remain of a pure heart and body, and forever be only mine. I will come back and make you my bride.'

"'I promise you that, my love', I said. And then I kissed him deeply and bit his lower lip and then mine drawing blood from both. He winced almost imperceptibly when I licked and swallowed the mingled droplets off his lip. I kissed him until I was certain his tongue tasted my blood. I whispered a chant of union between our two hearts and said we would always be able to reach each other with our thoughts and the language of our hearts.

"And then my head started spinning and I heard voices of his enemies who had started their search for him. I prodded him to hasten at once, and go in the direction in which they will not pursue him, for with my mind I was able to penetrate their evil intentions.

"'Go toward Glenda's Bluff but be careful not to get too close to the treacherous rocks. Trust me...you must leave and save yourself.'

"And he left, Kieran. He left me and all these years we have stayed connected. He has come to me many nights in my dreams where I have seen him happy, angry, and sad. I have seen him make love to many women sometimes hoping to forget me, but he could not. He had tasted my blood and that was his curse. No woman could take my place in his heart and memory. At times, he enjoyed his daydreams about me, and at others, he would curse me and ask me to set him free, but I reminded him of his promise to come and make me his bride. I was keeping my promise of chastity not allowing any man near me. I even spread a rumour that for me to preserve my healing powers I had to remain unmarried, and unsoiled by male touch. But I had so much love in my heart, so much fire in my body with no place to channel it, but toward healing others."

"How long are you going to wait for him?"

"The wait is almost over. Last night he came into my dream on a black stallion, and he was laughing and smiling telling me it was time...our time has come. Soon, he will be here to take me with him to England. I am to get ready."

"How will you get ready?"

"I will pack my herbs and medicine because people everywhere need healers. I shall leave this place with a heavy heart, but this place is full of unbearable sadness after Jilleen's death. I must tell you something. Aidan gave me all Jilleen's clothes. He said the pain of seeing her dresses was breaking his heart anew. His heart was bleeding from too many places...bleeding for his motherless son and himself. There would never be another love for him. He cannot even stand living here anymore and plans to move to England. So I want to show you the dress I will wear as my wedding gown. Can you endure the sight of it?"

Kieran nodded but his face turned moonlight white, and his lower jaw trembled. So many times he sought answers from me as to why my Goddess and his God allowed Jilleen's death, and I had no answers but could only try to reassure him they would find each other again. I was not always certain if my own belief was steady. There was just too much pain and suffering and no answers to the whys of wretched human fate.

When I spread the dress before Kieran, he kneeled and with a tremulous hand caressed its creases. It was a white dress with a laced-up front. The bodice of Jilleen's dress was trimmed with delicate blue dragonflies. The dress had drop sleeves made from mesh lace fabric. The back of the dress had a low v-cut, also laced up.

"I remember that dress. I remember peeling it slowly off her lovely shoulders."

He picked the dress up and buried his face in it inhaling deeply. He lifted his head, his eyes feverish with anguish.

"Why is her scent so faint? I mostly smell honeysuckle and I want to smell her. I want you to give me a piece of her clothing that still has her scent."

I went into my back room and pulled out a white chemise from the heavy chest.

He crumpled it and brought it to his nostrils, inhaling its fragrance. His face was contorted both in pleasure and heartache. He looked at me again and asked, "Aren't you afraid to wear her dress? Don't you fear it is bad luck to wear a dress of a woman who was killed?"

"I want to honour Jilleen by wearing her dress. She and I had a special bond and I feel her spirit around me. She wants me to wear it."

"I don't know what to think. I just know my life no longer has any meaning...or joy. I only say these things to you and no one else. We men cannot show weakness. Be happy, Ailionora. You are a good woman and Egerton is one lucky lad."

He stuffed the chemise in the pocket of his trousers and left. I could feel his pain, and I knew there was no cure for it. I also knew with certainty his life would be cut short. I saw it in the candlelight, but could not tell him his soul would soon leave this world in search of Jilleen.

With every new day, my excitement mounted. Egerton was getting closer and closer, and I heard his voice incessantly. He was not coming alone. My spiritual eye showed me a group of armed men riding behind him. A magnificent mare followed his horse, and my heart skipped a beat knowing the mare was for me.

I cleaned my house thoroughly and packed my belongings. I planned to leave in secrecy, but did not know if I would be able to hide my departure once Egerton and his men arrived. I was afraid of skirmishes between his men and the locals, but was hoping they would not be noticed if they arrive under the cover of night.

One night my dream was so vivid that I knew the day had come when I would meet my love in the White Circle, and leave this place forever. My hands shook from excitement and an undercurrent of fear was mingled with joy. Contrary to my habit to sit in stillness until my feelings offered clarity, I suppressed them and banished them. I went through the day dispensing medicine, but the fever of love dulled my healing powers. I felt guilt and remorse that I was failing the sick as a healer, because all my energy was focused on becoming a bride. Tonight in the White Circle, one of Egerton's riders, who was a priest, would perform the hand-fasting ceremony, and I would leave the Circle as a married woman. I would bestow upon my husband the gift of my purity, chastity, and virginity.

I arrived at the Circle wearing Jilleen's dress. It fitted me perfectly. The night was cloudy and chilly, and I wrapped a blue woollen shawl around my shoulders. My heart fluttered in anticipation of Egerton's riders, and horse hoofs pounded in my head disorienting me. I put my hands to my ears to dampen the sound and I leaned against a stone. The palms of my hands were hot, and my body started tingling with rising heat. I changed my position and moved to another stone, and at that moment I heard voices. Egerton must have already arrived. I ran toward the sound, and behind a stone gate I spotted three men sitting on the ground and drinking wine. Their horses could be heard but not seen.

My eagerness to be reunited with Egerton drowned out the voice in me warning me of danger, and telling me to hide, and turn invisible as I had learned to do while studying to become a High Priestess. I forgot the knowledge about how love could make me vulnerable, and strip me off my powers of second sight. I let myself fall into a trap the consequences of which I could have never foreseen.

The men noticed me and one of them was by my side before I could turn around and hide.

"Cad is ainm duit, cáilín? Ar mhaith leat deoch?"

While asking me about my name and offering me wine the man began to stroke my hair while his mates encircled me. They were neither Egerton's men nor the men from our village, or wider region. They reeked of sweat, rancid wine, and unwashed clothes. They laughed and joked about their good fortune to have come across a beautiful girl alone in the dark. The girl was theirs to play with now.

Two of them grabbed my arms and held me in their tight grip so I could not move, while the third one began to unlace my dress from the back. I expected him to tear it off, but his gaze was full of admiration for the silky white fabric. My blood froze from fright. I was at the same time incredulous that I would allow myself to fall into such a trap, ignoring my inner voice.

Once my dress fell around my ankles, the two men lifted me up, and I found myself standing between them wearing my chemise. The third man collected the dress gently, folded it and put it in a leather sack. He left us and disappeared in the dark. In my mind, I could clearly see him put the satchel on a horse and tie it. My dress was intended as a gift for someone.

When he returned, his expression was one of ferociousness and cruelty. He gave a sign to his companions, and they pulled me onto the ground and spread my legs. The man who took off my dress with utmost care, now ripped my chemise and undergarments with his knife slashing my inner thighs. Under his weight I could barely breathe, let alone move. When he penetrated me, I shrieked in horror realizing I would no longer be chaste for Egerton, and it would not matter that I did not succumb to these men out of my own volition. I started screaming and kicking hoping someone would hear me, but the Circle was too far away from the village for the sound to carry. I could feel blood trickling down my thighs, and when the odious man noticed it under the torch light one of his mates was holding over us, he dipped his fingers in it and licked it like a beast, saying that virgin blood was a source of man's virility. He laughed a demonic laugh, dipped his fingers again into my secret opening, and wiped his bloody hand off a stone saying he was painting a picture of a girl who just had lost her virginity. He called out to his mates to help him with his stone painting, and they raped me and dipped their fingers in my blood, and drew strange and meaningless shapes on the stones laughing in mirthful drunkenness.

Their laughter turned into a hushed conversation about whether to kill me or take me with them. As they were turning their backs to me and wiping their bloodied hands against their trousers, the heat I had felt earlier began to rise in me, yet on the inside I felt cold. I also felt I was rising above the ground. I looked up toward the heaven, raised my hands and with complete calmness asked the Goddess to strike the three assailants dead. I cast my eyes on them and saw a hawk swoosh down from the night skies screeching. With its talons, it went straight for the eyes of the man who stole my dress. He flailed his hands in defense, but lost balance and fell on his back. The other two men attacked the hawk with their knives, but the bird suddenly took off and vanished. The man on the ground was screaming that he could not see and was furiously wiping blood off his face. His mates picked him up and helped him walk by propping him up between them.

I shouted out to the Goddess again to not allow them to leave her sacred circle unpunished. She heard my entreaty, and a blue light descended from the sky like a sword of fire impaling the blind man. His screams and shrieks of agony shattered the night. When his body touched the ground, smoke rose from it. The other two started running, but stumbled as the blue light coiled around them like a snake. While one of the men died a horrible death by strangling, the other managed to escape, and in the distance, I heard gallop of horses, and knew my wedding dress and my life had vanished forever.

Moonlight drizzled in blue slivers onto the stones, and in spite of the wan light, I could see the marks my blood left on them. I screamed for rain, and a lonely cloud appeared out of nowhere and sprinkled the stones with rain drops that reminded me of bleeding tears. The stains stared and shouted at me, 'Shame, shame,' reminding me that I was no longer the same girl. I was no longer worthy of Egerton's love. I would never be a bride.

Fury replaced the self-pity consuming me. My ears were throbbing with the pain of hearing the word shame shouted at me by the stones, moon rays, grasses...I was losing my mind, and yet I was still desperately trying to clean the blood marks off the stones, and obliterate traces of my disgrace.

My palms started bleeding from scrubbing the jagged stones with the light fabric of my chemise. And my fury grew and expanded until I stopped scrubbing the stones and turned my eyes again toward the sky the darkness of which was sprinkled with starlight. My heart overflowed with supplication to the Goddess to prevent me from what I was about to do. Because at that moment I know with utmost certainty I had reached the point my grandmother had warned me about. She said there might come a time in my life when events of utter joy or extreme pain would provoke me to use for good or evil a special power I could use but once, and she hoped it would be for good. My seething rage was a clear sign that I was about to unleash this power and bring destruction, and the Goddess was not going to intervene. I also knew I could save myself, but my life held no worth anymore. I raised my hands to the sky and in a roaring and unrecognizable voice I summoned the furies of gods, skies, and demons.

Oh, Mother Goddess,

Giver of mercy and mistress of fury,

Look upon thy mortal daughter as she arises today,

Through the power of thy own wrath, fuel her own,

So all traces of her shame may be erased,

So no one remembers this cursed day,

So that the winds of oblivion erase the memory

Of all who knew of me

And the landscape remembers not my footsteps.

Oh Mother Goddess,

Let the bedazzling sunlight and iridescent moonlight

Wrap my home in impenetrable opacity

Until the curse can be broken with love and forgiveness.

My arms were raised toward the skies and the ire and passion of fire burned my palms and rose to meet the bolts of lightning striking upon the white stones. The noise was deafening as the ancient stones crumbled to dust, and the dust disappeared among the blades of grass.

With arms still outstretched, I was twirling in circles, and the faster I twirled the more the skies roared and split open showing white angry forms and faces of the gods offended by mortals. The White Circle was effaced not only from the face of the earth, but also from the memory of the people with whom I had shared this brief span of life. They would gradually forget Ailionora and her shame, and when Egerton arrived with his retinue, he would search for me not only in this lifetime, but also in all that follow. Until then, our soul light would merge with the starlight and add a sacred glow to eternity.

13

Weylin

Ariadne stopped speaking and her eyelids fluttered. Silence fell in the room as everyone was trying to process what they had witnessed. Keith was the only one who seemed to be at ease, as if what the experiments with Jacacia revealed were part of his everyday events at work.

Ariadne opened her eyes, looked at me and said with a smile, "Nice to see you again, Kieran. You never believed me when I said you'd be reunited with Jilleen, and here you are." She smiled at Leandra who, in turn blushed and said, "We may be Kieran and Jilleen, but we are not together."

"But you are still connected and always will be. I bring that knowledge back from the same lifetime. You are reconnected in this lifetime briefly, but there will be another one in which your time together will be much longer, and your fate and that of your son will be finally fulfilled. I had to say this now before I lose that knowledge."

I looked at her and said, "I have just heard things that make me want to pinch myself. I am aware of what I said during my own session, but for me to believe it, I think I need to find physical evidence of all of this. Maybe even then, I will doubt my own sanity. Who knows?

Maybe we have all fallen prey to some drug-induced collective hallucination and false memories. We may have influenced each other, and ushered each other into the same story through suggestion. I don't really know what to think anymore."

After I said that, I turned to Leandra expecting she would offer her opinion on another testimony of utter strangeness, but she just said she had to excuse herself, and go back to her office. She also added she could not spare more time, and would not sit in on the sessions with Keith's patients, but wished Keith excellent results, and eventual success with treating mental illness with Jacacia.

After lunch, we observed a patient of Keith's, a young woman suffering from schizophrenia. I found it hard to stay concentrated and kept tuning out, replaying in my mind my own experience with Jacacia and comparing it to Ariadne's, Leandra's and Annette's sessions. We all lived in the same lifetime? I kept shaking my head in disbelief.

Once Keith's patient came out of her Jacacia induced trance, she recounted an experience, which was very different from those the rest of us had. She did not connect to a past life, but was shown her current life with a clarity that left her shaken up to the core. She said she now knew all her mental problems arose from the fact that she ended up in a job she resented, because she had been discouraged by her parents to pursue a career in music.

But even though it was too late now for music, Jacacia showed her an alternate path toward satisfaction and healing. She had always had many interests, and her soul had called on her so many times to get in touch with her gifts, but she let the calls go unanswered never trusting herself to be good enough at anything.

The dissatisfaction of working as a receptionist at a podiatrist' office built over time and culminated in illness. Jacacia's message was to come back for another session in order to get in touch with her subdued creative impulses. She felt so optimistic about her future, and so certain she would no longer need drugs that all of us looked at her cautiously; however, no one dared say she should be careful and not do anything she might regret. We psychiatrists always feared our patients would stop taking the prescribed medications and cause their condition to worsen. Everything was simply too surreal, and the line between the rational and the insane suddenly became even more blurred.

After the session, Annette, Ariadne, and I went back to the hotel to rest before dinner.

I lay down with a massive headache after taking two painkillers. I sent a text to my wife letting her know that the sessions were highly intriguing and made me re-evaluate everything I had been taught and believed.

Her reply was the question about my arrival time and if it was still unchanged. At that moment, I knew I was going to ask for a divorce. The bond between us had dissolved a long time ago and there was nothing left. I could live without passion, maybe even with friendship only, but not with coldness and detachment. I wanted out of a dead relationship.

Over dinner, the three of us compared notes about what we had witnessed and were so overwhelmed with impressions that we did not even notice we had drunk two bottles of wine and were feeling quite tipsy.

"Are you concerned that your tests next week will confirm your cancer is still in the same stage?" I asked Annette.

"I feel so much better that I believe the results should also be encouraging, but then again there are moments when I believe I am in denial of the grim reality. What if the cancer has spread further and I will be dead soon? What if all of this was some kind of hoax and collective hallucination, as you said? I don't know what to think as nothing has ever prepared me for this kind of experience."

I texted Leandra feeling emboldened by my slight drunkenness asking her if she would join us for dinner the next evening. Her reply was curt and polite, and negative. I felt disappointed as I was hoping we could talk more about Kieran and Jilleen.

Even though during this week Leandra appeared at times reserved around me, I still felt connected to her. It was as if our hearts were tethered to each other via secret threads. I did not want us to turn into complete strangers, a state that ex-lovers so easily slip into.

Back at the hotel my headache returned, and I spent the night vomiting.

I felt nauseated the next day, too, so I let Keith know I would have to stay in bed. I texted Leandra again to tell her I wanted to see her before I left for Ireland.

Her response came three hours later saying that it was time for her to leave behind any past life in which she may have lived. She had to focus her energy and attention on her current life, work, and especially her family. She felt that by even discussing Kieran and Jilleen she was somehow betraying her husband again, and she never wanted to be the source of any marital stress, or be placed in a situation tempting her to transgress against her marriage anew.

I wanted to tell her there was nothing dangerous or tempting about talking about our experiences, and that we could be friends even though I could understand her husband's potential objection to that, but I decided to say nothing. Perhaps it was for the best that we severed all communication and abandoned trying to explain the inexplicable.

14

Leandra

My life had settled into a pleasant routine like a river in a perfect riverbed. The effects of shock I experienced witnessing Keith's experiment with Jacacia began to fade after a few months.

In the meantime, Keith wrote to say he had promising news to share. After subjecting his selected patients to the sessions with Jacacia, he studied with Phil their before-and-after brain scans and observed significant changes. He invited me to a meeting he organized at the hospital during which he planned to share his findings with the hospital managers and psychiatrists from the country and abroad.

Phil, as the head psychiatrist, would be the main presenter and would propose seeking approvals for further studies using Jacacia. The patients themselves reported they experienced true epiphanies, and disappearance of mental illness symptoms. Keith called it a breakthrough, a revolutionary finding, but his enthusiasm left me cold and indifferent.

In March, Adrian and I took a week off and went to the Dominican Republic for a dream vacation in a magical hotel resort. Our apartment had a breathtaking view of the ocean, a fully equipped kitchen, and a huge bathroom with a Jacuzzi in which we soaked our sunburned bodies every night while sipping cold white wine. Our vacation was pure pleasure until the last night when a dream awoke me in the middle of the night. It was so real that it took me twenty minutes of utter disorientation to start to convince myself it was just a dream. I dreamt about Weylin and me and the dream unrolled itself before my eyes as a film would.

Warm wind is rustling my hair as I am sitting under the flaming willow in my backyard. Swaying in the wind, the sun and heat-drenched trees and flowers are boasting their summer glory. It is Summer Solstice, the day I decided to mark in some small way, silently asserting that God is nature and nature is God, as Spinoza had said. I look around trying to absorb the essence of life surrounding me without mentally labeling each individual life form as a tree, a leaf, a dragonfly, or the wild turkey that has recently moved into the garden. I look at the lush vegetation, trying to mingle my spiritual energy with that of nature, as a Buddhist might. The rocks lying alongside the flowerbeds exude energy through their rough, rugged edges; the bark surface of the tree I am admiring feels rough under my sliding fingertips. Sunrays are licking my skin with their heat, awakening erotic desire deep in my belly. The desire burrows even more deeply in my body, shooting fiery sparks of wanting through my blood, making me gasp and drop the book I have been reading. I close my eyes and slowly let the wings of imagination take me to the world in which he and I, two separate halves seeking completeness, reunite once more ...

****

I hear the door leading from the kitchen to the garden open and catch a fresh whiff of soap, a mildly citrusy scent I cannot recognize. 'Perhaps it is Bergamot', I think inhaling deeply. I feel him approach me from behind my chair and I throw my head backwards, keeping my eyes shut. The back of the chair reclines with my movement and he bends down over me, kissing my eyes softly and suddenly parting my lips with his tongue, setting me ablaze with desire. I moan loudly as shivers of craving for him rampage through my body making my nipples harden and become visible under my white cotton dress. I still do not dare open my eyes in fear I would lose this sweetest of reveries and he would disappear like summer haze scattered to oblivion by gusting winds.

His fingers are now loosening up the laced-up front of my dress and sliding gently over my breasts and nipples. His breathing is thickening with the swelling lust. He takes the elastic band from my ponytail and spreads my hair across my shoulders, releasing the scent of tuberose shampoo. Like a staccato of erotic ripples turning into huge swells, desire is infusing all my senses; again the sensation is so overpowering that I feel faint, forgetting where we are and that neighbours might witness this scene of shameless abandon.

****

I swivel my chair toward him, rise from it and kiss him, flicking my tongue inside his mouth and around his lips. I gasp when I realize it is Kieran I am kissing. My incessant hunger for him has spanned lifetimes and has sprung from love that feels primordial. For I love him as much as I want him, if not more. It seems we have been wrapping our arms around each other for eternity, and in this moment, it feels again as if the heat of our bodies creates the most resplendent love poetry from erotic touches.

****

He takes my hand and gently pulls me toward the house, but I smile and pull him in the other direction, more deeply into the garden toward a weeping willow hiding a gurgling brook. The shade under the willow is cool and deep and provides refreshing relief from a hot summer day. The brook is shallow, only about a foot deep, but abounds in life, and during the long summer evenings, frogs can be heard croaking on its mossy banks, indicating the purity of the water.

****

He is walking behind me, unzipping my dress and then untying the string that goes through its midriff lace band. We wade into the water, and I step out of the dress and toss it under the willow tree. I have no bra, just white panties that stand out against my tanned skin. I sit in the water, scoop it in the palm of my right hand, drink it and splash a few drops over my breasts. He sits beside me, but at the next moment he starts kissing me and pushing me toward the ground. Lying on top of me he continues to kiss me, sucking on my lower lip and tongue, his eyes effervescent with love and desire. My panties are completely wet as from the waist down I am submersed in the cool water. I pull myself out of the brook onto the grass-covered bank, leaving my feet in the water. We fuse into a crescendo of fiery lovemaking that alters my consciousness like the most potent drug. In the dream, I wonder how the sharp rocks on the bank and in the water do not lacerate my skin.

****

We move out of the water and notice at the same time bleeding scratches on our arms. I place my arm over his and rub my rivulet of blood against his until the droplets become indistinguishable. "Now I am a part of you that you cannot lose or misplace in your heart", I whisper, kissing him.

Where the brook ends, the water is waist deep and forms a small dark pool. Holding hands, we wade through the water until we reach the pool and step into it. Our kissing is interrupted with raspy and breathy 'I love you'. I gently bite his lips, his ears, and lick his arms, chest, and then his lips again, whispering sweet words of love and desire. Lush foliage hides us, the summer solstice lovers, and it is only the solitary sunrays that find us, peering through the branches and caressing our naked skin. We make love again and I feel I am almost levitating above the pool, absorbing energies of water, earth, and air, becoming one with my love and the natural elements around me. 'I am dreaming a summer solstice dream', I think. I do not even finish the thought when Kieran vanishes and I find myself sitting forlorn on the rock against which we had made love. I notice a branch move and descend toward me. The leaves rustle and I hear a voice clearly say, 'Leandra, Jilleen, Juliet, Lola...you are that rare mortal who has been given answers about their purpose and destiny. Embrace the chance, my daughter, search for and find the answers in the past so that you may know the future. Your soul energy and that of Kieran, Karlo, Weylin and Waldon have been entangled for what you call centuries. Running away from him will not liberate you. Your dreams summon the sacred energy of lovers and reunite them. All the roads you take will only delay your destiny, and your destiny is to find the final answers and understand why this male soul energy keeps re-entering your life. Trust the path chosen by you. Trust it, Leandra.'

I awoke with a start feeling rattled to the core. My body felt the sweetness of lovemaking as if it had not been a dream, and my mind screamed at the return of my nightmares when I felt like a plaything in the hands of mysterious forces. My shivering woke up Adrian and he put his arms around me. I managed to say I had a nightmare and would get a glass of water to calm down. I asked him to go back to sleep.In the kitchen, I wrapped myself in the blanket I took from the armchair in our bedroom and sipped water looking out the window at the ocean. My laptop was on the kitchen table, and I turned it on to find a distraction. I went into my email inbox remembering a colleague had asked me to peer review an article she was planning to submit to a prestigious medical journal. I thought I'd read it and not go back to bed as it was almost 5 am. But instead of opening my colleague Christine's email and the attached article, my heart skipped a beat when I noticed Weylin's email in my inbox. I had not heard from him in a few months, but at that moment, I felt him deep in my bones and blood. The dream was so real that it made me question again my sanity. I felt tremor in my hand, as I clicked on the email and started reading.

Leandra,

I did not mean to write again but feel compelled to write if only for one last time. I have decided to take two weeks off work and drive through Ireland in search of traces of my past life or lives. The reason why I suddenly know what I need to do is the dream I had last night. You were in the dream, but that is all I am willing to share because I'd be afraid of your reaction if I told you how real it felt and what it was. However, one part of the dream sent shivers down my spine. You suddenly vanished and a voice told me I, unlike most mortals, have been given the opportunity to find answers to all of my destinies, in my previous and in my future lives, or at least in one of them. The voice told me your soul energy and mine are forever entangled and nothing we do will change that, only delay the fate etched in eternity. I know it sounds completely insane, and who knows if all is right with me. Maybe I have a brain tumour that causes all this strangeness.

Anyway, Ariadne also wants to come on this road trip. She feels the urge to uncover what happened to Egerton and if he is, in fact, Hugo. She says that Ailionora's wrath wiped out not only the White Circle from the face of the Earth, but also the memory of the place where the three of us had lived. She also feels there is a curse she needs to help remove in order to find Egerton in this life, or if Hugo is reincarnated Egerton, to make him come and stay with her. Yes, crazy! But what is crazier, Annette's cancer is in remission and her doctors are baffled. They call it a medical miracle. She has taken a year off work just to enjoy life with her family.

Something else is new, too. I am getting a divorce. When I came back, I told Maureen I wanted out. I trembled inside fearing how much I would hurt her and the kids. She broke down in tears and I froze ready to offer her another chance, to suggest we see a marriage counsellor, but her tears were tears of relief. She had also been considering divorce because she thought our marriage had been dead for too long and it was just an arrangement for the sake of keeping up appearances of a family. We both cried and hugged and decided to invest a lot of effort into staying friends for the kids' sake. I moved out two weeks later and bought a flat. The kids took it hard, in spite of our explanations and assurances we would always be a family of sorts. Things are calmer now that Maureen and I take the kids out for dinner every Saturday. We are planning a week-long vacation together with the kids as a test of this new arrangement. One day at a time until life assumes a new type of normalcy.

Now the main reason I am writing. In my last night's dream the message was clear that both of us should search for the evidence of our life in which we were Jilleen and Kieran. I do not know why, but it has something to do with our synergy, or their synergy that survived till now. Leandra, I cannot even begin to explain to you how real the dream was. I remember every detail of it, I who never remembers any dreams. Something is happening! Jacacia opened up a portal and there is no going back until the answers are found.

Hope you change your mind and come along. I do understand this is not something easily explained to a spouse. You know I would not do anything to jeopardize your marriage. Wrecking one is quite enough.

Weylin

The tremor in my hand became so strong that I dropped the glass on the tiled floor and it broke into smithereens. The sound of my scream woke up Adrian again who rushed into the kitchen but suddenly stopped seeing my raised hand. "

What the hell happened?"

"I broke a glass."

"Why scream? It's just a freaking worthless glass." "It has nothing to do with the glass. Let me clean up the mess and I will tell you the story behind my scream. I need to tell you." He helped me pick up the shards and then he brought the vacuum cleaner into the kitchen to remove the pieces too small for us to see. Then he made coffee and we sat down in silence. After I drank half a cup, I told him all the details about the Jacacia experiments and the same dream Weylin and I had. I let him read Weylin's email. I left out the erotic content of the dream feeling guilt over lying again.

"This is all so insane, Adrian. Such things do not happen, or if they do, there must be a rational explanation. I just cannot find one."

"What I will say is even more insane. I think you should go to Europe and satisfy your curiosity about the actual existence of your past life. If you find such evidence of us and Kieran and the high priestess, then we can finally accept that past lives do exist, and we reincarnate. And if you do not find anything, we shall close that chapter behind us forever. It is also insane that I will trust you to be alone with your ex-lover. I do not know where that trust comes from, because any normal husband would fly into a rage, and not allow you to mention that name again. But for whatever reason, I feel this story is unfinished and I want to see its end."

"Come with us. I know it sounds horrible to bring you face to face with Weylin. But you were my husband Aidan in that past life. If I find evidence of anything, it will be of you first because you were a prominent person."

"No, Lea, this is something for you to do. You can take pictures of whatever you find and report to me daily. As I said, I trust you not to cross any boundary with Weylin. I believed you when you said his visit made you feel uncomfortable, and you felt you were in the presence of a semi stranger."

"I am too awake to go to sleep now, so let's go to the beach and watch the sunrise." We dressed in no time and left the apartment holding hands.

PART II

15

The roar of the plane engines upon descent into Dublin jolted Leandra out of a shallow slumber. She had been awake the entire night tormented by renewed guilt over accepting Weylin's offer to join him on a wild goose chase of uncovering evidence of their past life in Ireland. How could she have agreed to that?

Why hadn't she categorically refused it and told Adrian that even though he suggested she get to the bottom of this insanely bizarre story, and said he trusted her not to betray him again, she never wanted to see Weylin again.

But there was something in her blood or her DNA, or in the lace of her soul that was spun from tangled fibres of her and Weylin's energies. The dream she'd had in the Dominican Republic impressed that knowing upon her skin and deeper, it incised itself in her soulscape. She had booked a hotel room for one night in a modern, five-star hotel located in the city centre. When she arrived at the hotel, she started feeling nauseated from nervousness and a lack of sleep. Without unpacking or washing up, she stripped off her tunic and leggings, and lay in bed. Before falling asleep, she noticed the bed was of a four-poster type, only modern. The room lacked the charm, warmth, and character of the room in Scotland in which she and Weylin had spent a weekend drugged with passion. She no longer believed it was love.

When she woke up, she felt better and was famished. She had not eaten for the past 24 hours. She could barely drink water on her knotted stomach. She knew Weylin was expecting her to text him once in town, but she postponed the moment. After a hot shower, she went to the hotel terrace restaurant. The afternoon sun was pouring warmth on her table, and she relaxed, taking in the verdant view. The leaves on the trees shimmered in the streaming sunlight, and in their rustle, she thought she heard a whisper welcoming her home. Perhaps in the end she'd turn raving mad.

As she placed her order for roasted pepper and white bean soup, an eggplant sandwich, roasted sweet potato, and rocket and tomato salad, her phone buzzed. She knew it was Weylin but did not want to check. Just not yet. She ordered a glass of pink champagne even though she did not think it was a good mix with jet lag. After she gulped down half of it, she looked at her phone.

"*Leandra, have you arrived? Your plane landed three hours ago. Where are you?*"

She texted back, "*I've just woken up. Having an early dinner on the hotel terrace and admiring the view.*"

"Done with work. Can join you in 30 min to discuss trip."

She realized it made no sense to avoid his company. She had agreed to this adventure with him and Ariadne. She gulped down the rest of the champagne and felt its effects on her empty stomach. She had texted Adrian as soon as she landed, and she now sent him a longer text attaching pictures of her colourful meal, and the tranquil view. He immediately texted back saying that one day they should visit that part of the world together. The words made her eyes well up and a painful ache for his company filled her heart. It was so foolish to agree to come here, and at the same time a feeling of something familiar infused her. Could it be she has returned home? She inhaled deeply deciding to surrender to the flow of life so her fate may be played out according to whatever divine plan was written in the stars for her. *"Yes, sure. Thanks for recommending the hotel. Quite lovely."* The food was delicious, and she savoured it slowly while waiting for Weylin.

When he showed up in the doorway leading to the terrace, the champagne almost made her choke as butterflies swirled in her stomach. Something in her recognized Kieran in him.

She stood up to greet him and he hugged her warmly. His hazelnut-coloured eyes sparkled with genuine warmth and affection. She noticed he had more grey hair in his black mane and had aged visibly. She also realized she did not see just his physical shell, but she also fully sensed the soul his body housed.

"How was your flight?"

" I couldn't sleep a wink so I watched four movies – don't remember any of them. How's your new life unfolding?"

He stuttered before answering: "It's unfolding, still getting used to my new apartment, but things are alright. Remember I wrote to you that Maureen and I have a very civil relationship and spend time together with the kids. Last night, the five of us went to a restaurant to celebrate my mother-in-law's birthday. I noticed Maureen was secretly texting under the table, so I assumed there might be someone new in her life. She looked pretty and animated. I'd be happy for her. And you? How have you been?"

"All's good. My elder daughter is engaged to be married next year. That will mean a new phase in our lives, especially once Adrian and I are grandparents."

"You'll be a terrific grandma."

"I hope so."

"I'm starving. Anything good on the menu?"

Weylin ordered seared halibut, creamed potatoes, a salad, and a bottle of white wine to share with Leandra. The sun went down and there was a chill in the air. Leandra put on her long black cashmere sweater and wrapped an emerald green shawl around her shoulders. "Cold?" He smiled.

"A bit. Wine should warm me up. Tell me about our road trip. What time do we leave tomorrow? I assume you'll drive, and Ariadne and I will enjoy the sights. As a former higher priestess, I'm counting on her to lead us to the places where we could unearth evidence of our past life here." Leandra chuckled as if it all were just a game played by silly adults.

Weylin looked uncomfortable when he said, "There has been a major development in Ariadne's life. Her lover came back and explained why he'd been ghosting her. He did not want any contact until he got divorced and until his test results confirmed full remission of his cancer."

"Strange, indeed," said Leandra. "So he's divorced now?"

"Yes, but unlike my divorce, his was acrimonious because of the division of assets. He also told her that another reason why he was avoiding her were the nightmares in which he saw her die a violent death before he was able to reach her and save her. The dreams had been so vivid that he took them as an omen of something horrible happening to her if he showed up again in her life. Anyway, he is in town and Ariadne decided not to join us now, but in a few days when he leaves. She wants to tell him everything about her experience with Jacacia, and the possibility that he had been Egerton in her previous life. Her intuition has been telling her there is a curse linked to Ailionora she must help lift, so she will definitively meet up with us. I hope it is not a problem for you to be alone with me for a few days."

Leandra's face went white, and then red, as words fell silent. The fork in her hand trembled. At that moment Weylin's meal arrived and he started eating ravenously. After a few bites, he looked at her and said softly, "Leandra, there is nothing you should fear...we are no longer what we had been...this does not have to be awkward or uncomfortable."

"Why the hell didn't you tell me, so I could cancel the flight?" Anger made Leandra's voice crack.

"Trust me, I just found out his morning. Here's her text message. Please read it." He handed her his phone.

Leandra put on her reading glasses and read, "*So sorry to bail out on you and Leandra. You won't believe what happened this morning and who showed up literally on my door. Will phone you soon to explain. So excited. Plan to meet up with you in a few days, so make sure you stay in touch and keep me posted. I know with certainty I am connected to a curse that needs to be lifted with my help. It is Ailionora talking to me through my dreams and intuition. And I am not mad, even though I sound it.*"

Weylin took the phone back from Leandra saying, "There was no time to let you know. You were about to land. Sorry." He raised his glass."Let's clink our glasses to a great trip!"

"It's easy for you, Weylin. You're free. You can travel with whomever you want. I'm a married woman who saved her marriage from the brink of disaster because I'd fallen in love with you. And now I'm supposed to drive around with you, wake up in the morning, and have coffee, wine, beer, lunches, dinners, admire sights, fields, and stone circles. Like...really!!!"

"I understand the strangeness of it, but don't you find what happened to you and me–what we revealed in my and your altered state of consciousness much weirder than this? You can trust me not to do anything improper...can't we just behave like friends, or good colleagues? We are way past the events of a few years ago?"

He sounded sincere and a bit impatient at the same time.

"I don't know what to say to Adrian. I have not lied to him since I told him about us. Now, I am not sure if I should tell him that it will be only the two of us driving around for a few days. Oh my God, this is so unsettling, but now that I'm here I feel compelled to go through this. It's as if I'm losing a will of my own... as if some force is playing with me again, pushing me toward... I don't know... some truth I need to discover," Leandra said, and her whole body shivered as if recoiling from some frightening scene. "Please, don't make it sound like something horrible. A few days of exploring Ireland with somebody you used to know is not the worst thing that could happen to you." he smiled mischievously and that helped her relax.

The rest of the evening they spent poring over a map he spread on the table after the waitress had cleared it. Weylin told

Leandra about the tips he received from Ariadne. They should be paying close attention to signs leading them toward the place where the White Circle used to stand, or toward the places or people who could help them unravel the mystery. She was certain they'd be able to see them and interpret their meaning. After all, reconnecting through Jacacia to her past life thinned the veil between this world and the other dimensions, and Ariadne felt she had regained some of her ancient high priestess abilities. She said that she now felt as a friend to the invisible world.

Weylin wanted to order another bottle of wine, but Leandra refused, saying she felt exhausted in spite of the nap she'd taken. He wanted to pay for her dinner, but she thanked him, saying she'd already charged it to her room before he joined her at the table. She also added she expected them to evenly split all the costs for the trip. "Weylin, this trip and exploration are to be considered a scientific project, and not a leisure trip or vacation. We are colleagues working on a project, ok?"

"Are you trying to convince me or yourself of the nature of our trip? You've nothing to worry about. It is a project. We are searching for evidence of our past life. I feel compelled...driven and almost obsessed with it. I need to do it. I've been aware for a long time I was missing something important...some vital piece of information, and now I know I'll find it and finally be able to live a life that had lain dormant in me."

His words made Leandra relax. And when he hugged her as a friend would, and the warmth of his eyes penetrated hers, she knew she would be able to deal with the reality of their spending the next few days together. She trusted him to be a gentleman and never cross the line of propriety. He also did not seem to be attracted to her even one bit, so there was no reason to feel any kind of alarm over the trip. She also knew she would not tell Adrian she was travelling alone with Weylin. That can wait. They agreed to leave the hotel at 10 am and she went up to her room. She expected a sleepless night of tossing and turning, but fell into a deep and dreamless sleep.

16

Weylin awoke with a start. His right leg had gone numb, and he shook it hard to restore the blood flow. He looked at the clock and got into a panic when he saw that it was 9:15 and he had told Leandra he would pick her up at 10 a.m.

He made coffee, showered quickly and then told himself to calm down and text her to tell her he might be a bit late. They were on no fixed schedule. He sipped his coffee on the small balcony of his flat on the second floor of an old stone building, viewing the rooftops of the surrounding houses. The small table on the balcony was dappled with sunshine, and Weylin could not believe their luck with the weather. The whole week was supposed to stay warm and dry, and mostly sunny. "How does that happen in Ireland?" he wondered aloud thinking that, perhaps, Ariadne's Goddess was intervening and would assist him and Leandra in their mission. Or it was an effect of climate change! He ate a banana and checked his backpack. Unlike Leandra who always travelled with a huge suitcase, he travelled light and tightly packed. He put on a white T-shirt, jeans, a pair of loafers and wrapped a light navy-blue sweater over his shoulders.

Leandra was waiting in front of the hotel. Her hair was tied in a high ponytail. She was wearing light blue jeans and a white sweater. He parked the car and stepped out to put her suitcase in the trunk. He remembered teasing her about travelling heavy and bringing uncountable pairs of underwear. He smiled at the memory and said: "Good morning. How did you sleep?"

"Wonderful. And breakfast at this hotel is just divine. Starting your day with champagne boosts optimism."

Her laughter warmed his heart. She put two bags on the backseat, saying the hotel packed some delicacies for the road, and they'd stop for lunch in some lovely spot along the way.

"Is that wine in the bag?"

"Yes, it was a last moment decision to buy a bottle of the sparkling wine they serve at breakfast. Also, after they offered all of that food for free, I felt I should buy the wine. They didn't charge me for the food because they mistakenly charged for a whole bottle of wine instead of a glass. Their apology is in these bags. They were so nice and embarrassed by the mistake they even gave me two glasses. Let's try not to break them because I'd like to return them. I am spending the last night here, too."

"Ready to roll toward Limerick and Cork? On the way we'll stop at many little towns, the first being Kildare, then wander around and check if we feel any special vibes. Ireland is small, and in the week we have, we can traverse it in every direction."

"We should also leave the beaten paths and wander deeper into the countryside. I'm feeling silly as normally, in any kind of investigation or search, we would know what questions to ask. In this case what can we ask? Was there ever something called Glenda's Bluff? Are there any books with references to the White Circle? We have nothing... no starting point, Weylin…"

"This is our starting point. My home city. And if we find nothing at all, we'll return, have one last dinner in Dublin and I'll take you to the airport the next day. It will be our final goodbye and we can become each other's memory–if that's what you want. I will always remember you with affection and will remember this experience as something mysterious, unsolvable, but beneficial. I have already begun to change my life and, perhaps that was the whole point of my experience with you and Jacacia."

Sitting in the car with Weylin made Leandra`s head spin with incredulity that she would find herself alone with him again. She looked at him and noticed he was relaxed, and his face was lit with a gentle smile. No wonder, because as a single man, any compunction over going on a road trip with his ex-lover had no place in his thoughts anymore.

The sunrays frolicked on the dashboard and the minutes melted into each other. She looked at the verdant fields and stone walls they were passing. They drove in silence, listening to a CD featuring Celtic music played on the harp. The sound was spellbinding.

"Weylin...this is more than surreal. What are we looking for? Why did I come here?"

"Let's not ponder that anymore, Leandra. Please try to relax. I can sense your tension. Let's look at this as one last adventure we are embarking on together as friends or colleagues, or both. Can you do that?"

Before she could reply, a dragonfly landed on the windshield, quivered for a fraction of a second before vanishing.

"That must have been a sign Ariadne told us to watch for," exclaimed Leandra. "Alright, this is an adventure and an exploration into our past lives. Sorry I'm not good company."

"Last time we drove together you were a much better travel companion." He winked and the implicit allusion to their road trip to the Ring of Brodgar in Scotland made her blush. "Sorry, Leandra. I should not have mentioned that."

His apology could not prevent the rise of the memory of their travel to Scotland during one stolen weekend. The memory was so vivid that he was afraid of losing control of the wheel. To remember in such detail must have been another sign of fate. The reverie of them unfolded before his inner eye and he felt like a voyeur in his and Leandra's memory of illicit love.

'Stall 37 in the Avis section', he remembered the sign on display. He hurried as much as he could, dragging her suitcase the size and bulkiness of a medium fridge. 'But then again, what's a girl in love to do when she's hurtling herself across the ocean to a breathless reunion with her lover', he mused while progressing along the corridor. He began to feel

the dizzying rush he knew so well from the previous encounters and trysts with Leandra. Loving her was distilled magic. Even though they tried their best not to take any chances of being seen together, nowadays with cameras placed everywhere, their encounters must have been recorded somewhere. Keeping their relationship a secret was a constant source of fear and frustration.

****

She was waiting for him in a restaurant while he went to pick up the rented car. Indian summer was shimmering across Scotland. Even though he was waiting in line for a car pick-up in a concrete building, he could sense the fragrances and sounds of summer when he looked through the windows. He remembered the dress she was wearing. A grayish summer dress that made him swoon and that made his eyes glaze over with desire for her. He had often wondered what it would take to make him NOT be turned on by her; maybe the East-German 70s-style "fashion" would do the trick. But then again, it seemed that whatever she wore made him start to overheat at the sight of her; his eyes seemed to penetrate whichever material covered her, and his hands became undisciplined creatures with minds of their own.

Her legs were bare, her feet looking comfortably casual in pumps. In a few minutes he would be with her on the road toward the Ring of Brodgar, and their clocks would stop and time would be measured by their heartbeats alone.

Once he picked up the car and parked it in front of the restaurant, he walked in to find her. When he saw her, he embraced her again with passion, wanting to breathe in her scent and keep it there forever. She had said the perfume was called Amethyst or some other gem. Inhaling her filled his soul with joy and a sense of pure wonder. They stayed there clinging to each other as if they had found one another after a century of frantic search. Incredulous of the intensity of their feelings, and the heat of the sparks flying between them, he laughed. He kissed her eyelids, her nose, her cheeks, her lips, her neck, her ears, and noticed an immediate change in her breathing. They kissed again and went to the car. On the way out of the restaurant they stayed in an embrace and stumbled on the street, prompting an angry car honk. Being together induced a trance-like state. They moved aside and the driver shouted something at them in an unintelligible language that sounded like one of the Scottish dialects. They got into the car and drove away.

****

Driving along a sunny road they absorbed the warmth of sun, feeling its blessings and smiles on their skin. 'So are we going to be there quickly, or are you still a Luddite?' Leandra asked him tongue-in-cheek knowing his dislike of GPS and his preference of getting lost on the way. 'It's all memorized up here', he said pointing to his head. 'It's an eight-hour drive and I will not get us lost, I promise'.

As they drove leisurely along country roads lined with fields and villages, they chatted and laughed and smiled at each other. They felt no need for incessant conversation. Being so close together, with a couple of days ahead of them, was sheer bliss. He looked at her again and put his hand on her knee. She smiled and scooted closer to him.

The wind was in their hair and her hand found its way to the nape of his neck; she stroked his earlobes and shoulders. She whispered to him that his white T-shirt stood in a delicious contrast against his tanned arms. She called him her pagan god and Celtic warrior, and he wondered if one could be both at the same time. She leaned onto his shoulder and felt his hand tense and tremble on her knee. She moved as close to him as the seatbelt allowed her, placing her hand on his thigh, just at the point where his shorts stopped. He felt the car swerve a little as he gasped with excitement. She kissed his neck and he feared he might have closed his eyes for a second as the car lurched precariously close to a ditch. She whispered into his ear asking him if he was able to drive steadily. 'I can try', he croaked hoarsely, and steadied the car. Her hand slipped inside his baggy shorts, and he let out a dark moan. She unbuckled her seatbelt and licked his neck and let her tongue, warm and wet, flicker gently in his ear. He put his arm around her and then turned the car onto a bumpy side road. After a few seconds, they found themselves surrounded by trees. He turned off the car in a quiet clearing. There was no one around, only bird chirps rippled the air. The sun was on them. They smiled at each other and kissed, and whispered love. His hand moved up her leg causing a shiver of desire in her. Softly as a dragonfly's wings, his fingers caressed the lace of her underwear eliciting a passionate sigh from her. His kisses turned ferocious as their tongues engaged in a slow, wet dance. Their eyes locked and they felt as if being submerged in warm water. 'I love you', he said and hugged her. 'Wait here', he told her and got out of the car. She heard him open the trunk and followed him. 'It's picnic time!' he exclaimed and spread a soft blanket on the grass. He took a basket from the trunk. It was filled with delicious Mediterranean goodies, several kinds of cheese, olives, tomatoes, Arancini, and wine. There were glasses and even an iPod he hooked up to the car so that soft jazz music suddenly welcomed them.

They toasted each other and ate with gusto. Birdsong enveloped them, and they caught glimpses of dragonflies hovering in the air and then moving on in little spurts. She was so beautiful and radiant, and looked content to the brim. And that made him happy. He had always worried too much about them; it was a constant weight in the back of his head. But in that resplendent little spot, everything seemed aligned and in immaculate order. He rested on his elbows, and her head was on his stomach; she was looking into the sky, and he was feeding her morsels of southern delights. 'Remember Barcelona?' she asked him. And they reminisced about the last day in that city, the first occasion they had to live out a brief and impossible dream, and the first time they had a chance to test whether 'they' even existed. They laughed and shook their heads in disbelief when they remembered casting furtive glances across tables, and secretly touching each other with their feet under restaurant tables. He caressed her hair and cupped her breasts with his hands. She stretched and sighed like a content cat catching a nap in the sun. The wildflowers around them were infusing the air with their sweet fragrance. Slumber crept upon them, but they chased it away knowing there was a lot of road to cover yet before reaching their destination.

They did not make any more stops until they reached the stone inn in Kirkwall, from which they would visit the Ring the morning after. The inn looked like something straight out of the Lord of the Rings; it exuded charm that survived centuries of hardship. 'How did you find this?' she asked staring at the walls. They entered the house through a creaky door and when they finally hoisted her heavy suitcase up the winding stairs, they could appreciate the room they were given. It was large, with exposed beams in the ceiling. The windows opened up to a small square, and there was even a balcony with a display of potted flowers, a small table and two chairs. The bed was a magnificent four-poster with a gauze-like canopy. The drapes on the windows were beige and heavy, and the fabric was imprinted with images of fairies and dragonflies. In one corner, an antique table with two chairs covered in yellow satin added exquisite charm to the ambiance. A large white wardrobe with painted flowers on the doors looked as if it might be filled with magic.

They looked at each other. There was nothing but happiness and harmony, and expectation of love in that room. They drank it all up in one big gulp of air. She went into the bathroom to take a shower. A few minutes later he joined her. He toweled himself off and went into the bedroom. When she joined him, he was sitting on the bed and hooking a finger at her. She slowly sauntered to him with a smile on her face and fire in her eyes. She fell into his outstretched arms, and he hugged her hips. Her hands tousled his hair. He stood up and loosened her towel. He then reached and took her soft belt from the nearby armchair and blindfolded her. She bit her lower lip and sighed. He let his hands glide up her toned legs, firm and slender, giving way to her buttocks. He got up, went around her, and cupped her breasts from behind her, kissing her neck. He pressed himself into her buttocks, and she responded with a little pant and pressed her back into him. Breathing heavily, he told her how much he loved her, and she replied with 'I know'. She was still blindfolded, and he pushed her gently on the bed. She stopped him, however, and bade him to stand still. Sitting on the side of the bed, she unwrapped his towel. She caressed and kissed his body all over and he felt himself entering a universe of intense colors and unbelievable pleasure as her tongue worshipped him. He moaned finding it hard to control himself. He squirmed and quivered under the touch of her flickering tongue feeling close to the point of eruption. Now she pushed him on the bed and pinned him down before mounting him. Time stretched lazily before them while they took pleasure in pleasuring each other. Their hands and lips and tongues took turns, and the room became a jumble of covers and pillows that flew through the air, beads of perspiration on their bodies, greedy kisses and insatiable licking. He was all over her and inside her, and sometimes he became arrested in movement, unable to do anything, his whole body one knot of concentrated tension. The crescendo of their lovemaking ended with a stupor of heaving breathing and tangled limbs.

****

Late evening they roamed the narrow streets at leisure, sipping drinks and coffee at quaint restaurants and cafés. Walking hand in hand or with their arms around each other's waists was bliss. They both remembered the first time they had been able do that; they felt happy but also awkward, like children caught doing something they were not allowed. They had late dinner at a restaurant on the square, and spent the entire time gazing into each other's eyes, but also enjoying observing the life of the town. That community became their own tiny retreat, a pocket of time where they lived out the secret side of their lives. When the stars came out that first night, amid the buzzing of late-summer insects, they strolled back towards the inn feeling sated. They neither hurried, nor procrastinated. They simply meandered their way towards their enchanting temporary dwelling. He looked into her eyes wanting to express a renewed desire for her. 'I know', she said without him having uttered a word. At a small candy shop he bought her a chocolate dragonfly wondering on which part of her body it would land later that night.

"Penny for your thoughts," Leandra's husky voice sent a ripple through his reverie. He looked at her and saw traces of slumber brush her features with youthful softness. Was it Jilleen's face he was looking at, he wondered? And then he remembered Jilleen from his Jacacia propelled trip, and did see a clear resemblance, especially in the eyes.

"I was replaying in my mind our trip to the Ring of Brodgar. My last memory before I heard your voice was the one of the chocolate dragonfly I placed on your body after we came back to our room. We had a lot of fun with it before it started to melt and disappear."

"Please don't remind me of that, Weylin. I don't want us to reminisce about our sinful and painful past."

"You look refreshed. Did you nap?"

"Yes, I did. Jet lag. Look at the time! I slept over an hour while you were daydreaming and driving. Luckily you did not get us into an accident driving under the influence of your musings."

"And you woke just before Kildare. We'd have arrived sooner, but the traffic is bad today. I suggest we walk around. I'd like to show you Castledermot Abbey. It used to be a Franciscan friary, but it's now in ruins. I'm sure you will still delight in it."

They walked through Kildare before visiting the ruins. The town was sunlit and the golden light seemed to run in rivulets down the quaint streets. They walked past charming cafés and restaurants and stopped for a quick coffee before visiting St. Brigid's Cathedral and climbing the tower to admire the breathtaking views. Descending the tower, Leandra felt dizzy and grabbed Weylin's hand. His grip was tight and warm.

Walking around Castledermot Abbey cleared Leandra's head. The stones of the ruins were warm to the touch. "I wonder what energy of love, pain, suffering, or joy these stones have absorbed over the centuries. I would like to learn more about the history of Ireland. You should tell me."

"I would if I knew much. History never interested me, but I guess if we want to find any traces of Kieran and Jilleen in this country, it might be useful to start some historical research. By the way, I'm starving. Where do you want to eat?"

"Is there a place somewhere by the river?"

"I remember coming here with my parents. We'll take the car, and I will take you to a place where we can go down to the River Liffey and picnic."

Half an hour later, Weylin spread a green blanket on the grass under an alder tree. Leandra sat down and leaned her back against the tree trunk. She let Weylin unpack the food and uncork the wine they'd purchased while she gazed at the river, enchanted. The buzzing of insects, the flitting of dragonflies and butterflies, the lazy moments that spread before her with the languor of golden summer created dreamlike effects.

"Hey, Leandra. Time to eat and not drift away on the wings of imagination." Weylin's voice sounded young and happy. His eyes sparkled with the specks of gold strewn around by the insouciant sun.

She smiled at him and their gazes locked. She turned her head toward the water again, feeling a jolt of connection with him that transcended the present moment. She no longer had any doubts about having known him from some previous time, a past life or... He interrupted her thought by saying he felt the same and she looked at him with her mouth agape.

"Yes, we've known each other for ever…denying it, serves no purpose. The events that have brought us to this moment were never random. I'm no longer dismissing the unimaginable and unbelievable as possible, if I'm making sense," said Weylin.

"Neither am I, even if we find no evidence of Kieran and Jilleen. They have now seeped into our blood and bones too deeply for us to ever ignore or obliterate them."

They ate in silence for a few minutes. When Weylin moved the food out of his way and lay down on the blanket with his head on Leandra's lap, she did not budge as if it had been the most usual and expected of all gestures. She felt an urge to stroke his graying hair, but resisted it. The intimacy of the moment quickened her pulse as she realized their spiritual bond was much deeper than the sexual one they had shared in the past.

"Time to break this spell and hit the road again." Weylin said. "We still have time to visit Blarney Castle and kiss the Blarney stone before enjoying Cork, and dining in a restaurant I remember from a visit with my family…or perhaps we should choose a different place?"

A shadow moved across Weylin's face as a painful memory of his marriage loss hit him.

"You have just remembered your life while you were married, right?" asked Leandra softly.

"Yes. We were doomed, unfortunately. We let our marriage die before intervening early enough in attempt to save it. From time to time, it feels like…. like my bones echo the ache of loss of our family, not her, but what we were as a family…if that makes sense…but then the feeling passes. I have to get used to being single again. Let's go and think happier thoughts."

"Just give me a moment to write to Adrian. I need to check in regularly with him." Leandra sat on a rock to write to Adrian. She also took a photo of the river to attach to the text message. She knew she would not mention that she was alone with Weylin. At the moment she pressed the send button, a dragonfly landed on her phone. Weylin noticed it and laughed, saying that it must be another of the dragonfly omens Ariadne asked them to watch out for.

They packed their picnic carefully, wrapping the glasses into napkins to prevent breakage, and strolled back to the car. Weylin offered his hand to help Leandra climb the bank and she accepted it, aware at the same time she needed no help.

They reached Blarney Castle late afternoon and spent an hour there before going into Cork. They walked for a couple of hours exploring the city and viewing the sights, such as the City Gaol that looked like a castle, St. Anne's Church, and St. Fin Barre's Cathedral. They stopped on a bridge to admire the River Lee glittering under the waning sun rays. On the bridge railing, Leandra noticed a brown bird with whitish spots on the belly. Just as she was going to point it out to Weylin, he looked at her and said, "Another sign. Maybe we are moving in the right direction."

"I feel tired. Let's go eat. Where are we spending the night, by the way?" replied Leandra.

"Silver Manor Hotel and we will eat at their garden bistro there. I stayed there a couple times with my wife and children in a happier period of my life. Something draws me there again."

Leandra was impressed with the hotel's exterior and interior. The word manor fitted its stately appearance perfectly. It was red brick, adorned with ivy. Her room was furnished and decorated in warm-hued luxury, and looked like a full suite with an elegant sofa, table, chairs, heavy drapes, bed linen, and carpeting. She gasped when she saw the room had a terrace with another lovely table. She decided to have breakfast there.

She took a quick shower and put on a green long-sleeved, mid-calf-length dress, brushed her hair and put on some lipstick. She opened her suitcase looking for her jewelry pouch but changed her mind about it. No need for dressing up more than minimally. The restaurant had wide ash rose-coloured armchairs, and she relaxed into one, feeling tired.

"Looking nice, Leandra. Red or white?"

"A glass of white, please. More than that would make me boring company and put me to sleep." She looked at the menu and felt hunger claw at her insides. She looked at Weylin and sweet tremors rippled through her body when she noticed his white T-shirt that looked identical to the one he'd worn years ago during their secret weekend in Scotland. Reading her thoughts, he said, "This is a new T shirt, if that is what made your eyes widen. Since then, I've bought quite a few of them and they all look the same."

The waiter placed a wine glass in front of Weylin and poured a bit, waiting for him to taste it. He raised the glass looking at the Petit Chablis, twirling the wine in its glass, and drinking it in two sips.

"Same old dry, light and citrusy taste that never disappoints," he said nodding to the waiter to fill Leandra's glass.

Clinking glasses, they looked at each other, smiling, before glancing at the menus again.

"You can't go wrong with whatever you order here."

"I already know what I want," said Leandra. "Seafood chowder, seared salmon, and chocolate mousse cake. I often skip dinner, but tonight I am in need of a substantive meal."

"I will have the same," said Weylin and moved his menu to the edge of the table. The waiter took their order.

"I suggest we buy breakfast at the English Market and pack a picnic again. You will be impressed with the selection of local foods and delicacies. Especially the bread."

"Well, why don't you buy breakfast and surprise me. We can have it on the terrace of my room," said Leandra wondering at the sudden she felt with her ex-lover. Being with him seemed as natural as breathing, as if they should never have parted, as if she had no other life outside of being with him. It felt as if all her longings gathered in a warm and cozy sense of belonging.

"What time does Madam want breakfast?"

"Nine. What will our next destination be? This feels like vacation and I'm afraid guilt will start to devour me."

"We'll drive to the Cliffs of Moher and stop in a couple of picturesque villages. And if this feels like vacation, let it feel so. Let's enjoy it fully…or as fully as we can."

They both burst into laughter, reading the same unspoken message between the lines. If they were still lovers, the experience would not only be full, but would be overflowing in every way.

The food arrived and the smells were tantalizing. By the time dessert was served, Leandra did not think she'd be able to eat another bite, but managed to eat half her mousse. Weylin finished it and insisted he pay for dinner, and she allowed him to do so. On the way back to their rooms he asked her if he should accompany her to her floor, but she thanked him saying it was not necessary.

"You can always call me if you feel afraid of the dark," he said flirtatiously.

"Stop it, Weylin! We are no longer what we were in this or in any past life, even though I find your offer tempting. 'Night." She pecked his cheek tenderly and took the stairs to her floor.

17

Leandra awoke suddenly, shivering. Daylight was streaming into the room as she had left the curtains partly open, not wanting to sleep in too late. She sat up in bed remembering a wisp of a dream in which a blond child was calling her from afar, 'Mommy, mommy, find me. You have come back to find me. I've waited so long to be found.' His tinkling and happy voice was still ringing in her head when she heard a knock on her door. She looked at her phone to check the time and it was quarter to nine.

She opened the door, not bothered that she was in her summer pajamas with dishevelled hair and puffy eyelids. She knew it was Weylin and a feeling of primordial familiarity with him erased any sense of embarrassment over her appearance.

"Good morning," he grinned, looking fresh in a long-sleeved white T-shirt and blue jeans. "Breakfast is ready. You just need to call room service and order coffee. I remembered you did not like coffee from plastic cups."

Leandra made the call and asked Weylin to wait for her on the terrace. She went to the bathroom, showered quickly, brushed her teeth and hair, and put her pajamas back on.

The terrace was washed in sunlight, but the air was crisp, and Leandra went back into the room and put on her long white sweater. Just as she was about to go back on the terrace, room service knocked with the coffee, and she directed the young woman who brought it to take it onto the terrace. Meanwhile she found money in her purse and tipped the smiling red-haired girl.

Having breakfast and sipping coffee with Weylin felt as if they were a happily married couple. As if reading her thoughts, he said, "I hadn't thought of you for a long time, even though our break-up was painful. I willed myself into forgetting you, I deleted our correspondence, all the beautiful stories we wrote for each other…I couldn't handle our affair any more…the fear of being discovered crippled and depleted me, but now that I'm divorced and our life paths crossed again, I feel it in my blood and bones that you and I belong together. My feelings are at odds with reality…you are married, and I don't wish to ruin anyone's marriage, but at the same time…words are failing me. Do you feel any of this?"

"I do, but this trip will end in a few days, and I'll go back to my life, and you will build a new one with someone who will awaken the most intense feelings in you. We'll forget each other, or at least partially. I hope you find another Jilleen in this life."

"You just uttered words you cannot possibly believe in. We'll never forget each other, and if we find any past-life evidence of us, it will mean we'll find each other again in another life. I have dated a couple of women since my divorce, but there was no magic in it. You and I had magic, and that energy is struggling to resurface, but we are pushing against it."

They ate and drank in silence, and smiled at each other.

"We should get going. How much time do you need?"

"Forty-five minutes. Meet you in the lobby", replied Leandra.

With windows open and wind in her hair, Leandra felt excitement and utter blitheness fill her soul. She felt young and at the beginning of life. Weylin drove whistling some old Irish tune and said he had no idea where that song came from. He only remembered hearing it in his childhood, but had no recollection of ever having memorized its melody.

On the way to the Cliffs of Moher, they stopped in Limerick for a couple of hours. Breathing in the brine-infused sea air, they had a lunch of mussels and hot bread on the terrace of a waterfront restaurant. Weylin again said how natural it felt to be with her, and how it should be like that always. Leandra changed the subject, refusing to look into the mirror of her feelings. She did not want to reconnect with him in fear of betraying Adrian again, and experiencing the agony of another heartbreak, but at the same time, she was aware they were bonded in inexplicable and mysterious ways, and perhaps there was futility of not acknowledging that bond. Perhaps there were divine forces or agents of fate that have brought them together again. She shook her head, not wishing to entertain such thoughts, and Weylin looked at her quizzically.

When they rose from the table, Leandra knocked over a glass, but caught it before it fell on the tiled floor. At the same time, Weylin reacted by grabbing Leandra's wrist in an attempt to help her steady the glass on the table. His touch sent a current of electricity through her and their eyes locked in recognition. Leandra blushed and left the terrace. Once they reached the car, the tension between them dissolved.

Before starting the car, Weylin offered Leandra a small box of chocolates and she opened it immediately.

"I shouldn't be feeling hungry right after lunch, but chocolate should not be resisted. Want one?"

As he had already started the car, she extended her hand and offered a chocolate to him, and he took it with his mouth. Feeling his mouth on her fingers sent another jolt of pleasurable shiver through her, and she began to feel panicky. Infidelity could be found in a myriad of gestures, thoughts, and feelings without the need to have sex to cross the line, she thought. Weylin did not seem to notice anything and focused on the road.

The traffic was busy, and it took them close to two hours to reach the cliffs. They purchased tickets and stepped on the stone walkway that seemed to usher them into the magic of the sunset. The view was spectacular: the ocean crashing against the shore, the water glistening under the kisses of the golden sun retreating to its celestial home, the cliffs towering over the water in defiance of time and change.

The wind was tousling Leandra's hair against her face, and she kept pushing the strands away from her eyes. As she raised her hand to tame her flying hair, the wind ripped off her scarf and it would have flown away had Weylin not caught it by both ends. He pulled the scarf back around Leandra's neck, and his move brought them face to face with each other. When he suddenly planted a kiss on her cheek, he said, "Don't take this the wrong way, I'm simply happy. I had not even noticed how sad I had been until I was able to compare it against this carefree feeling."

As if driven by a force outside herself, Leandra's hand trailed down Weylin's face. At the same moment, the wind howled and hissed, and the weather turned cloudy and bleak as if someone had flicked an invisible switch.

Weylin took Leandra's hand, and they ran toward the car feeling the whips of wind and drizzle against their backs. Giggling like two teenagers and breathless, they dropped onto their car seats, and took off their wet windbreakers.

"I suggest we spend the night in Doolin. It's a picturesque village not far from here. I haven't made any reservations, but can phone now. A while ago a friend mentioned staying at a B&B country house, and I just remembered it out of nowhere. I even recall the name of the place. How weird! Maybe it is a sign." He laughed shaking his head at the same time over another surreal moment.

"Sure. I just hope we finally uncover something related to why we embarked on this trip in the first place. So far, it has just been pleasant tourism, and I feel pangs of guilt gnawing at me and…"

Leandra did not finish her sentence when Weylin's phone beeped. He looked at the screen and read aloud a text message from Ariadne, "*You are getting closer...I feel it. I'm having difficulty breathing and keep thinking of you incessantly. Hugo is leaving in a couple of days, and I will join you. My Jacacia story astounded him.*"

"How's this for a synchronicity?" asked Weylin, showing the message to Leandra. She blanched and muttered she hoped Ariadne was right about them getting closer to some revelation, and would join them soon.

Weylin spent some time searching for the phone number of the country house recommended to him, and then made the phone call. Leandra listened to his conversation and was pleased to hear rooms were available as there had been cancellations.

As soon as Leandra approached the reception desk and locked eyes with a beautiful old woman wearing a long gray dress with a pink ruffled collar, she felt shivers of mystical anticipation run down her spine. The lady looked regal with her gray hair pinned up and her piercing blue eyes. Leandra's eyes were drawn to the beautiful dragonfly earrings the woman wore. The connection could not be overlooked; it was palpable.

"I have a lovely suite to give you. The view of the ocean is breathtaking. You are in luck as that booking was cancelled a few hours ago."

"We need two rooms," said Leandra with an almost apologetic tone.

"Oh, no problem. I do have two rooms, even though not quite as nice. Forgive my curiosity, are you here as tourists?"

"Not really...we are here trying to uncover some information...it's a strange story." Leandra sensed the woman's energy, and it instilled trust in her, and a feeling of comfort of the kind one experiences upon encountering a kindred spirit.

"I love strange stories. In fact, I collect them," said the woman.

Her smile made Leandra's heart flutter, and a knowing stirred deep within her telling her this inn was the beginning of their journey to their past life.

"Well then, I'd like to tell you the story - if you are willing to suspend disbelief."

Weylin was standing silently, fascinated by the unfolding of the conversation that left him feeling redundant.

"My granddaughter will replace me in an hour. Our small dining room is to the right. There is a round table in the window overlooking the garden. I'd like to invite you to have your dinner there. Our cook's culinary skills attract lots of visitors. I could join you after dinner for a glass of sherry, if your friend does not mind." She looked quizzically at Weylin.

"Of course not," exclaimed Weylin somewhat abashedly.

"By the way, my name's Jilleen," said the woman and proffered her hand.

Both Leandra and Weylin felt thunderstruck.

"A beautiful name," said Leandra hoarsely.

"It comes from a special book that has been kept in our family for many years. The name belonged to a distant ancestor. I will tell you about it later. Here are your keys. Enjoy your stay with us."

The house did not have an elevator and Weylin carried their luggage to the second floor. With excitement in her voice, Leandra told him how convinced she was they would finally uncover something significant. He could not help but agree, even though he warned her not to be overly optimistic in order to avoid disappointment.

In her room, Leandra unpacked her toiletries and her night gown, took a shower, and put on a light woollen dress, as the evening had turned chilly. She pulled her hair up in a messy bun, put on a touch of lipstick, and knocked on Weylin's door.

He opened it with a grin on his face.

"Remember the first time you knocked on my hotel room door in Barcelona? That moment is not only etched in my mind, heart, and soul, but also burned into my skin."

"Are you ready for dinner? And stop with your references to our past. I can't deal with the memories while also trying to find evidence of our previous existence here." Leandra's voice assumed a tinge of irritation.

"Can you deal with the fact that the bond between us is pulsating with renewed life?"

"No, I can't, and won't. I just can't…and you are making this hard for me."

She turned around and descended the stairs. He followed behind and passed by her in order to open the door to the dining room and let her through.

The table in the round window immediately caught their eye. The chairs were upholstered in light blue velvet, the wood inlaid with flowers and butterflies, obviously the work of an artisanal carpenter. The whole room was wallpapered in yellow with a discreet pattern of lavender coloured rose buds.

A young woman dressed in a long white shirt, called Léine in Ireland, under an open-sleeved green dress, a traditional Irish costume came smilingly to the table and recited the menu. Her smile had that sweetness of youth and naiveté, still untouched by life's hardships.

They ordered a platter of seafood and a bottle of white wine. Their conversation turned to discussing psychiatry and the potential use of Jacacia by Weylin's department.

"Isn't it amazing" Weylin said, "that so many people have had such different reactions to the drug? In his last email, Keith described the experiences of his patients and they ranged widely. Some claimed they had experienced blending with the cosmic consciousness, attaining knowledge that there was no death, or that death was another irrelevant piece of human existence. Other said they felt the ineffable "is-ness" of things when the experiencer knew the exact nature of matters, but could not put it into words. Keith said he had convincing evidence of patients overcoming anxiety and depression, and weaning themselves off drugs completely. I can't wait to start our experiments. Annette has begun to work furiously on the permits. By the way, she emailed me last night asking for an update of our gallivanting across Ireland."

"When I come back, I will discuss it with our department head and see if there is interest in conducting a limited study, too. I would absolutely ask for Keith's help. David would be an incredible asset, too," said Leandra.

Their conversation was interrupted when the food arrived. The scent wafting from the platter was intoxicating and they ate with relish.

"I do not remember when I felt so relaxed and content. It's as if…as if some circle has closed and my life is becoming whole and complete," said Weylin with a soft glitter in his eyes.

"Weylin, your life is not whole with me because I am still on the periphery of your life, where I will stay. I will be flying home in a few days, and you will move on toward new experiences, hopefully finding whatever it is you are still prospecting for. If it is true love, I hope you strike gold. As I've said before, I hope you find lasting happiness and peace."

"I struck gold in a past life, but fate interfered, just like in this one. What are my chances of finding another Jilleen or Leandra?"

"I can't answer your questions. I cannot talk about us because in my case, "us" is Adrian and I."

"I'm not so sure. We are here. Past lives and mystery connect us. We have not come here for nothing. But I won't talk about it anymore…at least not tonight." He laughed mischievously.

The waitress cleared their plates and a few minutes after brought an assortment of cakes, saying they were on the house. Leandra asked for the names and tried the chocolate flapjack first. The waitress also brought a carafe of sherry, saying her grandmother would join them soon.

Jilleen walked in just as they took their first sip of sherry. She had changed her dress and now wore a long black skirt with a long-sleeved lavender turtleneck and a string of pearls.

"May I?" she asked before joining them at the table. Leandra thought how Jillieen radiated nobility in her affect and speech.

Leandra offered her dessert, saying they were served much more than they could possibly eat after such a scrumptious and big dinner. Jilleen took a piece of moss pudding, saying it was always her favorite.

"Jilleen," she began, "I am spellbound by your earrings. They look so intricate and old, like a valuable piece of art. Are they heirlooms, by any chance?"

"Yes. We do not know how old they are, but I believe my grandmother told me they dated back to the 17th century. They belonged to a girl named Jilleen, who had been the daughter-in-law of one of our female ancestors who had been a chieftain's mother. All of that is written in a book that by some miracle has survived centuries. My grandfather always said the leather cover was of the highest possible quality, exceeding that of the modern leather binding practices."

Leandra and Weylin were rendered speechless by the revelation. Could it be just one mind-bending coincidence? Leandra could feel blood drain from her face, and her hand trembled when she picked up her glass. Jilleen was looking at her attentively before she removed one earring and placed it in Leandra's hand. The touch of gold burned Leandra's palm with a mysterious familiarity, and in a cracked voice she uttered, "These are my earrings," and then gasped in astonishment and turned crimson over her words.

She returned the earring to Jilleen, who put it back on. "Now, I am ready to hear your story," said Jilleen calmly, as if Leandra hadn't just uttered a most preposterous thing.

And the whole story of her affair with Weylin, her hypnotherapy sessions with David, her discoveries of her past lives in Ireland and Italy poured out of her, along with sobs and tears. She let Weylin tell Jilleen of his own experience with Jacacia, and of Ariadne and Annette's accounts of their own. When he mentioned how Kieran and Jilleen lost their son Conor, Weylin's chin trembled under the weight of the vivid memory.

The calm in Jilleen's eyes was replaced with disbelief in her widened pupils. She softly repeated the locales they had mentioned, Glenda's Bluff and White Circle, trying to jog her own memory.

"You must see my brother Fiann. He will lead you to the truth. He has special abilities…a second sight. He is a diviner, a seer, a poet, a shaman…someone with a deep reverence for our ancestors and the Celtic spirituality. He spent years researching our roots and chronicling our family's lineage. He has always said that a shaman must be able to connect to the ancestral wisdom, and walk the ancestral pathways in order to link them to the future. There is no divining of the future without the knowledge of one's roots."

"Tell us more about him and his abilities, please," asked Leandra transfixed.

"His second sight and shamanic abilities give him access to the otherworld from which he draws knowledge and inspiration for the poetry he writes. He claims to have encountered fairy folk from whom he has also gained knowledge, and that he has eaten of the nine hazels of poetic art, which according to legends grows by a stream in the otherworld. My brother has always been strange in the sense that he has always been enthralled by the Celtic mysticism. Once the town we grew up in witnessed his unusual powers, they started to believe him and seek his services. He became famous and our village attracted lots of visitors from wide and far."

"Where does he live?"

"On Valentia Island. He moved there twenty years ago. He has travelled and lived all over Ireland collecting writings about the Celtic spirituality and wisdom. He uncovered our ancestral roots dating back to the 15th century. He was the one who discovered the book I mentioned, the book that chronicles our family history. He found it in the attic of our parental home. But he will be happy to tell you about it, I'm sure."

"What does he use to divine? Cards, perhaps?" asked Weylin.

"No, he uses the well in his garden and also his cauldron. According to Celtic mythology, we are all born with three cauldrons. One of them is the cauldron of knowledge and one the cauldron of vocation and inspiration. He explained to me that the cauldron of vocation is often inverted, and some event of extreme joy or sorrow could upend it, thereby turning someone into a poet or artist. Does this make sense?"

Jilleen smiled and took a sip of sherry. Leandra and Weylin were drinking in her words, feeling their encounter was no coincidence, and that she was the one who would direct them to the mysterious truth.

Jilleen continued her story. "My brother became a poet after the woman he was madly in love with left him. She could no longer stand all the people knocking on their door seeking her husband's help, not to mention his prolonged absences gazing into the cauldron or the well behind the house. That was part of the reason. She'd also fallen in love with someone else, but that didn't work out. She did return to Fiann but he didn't want her back. He's never revealed all the details and has remained silent about it."

Jilleen stopped talking and nibbled on the dessert before continuing to talk about her brother. Her voice was laced with love and tenderness.

"My brother never charged anything for his healing services, saying that only fake seers and healers made money out of people's misery. But those who came to him left money and gifts anyway, grateful to have heard where to seek medicine for their ills, or to understand the reasons behind the devastating events in their lives."

"Do you think he will agree to see us and try to help us find what we are searching for?" asked Weylin.

"He has turned into a recluse and stopped receiving people several years ago. He is eighty-seven years old, and his health is failing him. He and I have always been close, and I have no doubt he'll agree to see you once I tell him your story. I will call him tomorrow morning and will let you know at breakfast what he has said."

She stood up to leave but stopped when Leandra asked her if she had always lived in Doolin.

"I spent most of my life in Dublin and taught literature at a college. My late husband was from Doolin, and he inherited this place from his parents. When we retired, we moved here, and our granddaughter joined us three years ago. My husband passed away last year. I plan to work here a bit longer until I either find a buyer for this inn, or convince my daughter and her husband to take over. I wish you a pleasant night." And with a nod of her head, she was gone.

Leandra turned to her companion. "I'm feeling so tired, Weylin. I need to sleep and stop trying to process all this information. I feel in my bones we are getting close to discovering something earth-shatteringly important, but I need to stop thinking about it because my brain cells are short-circuiting."

"I get it. I'm also ready to turn in."

Leandra barely touched the pillow when she felt enveloped in sweet slumber. As she was falling asleep, she inhaled the intoxicating scent of honeysuckle and wondered where it came from, because she had not smelled it in the room before. *The scent ushered her into a lovely dream in which she was walking barefoot on a mossy trail through an emerald green forest. What she noticed was the complete stillness and silence. Nothing moved, not even a leaf, and her footsteps did not make the slightest rustle. Her heart almost stopped beating when suddenly the silence was shattered by a child's cry. "Mother, mother, you have come to find me. Please, mother, find me! I have waited for so long for you and father to find me. It is time…it is time."*

Leandra followed the voice, feeling panic rise in her throat. The pain of having lost a child tore through her insides like a hurricane ripping her soul into pieces. The sharpness of her anguish made her feel as if she were suffocating or drowning. The air around her became hot, viscous, and unbreathable. The child's voice turned into sobbing before beginning to fade.

Leandra awoke with her lungs burning for air. Ice-cold fear was puncturing holes in her mind. The room was pitch black as she had drawn the heavy curtains to prevent light from streaming in. Now her panic grew as she sensed someone's presence in her room. She groped for her phone on the nightstand and almost dropped it on the floor. With shaking fingers she called Weylin, waking him up. She breathed laboriously and sobbed, unable to articulate her thoughts. The knock on the door made her realize it must have been Weylin hastening to help her. She found the flashlight on her phone, got up, and opened the door.

His face was contorted with worry and his pupils dilated with the question "What happened?"

"I…I had a nightmare. Conor was calling me…and … and it felt so real. I sensed someone in the room." She was gasping for air and looking frantically around her.

"It's ok, Leandra. It was just a dream."

Weylin put his arms around her and led her back to bed. He went to the bathroom and came back with a glass of water, which she drank in one long gulp. He helped her hold the glass as her hand was shaking.

It took her a few minutes to calm down and then she laughed, noticing that he had come dressed in his underwear and a white T-shirt. He smiled and said, "I had no time to even think of putting my jeans on. You're lucky I didn't run over naked or bump into another guest in the hallway. Now, let's try to get some sleep."

And he turned off the light and lay beside her, wrapping his arm around her, and threw one leg over her just as he had done in the past after they had made fiery love and relaxed into slumber. This time, however, there was nothing erotic about his proximity, only the warmth of a man wishing to shelter a frightened woman. The effect was instantaneous and close to miraculous. Leandra relaxed, turned on her right side and nestled her body into his embrace. Before she fell asleep, she heard him whisper, "It should always be like this."

She woke up with a slight headache, still wrapped in his embrace. She tenderly moved his arm and went to the bathroom to shower. She did not want them to be waking up at the same time in the same bed so she tried to be as quiet as possible.

When she came out dressed in a bathrobe with a towel wrapped around her wet hair, he was lying awake in bed looking at his phone.

She went to the window and opened the drapes, admiring the view of a lush garden, bursting with flowers and sunrays. On a small patio there were four white, wrought iron tables and chairs with red cushions. The chairs had a leaf and grapevine pattern and looked enchanting..

"You need to see the backyard. It is magical and I'm sure fairies live in it. I want to have coffee there. Let's meet in about 30 minutes. I have to dry my hair, ok? And thank you for helping me feel safe last night."

Weylin jumped out of the bed, smiled and said, "See you soon. I'll order breakfast for us and catch up on news while waiting. I won't need more than 20 minutes."

Leandra dried her hair and wished she could talk to Adrian and her daughters, but that was not possible due to the time difference. She looked at the crumpled bed sheets, incredulous that she had spent the night in Weylin's arms, and that it had felt like the most natural thing in the world. Their bodies had always fitted each other on a nano-level, as he had once said.

Just as she was about to leave the room, the phone rang. It was Jilleen wishing her good morning and informing her that her brother said he would consult a peregrine falcon, one of his ancestors who had been shapeshifting through centuries, and would then decide if he would receive them. Jilleen uttered all of this as if it was the most ordinary information, such as a comment on the weather. Leandra suppressed a chuckle of disbelief, and said she and Weylin would be in the garden.

They sat facing the sun as they sipped their coffee. Leandra took her sweater off as it was getting warm.

"We have been incredibly lucky with the weather. I thought we'd be driving in the rain all week. After all, Ireland is supposed to be rainy, isn't it?"

"Yes, it is, but we did luck out," said Weylin. "More coffee?"

"Yes, please. I still feel a bit shaken up by the dream. What if Jilleen and Kieran *did* have a son who died? I'm scared about finding out."

"We already know they had a son; you uncovered that during your hypnotherapy sessions with David, and I learned that on my Jacacia experience. We just need to find some physical evidence, such as his grave. Anyway, we'll find out whatever it is we have been destined to discover. And we will accept it for all it's worth, and see if there's anything left to uncover or do. I've always been rational and logical and I'm sure you have been, too. But now, I feel as if some higher force is guiding us, or manipulating us. There's no going back, but only toward what may be the final point in our fate together."

The door behind them opened and Jilleen stepped into the sunshine. "I have good news. My brother says he will receive you and reveal the knowledge you are seeking. His ancestor sent him a sign that your past is linked to a distant period in the history of Ireland, to a time of love, pain, and turbulence. He is looking forward to talking to you."

"How far is the island from here?" asked Leandra.

"Close to 4 hours by car and then a few minutes by ferry."

"I should book us rooms," said Weylin.

"No need for that," replied Jilleen. "My brother said you could stay with him. One part of his house is a wing that he had built ten years ago. It has a separate entrance, and a tourist agency manages it for rentals. Currently, it is empty, and you may use it. There are three rooms and you can have two of them."

"Excellent," said Weylin. "We will make sure we pay for our stay."

"I will ask the cook to prepare lunch and dinner for you to take. My brother is fond of certain foods, and it will give me pleasure to send some to him this way. We have not seen each other in a few months, but we do talk regularly."

"We'll go walk for a while," said Leandra.

"I suggest you visit Doolin Cave," suggested Jilleen. "It is quite famous."

The next couple of hours Leandra and Weylin spent admiring the stalactites in Doolin Cave and walking along the rocky shore. When they came back to their rooms, they found Jilleen's message that the packages with food were at the reception desk. They gave her a warm hug before they left, and promised to share with her their findings.

The next four hours passed quickly in light banter, during which they cast admiring glances at the landscape. Weylin teased her about their sleeping together the previous night by saying she had pretended to be shaken up by a nightmare only to lure him into her bed. He added he might use the same tactic. Leandra laughed, but told him about the recurring dream in which their son has been calling her, wanting to be found. She found the dream unsettling and was afraid of what they might uncover in connection with the lost child.

When they stopped at a restaurant for coffee, Leandra texted Adrian and her daughters. They were all fine and busy with their lives and said they missed her. She was grateful that Adrian did not ask any questions about her and Weylin, as he still believed Ariadne was travelling with them.

The ferry to the island left Reenard Point fifteen minutes after their arrival. The ride was choppy and windy, but it only lasted a few minutes. As soon as they stepped on land, they walked to the Town Clock building where a friendly local resident told them about the history of that lovely red landmark. Before they had a chance to interrupt the talkative stranger and ask him about the way to Fiann's house, he abruptly took leave, saying his wife was waiting for him for dinner, and he was not allowed to be late.

She and Weylin looked around admiring the breathtaking ocean and mountain views. The whole island was gilded with the warmth of sunset, and Leandra felt air around her turn into fairy dust. She looked at Weylin with eyes sparkling with delectable anticipation of what was to come. At the same time, they both began to walk toward the big white hotel called Royal Island, and inquired about Fiann's address with a young man working at the reception desk. They gave him the slip of paper with the address they had received from Jilleen before they left. Cheerfully, the young man replied that everyone knew Fiann, and that he used to be the biggest tourist attraction around until he stopped receiving visitors. The house was a five-minute walk from the hotel and would be easily recognisable by its heavy pale-yellow door with a large blue dragonfly-shaped brass knocker. The house itself was big and built from slate stone.

When they knocked on the door, it opened almost immediately, as if someone had been standing behind it. The man in the doorframe looked much younger than they had expected. He was tall and slim, with a shoulder long grey hair tied in a ponytail. His eyes were startlingly blue, and almost translucent. His nose was aquiline and there was an unexpected elegance about his features and his narrow face. He was dressed in black jeans and a black T-shirt. He smiled widely when he saw them and asked them to come in.

"I no longer receive guests, but after my sister told me your story I felt a flutter in my chest, a flutter of the kind that tells me I am about to uncover some vital piece of knowledge."

"We also hope to find out if there is any truth, or any real foundation to the bizarre experiences both Weylin and I have had," said Leandra.

"Please make yourself at home. I will first show you your rooms. My next guests will arrive in a week, but there is an agency that takes care of that. I hardly ever meet anyone and trust the agents to organize the cleaning of the rooms and make regular deposits of my earnings. They charge a pretty penny in commission, but they spare me the hassle of dealing with tourists."

"Oh, I don't think we will stay that long," replied Leandra. "We hope that two days is enough time to find out …whatever it is we need to learn.

"It was not a coincidence. You have come here because there is a circle of knowledge that needs completing. I still do not know what it is, but an inner voice is telling me that something important will be uncovered. I will let you settle in your rooms, and then we can talk. I'm afraid I'm not such a great host as there is not much in the way of dinner."

"Oh don't worry about that," said Weylin. "I would like to invite you to dinner at the hotel. I looked up their menu while we waited at reception and it is quite tantalizing. And your sister packed a box of delicacies for you, by the way. Here it is."

"In that case, I will decline the offer for dinner, but suggest you eat first and then we'll enjoy some tea and talk. You will find me in the room behind the green door," said Fiann.

Dinner was most delectable. Seafood chowder, pan-fried prawns and mushrooms served with rocket salad and soda bread, and raspberry tart for dessert. After the scrumptious meal and three glasses of wine, Leandra began to feel sleepy, but as soon as she re-entered Fiann's house her alertness was restored.

Fiann was sitting in a large red armchair holding a leather-bound book on his lap. The book looked ancient, and its cover was full of cracks. He asked them to sit down and offered them tea.

"Fiann," started Leandra. "Your sister told us a bit about you and your past. I…I feel as if I know you, or should know you …words have been failing me after so many strange experiences. There is a connection - I know there is one…" Leandra sighed deeply, unable to explain her feelings. Fiann smiled encouragingly and, caressing the book on his lap, began to talk.

"I do not have much life left in me. Soon, the time will come for me to shape shift or transmigrate. I see the puzzled look in your eyes. I believe, as my ancestors believed, that our souls transmigrate and turn into animals, birds, or fish until the time we can be human again. I have always been different from other people. I have always felt I have walked the pathways of two worlds, this one and the underworld. I am a seer and a shaman connected to the ancient wisdom. Ever since I was a child, I have felt a deep connection to something running parallel to our ordinary lives. When I was young, I dreamt I had descended into the underworld, reached a shining fountain out of which five streams were flowing. Nine hazel trees grew there, dropping their nuts into the fountain. I ate of the nuts, and when I woke up, I felt I was infused with divine poetic inspiration. I wrote my first poem that day. Then I started to encounter fairies and they imparted knowledge to me…mostly the knowledge as to where to find cures for the people in our village. I did not dare reveal much of my experience to my parents and family for fear they would consider me deranged. I hope you do not see me as a raving lunatic." Fiann smiled, looking at Leandra with a penetrating gaze, as if trying to bore into her soul.

"But are you feeling ill, or do you have a diagnosis that makes you believe you will die soon? Please explain," asked

Leandra, ignoring his revelations about fairies and the underworld in which he believed.

"My sister and I have always been extremely connected. She probably did not tell you this, but two weeks ago she called me to say she saw my Silver One. According to the Celtic mythology it is our spirit, or our double that walks parallel to us. The fact that she saw my double is a presager of my death. But death is just as natural as birth, a simple closing of one circle. It holds no fear for me."

Leandra did not know what to say as the strangeness of the entire experience made her feel she was the one straddling both reality and some fantasy world. To change the subject she pointed at a book among a few that lay scattered on the coffee table and asked, "That blue book with a fairy on the cover looks like a poetry book. Are you the author, by any chance?" she asked.

"Yes. As a matter of fact, I've just received a dozen copies today from my publisher. I did not even have a chance to tell my sister that I finally decided to submit my poems to a publisher. They were accepted and here they are." Fiann pointed to a box on the bottom shelf of his bookshelves adding, "This one I planned to mail to my sister as a surprise."

"May I see it?"

"Of course."

Fiann handed the book to Leandra and she opened it at random. Not understanding the sudden compulsion, she read aloud the poem on the page she opened.

A Prayer to the Fae
I close my eyes and see your smiling faces peering back at me,
From that glad place that only childish eyes can see.
In the twilight I can see your flickering flames like candles in the trees,

As I gaze upon your flitting shadows, I can hear your laughter in the breeze.
Joyful sprites whose gaiety can lighten the darkest days and nights.
Underneath the smiling moon I fondly gaze upon your joyous lights.
Help me face this tiresome world with hopeful, childlike trust.
Help me keep my heart alive to love, while doing all I must.
Show me how to face each day anew with innocence and mirth.
Let me see each soul around me with a knowing of their fragile worth.
Beauty is so soon besmirched by arrogance and greed,
Let them rest with you among the rivers guardian reeds.
When my trials are over and my exile in this cold harsh world is done,
Let me fly away with you beyond the setting sun.
When my time on earth is done, I nevermore will roam.
For I will once again return to that sweet western isle I once called home.

"Ah, how lovely. And that book you are holding? It looks so old," asked Leandra.

"It is so old that I am afraid it will disintegrate to dust any day now. It dates back to the 17th century."

Leandra looked at Weylin and his incredulous gaze revealed the thought behind it. She said to him, "You must also be thinking that this could be the book Jilleen's father kept as a diary, aren't you?"

Weylin stuttered when he replied, "Precisely my thought. If that is the book, we have uncovered maybe the biggest piece of the puzzle and evidence."

"Now tell me in detail what brought you here," said Fiann, ignoring their exchange about the book.

Leandra and Weylin alternated telling their story, not omitting their affair and the painful fallout after the break-up. Fiann was all ears when they told him about the hypnotherapy and Jacacia sessions.

"Have all of those who underwent the psychedelic experiment accessed their past lives?" asked Fiann with palpable curiosity.

"No," answered Weylin. "From the researchers' report, it seems only a small number of subjects claimed to have accessed their past lives, and one person said she visited a future life. Most of the accounts seem to describe the experience as one where all inner conflicts disappeared, and the subjects no longer viewed themselves as separate from their surroundings, but as blended with them. One of the subjects, a university professor of philosophy who had been suffering from a crippling depression, described his experience as a fusion of the observer and the observed, the experiencer and the experience, the knower and the knowing. He said he felt like awareness itself and part of the luminous life he could see flowing within the rocks, flowers, and animals. He also mentioned he had no sense of the past, only of the present moment. Does this make sense to you?"

"Absolutely. Without any chemical stimulation, my shamanic trance gives me similar experiences."

"My boss has begun applying for permissions to conduct the same experiment in our hospital after we received this report showing evidence of significant improvements in the patients' condition after a repeated Jacacia ingestion," added Weylin. "But please, tell us about the book you are holding. My palms are sweating from anxiety that it might be the same book I saw during my Jacacia-induced trip."

Fiann poured all three of them more tea before beginning to relate the history of the old book.

"I was fourteen when I found the book in a wooden crate in our home attic. The night before I began the search for it, I was sitting outside our house watching the moon. The moon and the stars could hold me spellbound for hours on end. My trance was interrupted by a sound — I thought it was the rustle of leaves, but the night was windless. I heard a voice, more of a whisper that turned into giggles, and I knew it was one of the fae I had kept encountering.

'There's a secret waiting to be uncovered. A secret spanning lifetimes,' she said. 'You, my boy, are part of the circle, one of many circles in the lives of men and women born and reborn in this dimension. There's a purpose that must be unveiled.'

"What secret? Tell me, guide me towards it." I implored the fairy. I also begged her to show herself to me, but she wouldn't.

"The secret lies in the book locked in the wooden chest in the attic. The book is swathed in three oilcloths. You need to read it and hold it in your possession because it cradles the answer to a future question."

"What question?" I asked, but she was already gone.

I went into the house. My parents, my sister, and my grandmother, who lived with us, were already asleep. I took a lamp with me and climbed the ladder that led to the attic. It took all my strength to push the hatch up and climb into the attic. Once inside, I could stand up straight because the ceiling was tall enough to accommodate my height. The attic was full of dust and cobwebs because no one used it, except to store old and broken furniture. In the far corner stood a large wooden chest, made from heavy and highly polished burgundy colored wood. It looked expensive and was fashioned with artisanal craftsmanship. I tried to lift the heavy lid, but it would not budge. Beads of sweat began to run down my face from effort. Just when I thought I would have to give up and ask my father to help me open it, there was a tiny scraping sound and I pushed the lid with all my might. It creaked some more as it gave way. When I lifted the lid, a cloud of dust flew in my face, blinding me momentarily and making me cough. I shone the light inside the chest and the first thing I saw was a white dress embroidered with blue dragonflies. Although it was not really white. What I want to say is that it must have been white before time yellowed it and poked holes in it. I did not dare touch it in fear it would crumble to dust in my hands."

Fiann stopped talking, eying Leandra with worry. "You've paled. Do you want to go to bed? You must be exhausted."

"Fiann, the dress you described…Ariadne, Weylin's patient who participated in the Jacacia experiment, described that dress as the one Jilleen had given her as a gift. It was the dress Ariadne, whose name was Ailionora in that life, wore the night she died while waiting for her fiancé in the White Circle. I am shaking at the thought that we will find the evidence we came to seek. And what do we do then?" Leandra looked as bewildered as a little girl lost in a huge, dark forest.

"Worrying about the future is futile. You'll discover what you are meant to discover, and life will unfold itself afterward the way it was meant to unfold. Trust the flow," replied Fiann.

"Please go on with your story," Weylin asked Fiann while handing a glass of water to Leandra.

Leandra nodded to Fiann, indicating she, too, wanted to hear the rest of the story, and he continued: "I rummaged in the space under the dress and immediately saw a square package wrapped in oilskins. I carefully unwrapped it and even more carefully opened it while my pulse quickened and my heart raced. I knew I'd discovered something of great importance. I closed my eyes and let my fingers gently trail over the rough leathery surface. The book emanated the energy of my ancestors. At that moment, I also knew beyond any doubt that I was born to be a druid, someone who is aware of the worlds, both visible and invisible. I could feel the turmoil, the pain and sorrow of loss ooze out of the pages without even reading the book. My soul shivered in anticipation, and my hands trembled trying to open it. At the same time, images, which I later recognized in the descriptions found in the book, flashed through my brain, surfacing from the deep recesses of my shamanic memory. Yes, at age fourteen I knew that my fate was one of a druid, and a shaman, and that my life path was determined."

Leandra looked at Weylin and noticed the darkness of his wide-open pupils. He returned her gaze and reached over to squeeze her hand briefly. She smiled wanly at him.

"On page one was a short introduction written by the author of the book. His name was Bartley O'Farrell, and he was a priest in the village called Ciorcal Bàn Sráidbhaile, the White Circle Village. He gave a vivid description of the place—let me read a couple of sentences to you."

Fiann pulled out a pair of white cotton gloves from the coffee table drawer, put them on, and opened the book as tenderly as one might touch a rose bud. Then he took the magnifying glass the top of a book pile on the table, and began to read.

'*In his endless mercy, God bestowed upon us this fertile land, forests teeming with beasts and a river in which fish thrive. The meadows in their glorious beauty soothe the weary eye and give birth to herbs that restore our health. And in its splendour, our White Circle never ceases to inspire awe in the eye of the beholder, while Glenda's Bluff bedazzles with its majestic beauty and warns visitors of the dangers of stepping too close to the edge and falling to their death in the eternally frothing sea...*'

"Glenda's Bluff?" said Leandra in a shaky voice.

"Yes, that's right," replied Fiann.

Fiann continued reading from the book and when Jilleen's name was mentioned as the indescribable blessing in her father's life, Leandra began to sob.

"This is the book, Weylin," she said, choked up by tears. It's the book you as Kieran took from Jilleen's father when you found him dead. How did it end up in Fiann's parents' house?" She turned to Fiann, her eyes sparkling with the power of her question.

"First of all, I can tell you that what is written in this book corroborates, for the most part, the information you gathered during your hypnotherapy and psychedelic experiences. The book chronicles Jilleen's trial as a witch, her disappearance from the village and her death. Her father wrote a long chapter about the loss of her second child and her ensuing madness. Later in the book, there is mention about Jilleen and Kieran's love affair —I will let you read the account yourselves."

"But how did your family get that book?" asked Weylin.

"I was about to tell you that, but I digressed. This may sound like a fairy tale to you, but this is what my grandmother told me the day I brought the book downstairs.

"She made tea and I helped her carry the cups to the table because she suffered from hand tremor that would only subside once I would hold her hands in mine for a few minutes. She was aware of the special healing energy I possessed.

"She said, 'Fiann, I have been the keeper of that book and I was going to pass it down to your mother, my daughter, but I shall give it to you now. The book tells a strange story of our origin. It was written by a priest before it was given to our ancestor Léan O'Fenelon, wife of the chieftain Conaire O'Fenelon and mother of Aidan O'Fenelon, who succeeded his father as the chieftain. The priest's daughter Jilleen was married to Aidan and the poor girl was murdered. Her father's heart broke and he stopped writing this diary in mid-sentence. A man by the name of

Kieran brought the book to Léan in hope that it would be safer in the hands of a powerful chieftain family, and she guarded it, making sure it was passed down from one generation to the next. Until now, it was mostly the female descendants who kept it safe, but because you, my child, are special, I am giving the book to you for safekeeping. It is important to stay connected in spirit with our ancestors, and this book is a link to our past.'"

They fell silent, letting Fiann's words wash over them. "What will happen to the book after you?" asked Leandra.

"I'll give it to my sister – she can decide if it'll go to her daughter or her granddaughter. I've already spoken with her about it – she wants to give it to a museum. She can make that decision.

"While you are here, you can read the book; however, you need to wear gloves and be very careful with the pages. The parchment is old and may tear. Miraculously, the handwriting is still quite legible except in a few places, so you can expect gaps in the narrative. Some of the words are smeared, but most of the writing has been preserved quite well."

Fiann stood up and handed the book to Leandra, who quivered ever so slightly upon taking it and cradling it against her. Her sigh was deep and pain-filled as she put her hand on her forehead. "This is getting to be too much. I need to rest…I…I am having difficulty processing all of this..."

Weylin stood up and extended his hand toward Leandra and she grabbed it to get up. She approached Fiann, who had also risen, and gave him a goodnight hug, thanking him for his hospitality. He said he would like to have lunch with them in his garden the next day. They readily accepted and said they would spend the morning leafing through the book. Fiann bid them good night and Weylin and Leandra left the room.

18

Leandra took the book to her room, but did not want to read it without Weylin. The agreement was to go through it in the morning in some quiet place.

Before she had closed the door to her room, Weylin hugged her, whispering to her not to worry and to keep her mind open. It seemed to her their hug lasted longer than expected, and she abruptly extricated herself from his arms because she sensed an involuntary reaction in her body - recognizing his touch and welcoming it. Reflexively, desire for him had seized her and surprised her.

He smiled, and in his smile, she saw that he felt her reaction. Flustered and embarrassed, she had rushed into her room and closed the door.

Alone now, she barely made it to bed when exhaustion overwhelmed her and she fell into a deep sleep. The dream into which she stepped was in no way distinguishable from reality in its vividness.

She was Jilleen, walking through the fields under a radiant sun. Summer pulsated and sang in her soul, and nature spoke to her. She reached a river that looked and felt so familiar. A voice whispered it was the same river into which she had been thrown when she was accused of witchery.

On both banks, the river was flanked by trees and shrubs. Trees were sacred to Jilleen and her ancestors. They were repositories of her people's collective memories, many of them painful remembrances of wars that left wasteland and fragmented souls behind. She could hear wailings, lamentations, but also verses of joy and celebration of life reverberating from the trees and the earth beneath them. Landscapes also had memory.

She did not know where her gift of communion with trees had sprung from, but she was grateful to be so in tune with Mother Nature.

She touched woodbine and the pliant shrub gave off an ambrosial fragrance, awakening memories of her and Kieran's lovemaking underneath this shrub. She kissed the blossoms on an apple tree and thought she heard the happy giggles of the tree's spirit bubble forth from its low-sweeping boughs. Then she touched a blackthorn and felt its desire to wander the world, and not be doomed to the spot by the river. When she wrapped her arms around a willow, she felt this sacred tree pour poetry from its bark into her heart, making it leap in joy. Touching the slender hazel, her eyes filled with tears, listening to the whispers telling her an ancient tale of a woman dying of heartbreak after her husband perished in battle.

She left the riverbank and went back into the fields, feeling intoxicated by the summer heat and the buzzing of insects. In front of her appeared a large stone with a flat surface and she stepped on it feeling blithe and carefree. She raised her arms toward the sun. Dragonflies flitted all around her in celebration of life. She felt inspired by the prospect of discovering something important. She looked around her expecting to see a familiar landmark and was surprised that it was not in her field of vision. She did not even know what it was she was seeking with her eyes, when out of the blue, the stone beneath her began to shriek, making her blood freeze in terror. She stepped off of it, wanting to run away, but some force held her captive.

'You are in the White Circle, but the stones have vanished. She destroyed them in rage and vengeance, severing the thread of the sacred ancestral memory' shrieked the stone, and Jilleen remembered that she used to come to the Circle to enjoy moments of solitude among the white stones. Then she also remembered in horror that near the Circle, on Glenda's Bluff, where she had stood talking to Kieran, Jane, who was also in love

with him and jealous of her, had pushed her off the cliff - and killed her.

The stone kept shrieking and in its words, she heard her and Kieran's names. She also heard something about a curse that must be lifted so that the darkness of oblivion could be dispersed and the holes in the tapestry of memory stitched. She understood that she was getting closer to the answer about her own past and her future, and that she was one of the few fortunate souls to be given the gift of such revelations.

She woke up startled, but remembering the dream in its entirety. She got up, found her phone and in the notes app wrote down what she remembered of the scenery she saw in her dream, hoping it would help her find the place where the White Circle had once stood.

It was seven thirty and she was eager to open the book and delve into its secrets. She texted Weylin to see if he was awake but there was no reply.

She quickly showered and dressed and went out. She spent an hour walking, breathing in the sea air and admiring the views. It was a sunny, but cool morning, and Leandra was grateful for a thick sweater in which she had wrapped herself. She ended her walk at a quaint town café where she bought coffee and pastries.

On her way back to Fiann's house, she found Weylin's message letting her know he was awake and waiting for her.

She answered that she was on the way back with breakfast. He wrote back immediately saying he was dying for a cup of coffee, and suggested they eat in his room as it had a sunny corner with a table for two.

Leandra brought the book into Weylin's room. He still looked sleepy and had dark circles under his eyes.

"Did you sleep well?" she asked.

"I had strange dreams and kept waking up. The strangest part was dreaming about talking stones…imagine. I remember reading about them in a book of Celtic mythology when I was a teenager, but to dream about it is more than bizarre. We must be getting closer to the knowledge we came here for."

"I had never heard of the talking stones before until last night when I also had a dream about stepping on one that shrieked its truth about Jilleen and Kieran, a curse that had to be lifted, and the answers about my past and my future. I took some notes upon waking with the hope that they would help us find the place where the White Circle had once stood," said Leandra.

"You're talking about it now as if it were the most normal thing. What we both considered insanely ludicrous we now accept as a parallel reality, it seems," said Weylin.

"My head is still spinning, but I'm no longer reacting to the events with utter incredulity, denying their possibility. We'll get to the bottom of this and go back to our normal reality. We've come too far to abandon it now. Let's see what's in the book. We have about three hours before meeting with Fiann," said Leandra.

With her hand slightly trembling, she opened the book and turned to page one. The first few pages showed a handwriting that looked like an undecipherable scrawl. Intuitively, she ran her hand across the page and shivered as if touched by a mysterious energy.

"Why that reaction, Leandra? Did you feel something when you touched that page?" asked Weylin.

"A jolt of electricity just went through me, but nothing unpleasant, like a surge of something warm and familiar…so love-like."

Leandra flipped through the first few hand-written pages and moved her chair closer to Weylin's so that they could read together. While looking at the writing, their arms and knees touched, and Leandra felt wrapped up in cotton-like soft coziness and familiarity.

She began to read aloud from the book and her heart quivered with fondness for the man whose entries from centuries ago she was reading. The man adored his daughter Jilleen, but was also concerned for the safety of a child who ran wild, saw God in every breath of wind, in every leaf, flower and animal. She grew up into a beautiful young woman, who enjoyed helping others through her knowledge of medicinal herbs, and who seemed to be a daughter of some pagan deity.

As a priest whose mission was to ensure that the Church doctrine was followed, he felt that Jilleen had embodied the spirit of the druids, fairies and other creatures that many of the superstitious villagers still believed in.

Jilleen's father chronicled in detail her wedding to the chieftain, mentioning that marriage had not changed his little girl. He was surprised her husband allowed her to preserve her freedom and roam the fields and meadows, and to spend time alone in the White Circle, where, according to gossip, she was seen communing with a wolf.

When she was accused of witchery and thrown off the village bridge, he spent hours kneeling and praying to God to bring his daughter back and God heard his prayers. When she miraculously reappeared, her husband had ordered many men and women killed, looking for the one who had accused his wife wrongfully of witchery while he was away.

As always, life returned to its regular rhythm after it was shattered by turbulent times. He was looking forward to becoming a grandfather again, but not only did his grandson die during birth, but also Jilleen almost followed him. Her grief became his grief. There was nothing he could do or say to comfort her.

Any mention of the word *God* would make her flinch and shudder, as if in revulsion. Her spirit was so weakened by the loss that he was afraid madness would completely overtake her mind.

Miraculously, she began to recover and leave her house gradually to romp in the fields again. She still visited her son Conor's grave often, and wept inconsolably at his tombstone, but he dared hope she had escaped the clutches of madness.

And then, his world shattered. His daughter, his very life, was found dead at the bottom of Glenda's Bluff. The last paragraph in his entry had several inkblots. The few legible words revealed that he was aware he was dying of a broken heart, and prayed to God to take him so that he could reunite with his only child and his late wife.

Leandra left the book open, went to the window, and gulped in fresh air. She felt she was suffocating with pain. From somewhere deep within her, knowledge that once upon a time, the man who wrote that diary had been her loving father constricted her throat and chest.

Weylin brought her a glass of water and she managed to take a few sips. She cried, placing her head on his chest. He caressed her hair gently, whispering that he also felt he had known him.

"It is almost time to meet Fiann," said Weylin.

"I need to read the next chapter. I must know more…what happened?" said Leandra going back to the table, clearing her throat, and continuing to read aloud.

She sat in the chair while Weylin lay on the bed listening to her voice as if transfixed.

19

My name is Léan O'Fenelon. I am the wife of the former chieftain Conaire O'Fenelon and mother of Aidan O'Fenelon, who succeeded his father, my husband, as chieftain after my husband suffered a grave wound in battle.

On this day of July 17, 1644, I am writing for the first time in the book our neighbor Kieran brought to me asking me to protect it from the ravages of time. He chose me as the protector of the book and the memories of our place, because he knew I could read and write quite well, thanks to my daughter-in-law Jilleen, who taught me the skill.

To be able to read and write was seen by many people as spell craft, and I had shared that belief. My daughter-in-law, however, gave me the worlds of fairy magic by teaching me these divine skills.

Kieran was haggard and he looked unwell. A dark foreboding gnawed at my soul upon seeing him. I feared his days on earth were numbered, and God would soon call him to his heavenly abode.

"If this book is destroyed, no one will ever know that we existed."

"Are you certain I should be its keeper, Kieran?"

"You are the only person I know who writes as well as our priest, Jilleen's father, had. You and I are also some of the few folk left who remember our past, who recall the magnificence of the White Circle. I know not why it is that not everyone recalls what we used to have. How could they have forgotten the Beltane celebrations we held among the stones?

When the White Circle vanished as if it had never existed, it began to fade from our collective memory. Even your own son seems to have no recollection of it, although it was in the White Circle he had asked Jilleen to marry him.

"How do you know that, Kieran?"

"Jilleen told me..."

He blushed and stopped talking, realizing he had said too much, for my daughter-in-law would have had no reason to confide that in him. But I knew she must have said much more to him, for Jilleen loved him. It was time for me to reveal my secrets to him, for time was running out, and I felt we were all slipping away into the oblivion of history, or into the charcoal blackness of the curse many believed Ailionora had cast upon us before she disappeared. I always had difficulty believing she would have wished us harm, for she was one of the kindest souls I had ever met.

"Kieran, firstly, I vow to keep the book well protected to the best of my ability. I shall try to add entries to it in hope our existence is not completely erased, but I fear my success may be short-lived. And yes, I am aware that most people have forgotten about the White Circle and I know the answer why.

Alionora's grandmother Etain imparted some of her knowledge to me before she died. She told me about the tradition of high druidesses in her family, about the tragic death of her daughter, and Ailionora's special powers that she developed after her initiation into the art. She confided other secrets in me, and they will die with me. Etain's powers were even greater than those Ailionora possessed, but both had to hide them.

Etain told me one evening that she had a premonition that something horrible would happen to Ailionora in the White Circle. Etain saw visions of blood in her dream, and tried to fend off the evil that had befallen Ailionora by shape-shifting into a hawk, and attacking the demons that had pounced on her granddaughter. But she knew she could not save her, and she also had no heart to share her premonition with her, but tried to warn her indirectly of the dangers. In her dream, she saw that the men who attacked Ailionora violated, both, her body and soul, provoking thus her fury, and making her use her one-time power, a power capable of causing great ruin.

I believe Etain's dream came true, and it was Ailionora who destroyed the White Circle and cursed us. Not only do I believe in that, I feel it. Perhaps the rape made her feel too ashamed of having lost her virginity and she cursed us with forgetting the events, but whatever higher power heard her and obeyed her, must have also expanded the circle of forgetfulness to encompass more than the event of her rape. I believe this is what happened because my son's friend Egerton and his suite arrived the day after the Circle was destroyed, and spent a few days with us. He told us he had come to marry Ailionora and was frantically looking everywhere for her.

He told me he and Ailionora had communicated through dreams and thoughts during the time they had not seen each other, and that she was ready to leave her home and go to England with him as his bride. Seeing him in so much distress, I told him about Etain's premonition and dreams that presaged the fate that would befall her granddaughter. His eyes widened and his nostrils flared up in rage. He believed what I told him even though I had said it was just my supposition based on what Etain had confided in me.

After learning what he considered to be the truth, he and his men went in search of the rapists. Their search lasted for a fortnight, and then one morning, by sheer chance, as Egerton told Aidan and me, they stopped at an inn, tired and hungry. As they dismounted, a stable boy appeared leading a horse. From the saddlebags, a piece of white silk embroidered with blue dragonflies was protruding and it caught Egerton's eye. He seemed to remember how much Ailionora had admired the dress with dragonflies Jilleen wore while Egerton was visiting us on

Aidan and Jilleen's wedding. Led by an inner voice, he stopped the boy, opened the bag, and pulled the dress out. Then he looked at the horse admiring the magnificent white stallion, and wondered who owned such a prized animal.

The stable boy turned white with fear and began to stutter when Egerton asked whose horse it was. The boy muttered a name, mentioning the green breeches the owner was wearing. Egerton went into the inn and spotted a large man with dark hair, dressed in a brown jacket and green breeches. The man was drinking ale and talking to the girl serving him. He was promising her a beautiful white dress if she gave him a kiss. The girl laughed coquettishly asking him whose dress he had stolen. He said it had belonged to a wild but bonnie lass who no longer needed it.

Egerton's blood roiled. All of a sudden, he felt the hatred of the English toward the Irish course through his veins, and he wanted to kill the man on the spot, but knew he had to preserve his calm. He gave a sign to his men, and they pounced on the man, grabbed him by the limbs and dragged him outside.

Everything happened too fast for any of the local people to react. They threw the man on his horse, tied him, mounted their horses, and took him into a nearby forest. Egerton did not tell me what means of torture they employed to get the man to talk, but they found out what had happened. The man talked about fire bolts tumbling down from the skies and killing his mates. He talked about the girl twirling in the moonlight and praying to some demonic power. Her prayer sounded like a curse that unleashed supernatural powers.

He heard a plea in her words asking for her shame to be erased and forgotten. He admitted to the rape of Ailionora, saying they were drunk. He believed that Ailionora's wrath and shame over losing her virginity made her destroy the White Circle, as he witnessed the stones tumble down to dust. He broke down and cried, begging for mercy, but Egerton killed him slowly, making him suffer until the man drew his last breath. I never asked what they did with the body, and I never had reason to doubt that Ailionora destroyed the White Circle. My heart wept for her and her fate.

Egerton returned Jilleen's dress to me as he could not bear to keep it as a reminder of Ailionora's tragic death. I will never forget the wild look in his eyes, the look of pain mixed with rage. I never heard from him again.'

Kieran's face turned even whiter upon hearing the story. He then begged me to give Jillian's dress to him and began to stutter, struggling to find an explanation for such a bizarre request. But I knew more than he suspected, and decided to reveal that last secret. He looked so gaunt and drained of life that I feared he would not live long, and I wanted him to know.

"Kieran, I shall give you the dress, for Jilleen loved you more than she loved my son. You are looking at me with fear and astonishment in your eyes, but there is nothing left to fear. I have never breathed a word of that knowledge to anyone. I could not bring such shame upon my own son and his house."

"How…how did you know?"

And Kieran broke down before my very eyes. His body shivered and his mouth twitched. Again, I sensed there was not much life left in him.

"When Jilleen came back home miraculously after we had all thought she had drowned in the river as punishment for her witchery, I expected her to stay home and stop roaming around like a wild beast. I was not happy when Aidan chose such a queer girl for his wife, but I could not do anything. He was smitten by her. I tried to stay cold toward her, but she thawed my heart with her genuine warmth and love. And not only that! She was the one who taught me to read and write, and that was the gift against which few gifts could measure.

When we heard she had been accused of witchery and thrown off the bridge, my heart broke. I knew that upon his return from England my son would search high and low to find his wife, and he would start killing mercilessly. Jilleen had a soothing effect on his temper that could flare up without any warning.

When she returned, I was overjoyed that my son had his wife back, and especially that my grandson Fiann was not motherless. Jilleen was a mother full of tenderness who would spend hours on end with Fiann singing to him, telling him stories, and teaching him kindness toward all creatures.

When she returned by God's miraculous grace, I expected her to stop disappearing into the wild, and she stayed home for a few weeks. One day, I noticed a strange light and longing in her eyes, and she began leaving the house again. I could not understand what it was that was calling her away from her duties as a mother and wife. When I asked her, she said it was the owl that she had saved while being held captive in the woods. She must have told you the story of her captivity and how the inquisitor who had saved her from the mob that wanted her death, kept her captive in his friends' cabin in the woods."

"Yes, Jilleen told me the story of her ordeal! Aidan was never able to find the inquisitor, for he would have killed him."

"One day, when Jilleen said she would ride out to the lake, I surreptitiously rode behind her. That is when I saw the two of you making love on the rocks. I was aghast at first, and my first thought was to go back home and tell my son what treacherous snake he had married, a snake that deserved being stoned to death. But I stayed, watching you - and I was transfixed. Your lovemaking was like a dance of two bodies and souls coiled in rapturous love. I felt envious for never having known such passion, or such sin and devilry. I had only known brief moments of copulation with my husband and believed there was no more that happened between a man and a woman.

When the storm suddenly split the sky, I saw you climbing the hill and fighting the wind to find shelter in our guesthouse. I felt brave enough to follow you in that raging weather and I stood in front of a window, trembling in the rain, but watching you light a fire in the fireplace and make love again looking at yourselves in the huge mirror we kept there. Rain was pouring down my face, the wind was whipping my hair, but through that fury, I could still see the flames of fire flicker playfully in the mirror in which your two bodies swayed in love-infused drunkenness. I do not remember how I got home, or even how I found my horse that hid in a thicket, neighing in terror. The storm blew over as suddenly as it had started, and my stallion calmed down and brought me home.

I had to tell someone what I witnessed, and I confided in Etain, Ailionora's grandmother. I was shaking from cold and shock, and she made me a cup of tea and wrapped me in her heavy woollen shawl. She told me she knew of your love because she had seen you together many times. She claimed she saw you and witnessed your secret encounters during the times she had shape-shifted into a hawk. She said your love was not of this world only, but also of many incarnations, and that you would meet again in the future, in an incarnation that would be of significance for the whole world. She was not able to tell me more, but what she had told me, I believed."

"Ailionora said the same...that we would always find each other, that our souls were entwined. I would like to believe that," said Kieren in a dark and shaky voice.

"So I have carried that dark secret in my bosom and shall take it with me to my grave. But you are looking unwell, Kieran. What ails you?"

"The loss of Jilleen and the fear I shall forget her. Since Ailionora and the White Circle disappeared, most of the people, as you know, have forgotten about both. My memory is still intact, but I fear it might wane."

"I fear the same and that is why I shall continue to write in this book. I owe it to Jilleen's father. He was a kind man and a good priest, and one that suffered deeply when he almost lost his daughter to drowning, and then to madness after she lost her baby. And then that final blow when she was found dead.

"I also want you to know that I held Conor in my arms. I wanted to see the baby. I was relieved it was stillborn because the thought of my brave and honorable son raising his wife's bastard was too much to bear. It was your child without any doubt. Etain said it was not Conor's time to be born, but that in a future lifetime, his role would be larger than that of all our valiant chieftains together. She saw that in the sacred well behind our house, but said the vision offered to her was limited. A druid with much more visionary power would one day look into a well and be given answers."

Kieran left looking crushed, and a flutter in my breast told me I would never speak with him again.

Days and years passed, argent moons and golden suns set and rose, and my grandson's happiness became my purpose of living. I did my best to replace a mother to him. Aidan did not remarry, even though rumours reached me about his many dalliances abroad. He rarely came home, and spent most of his time in England, and the fury over what the villagers perceived as his betrayal, was palpable in the air. Their reproachful gazes made me blush, but I'd had little influence over my husband, and even less over my son. My heart was breaking because of my grandson Fiann, who had neither a mother nor a constant father presence in his life. What a cruel fate to befall a child!

Nevertheless, Fiann was a happy spirit. He inherited his mother's beauty and his father's stature. He grew up into a strong and fearless lad, and whenever Aidan would come for a visit, he would take him hunting, and from time to time, he'd invite him to join him in his visits to England. Aidan hired a tutor for him to educate him in history, sciences, and literature, but Fiann was not like his mother, and disliked books and learning. I would often take him to the place where the White Circle used to stand, and would tell him stories of our Beltane celebrations, of how his father had asked his mother to marry him there, of the rumours of a wolf following his mother around the Circle, and Fiann's eyes would light up in fascination over these tales. I told him about the Circle's disappearance and Ailionora's curse, and told him about the book, and the memories of our quaint village I was trying to preserve. I showed him his grandfather's book and told him that he died from a broken heart of losing his only child, Fiann's mother Jilleen.

Fiann was spellbound by my stories and decided to invest effort into mastering the skill of writing so that he could be the next memory keeper of our small world. He even began to write stories and poetry of his own and discovered he was quite gifted. He searched for knowledge about the history of Ireland, its myths and beliefs before the advent of Christianity. I told him all I knew about Etain and Ailionora and their powers as druidesses. I was happy to see that my storytelling seemed to have aroused his curiosity and inspired him to seek new knowledge.

Meanwhile, in the village, there was no one left who remembered the White Circle. Ailionora's curse was so potent that I wondered why my memory was spared. There were many moments when I questioned it, when I felt uncertain of my own recollections. But then, I would reread the entries Jilleen's father had made in the book, and would be reassured that the White Circle had indeed existed until Ailionora destroyed it in the effort to obliterate evidence of her shame.

Writing in this book has given me much joy. Even chronicling some of the most trivial moments of the day has given me hope that some memory of our village would be preserved for posterity. Often, Fiann has sat by my side dictating what he wanted me to chronicle. Sometimes, it was the story about a successful hunt he had taken part in, another time about a festivity, during which he exchanged glances with pretty girls. And

I wrote it all down without even understanding why it was important for the memory of us to be preserved, because the transience of life turned everything into dust. But then I would remember Etain's words about the importance of preserving ancestral memories in order to keep the Celtic spirit alive. The ancestors' wisdom showed us the deeper way in life and had always helped guide us.'

Leandra began flipping through the pages, reading entries voraciously. Her hands were shaking, and from time to time, she would stop reading and look at Weylin with eyes wide open and brimming with questions. Her incredulity found its reflection in Weylin's gaze. They alternated reading the pages aloud to each other.

Kieran's body was found on the rocks at the lake where Jilleen and he used to meet in secret. At first, it was thought he had fallen to his death, but his body bore no marks of scratches, injuries, or signs of a violent death. He looked peaceful even though his eyes were open. He was lying on a rock with his head on his coat, and in his hands, he was clutching Jilleen's white dress.

His wife buried him beside her own father. Before she buried him, she pried the dress from his stiff fingers and witnesses swore her gaze was filled with savage jealousy and hatred. She now knew what her female intuition had told her many times - the suspected truth about her husband's infidelity. He had loved Jilleen, and not her. And so the dress found its way back to me, and I laid it carefully into a wooden chest, showing Fiann where I kept his mother's jewelry, books, and this special dress.

Kieran's wife visited his grave almost every day, and her wailing chant of sorrow could often be heard by the passers-by. She never stopped wearing black. As a wealthy middle-aged woman, she soon had many suitors, but refused them all. She hired more help to till the fields and help her with household chores. Her sons were now grown men, and they both married girls from a nearby village. The younger one was the spitting image of Kieran, and it was said that whenever she would set her eyes on his handsome face, the pain she felt was palpable.

Upon reading about Kieran's death, Leandra began to sob, saying she could feel how much Jilleen had loved him. Weylin took her in his arms, held her and whispered, "I am here, Leandra. We have met again, remember? I am here."

With his arm around her shoulder, Leandra continued to read entries made by Jilleen's mother-in-law.

Fiann fell in love with a most beautiful girl from a neighboring village and married her. Her name was Liban and she believed in fairy folk as most of the people, even though they did not dare admit it before priests. Her father was such an unsightly man, and her mother a plain looking woman, while Liban was so alluring that it was believed her real father must have come from the land of the fae. Evil tongues in the village began spreading the rumour that sooner or later the fae would come to claim her and take her back to their realm.

Their first child was born on a hot August day, and they named him Nede because his name meant a gift from God and Liban believed unwaveringly that he had been sent by God. She was the happiest mother I had ever seen. She sang to her son every day, held him in her arms day and night, saying she was afraid to put him on the ground in fear the fairies might snatch him as he was an inordinately beautiful baby, a replica of his mother.

Soon after Nede's fifth birthday, Liban fell ill. After Etain and Ailionora died, the village had male healers in whose craft I did not trust. They gave Liban tinctures and potions, and her condition was deteriorating by the day until she took her last breath and died. I felt deep regret that I had not asked Jilleen to teach me the art of healing, along with the writing and reading craft. To allow such knowledge to die was a sacrilege.

Fiann cursed his and his father's fate that they would both lose their wives. However, unlike Aidan, who never wanted another wife after losing Jilleen, Fiann remarried after six months. Maeve, his new wife, was not adorned with beauty, but with a heart of gold. She could not conceive, but did not wallow in sorrow. Instead, she embraced Nede as her own child and would get furious if anyone mentioned he was not of her own flesh and blood. Meave was a high-tempered girl, who soon imposed her will on the household. She was kind to me, and as my health was failing me and joint pain barely let me hold the quill and write, she massaged my hands, and her devotion could not have been greater had she been my own daughter.

Leandra stopped reading coming upon an empty page with inkblots splattered across it. The page was yellowed and crinkly, and she turned it over with great care. She held the book in her hands as if were the most fragile and precious object.

"Weylin, we have found what we came to find. After we have read the book, all that will be left to do is locate the village where we had lived and loved each other once upon a time. Perhaps Fiann can help us find the way, as he already knows its name. We know with certainty there is a Glenda's Bluff, even though it may not be called the same name anymore, there is a lake at the foot of a hill, and on the same hill a guesthouse had once stood. Perhaps it is still there, or its ruins are still recognizable. Perhaps even the mirror which reflected Jilleen and Kieran's love dance still stands there untouched, even though that should not be possible. There is a river and a bridge from which Jilleen had been thrown into the water. All these landmarks must be in close proximity to each other."

"Let's read some more and then it will be time to meet Fiann for lunch. This is really blowing my mind," said Weylin.

The following page was also empty, and Leandra began to think they would find no more entries, but the next page revealed new handwriting, large and elaborate, with letters written out with what looked like great care and precision. She began to read aloud.

My name is Fiann. I am continuing this journal in honour of my mother, my grandmother, and my grandfather who was the first one to write in this book. By writing in the book, I am also honouring our ancestors, as my grandmother instructed me. It has already been two years since she died in her sleep and that is how long it has taken me to continue her legacy of preserving the memory of our clan and our village. My son Nede is seven years old, and I pray he grows into adulthood and extends our lineage.

My father Aidan also no longer walks this world. He and I participated in the uprising against the English invaders, defending our Catholic faith against the Protestants, and he died fighting valiantly for our land. He came back from England lamenting having ever trusted the fiends and deserting his country.

In the battle, I was wounded, but the wound healed and the scar on my inner thigh reminds me of the horrific experiences. Many good men and women died last year. The earth was soaked with blood and anguish. Famine erupted after the battles, followed by plague. A druidic seer I met on my way back home said during a trance the earth was suffering and wailing, and it would take her a long time to heal. Meanwhile, suffering would spread, and many more people would perish.

***

My memories are now swirling and are anchoring me in a moment in time when I believed I would die, felled by the English sword, but a hawk swept down from a tree, and pierced the Englishman's eyes with its talons. He fell on me screaming and drenched my shirt with his blood. I extricated myself from under his body and kept plunging my dagger into his back until he gave no sign of life.

The plague followed me home and reached our village, but our household was spared as I forbade everyone to leave the estate or allow anyone in. We had enough food reserves to sustain us for two months with careful rationing.

When the dark times were dispelled, life and peace returned to the village. Then a miracle happened, a miracle that felt like an explosion of the sun in my heart. Maeve told me she was carrying our first child. It was then that I noticed how large in her waist she had gotten. I lifted her off her feet and swung her in the air. We laughed like children and when she said, 'I hope I can love this child as much as I love Nede,' I almost cried over my good fortune to have been blessed with two good wives in one lifetime.

***

Years are flowing by like rivers, in one direction only, with no return. Nede is nineteen years old, and his brother Cormac is twelve. The boys are the best of friends and their mother's smile never leaves her face, or eyes upon seeing them. She decided not to tell Cormac that Nede was not her natural son, but he heard it from the villagers. She vehemently stood her ground saying he was as much her son as Cormac, and to stop listening to evil tongues.

There was another uprising and I took my men to join it in spite of Maeve's wailing that her children would be fatherless and we would lose everything. Fortune smiled upon me once again, and in spite of another cycle of devastation, bloodshed, and ineffable suffering of the people and the land, I came back home.

The English had scorched the land, massacred both the people and the animals, crushing the rebellion. The English kept searching for the rebels who had survived, killing them off one by one. Famine and disease ruled again, and I feared we were doomed. My wife was terrified both I and our sons would be killed before her very eyes once the English enter our village in search of the rebels. She persuaded me to pack what we could and flee. Many of our neighbors had already left in search of a new and safer life. My heart bled knowing I would leave the family home that had been in our possession for generations, and I felt like a coward and a powerless wretch, unable to defend neither his country nor his home and family. I knew the English would take possession of our lands and colonize them, and I hated them with a fervor that made my blood roil. We decided to begin packing right away, and one valuable to pack and keep safe would be this black book to which I have developed an attachment as if it were a person. I wrapped it in oilskins and placed it carefully in the chest under my mother's white dress and her jewelry box. I might have to sell some of her jewels in order to give my family a new home. I knew my mother, who must be watching us from above, would approve of that.

Before I left the only hearth I had ever known, I visited once again the place where the White Circle had stood. I no longer remembered it, but I trusted my grandmother's word that it had existed for centuries. Perhaps, one day, someone would rediscover it after reading this diary. Perhaps the solitary stone that remained there would turn out to be the repository of all secrets of this place, and it would reveal them to a worthy visitor. Someone might be able to discover what the J&K etching on one side of the stone meant. J could stand for my mother Jilleen, but who was K? It could not be linked to my mother in any way. There was also a faded inscription under the initials, and the only words I can make out is that they would always find each other.

***

I am getting weary of life, of fighting the demons who keep invading this land of ours, but I must go on for my family's sake. The day will come when the sons of this land will be their own overlords, and masters of their lives and nation. One day, freedom will be a thread of glitter woven into our destiny and no one will ever dim its light again.

When we leave the village boundaries, we stop and turn back to cast one last look at our small piece of homeland and say goodbye, but suddenly a wind rises and darkness full of wisps of mist falls, diminishing the visibility. We move away quickly, looking for shelter from the whipping wind, and find it in a large rocky outcrop. We spend the night there and, in the morning, we look again in the direction of our village, but we can see no signs or landmarks that look familiar. The landscape looks foreign and unrecognizable, as if the part of the world we grew up in was ripped off the face of the earth. We shudder in fright and move eastward in search of a new beginning. I shall stop writing now...

Leandra closed the book once she came to an empty page and Weylin gently took it from her hands.

"You realize," Weylin said, "that our host Fiann seems to be a descendant of your and Aidan's son Fiann. And the solitary stone in the White Circle must be the same stone that appeared in your dream. If the J&K etching still remains, it will be easy to recognize it? Quite insane, isn't it? And we have been brought here, obviously to learn something important. We are yet to discover what it is."

"I'm finding it hard to form any coherent thoughts, Weylin. This feels like a dream from which I'll awaken any moment. And how do you find a stone among millions of stones? I assume it will be large and visible if we happen to stumble upon the White Circle site."

"Whatever it is that has brought us here will show us the way to the stone. It's noon. Let's look for Fiann and give the book back to him. I'm sure he won't mind lending it to us again," said Weylin.

"Perhaps he can just tell us the rest of the story," replied Leandra.

They found Fiann in the kitchen, which was filled with ambrosial smell of freshly baked bread and fried fish.

"I felt like cooking and hope you are ready for some lunch. Let me just finish the salad."

"The bread smells divine," said Leandra.

"It is my grandmother's recipe for soda bread. Can you help me carry the plates out onto the terrace, please?"

"With pleasure," said Leandra, and continued, "Fiann, we read quite a bit of the book and neither of us can express just how incredible this all is. Weylin also pointed out that if you are a descendant of Jilleen's son Fiann, then you and I are related, provided I was, indeed, Jilleen in the 17th century. The strangeness of this all is so hard to process."

"We must be related and yes, I am Fiann's descendent. I spent five years tracing back the family tree and roots through nine generations. I will show you the drawing of the lineage, including all the names starting with Aidan's son Fiann. The lineage goes through my father's side of the family."

"I am so, so confused, Fiann. If I was Jilleen and Weylin was Kieran, and we met someone who seems to have been Ailionora, and she loved Egerton, who showed up in this life as her lover Hugo, with whom she has just reunited…and we met Annette who had lived in the same period as Lady Tyrone, I am wondering how many people I have met in life not knowing we had past-life connections?"

"Souls come into each other's lives when there are important lessons to be learned. You can never know for certain what the past connections were, but most people sense their specialness."

The sun was blinding on the terrace and Leandra went back to her room to fetch her sunglasses. When she returned, Weylin and Fiann were drinking beer and Fiann offered her one.

Her first instinct was to refuse, but her nerves were frayed, and she hoped beer would have a calming effect.

They ate in sunlit silence. Whenever Leandra would lock eyes with Weylin, she could read reassurance in his gaze.

She broke the silence by asking Fiann where the village was in which she had lived as Jilleen because he must have discovered it during his attempt to trace back his family roots.

Fiann took a sip of his beer and said, "I do not know if I mentioned that my family was from Connemara, from a small town near Clifden. After I discovered and read the book, I became obsessed with tracing back our family roots and especially, rediscovering the White Circle.

In my dream, the same hawk that appeared in my waking times occasionally was telling me there was a village to be rediscovered, and a curse to be lifted in order for the flow of ancestral memories to be restored.

The hawk also said that dark energies hid the village from the rest of the world, and that as a shaman it was my duty to dispel them. However, I could not do it alone, and had to wait for the person who would assist me in that task.

"So, to go back, I could not understand fully what the hawk was telling me, but it was persistent, following me day and night until one evening, as I was chopping wood behind the house, it screeched into my ear, 'Listen.'

"I wiped off the sweat off my forehead and sat on a stump. The hawk circled and circled around me, and I felt I was falling into a trance. In the trance, I experienced a symphony of colours twirling around me and a sense of being enveloped not only in love, but in an energy of a higher intelligence, or consciousness. I even felt as one with the stump I was sitting on. In my mind, a whole world exploded, giving me another insight that I was, indeed, a shamanic healer, a druidic seer, and that my mission in life would be to help people deal with illness or access the knowledge that would be of help to them.

"I looked around me and everything seemed to be magnified. A spider that I would normally find hideous, appeared to me as a creature of most intricate beauty. Everywhere I looked, I could see a pattern, or a web ruled by order and intention. When my focus finally shifted to the hawk, it was perched on the lowest bough of our apple tree.

'Who are you, and what it is you want me to do?' I asked.

'I used to be Etain, a druidess before I shape-shifted. Centuries have passed since I lived a life of a woman. Soon, it will be time to transmigrate into the human form, but not yet.'

'Why have you been following me?'

'To help you find your purpose in life, and for you to carry out a mission.'

'What mission do you wish me to carry out?'

'Remove the curse my granddaughter Ailionora cast on a place so that it might gradually become visible again to the outside world. The black winds of oblivion have kept it veiled for too long. The spirits of the people who died there are clamoring to be found and remembered. That is one part of your purpose. The other is to use your shamanic powers, along with Ailionora's help, to reveal an important truth about a future incarnation of the two people you will meet. That incarnation will be pivotal in the survival of humans and earth itself as we know it.'

'Is that place the White Circle village mentioned in the book I found?'

'It is. You are descendant of a chieftain who had lived there. In your blood courses the valor and wisdom of your ancestors. Soon, your second sight will become even sharper, and your healing powers will bring relief to many people. It is your destiny. The book in your possession asks for the memories to be resuscitated. Our ancestors' memory paths must not be broken because without memory, there can be no knowledge and wisdom passed on to the new generations. The village you are from holds important knowledge not only of the past, but the future, too. It is a shaman's duty to recover lost knowledge and reveal what is crucial for a future time.'

'How do I make it visible again?'

'When the time is ripe, I will reveal to you what should be done. You will wait patiently until you have met the reincarnated druidess, and the lovers from a past incarnation. Once the four of you have gathered, I shall appear again and offer guidance.'

Leandra was listening to Fiann with eyes filled with wonder. She felt like a little girl who had just discovered that magic was real and co-existed with her world of science and rationalism without any need for competition.

"Fiann, sorry for interrupting your story. I feel all shivery with anticipation. But can you please tell me first about the lineage you discovered? Was Jilleen's son Fiann your direct ancestor?" she asked to be sure she had understood correctly.

Fiann opened the black book and turned it to the last page. He handed it to Leandra to look at and she pulled her chair closer to Weylin's so that they could both look at the page. They were both in awe over the clarity of the chart outlining the family tree of chieftain, Aidan O' Faolán.

With her finger, Leandra traced the lineage line trying not to touch the paper in fear of damaging it, and gasped when her finger hovered over Jilleen's name.

"Who created this chart?" she asked.

"The person who made the last entry in the book. After Fiann's death from old age, only brief entries were made by his descendants. Fortunately, each identified him and herself by name, so I was able to reconstruct a large part of the family tree. If you turn the page, you will find it done in my own handwriting. As I mentioned before, my sister and her daughters will be the future custodians of the book. She and I also discussed the option of offering it to the National Museum of Ireland. A close friend of mine is one of the curators there and has already expressed interest in adding it to their collection of ancient books. But now that I have met you, I plan to write in the book about our findings in the village of the White Circle if we succeed in locating it and fulfilling the mission the hawk outlined."

Leandra shook her head swallowing hard. She began to read aloud the names starting from Jilleen and Aidan, whose son Fiann married Liban and then Maeve. Fiann's son Nede married Tara and in 1682 their son Dil was born, who married in 1701 and had three sons.

The names danced before Leandra's eyes as she became more and more conscious that she was holding in her hands evidence of her previous life as Jilleen. Could she still doubt her own experiences? Could all of this be explained as some coincidence of the most bizarre kind?

"I need to go out for a walk," said Leandra, getting up and dropping the book on the floor. Aghast over her clumsiness and the possibility of having damaged the book, she began to cry in despair, but Weylin lifted the book quickly assuring her there was no impact as it had fallen from a low height onto a thick oriental rug.

He followed her out, saying he would join her, and they spent the next two hours wondering around the village and climbing a hill. Once they sat on a large rock on the hill and looked at the ocean, Leandra began to cry again.

"My nerves are getting so threadbare that I did not even allow Fiann to finish his story. I wanted to ask him how he would remove Ailionora's curse and the veil covering the village. Is it even possible to repair the rupture in the collective ancestral memory?" She sighed. "Now I wonder what that veil was. How can a village become invisible to the outside world? He said black winds prevented visitors from coming near it. I cannot wait to hear more. We must go there and touch that solitary stone with our initials etched in it. And I know, Weylin, life would not have allowed our paths to cross had it not been for that past-life connection. That is why I could not resist you and this is not a lame excuse for adultery. The bond between us is so alive, so vibrant and palpable. The interflow between our souls is so viscous, for lack of a better word."

Weylin put his arm around her and said it was the reason neither of them could forget each other and never should. Leandra got up, saying she was restless and needed to do something constructive to calm down. She recognized that it was an excuse to extricate herself from his embrace.

"I know what I want to do. I'll buy groceries and cook dinner for the three of us. Cooking has always had a calming effect on my nerves. Agitation, just like any other negative emotion, should be turned into something positive. That's something I tell my patients."

The stores were still open, and she bought vegetables for roasting, fruit for fruit salad and eggs for a frittata. Weylin bought two bottles of expensive vintage wine.

They found Fiann in the kitchen making a cup of tea. Leandra asked him if it would be alright for her to prepare dinner and he smiled, welcoming the idea. He said he would relax in his room and come back in two hours.

Weylin offered to help as he himself enjoyed cooking. He reminded her how, once upon a time when they were lovers, they had dreamed about cooking together one day. Chopping and peeling turned into a light banter, laughing, and accidental touching that provoked blushes. Leandra's eyes sparkled in response to the reflection of his.

Weylin opened a bottle of white wine and poured them a glass each. They clinked their glasses giggling, and he said, 'To my lovely Jilleen, mother of my son Conor!' Leandra looked at him in astonishment and then whispered, "I am still in disbelief that we were Jilleen and Kieren."

"But we are and we were. Doubt has no more place here. I simply know it with certitude. And the yearning for something I could not define that had made me feel unsettled for so long is now diminished. I feel everything in my life is falling into its proper place, and there is just another piece of puzzle to be solved for the circle to close…and for us to find the White Circle Village. And I feel strongly that will happen soon. At least one big piece of my life is currently where it should be — it is you, Leandra."

"It cannot be me, because I am not, and will not be available," she replied with softness in her voice and shimmering moistness in her eyes.

"I let you go in the past lives we have shared, but this is the only life I have now. I do not want to wait for other, future lives for us, even though Ailionora told me there would be more incarnations, in which we would meet. Please reconsider."

Their talk was interrupted by Fiann, who walked into the kitchen looking rested. Weylin offered him a glass of wine, but he declined. He added he would set the table while they finished making dinner.

Once at the table, Leandra asked Fiann to continue the story she had interrupted and tell them if he was able to find the village. She also wanted to know if he could take them there.

"I cannot give you a definitive answer. I thought I had visited the village, but I cannot be certain. I see incomprehension in your eyes. When my wife left me suddenly, I thought I would go insane with pain. Despite being a seer, I had not seen it coming. My intuition had remained silent, so her decision caught me unaware and unprepared. I pleaded with her, promising her I would stop receiving patients, and we would travel and start anew, but she could not be swayed. Later, I found out there was someone else in her life.

So after she left, I found myself in a state of catatonia, a trance that lasted for a few days. In that trance, I felt myself shape-shifting into a bird and looking for the White Circle Village in hope of finding answers to the questions to why my wife, who had been the love of my life, had left me so abruptly. I could not explain to myself why I was seeking that village expecting to find answers.

Perhaps I remembered what the hawk had previously told me, and I felt compelled to seek the unknown. I don't know. The hawk appeared by my side and guided me to the village, but we could not enter it, for strong winds rose, created darkness around us, and prevented further travel.

The hawk had repeated again that alone I could not enter the village; however, I did not give up and tried again to fly against the winds. For a moment, it seemed I had succeeded as I caught a glimpse of a jagged shore, bluffs, and distant ruins above a lake.

I also saw a well behind the ruins of a house, descended upon it and asked the question whether my wife would come back to me. The water in the well rippled, showing me the image of my wife and a man with a beard. That is when I knew she had found someone else.

It all happened in what felt like an instant, and I found myself again tossed in a strong wind and disoriented. When I came out of the trance, I found myself sitting beside the well in my garden, so at the time it seemed I had never actually left my house. I cannot even claim with certainty it was not just a dream I had dreamt under the huge distress of loss.

"So you cannot tell us for sure if in your trance or shape-shifted state you saw Glenda's Bluff or found the village?"

"Unfortunately, I can't. At this moment, all we can do is to wait for a sign for where we should begin to search," said Fiann.

Leandra's sigh reflected impatience. She stood up and began to pace the room.

"I have no more time to waste. I cannot stay on this island indefinitely, hoping for a sign. I have to go back home to my family and my job." She turned to Weylin. "If there is no sign tomorrow, I am ready to abandon the search and go back home. The book in itself is much more than I ever expected us to find. So, the day after tomorrow we go back to Dublin, alright?"

The sudden change in her mood took both Weylin and Fiann by surprise.

"Alright, don't worry. I'll take you back," Weylin said in a subdued voice.

They sat in silence for a few minutes. Leandra looked more relaxed now that a decision about the return to Dublin had been made. She poured herself a glass of wine and asked Fiann to tell them about his life after his wife's departure.

"After she left, I became restless and could not stay alone in the house. I stopped receiving patients and decided to travel around Ireland on foot. I felt I needed some sort of inner pilgrimage, reconnecting with myself.

The grief over lost love seemed to have sapped my energy. I was feeling lethargic and at the same time fearful that I was losing my shamanic sight and healing powers. My parents were still alive at that time. They were both religious people who were not spiritually too connected to the Celtic past. I phoned to tell them I would be travelling and they would not be able to reach me for a while, but I would occasionally call them so they would not have to worry. So, I set off on a journey without a destination.

"The hawk would appear from time to time, but would not talk to me. Occasionally, she would lead the way, and I would follow without questions or doubt that she knew where I needed to go. I slept in the fields, as it was summer, and when it rained, I asked shepherds to allow me to sleep in their huts.

"And it was at that time the healer in me awoke again after a dream in which a voice told me that the weave of my destiny held a healing mission. The healing would encompass people and places because there was a place that needed to heal, too. I did not comprehend the full meaning of the message, especially its reference to a place that needed healing. But now that you are here, I know what that place is.

"My healing gift seemed to be one of the reasons for my inhabiting this point in time. And the voice I mentioned just repeated what the hawk had already told me when she spoke of my fate.

"It felt as if a supernatural force directed every movement I made. When I planned to follow the hawk and go straight down a road, all of a sudden, I would feel a pull toward a different direction. The hawk would screech in alarm at first, and then calm down as if she understood. I would begin to hurry and arrive at a hut knowing there was someone ailing gravely and needing my help. I would go in and place my hands on the man's or a child's head, feel the illness - it always felt like darkness, and then, I would place my mouth on the patient's chest, suck the darkness out being careful not to infect myself, and then spit it out. Sometimes, the ground would burn upon the touch of the noxious substance. That was only one method of healing, because with time, I developed a few other methods without any conscious involvement or planning.

"Not only was I healing people, but I was also directing them toward sources of healing, or instructing them what to do to stay healthy. My second sight also grew stronger than before, and I would warn them of approaching storms, so they could bring their cattle into shelter, or not take their boats out to sea. I would tell them where to dig for buried treasure, or where to find medicinal herbs, and how to prepare them. I cannot explain where this knowledge stemmed from; it was just there for me to access when I needed it. By coming on this journey, I strengthened my healing powers. I thought, perhaps, this was the reason behind my wife's leaving me. It felt that I had grabbed all that grief, and like clay, molded it into something higher, something that transcended me, something of value that I could give to others. To be of service to other people felt like a noble cause, a cause worthy of being deprived of a woman's love."

"How long were you on the road like that?" asked Leandra.

"Six months. One evening, as I was gazing at the night sky through the window of a house at which I was offered a room after treating a baby, a clap of thunder shattered my reverie. At that moment I knew it was time to return home, because something important awaited me there.

"The next morning, instead of walking, I took the bus. I arrived home late in the evening and saw the lights were on. When I unlocked the door, I heard noises in the kitchen. Before I could even feel the alarm that someone might have broken into the house, my wife appeared from the kitchen. She wanted to embrace me and began to cry, but I stood there like a statue. She had changed. She looked aged and miserable.

Through her sobs, she told me she had worried that something bad had happened to me, and that I would not be coming back. She said that her lover turned out to be an alcoholic, and after a few weeks she could no longer recognize the man she had fallen in love with, and for whom she had left me. She was contrite and apologetic, but I was unmoved.

"Without uttering one single word, I went out into the backyard and sat by the well. As a diviner, I often sought wisdom in the well's mirror, and I gazed into the moonlit water asking the Goddess for advice on whether I should forgive my wife and try to build our life anew. After all, I had been a neglectful husband who had paid more attention to my patients than to her.

"I sat still and slowly fell into a trance. In that altered state of consciousness I saw myself burying a heart under one of my rose bushes.

"My trance was broken by my wife's voice calling me inside. I went into the house and looked at her in silence. Her eyes were full of sadness in which hope flickered, hope that I might forgive her. And I was tempted to embrace her, but then I realized she had come back not because she loved me, but because she was seeking solace in me," said Fiann and looked at Leandra.

"You suddenly blushed, Leandra. Did I say something embarrassing?" asked Fiann.

"What you just said, Fiann, triggered a painful memory. When Weylin and I broke up, I was in excruciating pain…and there were moments when I was seeking solace in my husband's arms. All the time I was aware that I was adding another layer of betrayal to the high treason of adultery. We came to the brink of divorce, and it was only after he had undergone hypnotherapy was he able to forgive me. Did you ever regret not forgiving your wife?"

"I thought of her often, but something in me went cold…something hardened. I heard that she remarried and then divorced, and news of her never reached me again after that. Little by little, I stopped thinking about her and opened my house to patients again. Changing people's lives by restoring their health restored me also from within."

Fiann began to cough, and Leandra handed him a glass of water. He drank it and then said good night. Before he left the room, he asked Leandra to reconsider her decision about going back to Dublin and leaving Ireland so soon. He said he felt clearly that in the next few days they would finally discover what was meant to be revealed for a long time.

Leandra said good night to Fiann and gave him a hug. She added that she would not change her mind and would leave in two days, and that she thought coming to Ireland may have been a mistake in spite of the staggering discoveries.

After Fiann left the room, Weylin turned toward Leandra and said, "How could you say this trip might have been a mistake? Did you forget what was revealed in Keith's experiments? Did you forget what I revealed? What about the book and…and?"

"Weylin, as I said before, I'm no longer sure all of this is anything more than a most weird coincidence or a collective hallucination. I don't know."

"How can you say that after so much has happened, after we have read the book, after…" his voice cracked with impatience and irritation over her words.

"There is an infinite number of coincidences happening every day, and the fact that some of them are meaningful to us still does not make them anything more than a coincidence. There must be some rational explanation for everything irrational we have experienced so far."

"I'm sure Keith would have no problems making sense out of this. And David as well. He uncovered so much during the hypnotherapy sessions with you. You can't say you no longer believe your own experience." Slight stutter colored Weylin's voice and noticing it, he blushed.

"At this moment, my head is spinning, and I'm no longer able to even tell what's up and what's down. I'm going to bed now, and tomorrow is definitively the last day I'm spending on this island. I've had enough of this, Weylin. I'm exhausted, and there is a feeling of senselessness about all of this. We are doctors and we should go back to our professional lives, and remember this as something crazy and fun, and out of the ordinary. Good night."

Weylin reached over and grabbed her hand before she could leave the room. Gazing into her eyes he said, "You will miss the unique opportunity of finding something truly mysterious if you give up now. You cannot betray Jilleen and Kieran by leaving."

"Really! You are brazen enough to tell me I can't betray Jilleen and Kieran while you already betrayed them by breaking up with me in this lifetime, and going crazy over Jorunn. Have you forgotten that little detail? Have you?"

A solitary tear trickled down Leandra's cheek as she turned her back to him and left the room.

20

Monotonous rain patter woke up Leandra. She looked at her phone and it showed seven a.m.

She found an email from Adrian telling her he missed her, and could not wait for her trip to end. He asked her about her discoveries, and she wrote back that they were strange and unexpected, but that she wanted to wait until they could sit down, so she could relate to him all the details. She added that even though she felt enough had been unveiled, she also thought there must be some rational explanation behind all the bizarre experiences, but she was no longer willing to explore the events more deeply, and was ready to come home. She was ready to finally close that chapter of her life. She was planning to return to Dublin the next day and would keep him posted.

She got up and looked through the window, planning to start packing her suitcase. Impatience began to course her veins telling her there was nothing else to discover and it was high time to go back to a life of normalcy. And once she has settled back down into her routine, she would ponder the events of this trip.

Before she turned away from the window to begin packing, she glanced at the roof of the house across from Fiann's and saw a hawk perched, unperturbed by the wet and windy weather. She immediately thought of Etain and shivered lightly. After throwing a few pieces of clothes into her suitcase, she took a long hot shower, dressed, and went to the kitchen where she found Fiann and Weylin drinking coffee. Sunlight was streaming through the large bay window into the kitchen and she was perplexed that there were no signs of rain anymore.

Weylin handed her a coffee mug and offered her a plate filled with pastries. "I was up early and bought us breakfast."

"Thank you, but I will just have coffee." Her voice lacked its usual warmth and sounded strained and reserved. "You two look as if you had a serious talk before I came in," said Leandra.

At that moment, Weylin's phone gave off a ping and he excused himself while he checked his message. After a few moments, he said he wanted to read aloud the message he received from Ariadne.

'Good morning, Weylin. Hugo left last night and it is time for me to join you. Send me your whereabouts, please. I will be there as soon as I can. I will explain when I see you. It seems we are about to reach the end of our peculiar story in which we are interconnected, or perhaps start a new one.'

Leandra and Fiann were silent while Weylin texted back Fiann's address to Ariadne. She replied immediately saying she would leave her house within the hour. She should reach the island in about six hours, if all went well. Fiann and Weylin exchanged glances that revealed that Ariadne's announced arrival was something they should have expected, as all the pieces of the secret mosaic were falling into their right places. It seemed Ariadne was the last missing piece before they could set out on their journey to the White Circle Village. Weylin looked at Leandra with anticipation, waiting for an answer to the question she could plainly read in his eyes. She said with a sigh of surrender, "Alright, this was unexpected, and I'll change my mind about going back tomorrow. I will change my flight, if I have to, so that we can get to the bottom of this. But I'm losing patience, I must admit, and longing for home and my family."

"Thanks for changing your mind," said Weylin in relief.

Shivering restlessness infused Leandra, waiting for Ariadne to come. In spite of her recent feelings of doubt, the mystery continued to unravel, and it seemed nothing could stop it anymore. The time had come. Suddenly, every cell in her body began to pulse with delicious anticipation. Now, she could not wait to visit the village in which her destiny unfolded in so many dramatic ways. She wanted to sit on her son Conor's grave, roam the fields again, and feel the spirit of the wolf who was her friend centuries ago. Perhaps more memories will come to the surface once she treads upon the long-forgotten landscape. She did not dare think what would happen if they failed, and the village remained forever hidden by the winds of oblivion.

Weylin invited her out for lunch, and they sat on a terrace overlooking the sea and enjoyed the breezy weather. Fiann had declined the offer, as he wanted to rest more. They did not talk much, overwhelmed by the revelations and the impatience to get to the bottom of their discoveries. Leandra remembered she had forgotten to ask Fiann about Jilleen's jewelry and if he still had her box. She wanted to touch the pieces for remnants of energy.

When they returned to the house, they found Fiann in the garden lying asleep in a reclining chair. He opened his eyes when he heard them, and Leandra apologized for disturbing his rest. He said he had awoken before they arrived, and the nap reenergized him. She asked him about the jewelry that he had found in the chest with the book and the dress, and he said his sister took the dragonfly earrings, and, as far as he knew, she wore them a lot. A few other pieces were in his safe because his sister did not want to keep them for fear of losing them.

He left the chair and went into the house. A few minutes later he returned with a black wooden box that had a golden coloured dragonfly engraved on the lid. "There are only five pieces of jewelry in the box. Jilleen must have had many more, but it is a miracle that even this many have been preserved. Feel free to take a look."

With a trembling hand, Leandra lifted the lid and looked into its red velvety interior. Gently, she took out a string of pearls and held them against her neck. Then she placed a dragonfly brooch on the palm of her hand and admired its intricate design. Its eyes were blue, and she assumed the stones were sapphires.

Another piece was a necklace made of green and blue stones. It looked regal and expensive. The last piece was a ring with a cluster of multi-coloured stones set in gold. When she put it on her ring finger, an awareness that it was a special ring given to Jilleen by her husband washed over her, knocking the breath out of her.

"Keep the ring, Leandra! It used to be yours and it has found you again. I felt your reaction and that ring, unlike the other pieces, made an energy impact on you. My sister will not mind."

Leandra looked at him with tears in her eyes and thanked him by nodding her head. At that moment, the doorbell rang and Fiann went to answer it. She could hear him welcoming Ariadne who came in talking excitedly. Leandra stood up to greet her and Ariadne hugged her warmly."I just knew I had to join you. My grandmother Etain appeared in my dream telling me it was time for me to lift the veil of the curse. She said as Ailionora, I had severed the continuity in the collective memory of the village. With Fiann's help, I, Ariadne, am now to break the curse. If successful, my fate with Egerton, who has reincarnated as Hugo, will be able to unfold." Ariadne stopped speaking to catch her breath, and then continued. "During Hugo's last visit, he told me he had often dreamed about looking for me and finding me dead. His dreams were so vivid that he did not dare phone me in fear of learning I had died. That was the reason behind his ghosting me."

The rest of the evening they spent in animated conversation about their plans for the next day because they decided to leave without further delay. Leandra told Ariadne everything that they had learned from Fiann, and how they found him. None of them thought any longer that it was all a web of inexplicable coincidences. They just did not know how Fiann would be able to locate the village, and if the winds protecting it would allow them passage, or how Ariadne would be able to lift the curse, and what truth would be revealed to them. But then, they remembered the messages Fiann had received during his first visit to the village in his trance, and knew that they would receive guidance at the right time.

21

Weylin woke up in the middle of the night to a heavy rainfall. He looked out the window into the dark and blustery night wondering if they would be able to leave on their trip in such a downpour, and if the ferry would run in the weather that threatened to turn into a storm. Gazing at the dark sky, he thought even the heavens had need for cathartic weeping.

He fell back to sleep again and awoke with a start when he heard a knock on his door.

"Weylin, are you awake? Fiann would like us to leave in about an hour. Breakfast is ready."

"Yes, Leandra, I will join you in a few minutes. It seems I slept much longer than I'd intended."

It was still raining when they left the house. The ferry was fifteen minutes late, and the choppy seas made Ariadne's stomach heave just by looking at the roiling water. Just as the ferry docked and they were ready to go aboard, Fiann, who had looked deeply pensive ever since they left his home, said in an urgent tone: "We must go back to the house and seek the truth in the well. The well in my garden will lead us to another well, which will reveal all that until now was unknowable. I'm sure of it."

"What! This is getting insane. What you just said about the wells…what do you mean?" Leandra exclaimed, but he just repeated they had to go back. They felt they had no choice but to follow him back. Once they took off their wet coats and jackets and sat at the kitchen table, Leandra asked Fiann to explain the sudden change of plans. Her voice had a tinge of frustration and impatience, and Weylin was afraid she would say she'd had enough and insist he take her back to Dublin.

"I suddenly heard a voice telling me to go back, and look for the answers in the well in my garden. Another well was mentioned. Like a well within a well that leads us to what we're seeking. The voice also said it was still not time to physically visit the White Circle Village, but the time was ripe to lift the curse off it. So we need to wait for the rain to stop and go to the well."

Fiann said he needed to spend some time in stillness, and wait for more insight as to what needed to be done. Without further explanations, he left the kitchen. Leandra looked at Weylin wanting to say something, but before she had a chance, he interrupted her. "I see your impatience rising again. I see clearly your renewed disbelief, but please do not do anything rash."

"I've already done something rash by coming here. I don't understand this sudden shift and Fiann's erratic behaviour. Nothing is making sense anymore. Look at us! Three medical doctors on a wild goose chase!"

Ariadne laughed and said she understood Leandra's disappointment with the change in plans, but trusted Fiann, and her intuition was telling her important answers lay before them.

"I feel as if there is a pendulum in my head," continued Leandra. "One day, all this craziness seems normal, and the next day, I shake my head over my belief in the irrational and fantastical, and just want to go back home and never give it another thought. At times, I begin to doubt my own sanity and my ability to think."

They made coffee and the atmosphere became more relaxed. Leandra went to her room to Skype with her family, and Weylin said the rainy weather made him sleepy, and he would take a nap. Late in the afternoon, they gathered again in the kitchen, engaging in a light banter about politics, climate change, and other topics unrelated to their reason for finding themselves on the island. Fiann joined them soon and said he was ready for dinner, and suggested they go out.

They walked the empty streets in silence looking for a place to eat. The rain was letting up and turning to drizzle mixed with mist. Fiann suggested they walk a few minutes longer and have dinner in a relatively new restaurant, the owner of which was an accomplished chef, known for delicious seafood concoctions. They reached it in a few minutes and felt lucky to be immediately given a table, as the restaurant was unexpectedly already full.

After a bottle of wine, they all felt more relaxed, and Leandra felt giddy. Her laughter was tinkling with mirth. Jokes flew about the insanity of the trip, and their belief in fantasies. Soon, they ordered a second and a third bottle of wine, and tipsiness fuelled more laughter.

On the way back to Fiann's home, they continued joking, and just as Fiann put the key in the door, a screech pierced their banter, stopping them dead in their tracks. They looked around and then up. A solitary streetlamp cast just enough light for them to discern the shape of a bird sitting on a low branch of a tree.

"My grandma Etain is here," whispered Ariadne.

The bird flapped its wings several times, and Fiann went up closer to it. He gazed at its eyes for a few moments standing completely still. When he rejoined them after about fifteen minutes, he said, "Tonight's the night. We need to go to the well now, she says. The rain has stopped and our synergy is strong enough to lift the curse and see the village in the well water."

"But we are all semi-drunk and tired," protested Leandra, but Weylin said he would make them coffee, if it was alright with Fiann, and that should help clear their heads.

Fiann said he would wait for them in the garden, by the well. All of a sudden, his expression was sombre, and there were no traces of tipsiness in his voice or demeanor.

"I did not hear you talk to the bird, nor did I hear the bird make any sound," said Leandra.

"I could still receive the bird's message. She will be waiting for us at the well."

Leandra asked Fiann a barrage of questions to which Fiann had no answers. He said everything would be revealed in good time and left the kitchen. Weylin poured coffee for the three of them, and they sipped it slowly. Through the kitchen window, they could see the moonlight gently part the clouds and stream its silver cascade upon Fiann's garden.

"I'm feeling nauseated," exclaimed Leandra suddenly, and excused herself. She barely made it to the bathroom before she began to retch and vomit violently. Her head was spinning, and she was cursing herself for having drunk too much. She brushed her teeth and lay on the bed exhausted. She lost all track of time and was drifting off to sleep when a loud knock startled her. It was Ariadne calling her to join them in the garden. She said that Fiann was ready to start a shamanic ritual that would lead them to the knowledge they came to find.

Leandra still felt unwell, but dragged herself out into the garden. She and Ariadne joined Fiann and Weylin who were already sitting on a low circular wall surrounding the well. The rain had completely stopped, but the ground was still wet. Moonlight streamed its argent brightness over the well, and Leandra peered into it, trying to see the water. The well did not seem too deep, as she could discern water ripples on its bottom. Peering into the well made her feel dizzy and nauseated again, so she lifted her gaze. They sat in silence not knowing what to expect. Everything around them was quiet, and the tranquility of the garden helped Leandra calm herself.

After a few minutes, the silence was broken by swooshing sounds of wings, and a shrill screech. Upon hearing it, Fiann nodded his head in understanding. He extended his hand toward Ariadne and asked them all to hold hands, saying their synergy would take them where they needed to go. Time passed imperceptibly between their breaths filled with excitement.

Impatient and shivering from the chill that permeated the air, Leandra asked, “What now?”

“We have to wait,” Fiann replied.

Moon rays mingled with their renewed silence, creating an aura of mystery and anticipation. Leandra began to feel fidgety and irritated. Just as she was about to ask another question, she felt the rising of a wind. At first, it was a light and caressing breeze that twirled around them as if in a dancing motion. It almost felt as if it were checking them out, curious about their presence so late at night. Fiann sat like a stone statue gazing into the well. His sudden chant startled Leandra and when she looked at him, she could clearly see he was in a trance. She tried to relax by looking into the well water, but her dizziness returned. She closed her eyes, and after a few minutes felt tension leaving her body and slumber overtaking her. After a few minutes the wind’s strength increased, and in no time turned into a violent eddy of air, threatening to knock them over. Leandra screamed and grabbed Weylin’s hand. With her left hand, she grabbed Ariadne’s, and the four of them sat in a tight circle holding onto each other.

The onrush of wind was followed by a tide of blackness obliterating every beam of moonlight. The billows of biting air soared around them, enveloping them in darkness that howled, roared, and wailed in fury, or in pain. Every now and then, flickers of light would pierce the blackness and vanish. One moment, the lights seemed to be winking at them, another, they would appear as balls, or arcs of bluish fire. Leandra felt terrified and dug her nails into the palm of Weylin’s hand, screaming. She believed the demonic hawk had lured them into this ritual in order to harm them.

She wondered against what kind of divine order they had all transgressed to summon so much wrath. Just as she thought she would lose consciousness amidst the inner and outer turbulence, she heard Fiann and Ariadne’s voices chant in unison. It was utterly incomprehensible to Leandra how she could discern words in what now sounded like a prayer, but their voices rose above the furious whistling of the wind, and lost their initial quiver. Leandra's left hand was clutched in Ariadne's, and she could feel Ariadne squeezing her hand in rhythm to the prayer.

Leandra could no longer distinguish between the sound of Fiann and Ariadne's voices as they had begun to sound like each other's echo. She could discern words begging for forgiveness over Ailionora's destruction of the sacred circle to obliterate traces of her shame. The prayer for forgiveness flowed into an uplifting blessing upon the winds. She could make out words of appeasement, names of places unknown to her that were kissed and christened by the winds, words expressing worship of divine forces, and the magic of the natural world. The blessings turned into another supplication to the winds to protect them, and allow them a glimpse of the White Circle village, and their intended fate.

Leandra could not fathom how Fiann and Ariadne knew what to say to appease the wrath of nature or some divine force, but whatever it was they had uttered had a calming effect on the winds. Gradually, they died down with what sounded like a deep sigh of surrender, and the darkness was lit by multitudes of lights. Leandra thought it must have been fireflies, but knew it was something else because the air itself had become warm, moist, and glittering.

Fiann and Ariadne continued to pray, rising and extending their arms toward the velvety skies. Leandra gazed again into the well and saw a shimmering opening in the glassy water surface. Around the opening, it seemed as if layers of air were quivering and bowing to them, even though the mere notion of air visibility was preposterous.

Fiann bent lower over the well with his eyes closed. They followed his movement, straining to better discern the shapes on the water's surface. The opening at the bottom of the well widened, and a most bedazzling view burst open before their eyes.

22

Bathed in golden sunlight, a village lay under a hill. In the distance to the west, they could see sun-bleached bluffs towering over a sea. The sound of the chorus of the waves crashing against the rocky shore reached them.

In the opposite direction, they could behold a circle of stones standing proud and erect. How an image that sharp could appear in the well water was a mystery that made everyone except Fiann let out a loud gasp of disbelief. It was as if a film were rolling before their eyes, and at the same time, they were part of it.

Leandra looked at Ariadne, wanting to say something, but stopped before she could utter a sound, astonished over her changed appearance. Her hair was waist long and flax blonde, and the white sweater she had worn, when they sat around the well, had turned into a long white dress. Leandra quickly looked at Weylin, and was shocked to see his hair was the colour of golden wheat and his eyes were no longer dark, but greyish blue. How she could detect all of that in the darkness-enveloped garden, was another source of mystery. Weylin was also taller and slimmer. His arms were sinewy and muscular.

"Kieran," she cried.

He took her hands in his and gazed into her eyes. In his eyes, she could read the whole story of their love that had straddled centuries. They were a mirror in which she saw the reflection of her own soul. Love for her floated in the blueness of his gaze.

"I have waited for this moment for centuries, Jilleen. Ailionora did promise we would meet again and here we are. Our fates are twinned."

Leandra continued gazing at the well water and noticed the hawk sitting on Fiann's shoulder and screeching something into his ear. Ailionora extended her hand toward the hawk and whispered, "Grandmother, we finally reunite. Thank you for trying to save me from rape, and thank you for bringing me back home."

An unexpected fragrance of honeysuckle reached their nostrils, infusing them with an unmistakeable sense of familiarity, mooring them in the moment, and in a circle of belonging. Everywhere they looked, the landscape was suffused with ethereal beauty. They inhaled the sweet air and followed Fiann down the hill. When Leandra tried to reorient herself, and look for Fiann's garden, she could no longer see it. It now felt as if she were dreaming, and looking at the dream from the outside, at the same time. She expected to be fearful, but all she could feel was sweet anticipation, as she watched in the mirror of the well all four of them hurry down the hill. She was now observing herself and Weylin as Jilleen and Kieran, and wondered how that no longer confused her.

On the way down, Kieran asked Fiann if they would visit the White Circle, and he replied that Kieran should take Jilleen to the Circle, and he and Ailionora would look for Aidan and Jilleen's home, and specifically for the well behind it. Kieran and Jilleen would find them there. Once they found the well, they would get ready for the ritual of blessing the village, and pray for its healing and its emergence from behind the veil of oblivion. Jilleen said that she also wished to find Conor's grave. Her heart was clamoring with whispers that urged her to seek her lost son.

Kieran grabbed her hand and laughing, they began to run toward the Circle, feeling young and carefree. Jilleen was no longer dressed in jeans that Leandra had worn, but in a blue dress with a laced-up bodice. "We have found ourselves in a collective dream, Kieran. We shall wake up and not even remember any of this, but let's enjoy it while we are here."

They continued running and reached the stone circle breathless.

"I wonder how we can see the circle if Ailionora destroyed it? It must be a mirage in our dream," said Kieran softly and continued. "But it does not matter, it feels as it had always felt, the scents are the same, you smell like Jilleen, and the stone in the middle looks exactly like the one Ailionora had used as an altar, and performed the hand-fasting ceremony on us, tying us to each other forever. Jilleen, forever does exist, now we know it."

And the dream rushed forth and they went from stone to stone touching them; however, they could feel no texture under their fingers and that puzzled them. It was as if the image existed as a hologram.

Back at the stone that stood in the middle of the circle, they crouched and began examining its sides carefully, until Jilleen cried in delight. "I found our initials…here they are." Etched in the grey stone surface, the initials J and K were easily recognizable. There was no doubt in their minds that the initials had belonged to them.

They lowered themselves on the grass beneath the stone and rested their backs against it.

"This is the stone I saw in my dream as Leandra," said Jilleen. "In my dream, the stone was shrieking as if wanting to relay important messages to me."

"Stones are tabernacles of collective memories and oracles of the future, according to Ailionora. Perhaps we should listen to what this one needs to say to us," whispered Kieran.

He extended his hand and pulled Jilleen toward him, and she found herself on top of him. At that moment, the love and passion they had felt for each other centuries ago engulfed them in a flame that took their breath away. Their lovemaking was feverish, intoxicating; they were entangled in each other's bodies and souls, feeling as an inextricable part of the divine. Their desire for each other was threaded with the echoes of longings spanning hundreds of years; his lips and his skin were grafted on hers; their kisses were interspersed with rasping whispers that they were inseparable, and that they would always search for each other in the stars, the winds, the ocean tides and grains of sand. They were tongues and mouths exploring every crevice of their bodies, recognizing each other's scent from centuries ago.

"You're cleaved in my soul, Jilleen. I will not let you go again." Their love was as verdant and succulent as the springtime grasses and flowers at their peak in May. In every incarnation, their bodies and souls were reflections of each other. Such mirroring of souls stayed imprinted in their blood.

Their lovemaking left them breathless and fatigued. Caressing her hair, Kieran said that he felt whole again, his yearning was fused with a sense of belonging. Now, he realized that he had always been hearing ripples of this place in his heart, and could never decipher the message and understand his restlessness. It was now stilled because their lovemaking felt like coming home.

Sweet slumber crept over them, and just as they closed their eyes. entangled in an embrace, the stone began to whisper. Startled, they pricked their ears, trying to understand the words until the words flowed with incisive clarity. The stone spoke of the history of the region, the wars, the rule of the chieftains, the disappearance of the White Circle after Ailionora summoned the forces of destruction. They listened to the whisperings spellbound, and when the stone began to narrate the story of Jilleen and Kieran, they gasped in disbelief almost not daring to breathe, in fear of interrupting the mysterious narrator. The voice coming out of the stone urged them to find Fiann, because it was time for Jilleen and Kieran to learn the story of their future.

In great haste, they dressed and ran toward the village. The village was devoid of people and had a dream-like quality.

Jilleen recognized the house in which she had lived with her husband Aidan, but before turning toward it, she pulled Kieran in the direction of the cemetery. The wrought iron gate opened with a loud creak, and they headed toward a grave at the end of a row, knowing with certitude it was their son's grave. Once at the grave, they sat on the ground and placed their hands on the tombstone.

"Mother," a voice rang with sharp clarity in Jillian's ears. "You have found me. I am happy."

Both Jilleen and Kieran looked around hoping to see the child whose voice they heard, but silence descended upon them. Kieran helped Jilleen get up, telling her it was time to find Fiann and Ailionora, and they left the cemetery. Jilleen felt frozen and unable to connect to any emotion.

In front of the house where she had spent so many happy, as well as turbulent years with Aidan and her son Fiann, she stood immobile inhaling the scents and absorbing the sights.

"Come, Jilleen," said Kieran taking her hand and leading her around the house. "If Fiann and Ailionora are not here, we need to go back to the White Circle."

A beautiful garden sprawled before them. It was flanked by rose bushes, most of which were full of white blooms. Jilleen remembered having planted them with love. She also wondered how the garden was not overgrown with weeds, but looked instead as if someone were still tending to it.

In one corner they spotted Fiann and Ailionora sitting around a well, and the sight of the well jogged Jilleen's memory, too. All her senses were awakened by the familiar surroundings. The well reminded her of Fiann's words about the revelations waiting to be found in *the well within the well.*

She and Kieran sat on the round bench by the well, and looked into its darkness. The water was shimmering under the soft rays of sun and they looked at it, transfixed.

"We are ready to begin," said Fiann softly, and he and Ailionora rose and began an incantation summoning the Goddess.

"In this tapestry of divine spirit

Connecting all and everything,

Mother Goddess who pulsates in our blood

Let yourself be known

In the ripples of this water..."

Again, Ailionora begged for forgiveness for the sacrilege of destroying the White Circle, and offending the gods who had helped create it. Both she and Fiann fell into a trance and swayed in unison until a thick ray of sun, like a bolt of lightning or a sword of fire descended from the skies and fell into the well. The four of them gazed at the water that began to ripple and then churn. The earth beneath their feet was shaking with light tremors. The roiling water was now moving in soft swells before freezing into a mirror. A voice whispered, "Look carefully, for destiny shall unfold before you."

Images of the White Circle Village began to appear as if in a slide show. The village was teeming with people and activity, and the people wore modern day clothes. There was machinery everywhere as roads, houses, and buildings were being built. On one building, the year of its construction could be seen clearly: 2034. From the images, they inferred that the village would become visible to the outside world, and would be enlivened.

One building was a library and they witnessed a room full of students listening to a lecturer talk about the Celtic history, the pre-Christian times, the wars against the English, the Great Famine etc.

"The thread of the ancestral memory has been restored. There is continuity in the ancient wisdom again," whispered Ailionora.

"Thank you, Goddess, for lifting the curse," Fiann exclaimed, looking smilingly at Ailionora.

Just as Jilleen was about to look at Kieran, Fiann said, "There is more."

The face of an old woman appeared in the mirror. Ailionora recognized her grandmother, Etain. A child's face appeared beside her, and Jilleen began to weep, recognizing Conor.

"Don't cry, mother. It was not my time to be born then, but you will be my mother again." The child laughed and disappeared, but Jilleen could feel his small arms around her neck for a brief moment.

Etain's image appeared in the well's mirror again, and she looked straight at Jilleen and Kieran. Her prophetic-sounding words and sent shivers down Jilleen's spine.

"You and Kieran shall conceive Conor again in another time, the period in which you will stay together for a full incarnation," they heard Etain's voice narrate the story of their future. "That time will be one of the most important epochs in the history of the human species, because Conor will be born so that he may reverse the cataclysmic events threatening human existence. The Earth will be burning, but he will invent ways to soothe its pain; people will be dying by the millions, until he finds solutions that would slow down death and destruction; contamination and pandemics will spread everywhere until he leads others in the discoveries of how to clean the poison out of the soil and waters and find cures for the illness that was ravaging the world; he will be the leader who will be followed by multitudes of people in his attempts to save the Earth, and its animal and human inhabitants. There will be a shift in human consciousness, there will be more compassion and love. Humans will coexist with animals and will no longer eat them. The animal world will regulate itself. What you have heard now you will partially remember once you incarnate again. You will recognize each other, and know that your son will be born out of your love, and that he will grow into a man of unique qualities, a man who will be desperately needed by the time in which he is born. And you, his parents, will be healers of bodies and souls."

Leandra and Kieran were looking at each other as if awakening from a dream, but their gaze reflected a new understanding. Just as Leandra turned toward Fiann with a question about the prophesy, the mirror in the well shattered as suddenly as it had appeared, and was replaced by stagnant water.

"Our mission has been accomplished here," said Fiann. "We need to leave now, and let the village become gradually visible to the outside world. Unlike us, those who discover the village will find ruins and rebuild it. An archaeological dig will uncover the remnants of the White Circle. I simply know all of this."

Wan sunlight was trying to penetrate the misty air of early morning. Leandra was the first to stand up, feeling cramps in her back and legs. She looked into the well, but all she could see was still water. She looked at Fiann in confusion, and asked, "Which well showed us the images of the village, and which one foretold our future?"

"This well in my garden and the one behind your husband Aidan's house seem to be interconnected, and this one was the gateway to the other one," said Fiann. We found truth in both of them.

The winds rose again, and the skies were suddenly covered by a veil of opaqueness, but the darkness no longer felt menacing. Feeling pushed by an invisible force, they hurried out of the village, climbed the hill, and soon found themselves sitting in Fiann's garden by his well.

An expression of scepticism replaced the look of confusion on Leandra's face, and she said, "This, in fact now feels as if we had all drunk too much, and we did. We all got quite tipsy after the last night's dinner...was it last night? I must have hallucinated all of this. I feel I need to pinch myself."

They went inside, and spent the next hour comparing their experiences, and gasping every time they discovered a perfect match between their reports. Leandra participated in the discussion, still unwilling to admit that she could not have hallucinated the same experiences as the other three. In his account of the events, Weylin did not mention their lovemaking in the Circle, but only their visit to the cemetery; however, the glances they exchanged reflected the unspoken secret. Weylin highlighted the recurring message telling him and Leandra they would recognize each other in a future incarnation. They all confirmed learning that in that future incarnation Leandra and Kieran's son Conor would be reborn. It seemed all the other incarnations had happened as preparation for the most important one, yet to come.

Feeling exhausted from staying up all night, Leandra, Weylin, and Fiann went to bed while Ariadne stayed to reply to a message from Hugo. He was asking her if she would be willing to move to England and marry him. He had apparently spent a long time thinking about their relationship, and was ready to commit. All of a sudden, there was clarity in his mind, and all doubt and fear had been dispelled.

They slept until 2 p.m, had a late lunch at the same restaurant where they had gotten drunk the night before, and when they returned to Fiann's house, Leandra said she was ready to leave for Dublin, even if it meant arriving there late. She and Weylin agreed to leave in 45 minutes, or as soon as they packed their suitcases. Ariadne said she would leave the island in the morning, as she felt too exhausted to drive.

When Leandra hugged and kissed Fiann, thanking him for the most unique experience and his warm hospitality, she began to cry, feeling rattled by the events of the last few days. She invited him to visit her, but he said he was too old, and tired of living, and what little life he had left, he planned to spend with his sister and her family. Ariadne offered Leandra a stay of an extra couple of days in Dublin at her house, but Leandra thanked her and said she was eager to fly back home. She promised to stay in touch, and wished her happiness with Hugo. Ariadne said that once dust of all the excitement over the mystical experiences they had shared has settled, she would like them to talk over Skype, and consolidate their impressions once again. She promised to keep both Leandra and Weylin posted about the new phase of her life that would soon begin in England.

Upon Leandra's insistence, Weylin drove to Dublin without stopping. She was eager to get to the hotel and fly home the next day. She looked pale and dishevelled, and kept opening the window to inhale fresh air because bouts of nausea plagued her. The first twenty minutes of their ride they spent in complete sentence. Leandra broke it by saying, "There must be a rational explanation for these irrational events. There just has to be one, and I want to shed some light of sanity on these experiences."

"I feel at a loss for words over your renewed questioning the reality of what we had witnessed," protested Weylin. "How in the world can you cast even a shadow of a doubt on what you and I experienced? Why can't you accept that some things are inexplicable…science cannot explain every phenomenon." Weylin sounded frustrated and his stutter returned.

"We humans build lots of defences against reality. We resort to delusion to assuage our fear of life…our existential anxiety. We want to give our lives meaning, and we sometimes try to find it in symbols, myths, signs…," said Leandra gesticulating nervously with her hands.

"What? Are you now trying to convince me I hadn't seen what I saw, I hadn't held the book in my hands in which our names from a past life were mentioned…?"

"I'm trying to analyse it scientifically or psychologically, taking into account a wider picture of the human condition. The fact that we felt compelled to search for evidence of our past lives, and the fact we witnessed certain inexplicable things, still does not mean they actually exist. Perhaps it is all one huge coincidence, and by believing in the magical and the unreal, we are weakening our scientific minds. Maybe what we saw as reality are false memories implanted into our minds by Fiann's shamanic power of suggestion. Perhaps what we thought was true was just our collective false interpretation of truth."

"Leandra, you're making little sense. You're rambling. There are no false memories that we could collectively experience. We did not become delusional because of some existential dread we both felt at the same time. Yes, perhaps we were drunk, and fell under Fiann's influence, but even if we had, we would not have had identical experiences. That is just impossible!"

They sat in silence again. Leandra's breathing was heavy.

"Shamans must possess great powers of suggestion," she persisted. "Wouldn't you agree with the possibility that it was not only the effects of Jacacia that made you believe you accessed a past life, but that it could have been Keith's suggestive influence that planted false memories in you?" She inhaled deeply and asked Weylin, "Remember our weekend in Scotland?"

"Of course I do."

"Do you recall our conversation about existential psychotherapy?" Without waiting for his reply, she continued, "We both agreed that many symptoms of anxiety our patients exhibited might be rooted in a deeper fear of death, the meaningfulness and absurdity of life, feelings of isolation etc. You and I recognized that, perhaps on a subconscious level, we ended up having an affair in order to find a temporary antidote to mortality, or to infuse life with a deeper stemming from love."

"I remember our conversation, but what has it got to do with us?" asked Weylin.

"Well, maybe our search for evidence of our past lives, our belief in synchronicities, symbols and omens, such as dragonflies, maybe, just maybe, it all originates from our subconscious mind, from our unconscious fear of death, of being annihilated, of vanishing without leaving a trace. What if we somehow invented all of this or misinterpreted it to suit our subconscious belief that there was more to life than meets the eye?"

"Your explanation and supposition still do not make much sense, even though I agree that what happens in our subconscious may drive us in ways we can never understand."

"But Weylin, just consider this. Remember how at the peak of our love affair we said we must have known each other from some past life because of the depth and intensity of our feelings of familiarity? Remember how we saw synchronicities and magic everywhere? Remember the sense of vibrant aliveness our intoxication with each other created? I'm sure all people who fall in love experience the same sense of having known each other from times primordial. But, maybe, you and I just took it to the next level by exploring these mystical possibilities, because we could no longer go back to the everyday reality, because we could not accept life in its existential nakedness. We are born and die and there is nothing much more to us, so to escape the harshness of our biological nature, and to romanticize life, we co-created with others this whole new world of past life connections."

"Leandra, but that still does not make sense, as we never pursued these mystical venues consciously or believed in them. I had even almost forgotten all about you and us, frankly, until I met Keith. I never believed in the nonsense of reincarnation until I listened to the recordings of your own hypnotherapy sessions. My experience with Jacacia shook up the foundations of any rational belief I'd had up to that point. Yes, I've felt existential dread and anxiety before, but I'd never consider them reasons for going on this trip to seek evidence of our past lives. Your theory is just too out there. You just sound like someone trying to force a square peg into a round hole."

"I still think there must be a way to explain all of this. There is still so much we need to learn about the workings of the brain, and its reaction to hypnotherapy, psychedelic drugs, shamanic chants, and other methods of altering the state of consciousness."

"Well, we'll soon arrive at your hotel and we can dissect this further over drinks," said Weylin.

For the rest of the drive, Leandra tried to analyse the events from more perspectives, but the more she tried to find scientific basis to the experiences that defied logic, the more convoluted her explanations became.

Once they reached her hotel, Weylin reiterated he would like them to spend the last evening together, and discuss further the surreal experiences, but Leandra said she felt too exhausted and sick to continue processing and dissecting events.

"Perhaps we could research the topic of collective hallucination," Weylin tried again, but Leandra repeated tersely she was too tense and too tired to talk about it anymore, but once she has recovered psychologically from the trip, they could revisit it together with Ariadne.

"You realize we are connected and have been connected forever," he continued. "You can't just deny it and ascribe it to a phenomenon that can simply be reduced to a dry scientific explanation. Perhaps your denial of still feeling attracted to me makes you deny what we saw and heard this week with our own eyes and ears. How can you just leave after our lovemaking in the White Circle"...but she did not allow him to finish his sentence. She opened the door, asking him to help her with her suitcase.

He got out of the car, hauled her suitcase out, and brought it to the hotel entrance. He looked dismayed by her reaction. She hugged him perfunctorily and disappeared into the hotel.

Alone in her room, Leandra showered, sent an email to Adrian confirming her flight details, and went to bed. Sleep would not come.

Her phone rang and she picked up. Weylin was begging her to reconsider and let him come up her room to talk one last time. He was at home but could not settle down. It was important he saw her again. He said he could present an array of arguments about the reality of what they had experienced, and he reminded her again of their lovemaking as Kieran and Jilleen, and asked her if she remembered the volcanic passion between them. When she finally relented and said he could come up to her room to talk, he let out a jubilant cry on the other end of the line and hung up.

Exhaustion overtook her and she slipped into a shallow dream. She was awoken by the screeching tires of an automobile, and the sounds of people shouting and screaming in what sounded like distress and shock. A few minutes later, she could hear the sirens of police cars and ambulance.

She got up to peer through the window. There was commotion on the street. She opened the window and could hear someone shout that a man had been run over as he tried to cross the street toward the hotel entrance.

Her heart lurched into her throat, and then seemed to stop beating. Her scream stayed frozen on her lips before she could articulate it and shatter the silence in the room.

Staring through the window in a catatonic state, she saw a child's face high up in the air. It was looking at her with sorrow and love in his eyes. In its blurred features she recognized Conor. His voice had a tinge of encouragement in it when he said, "Don't be sad mother. Father and I shall be waiting for you."

About the Author

As far back as she can remember, Jana has been fascinated by storytelling. Her love of reading and writing propelled her toward studies of languages and literature resulting in B.A. degrees in English and German Languages and Literature, an M.A. in Literary Criticism, and B.Ed. in English and Dramatic Arts.

Among her publications are academic articles published by *Cambridge Scholars, UK*, and the *Journal for Distinguished Language Study*, USA, the novel *Poisonous Whispers*, published by *Roane Publishing*, N.Y., poetry, short fiction, articles, art reviews, and blog posts featured in literary journals, such as *Ariel Chart, Chantwood*, the *Pangolin Review, Abstract, Canada Fashion Magazine and Authors Publish (*Facebook page*)*.

Her short story, *Purveyors of Magic* appeared in the December 2020 issue of *The Black Shamrock,* and her short story *2148* was published in September 2020 in the anthology *Thin Places, by Broken Keys Publishing (*winner of the Best Year Award in the Ottawa Faces Magazine*)*. Her short story "*The Gift in the Box Full of Darkness*" was featured in the anthology *Sunset Rain* and her poetry in the collection *As Darkness Falls,* both published by *300 South Media Group*. She also contributed an inspirational poem to the *Thoughts and Prayers* anthology published in 2020.

She acts as a senior editor for *Ariel Chart* literary journal and contributing editor/writer for *Canada Fashion Magazine*. She has been nominated for the *2019 Best of the Net* and the *PushCart* awards for a piece of non-fiction and a short story published in *Ariel Chart*. In addition, she was the first runner-up with an honourable mention in the Oyster Art Flash Fiction Contest of March 2021. She lives in Ottawa, Ontario and works for the Government of Canada as an education specialist in the field of military language training. She can also be contacted via her Author Page at www.facebook.com/J.Damselfly

Manor House
www.manor-house-publishing.com
905-648-4797

CPSIA information can be obtained
at www.ICGtesting.com
Printed in the USA
LVHW052051141222
735146LV00006B/293

9 781988 058900